the
dark pageant

Also by Edward Lucie-Smith

Poetry:
A Tropical Childhood
Confessions and Histories
Towards Silence
The Well-Wishers

Anthologies:
A Group Anthology (with Philip Hobsbaum)
Penguin Book of Elizabethan Verse
The Liverpool Scene
A Choice of Browning's Verse
Penguin Book of Satirical Verse
Holding Your Eight Hands
British Poetry Since 1945
A Primer of Experimental Verse
French Poetry: The Last Fifteen Years (with Simon Watson-Taylor)

Art History and Criticism:
What is a Painting?
Thinking about Art
Movements in Art Since 1945
A Concise History of French Painting
Symbolist Art
Eroticism in Western Art
The Invented Eye
World of the Makers
How the Rich Lived
Arte Oggi
Work and Struggle

Other:
The First London Catalogue
The Burnt Child
Joan of Arc

the
dark pageant

EDWARD LUCIE-SMITH

First published in 1977 by Blond & Briggs Ltd.
First paperback edition published in May 1986
by GMP Publishers Ltd, PO Box 247, London N15 6RW.

British Library Cataloguing in Publication Data

Lucie-Smith, Edward
   The dark pageant.
   I. Title
   823.914[F]   PR 6023.U42
   ISBN 0-85449-006-X

Printed by The Guernsey Press, PO Box 57, Braye Road,
Vale, Guernsey, Channel Islands

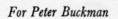
For Peter Buckman

PREFATORY NOTE

Since this book is about one of the most famous criminals in history, there is some risk that I may be accused of exaggerating his crimes. Every detail of what Gilles de Rais did to his victims is, in fact, based on the contemporary record of his trial, and there are even certain sickening details I have not used. Gilles's final address to his two confederates, together with many of the words attributed to his companion-in-arms, Joan of Arc, are also firmly based on contemporary document-ation. There is a list of the people mentioned at the end of the volume.

E.L.-S.

part one

1

I have not been a great sinner, at least in comparison to the sins I have seen committed. But there is something within me still which muddies, not the soul, but the intellect. I can never be rid of the past. Each day some fragment of it floats into my consciousness. I am now an old man, and I should like to go, when my time comes, with complete clarity of mind – the floors scrubbed, the linen aired, all the cupboards turned out. Away with all this rubbish! I sense that we are entering a new age; men speak and think in a different way from the one I was used to as a boy. That young ruffian Francesco Prelati was the first man I heard talk of knowledge and reason in that particular tone, and he did not mean what he said. But nevertheless he brought the first echo with him from Italy of the ideas which every man of learning in the kingdom now begins to discuss. Old as I am, I prefer the new age I glimpse to the old one in which my story was enacted. Blotting out memory, I commit myself to the future.

Which scene shall I blot out first? Perhaps this. I see a large room, high and white. At the end, against the wall, there are two thrones of black oak, of the kind you see in every noble-man's hall – the chair of estate under a canopy where a lord sits to give justice, as is his right. In one of them sits a man in bishop's robes, with a great sapphire ring on his hand. In the other, a Dominican monk. I know well enough who they are: Jean de Malestroit, bishop of Nantes; and the reverend Jean Blouyn, vice-inquisitor. They are judges in a matter of heresy. Before them stands the accused, a man of some thirty-six years old, with a slender figure. He is dressed in black, but very magnificently. Gold stars twinkle on the sleeves of his velvet doublet, and his belt is a wreath of golden roses. This man is speaking endlessly, rapidly. The words pour out of him so fast that you wonder how he draws breath. And yet he never raises his voice. The notary sitting at the judges' feet is straining to hear, and at the same time straining to write swiftly enough. The only sound, besides that voice, is the scratching of the notary's pen. Now and again there comes a sigh, an intake of breath, from the two hundred or so packed into the room, and who are also listening. I see how the bishop's fingers grip the arm of his chair, and how the light in his ring shifts as the muscles tighten. Suddenly he is on his feet, fumbling with his robes, ripping away a panel of cloth. 'No, no,' he exclaims. 'It is not fit that such things should be said in the presence of the image of God!' And he turns his back on us, and veils the crucifix which hangs on the wall between the two thrones. Then he seats himself once more. 'You may resume your testimony, messire Gilles de Rais,' he says.

But I am going too far and too fast. That scene took place more than thirty years ago, but we must go back further still. Tonight France is ruled by King Louis XI, whom some men call 'the spider', and some 'the father of his people'. From his house at Plessis-les-Tours the king's couriers ride with his orders, and almost always those orders are obeyed. Every now and then, to be sure, it seems as if the old days might return. It is not so long ago, for example, that the king allowed himself to fall into the hands of his bitterest enemy, once his best friend, Duke Charles the Rash of Burgundy, and only got away after licking the duke's boots for him. I hear the Parisians, who have never loved our monarch, any more than he loves them, have trained their parrots to cry 'Peronne! Peronne!' to remind him of where his misfortune took place. But our king is a patient man, and even a forgiving one when it suits him. He knows that both he and the kingdom grow stronger every day, and he takes comfort in praying to the Virgin, in the church he has had built for her miraculous image at Cléry, on the south bank of the Loire. Recently I went there, and saw the oratory he has had made for himself, high up, with a little window overlooking the altar, so that he can spy on God as he is reputed to spy on his own kingdom.

Let me begin again, much further back. It is the very end of September in the year 1415. I am a boy of twelve. My name is Raoul – Raoul de Saumur. It is a name with a fine ring to it, and good ancestry behind it, but I have already been made to realise that I have only a humble place in the scheme of things. Our family can lay claim to nobility, but to little else. My father never held much land, and what he held he mismanaged. He died when I was five. My mother cannot protect the property we have in the troubles which are gradually engulfing the realm under mad King Charles VI and his German wife, Isabeau of Bavaria. We get little help from our immediate overlord, Jean de Craon, the greatest nobleman in the smiling Duchy of Anjou. Jean de Craon has the reputation of squeezing vassal and serf alike for every penny he can get out of them. My mother hopes, indeed, that he has forgotten our existence, as the two of us try to eke out a living in the tumbledown manor-house which is by this time little better than the hovels the peasants live in. The roof leaks, and our few chickens wander in and out of the place at will, leaving their droppings on the dirty floor and sometimes even nesting in dark corners. Since my tenth birthday I have had no shoes. There has been no money to buy a new pair, nor even the goods to barter for them. 'I'll go to the wars and make our fortune,' I say, and my mother despairingly covers her face with her hands.

When Jean de Craon's messenger arrives, picking his way through the dung-heap that stands before our front door, my mother is scouring a pot with a handful of sand, in the crazy lean-to we use as a kitchen. She comes to meet him, wiping her hands on her apron. He is a big man, blunt-featured, well set-up, clad in plain woollen stuff and in leather. A sword hangs by his side.

'Are you the maid or the mistress?' he asks.

'The mistress.'

'Good. I have a message for you. From messire Jean de Craon.'

As he holds out the little scroll towards her, I see my mother's eyes drop to the ground. The moment she has feared for so long has arrived.

'Can you read?'

'Yes, a little. Enough for this.'

'Just as well,' he says, smiling, 'for it's more than I can do. Better read it aloud. I think there's something that concerns me in it, as well as you and the boy.'

I see my mother slowly unrolling the parchment, conning it over, while the colour floods into her face and drains out again. She clears her throat, and begins to read:

'Madam, I have need of your boy. Send him to me at my castle of Champtocé. You may be certain he will not lose by it. The bearer of this is called Guy de Roye. He will bring the child to me, and then return to you. You have my permission to marry him. He will set your affairs in order, something that has too long been necessary. In particular, he will be able to perform the knight-service you owe me for your estate. In these hard times I cannot have a fief lying idle in the hands of a woman. Jean de Craon.'

'That seems plain enough.'

'Yes.'

'I have orders to take the boy with me at once. My lord is impatient to have him.'

'When will you be back?'

'In two days. You had better speak to the priest.'

My mother bows her head silently, and the big man looks at her.

'Come now, woman. A marriage should be a time for rejoicing. I confess I had hoped for something fresher and younger, but beggars can't be choosers, and nor can soldiers of fortune. My lord owes me something for my service to him, and you need a man to protect you. Your land looks very neglected, what I've seen of it, but I'll soon put that right. We ought to get on together quite well.'

This was how I left my mother, and went to the castle of Champtocé.

2

When I first saw Jean de Craon's castle, from the crupper of my future stepfather's horse, it seemed to me the largest building I had ever looked at, and also the most threatening and sinister. Champtocé is built on a mound, set a league or so back from the banks of the Loire. After riding downstream, we had reached the town of Ingrandes, which was also, Guy told me, one of the many possessions of the formidable man who had so abruptly sent for me. Ingrandes stands at the point where, for a short distance, the river forms the frontier between the two duchies of Anjou and Britanny. A long bridge with many arches crosses the Loire.

As we approached, I could see great strings of pack animals approaching this bridge, then pausing at a structure which stood at the end of it, on the near bank. There was a great bustling and shouting as they arrived at this building, then left it again.

'What are they doing?'

'Paying their customs' dues,' said Guy.

'To the king?'

Guy laughed heartily. 'No – to our master. The customs' post at Ingrandes is one of the reasons why Jean de Craon is such a rich man. Sometimes the merchants try to bilk him by swimming their beasts across the river, or crossing at a ford when the stream is low. But his men keep a good watch, and if they do not pay here they are made to pay twice as much when they get to Champtocé.'

'What are they carrying that's so precious? Silver or gold?'

Guy laughed again at my ignorance. 'No, lad. Those saddle-bags are full of salt. A human being can't do without salt any more than a cow can, and my lord Jean controls the road whereby most of it comes from Britanny into the kingdom of

France. He could teach those rascally alchemists a thing or two about turning salt into gold.'

He turned his horse to follow the pack-trains on their way inland. The road was so dusty from all the traffic that it carried, that the castle seemed to rise up quite suddenly out of the clouds that surrounded it. We trotted along, by-passing the other beasts where we could, but all too often wrapped in the choking powder that billowed from their hooves. My eyelashes and lips were coated with the gritty stuff, and my hair was full of it.

The dust died a little as we started to cross a marshy water-meadow by means of a raised causeway, and there, on our left, was the stronghold, lifting its towers and walls a little distance from the road, with a scummy lake in front of it. From the tallest tower flew a banner which showed that the lord himself was in residence, while on the ramparts I saw the scattered gleam of steel as the watch moved, and looked out from their posts. Apart from that Champtocé remained closed, blind, forbidding, in the glow of a fine autumn afternoon.

Guy branched off from the main road, and rode directly towards our destination, along another and narrower causeway that crossed the lake. At the end of this a lowered drawbridge indicated that the castle, for the moment, had no fear of hostile visitors. As the horse's hooves struck the wood, two men emerged from the shadow of the gateway arch, and crossed their lances so as to bar our way, then lowered them again when they saw who the rider was. We moved forward into the main courtyard.

This struck me as being little better than the dung-heap outside our own doorway at home. The ground was littered with rubbish, dog-dirt, horse-dung and old bones. A cow was tearing at some scrubby grass in a corner, a hunting-dog was searching for fleas, and a man-at-arms was drowsing in the sun, leaning against a doorway and scratching his crotch. As Guy slipped from his horse and I followed him, the guard opened his eyes and jerked his thumb inwards. 'He's waiting in the solar. Through the hall, and go right in.'

We passed through the door into the coolness of the great hall of the castle. The air was dank, and smelt of sweat and stale food and spilt wine. The long trestles were still littered with the remains of the last meal. My bare feet scraped through the dirty straw that covered the floor, and another dog peered from under one of the tables and growled at me.

Guy was obviously familiar with the place. He walked the

length of the room, and mounted the low dais at the back, making for a door at one corner. I followed him. As he knocked, a voice murmured indistinctly, and we mounted three steps to find ourselves in a smaller, square chamber. Tapestries hid the stone walls, and, despite the golden weather outside, a sulky fire smoked in the hearth. Guy drew himself up stiff, then made a low bow. Seated at a table beside the fireplace was a tall, thin man in a long russet-coloured robe. He seemed to me quite old – at any rate his thin hair was white. Grey eyes looked at me from either side of a high-bridged nose, and, after a pause, the thin mouth opened to speak.

'So this is the boy?'

'Yes, my lord.'

'A ragamuffin. His mother must have been worse off than I thought.'

'The land will improve with a bit of care, my lord.'

There was a pause as the grey eyes continued to survey me.

'Your name is Raoul de Saumur?'

'Yes, sir – I mean, yes, my lord,' I stammered, finding my tongue had almost ceased to obey me.

'Don't be nervous, child. Your father had good blood, even if not much luck. Have you been told why I've sent for you?'

'No, my lord.'

'I wish you to live here as companion to my grandson who will be arriving in a few days. A boy needs playmates of his own age. You will do the same lessons, and learn the profession of arms together. I will provide you with whatever I think necessary.'

I felt Guy's elbow digging me in the ribs, then his hand on the nape of my neck. I bowed and said, 'Thank you, my lord. As you please, my lord.'

'You may ride over and see your mother in the Christmas season. For the next few months she will no doubt be busy with this man here.'

As the words were pronounced, I knew the promise would not be kept. My mother and I would not see one another for a very long time.

'One thing more. My grandson is a great nobleman, and will become a still greater one as he grows up. I will not have him touched by those I appoint to teach him. You will be beaten for whatever faults he commits. See to it that he does not commit too many.'

'I'll – I'll try, my lord.'

Jean de Craon had abruptly lost interest. He addressed himself to Guy. 'Take him away and scrub the dirt off him. See what clothes you can find to fit, and get rid of the others. And tell the cobbler to make him a pair of shoes.' His eyes returned to the ledger he had been studying, and together we backed out of the room.

Two days later I was comparing the lot I had left with the one I had just tumbled into. I had a secondhand doublet and a pair of hose, both much better than those I had been made to discard. At Guy's hands I had undergone a thorough cleansing beside the castle well. Several of the garrison had gathered to watch my discomfiture as I shivered and spluttered under the repeated bucketsful of cold water he poured over me. The castle cobbler had made me a new pair of boots in stiff leather which pinched abominably. Though everything fascinated me, I felt very much at a loose end in this bustling community of people, all of whom had their own tasks to get on with. And I was suffering from lack of sleep.

That first night I had been handed a moth-eaten fur rug and told to find a place for myself in the great hall. This was easier said than done. Half the garrison seemed to sleep there, sprawled on the tables or curled in the straw. I managed to find a corner on the dais, close to the solar door, but even so the big room was loud with the breathing and muttering of those I shared it with. Every few hours there would be a general upheaval as the watch was changed, and as more men clattered in to replace those who came groaning to their feet. The rug I had been given was full of fleas, and I was thoroughly bitten by them.

It was on the evening of the second day, when dusk was just beginning to fill the courtyard, that Gilles de Rais arrived to be taken under his grandfather's protection. I heard the clopping of hooves over the wooden bridge, and ran out of the kitchen, where I had been hanging round the cooks as they prepared supper, to see what was happening. The first to emerge from under the arch was a slender boy of my own age with blue eyes, a smiling mouth and blue-black hair, riding a spirited little pony. He made it rear and lash out with its hooves like a real warhorse as it reached the centre of the courtyard.

After him, and riding at a more leisurely pace, were two churchmen, one stout and one thin, mounted upon mules. The stout clerk had an equally plump child seated before him on his saddlebow. After these three came a considerable train of pack-animals.

Jean de Craon had come down from his room to welcome his grandson. The meeting was formal enough. Gilles dropped to the ground from his horse, knelt in the dirt, and kissed the old man's hand. The latter scarcely looked at him. His steely eyes were fixed on the two clerics. The thin one tried to outstare him, but was soon forced to shift his glance.

'It is good of you, fathers, to bring your charges right to my door,' the old man said.

'My lord, you know that we were appointed master Gilles's tutors in his late father's will,' the thin clerk replied, rather defiantly I thought. 'It is our duty to be with him at all times.'

'I scarcely think that will be necessary, now that I have decided to intervene.'

'His father's wishes . . .'

'Have now been set aside. Have you anything more to say to me, master Michel?'

The thin clerk bit his lip, and the fat one mopped his face with his sleeve.

'In the circumstances,' said Jean de Craon, 'I shall be honoured to offer you a meal and a bed for the night. My steward will look after you and arrange for your departure in the morning.'

As if he had given some kind of signal, there was a sudden bustle round the newcomers. The fat child was lifted down, and carried off wailing in the arms of one of the women. The clerks were helped from their mules, and the pack-animals were unloaded and led away. The boy whom I now knew to be Gilles de Rais was left standing in front of his grandfather. For the first time since I had met him, Jean de Craon seemed a little at a loss.

'Gilles, this is your companion, Raoul. He will do all that you do while you are here, and learn from the same tutor and master-at-arms. I ask you to remember that he is as noble in blood as you are yourself.'

The boy answered with a shrug.

'You will share the same bed,' Jean de Craon added. I was not sure if this was good news or not. It meant a more comfortable berth than the one I had had last night in the hall, but Gilles was already looking rebellious.

'I don't want to do that,' he said. 'I'd rather sleep with my little brother René.'

'You will do as I tell you,' the old man answered. Quite deliberately he drew back his hand and caught his grandson a ringing slap. Then he spun on his heel and entered the doorway which led into the great hall, the long skirt of his gown flicking the jamb as he passed.

Slowly Gilles's finger rose to touch the angry red mark on his cheek. I could sense any number of eyes regarding us, from various points of vantage. All at once, I felt sorry for him, though he had behaved superciliously.

'Come on,' I said. 'Let me show you something in the kitchen. They've got a dog there that runs round and round inside a cage shaped like wheel. They use him to turn one of the spits. His back's all bent because they never let him out.'

3

That night, Gilles and I stood and faced one another across the bed that almost filled the small tower room that had been assigned to us. It was late, and the smoky rushlight flickered in the gusts of air from the slit window, casting strange shadows on Gilles's face. This, with its winged eyebrows and high cheekbones, already had a recognisable contour. You could guess at the handsome man he would become. Now, from moment to moment, he looked sometimes like a devil, and sometimes like one of those carved angels you see in church.

'What else did my grandfather tell you?'

I hesitated, wondering if I should give him the information or not.

'Only that I am to be beaten for whatever faults you may commit.'

'He hit me hard enough himself today.'

'That was because you are the same rank. He won't have you touched by anyone inferior.'

'Bravo for grandfather. It's the first nice thing I've heard said about him.'

Now Gilles himself seemed to hesitate, though in fact we'd grown quite friendly as I'd attempted to show him over Champtocé, which after all I had not had much time to explore myself. I noticed how much more quickly the guards and servants stepped aside for him than they did for me.

'Come here. Bring the light. I want to show you something.'

I picked it out of its socket, and started to walk around the bed. Meanwhile, Gilles had turned his back to me, and was slipping off, first his doublet, then the shirt he wore beneath it.

'Closer. But hold it so you don't burn me.'

I saw the flesh was criss-crossed with thin weals. Some were quite old and already fading. Others looked nearly fresh.

There was a crust of blood on some, where the cane had cut the skin.

'Who did that?' I asked.

'My tutor, messire Michel. He used to beat me every day. For my soul's good, he said.'

'Why don't you tell your grandfather about it?'

'After the way he treated me this afternoon?'

'He didn't seem to like messire Michel much.'

'That was only because the monk had been trying to hang on to something grandfather wanted. To me, in fact.'

I was shocked by the coolness of his tone, more shocked in fact than by what I had just seen. I made a sound of protest.

'Careful with that light, you idiot! My back is sore enough as it is.' Gilles pulled his doublet on again, and turned once more to look at me. Our faces were now very close.

'I have a lot of lands,' he said quietly. 'While I'm here, grandfather controls those lands as well as his own. He didn't want me because he's fond of me. Oh yes, messire Michel was careful to let me know all that.'

I gaped at him. He was going too fast for my understanding. Seeing my expression, he burst into an apparently unforced and genuine peal of laughter.

'Poor Raoul! You're a real country bumpkin, aren't you? Well, blow out that light and let's go to bed.'

The bed itself was larger and a lot softer than anything I'd been accustomed to at home. There what I slept on was a bale of straw – one which got pretty musty towards the end of winter. This mattress, I realised, was pure goose-down. Its softness made me restless. In addition, it seemed determined to roll me inward, towards my companion. I dozed off, still clinging to the outer rim, like a man crawling up a steep hill. As soon as I relaxed I felt a savage pinch which jerked me awake again.

'Keep your distance!' Gilles hissed. 'There's plenty of room for both of us.'

I lay rigid in the thick darkness, listening to his regular breathing. I wondered if he had now fallen asleep. The goose-down was warm as well as soft. I could feel myself starting to sweat, and moved to loosen my clothes a little. Beside me, Gilles was completely naked – I had heard him strip off his hose in the sudden darkness after I had blown out the flame. The bare flesh, so close, and yet not touching me, seemed alien, threatening, more menacing than a man in armour would have been. As I held myself away from Gilles, trying to stop sleep from overcoming me, I had a desolating sense that I had embarked on a new path from which I could never turn back. For the first time I had arrived at Champtocé, I felt truly homesick.

The next morning, inevitably, we woke huddled together in a tangle of limbs in the middle of the vast mattress. To my relief, and also to my surprise, Gilles accepted this without anger, smiling at me sleepily as he freed one arm which had strayed beneath my shoulder.

'Come on,' he said, 'we'd better get up and see how things work around here, and whether my grandfather has really got rid of messire Michel and his companion.'

They had not gone yet, but they were about to depart. Their mules were saddled and waiting, and the two priests were climbing sulkily aboard them, under the eye of the captain of the guard. It was clear that the latter had been ordered to see that there was no attempt at delay.

'I must at least say goodbye to the pupil who was entrusted to me,' Michel de Fontenay was saying huffily, 'even if I am not permitted to continue his education as his late father wished.'

'Get going, priest,' the soldier replied. 'Don't make matters difficult for all of us. My lord wants you off the premises. He gave no orders about farewells.'

It was at this moment that Gilles sauntered into the sunlight.

'You were asking for me, messire Michel?'

The priest seemed disconcerted by his arrival, and at a loss for words.

'You may be sure,' Gilles said, 'that I shall never forget you. I think you would be unwise to let me catch you, once I am grown.'

Michel de Fontenay jerked his chin upward, and his hands tightened on the reins. Gilles laughed, and even I could tell this was not a child's laugh. It sent a shudder through me. Then I saw Gilles wink at the captain, who pulled out his sword and brought the flat of its blade down with a thwack on the rump of the thin priest's mule. The beast let out an outraged whinny and bolted across the drawbridge, and then along the causeway. A moment later, the second mule, similarly urged, followed at the same breakneck pace. Watching the two priests jouncing in the saddle, clinging on for dear life, Gilles and I let out a simultaneous shout of mirth. This time it was the kind of *fou rire* which only seizes the very young – a racking, tearing spasm of merriment which made us weep great tears as we clung to one another in the castle gateway.

We soon found that Jean de Craon meant to have as little to do with us as possible. A tutor arrived, and we began our lessons. I found that Gilles already knew a good deal of Latin, while I could barely struggle through the simplest reading and writing in French. Gilles took a certain pleasure in showing off, and mocked me impatiently for my ignorance. Whether we studied or not, the tutor was too timid, too overawed by Gilles's exalted rank, to impose any discipline on us.

Where training in arms was concerned, we were more nearly equal. Gilles had a litheness and quickness I could never match, and his suppleness and sense of balance made him more at home on a horse than I. But even now, at twelve, I had greater reserves of physical strength than he, and, though I rode less well, I could get more out of a horse than he could. I noticed from the first that Gilles often had a rough, impatient cruelty with animals. He would stick spurs into a horse, then harshly rein it back, just to feel the beast writhe between his legs.

For ten days or so, however, we seemed to get on so well that I almost forgot what Jean de Craon had said to me when I first came to Champtocé. Then I was painfully reminded of it. It happened like this. One of the bitches that hung about the courtyard had whelped, and orders were given that the pups were to be drowned in the moat. They were put into a sack and thrown into the stagnant water. But the sack was not weighted, and somehow the wriggling bundle drifted to shore again. It was here that Gilles found it, and I only discovered what had happened when he and I were summoned to the solar, into Jean de Craon's presence. The man who brought us the message was Jean's body-servant, François. I thought the look he gave me was slightly shamefaced.

When we arrived, the atmosphere was menacing. The captain of the guard and two of their garrison were present. On the floor was a small dank-looking bundle of cloth.

'I have heard something I do not like,' the old man said, addressing himself to Gilles without any preliminary greeting. 'Did you do this?' He nodded to one of the soldiers, who moved forward and teased open the bundle with the toe of his boot. What I saw within made me gag back the bile in my throat. Two newborn pups lay inside it. One had had its belly ripped open. The guts had been pulled out of the slit, and trailed glistening from the body. The blind eyes of the other had been roughly put out, perhaps with a pointed stick.

Gilles nodded, and a small, tight smile appeared on his lips,

'Why?' rapped out Jean de Craon.

'No reason. It amused me.'

'You may amuse yourself thus in war, with your enemies. But not here with the castle curs.'

Jean de Craon turned to the soldiers and gave them a sign. For a moment I had forgotten that all this might have anything to do with me – that I had not merely been summoned here as a spectator. Now I felt myself being lifted off my feet. One of the soldiers grabbed my arms and swung me face down on his broad back. The other loosened the points of my hose, then he rolled them down over my buttocks. Then he took my ankles in a firm grip. Out of the corner of my eye I could see the captain of the guard loosening his broad leather belt. The blow, when it came, knocked the wind out of me. My whole body clenched itself against the pain. The next blow shocked me just as much, though now I knew what it would be like. Four other blows followed. When the two soldiers set me on my feet again, with my hose still trailing around my calves, my legs trembled violently, and I had bitten my tongue in the effort not to cry out. I turned my back in order to make myself decent again, and to hide the tears I could feel brimming in my eyes.

'Now you may both go,' said Jean de Craon in the cold, precise tone I had come to associate with him.

At first I merely hated Gilles for the pain he had caused me. He offered me no apology. We said nothing to one another that night when we went to bed, and we rose in the same heavy silence the next morning. I was trying to plan some kind of revenge – a ducking in the castle moat, a few burrs under his horse's saddle. These repayments seemed not only underhand but inadequate. As I slouched brooding in a corner of the ramparts, still stiff from the beating, I heard a man humming to himself as he strolled along the walk that joined one tower to another. Round the corner came one of the soldiers who had held me the previous day, while I took Gilles's punishment. Seeing me, he paused in mid-stride, then came up and touched my arm.

'It's you, lad, is it? Still sore? Don't worry, our boys will look after things for you. Just wait a day or two.'

I didn't really believe the promise, though I was glad to have his sympathy.

It was immediately after this that I noticed the people of the castle had begun to ostracise Gilles. It was nothing that could be construed as open disrespect. If Gilles gave commands, they were always obeyed, within the limits of his grandfather's orders. Any request which contravened these was simply ignored, passed over in silence and without explanation. For the rest of the time everyone behaved almost as if Gilles was not present, saluting him if this was necessary for respect, but turning their eyes away as he passed. I myself avoided him as much as I could, and never spoke to him unless I had to. This went on for nearly a week.

One afternoon I was again perched high on the ramparts, this time in a spot which gave me a good view of the courtyard. The weather was still warm and fine. Looking down into the sunlit enclosure, I saw Gilles moving across it. His shoulders were hunched, and he was kicking a stone in front of him. The usual quota of guards, or perhaps rather more than usual, were lounging about. I heard one of them whistle, and saw him bring his hand from behind his back. In the broad palm was a ball made of straw covered in leather. The guards often played with one of these, and until recently Gilles and I had been allowed to join in. Adroitly the man tossed the ball to one of his companions, who twisted and threw it between his legs to another guard. Gilles had stopped, and was looking at the game rather wistfully. With a wink, the man who was now holding the ball tossed it straight towards him – an easy catch. In a moment he was in the thick of things.

As I watched, I wondered why he had suddenly been forgiven. Then I realised that I could see a pattern in the activity below. Among the seven or eight men who had joined in the game were the two who had held me while I was being beaten. Their movements were purposeful rather than random. The whole group, with Gilles in the middle of it, was slowly edging its way across the courtyard to the place where a horse-trough stood beside the kitchen door, with a pair of huge crocks next to it. Into these crocks went the scraps and swill which were afterwards used to fatten the pigs. Now the whole group was pressed against the rim of the trough, struggling for possession of the ball.

I did not see who was responsible for tripping Gilles up. From the midst of the knot of bodies came a sudden cry and a splash. At the same time, one of the huge crocks tilted, and emptied most of its contents into the already slimy water of the trough. The next moment all the soldiers had vanished, and the only person left in sight was Gilles, sprawled in the muck, his doublet soaked, his hair sticky with swill. Somewhere out of sight I heard a shutter opening, and a long peal of feminine laughter, hastily cut off.

4

After Gilles's ducking, we were reconciled. Nothing was said, but somehow it was understood that he would never get me beaten again. Indeed, as things turned out, so little supervision was exercised over us that it would have been difficult for either one of us to be caught doing something which would earn Jean de Craon's disapproval. Gradually, too, Gilles made his peace with the men of the garrison, though I noticed that they never trusted or confided in him as they sometimes confided in me.

In early November, news arrived at Champtocé. It was the news which was to change everyone's life in France.

It happened before dawn, in the mist of early morning. A rider came right up to the edge of the moat, and started shouting to the guard. Soon the whole castle was awake, and we lined the walls to learn what was going on. Jean de Craon appeared, with a torch in his hand, and climbed stiffly to the top of one of the towers. After a certain amount of bellowing back and forth, it was decided to lower the drawbridge and let this unexpected messenger in.

When he came into the courtyard, it could be seen that both he and his horse were completely caked in mud. The horse stumbled as it entered, and the rider reeled and toppled from his saddle. He grovelled at Jean de Craon's feet, mumbling incoherently. The one word the rest of us could hear was a name completely strange to us – 'Agincourt'. The syllables ran round from tongue to tongue, till at last someone was found who seemed to remember that Agincourt was an obscure village in northern France. Still holding his torch in his hand, Jean de Craon leaned closer and closer, trying to hear what the man had to say, until his tall figure was bent almost at right angles. Then at last he seemed to understand, and seized the messenger by the arm, dragging him to his feet. The two of them disappeared into the darkness of the great hall.

The morning, after the weeks of golden weather that had preceded it, was grey and rainy. Jean de Craon remained shut up with his visitor. At last, when it was nearly the dinner-hour, the captain of the guard and one or two others were sent for, and it was from them that the rest of us at last heard the news. The king of England had invaded France, and had taken Harfleur, at the mouth of the Seine. Later, his small army had begun to march across country, pursued by the much larger French host. The English, finding the French uncomfortably close to them, had taken up a defensive position between two belts of woodland in the fields near Agincourt. The French knights, pressed together by their own overwhelming numbers, and with no room to manoeuvre, had been mown down by the arrows of the English longbowmen as they tried to charge. Half the great lords of France were now either dead, or else prisoners in English hands.

Jean de Craon did not dine in hall that day, and for the rest of us it was a gloomy meal, with each man speaking in whispers to his neighbour. More news arrived before we had finished eating. There was a hail from outside, as the guard challenged a fresh arrival. Within moments the newcomer was stalking between the tables, with every eye following him. He mounted the dais like a man going to the scaffold, and knocked on the door of Jean de Craon's room.

Soon after dinner, Gilles was sent for. 'You come too,' he said to me.

'Your grandfather didn't say that,' I insisted. I had unhappy memories of Jean de Craon and the solar since my beating, and wanted to stay as far away from both as I could. But Gilles was determined that I should go with him.

When we presented ourselves, the two messengers were still with Jean de Craon. They were as dejected and dispirited a pair of men as I have ever seen in my life. The old man's eyebrows rose when he saw me. 'I did not send for you,' he said. Then he gave a heavy sigh. 'No matter. You may as well stay. The part of the news which is not yet known will be common knowledge soon enough.' Then he turned to the two strangers.

'Gentlemen, I thank you for the pains you have taken in coming so rapidly to inform me. Refresh yourselves and show these to my treasurer in due course.' To each man he handed a parchment slip, with a few words and figures written on it.

They bowed painfully, and backed out of the room. Gilles and I were alone with the master of Champtocé.

For a moment, it seemed as if Jean de Craon did not know how to begin what he wanted to say. He sat down at his table, turning a goose-quill slowly between his fingers, his eyes fixed on his hands rather than on us. Then he looked up.

'You have heard the news, Gilles?'

'Yes, messire.'

'A heavy defeat. I am glad I sent so few men to the host.' He continued to turn the quill absently in his hands. 'There is one important loss.' Still he could not bring himself to pronounce the words.

'My son Adhémar is dead. The second messenger brought definite news that he was killed, not taken. I suppose the ransom might have crippled me. Gilles, do you know what this death means?'

'That you have lost your only son, messire.'

'It means that you will now inherit all my lands as well as those that came to you from your father and mother. You are already rich. When I die you will be amongst the two or three richest men in France. Think about it. Some people say that money and lands are a burden, and that the more of both you have the more troublesome your life becomes. I must say to you now that I have never agreed with them.'

And with this he dismissed us. A requiem mass was sung in the castle chapel, and we all wore mourning for a while (my profit from the battle of Agincourt was a handsome new doublet), but Jean de Craon never mentioned his dead son again.

His attitude towards his new heir was strange. It was almost as if he avoided Gilles, though they both lodged in the same castle. Yet occasionally there were signs that he kept himself well-informed about our activities. In some respects, surprisingly, he had little need to worry. Gilles was an eager scholar. Out of pride, I struggled to keep up with him. Neither of us needed any urging in lessons that concerned the profession of arms. We learned the uses of all weapons, but particularly how to handle the sword and the guisarme. We also learned how to handle a lance on horseback. The master-of-arms made us ride against a dummy which pivoted on a post which raised it to the same level as a mounted man. If you failed to catch the dummy precisely in the centre of its body with your lance. point, it swung round under the impact, and its extended arm caught you a painful crack on the head. The harder you charged at this device, the likelier it was to knock you from your horse – but we made it a point of pride to charge full out. As a result Gilles and I took any number of tumbles in the practice-lists which were laid out to one side of the castle. In the end, however, we became passably skilful jousters.

As we grew up, we rode out hunting more and more often, and for greater distances. Sometimes we were absent from the castle for several days at a time, though on these occasions the rule was that we took an escort of three or four men of the garrison along with us. Though Anjou was not as yet plagued by the robber bands which had begun to infest northern France, it would not have been prudent for us to ride out alone.

Ever since his ducking in the horse-trough, Gilles had been circumspect about the way in which he behaved towards the men of the castle guard. He accepted the deference due to his rank without comment, just as they gave it without apparent effort. But there was something more than this. Gilles now seemed to want to dazzle them, to win a more personal kind of regard from the tough soldiers whom Jean de Craon kept on the payroll, and whom he was careful to feed well and pay regularly.

When we rode out into the countryside, our hawks on our wrists, our hounds running beside us, Gilles also showed another aspect of his nature. He was ruthless about the way in which he trampled down the peasants' crops. Often, indeed, it seemed that he was happier to ride through a field of standing corn than to take the path that ran beside it. For the most part, the peasants themselves took the damage we did quietly enough – Jean de Craon was known to be a harsh overlord – but I noticed, even if Gilles did not, the look of sullen despair on their faces as we trampled their crops flat.

Hunting parties were not the only expeditions that set out from Champtocé. Jean de Craon was not content to sit safe in a strong castle, while the kingdom tumbled to pieces around him. In the weakness of royal authority, he saw his own opportunity. He was constantly extending his own powers, creating rights for himself where they had never existed before. He harried his own peasants, and he harried other people's. All the villages around paid him for his protection, whether he was overlord to them or not. When the mood took him, or when he wanted to give his men something to do (it came to the same thing), he raided deep into neighbouring fiefs. Jean seldom accompanied these raids himself, though, as Gilles and I grew up, he encouraged us to do so. I soon grew sick of seeing peasants strung up by their thumbs to make them tell where their savings were hidden. So much the worse for them if they had accumulated nothing since the last raid. Gilles, on the other hand, would watch the proceedings with placid interest. One reason for undertaking enterprises of this sort, though no one admitted it openly, was that they provided sexual diversion for the garrison. The peasant girls the men tumbled were for the most part not particularly unwilling, though it would have made no practical difference had they been so. They raised their skirts when they were told.

Gilles and I were now fast growing up, and Jean de Craon may have felt that, by encouraging us to ride out in this way, he was providing for our sexual initiation. In my case, he was right. When I was fifteen, a bouncing peasant girl some three or four years older than myself relieved me of my virginity at the same instant the men-at-arms were relieving her father of his money. The event took place in her father's barn, and we were flushed out of the straw the moment after we had reached climax by the rest of the troop coming to set fire to it, since the owner had proven resistant to their demands. The roar of laughter as I emerged with bits of straw in my hair and clinging to the hose I was still lacing up made me blush to the tips of my ears, but secretly I wasn't sorry to have what I had done known publicly.

In matters of sex, Gilles was reticent, and I believe kept what Jean de Craon wished him to lose. He and I continued to share a bed, and the heat of summer in our tower room had taught me to act as he did, and to strip to the skin before retiring. During the summer months just before my sexual initiation, he and I had begun a series of fumbling experiments with one another's bodies. These took place, not when we first went to bed, but in the small hours when one or other of us would stir into semi-wakefulness with an adolescent erection. What had taken place was never acknowledged by either of us in the morning. After I had been with the peasant girl I resumed my hose for a few nights as a sign that things were not to be carried further. Gilles accepted the hint without comment.

It was from this moment, however, that he began to conduct a kind of courtship of the captain of the guard, whom previously he had treated as a sort of servant, even though it was Pierre Cardinal's duty to act as our military instructor, and we were therefore much in his company. Pierre was a Fleming – broad, fair and muscular. The men he commanded liked him; and the girls who worked in the castle kitchens liked him still more. When he washed himself, on summer mornings, in the castle courtyard, they would cluster in the doorway to see him do it, and he swaggered a little, and also blushed a little, as he felt their eyes fix on his solid torso. It was rumoured that he never had to spend a night without a companion, and certainly when we rode out, the peasants didn't need to be asked a second time if he cast an eye on them. It was said you could find unexpected fair-haired children, quite unlike their sisters and brothers in looks, within many miles radius of Champtocé.

Now Gilles began to make every possible opportunity for physical contact with Pierre. When we practised archery with the English longbow, he would insist that Pierre stood behind him to guide his arms and show him the right position. When he failed to hit the target square in the centre, on the days when we practised in the lists, it was into Pierre's embrace that he tumbled as he fell from the saddle. Once or twice, indeed, I thought that he could quite easily have maintained his balance if he had tried a little harder to do so. And on these occasions I thought I saw Pierre blushing, just as he did when the kitchen-girls looked at him.

One hot summer afternoon I was drowsing by myself in an almost deserted castle. Most of the inhabitants had gone to the fields, to help with the harvest. Those members of the guard whose turn it was to keep watch also drowsed and nodded on the walls, and from somewhere deep within the stonework came the humming of bees which had found a crevice within which to build a hive. At that moment they were the only industrious creatures left in Champtocé. But suddenly I was aroused by what sounded like the impact of a blow, followed at an interval by another, and then by another. The noise was so strange and unexpected that I began to hunt for its source, finally tracing it to a room in the base of one of the towers. I made my way round this until I could look in through a low window, left open like all the rest because of the heat. But at first the space within was too dark, in contrast to the dazzle of sunlight outside, for me to be able to make out what was happening. Then I heard Gilles speak.

'More, Pierre,' he commanded. 'You know I can bear more.'

'Messire Gilles,' answered Pierre Cardinal, in a voice simultaneously thickened and pleading, 'I am only flesh and blood. You will lead me into mortal sin.'

'Never mind. That part of it doesn't matter. Now teach me to be a man.'

I could now see what was going on, and a strange sight it was. Gilles was trussed face downward on a wooden bench like those we sat on in the dining-hall, with his hose lowered and trailing round his calves. Across his buttocks and thighs were a number of fresh weals. Standing over him was the captain of the guard, stripped to the waist and sweating profusely, with a familiar leather strap in his hands.

'Again!' said Gilles. With a kind of groan, Pierre swung the belt and brought it crashing down with the full force of his arm. The memory of the beating he had once administered to me made me clench my own muscles involuntarily, and I could see Gilles shudder under the weight of the blow. Pierre raised his arm once more, but seemed to think better of what he was going to do. He dropped the strap, and began to fumble urgently with his own hose. Then he threw himself on top of the prostrate figure before him.

'Too soon, Pierre, too soon,' was what I thought I heard Gilles murmur as he accepted the assault.

I was in two minds as to whether or not to mention what I had seen to Gilles, and perhaps I wasn't very good at concealing my curiosity. One night, as we were preparing to go to bed, Gilles suddenly turned his naked back to me.

'All right,' he said. 'You can take a good look.'

'But for what reason?' I said, my voice cracking.

'You should have asked me who was responsible, just as you did last time. Would you prefer our friend Pierre to mark you instead of me? After all, that's the way my grandfather would have it.'

'Why did you make him do it?'

'We must all learn to bear suffering. It's not something you can find out about at second hand.'

'And to bear pleasure, too?' I retorted.

Gilles looked at me soberly. 'Ah,' he said, 'you've been busier than I thought. I had to let him do what he wanted, in return for doing what I wanted. There's a bargain in everything, as you know.'

'But Pierre likes women,' I protested.

'Pierre is like the animals. He needs the act itself. And like the animals, he knows how to forget what he has done.'

5

1420 was a year of disasters. The Duke of Burgundy signed a treaty with the King of England. Queen Isabeau of France signed it too, on behalf of her husband the mad King Charles. She thus disinherited her own son, the Dauphin Charles. And in that same year Gilles de Rais got married. His grandfather arranged it, as he arranged so many things, and it was a dynastic union. The bride was Gilles's cousin. This may sound simple enough, but there was more to it than appeared on the surface.

One reason why Jean de Craon had taken his grandson to live with him was that he wanted, not only to control Gilles's lands while he was a minor, but to see to his marriage. By marrying Gilles to the right girl, Jean could extend his own influence still further. Almost from the moment his grandson arrived at Champtocé, he was busy with negotiations. On the infrequent occasions when he sent for Gilles, it was usually to tell him about some matrimonial project. But these were always being called off, as the political situation altered.

On the day he sent for us, neither of us suspected that there was anything unusual in the wind. But Jean was unexpectedly genial when we presented ourselves before him.

'Good morning, grandson,' he said. 'I have asked you to come and see me because there is something to be settled. How old are you now, by the way?'

'Sixteen, messire.' Gilles knew his grandfather was well aware of this fact.

'About time you were married, then?'

'I have heard you say so before, messire.'

'Yes, as you know I have made a few enquiries on your behalf.' Jean waved his hand, dismissing previous schemes. 'But now I have something more definite in mind. You remember your cousin, Catherine de Thouars.'

'I don't think I've met her,' said Gilles, dubiously.

'You will, shortly. A pretty girl with a tiresome mother. She is also the heiress of lands which march with yours. Just the person for you to marry.'

'If you say so, messire.'

'However,' Jean de Craon continued briskly, 'I foresee one or two problems. There is the degree of consanguinity, which will mean difficulties with Holy Mother Church, and delays while we get a dispensation. And the girl's mother has foolish ideas of her own. Too much delay might give her time to do something about them. On the whole, it would be best if there was an elopement.'

'An elopement, messire?'

'Don't keep echoing me, boy. You know perfectly well what I mean. You must carry her off. Once she's wedded and bedded her mother can make as much fuss as she likes. And the Church will soon come round. I've made a few enquiries about that already. I've also found out what the girl's routine is. She's shockingly badly guarded. She lives only about twenty leagues from here, and it ought to be easy enough to kidnap her. You and Raoul, with a few of my men to help you, ought to be able to manage it without any trouble. It's all settled. We can do it at the beginning of next week.'

As always when his mind was made up, Jean de Craon was quite inflexible in carrying out his plan. The horses were saddled early one morning, and the two of us rode out with Pierre Cardinal and four of his best men. As we trotted through the springtime countryside, the peasants tilling their fields looked sullenly away from us, and one of them spat in a furrow.

After we had ridden for most of the day, and had gone well beyond the boundaries of Jean de Craon's territories, we arrived at a large fortified farm. The farmer appeared to greet us only after prolonged hammering at the door. He was a shifty-looking individual, not the kind of man one would expect to find as tenant of such a handsome-looking property. He was a widower, and had a son of about twenty who seemed as shifty as himself, and a somewhat older but not unhandsome daughter who kept house for him.

It was at once apparent that she and the captain of the guard were acquainted. Jean de Craon's plot, unknown to us, had been in the making for a period of time, and, as the threads were being drawn together, the girl and Pierre had inevitably reached an understanding of their own. Gilles watched their manoeuvrings sardonically.

The farmer fed us – good rough fare – and we bedded down in the outbuildings. He offered to turn out of his own bed for 'the young lords', as he dubbed Gilles and myself, but we preferred to sleep with the other men in the straw. Soon after we had settled ourselves for the night we heard a slight scraping as the barn door opened and then shut again. Though she did not carry a light, I thought I recognized the silhouette of our host's daughter in the pale beam of moonlight which stole in with the intruder. Soon there were subdued but unmistakeable sounds of love-making from the spot where the captain had settled himself.

The next morning, though we rose very early, the woman was already gone. She greeted us in the kitchen with hot barley broth, and scraps of mutton from last night's dinner. We rode out into the pearly spring dawn, and this time our host's son came with us. An hour or so later we were holed up in a small wood which overlooked a winding pathway beside a lake. It was a good spot for an ambush, and the youth assured us that the girl and her duenna had to take this route when they left the nearby castle to go hawking, as they did every morning. There was rather a long wait after this. It seemed that Catherine de Thouars liked to lie in bed for a while, even after the sun rose. Our horses grew restless, and I could hear the captain of the guard cursing them under his breath.

At last we heard the sound of hooves and the jingle of harness, and the quarry came into sight. There were two women with hawks on their wrists and an escort of two mounted archers. Because of the narrowness of the path they were strung out in single file. First came one of the archers, then a plump, blonde girl whom I guessed to be a little older than myself. She wore a green dress and there were bells on her bridle. Her fair hair flowed on to her shoulders – the emblem of virginity. 'Gilles will soon put that right,' I thought to myself, with a little stirring of excitement. The duenna was more than plump – she was massive, with a tall headdress balanced by a cascade of wobbling chins. Her appearance made me groan, as it was I who had been assigned to take care of her.

When the procession was clear of the woodland ride from which it had come, and the individual riders could be seen clearly against the still water of the lake, the captain of the guard dropped his hand. Two crossbow bolts whirred towards the quarry and the soldiers of the escort dropped in their tracks. The four horses – two of them now riderless – started to buck and rear as our party swept down on them.

Gilles grabbed Catherine de Thouars's bridle, and I did the same for the duenna. As I took it, she started to scream, chins wobbling violently. For a moment I was nonplussed. The noise was very loud, and it was all too evident that she had the lung-power to keep it up. At the same time, however, I noticed, out of the corner of my eye, that our men were busy with the two archers who had been so neatly tumbled from their horses. One was dead – the bolt had got him in the eye. The other, wounded in the leg, had pulled himself to his knees and was trying to crawl away into cover. As he made for the nearest bush, Pierre Cardinal seized him by the hair, jerked his head back, and neatly cut his throat, as if he were a stag we had brought down while hunting. I leant close and hissed in the duenna's ear: 'Stupid bitch! Do you want that to happen to you?' She took one look, turned clay-coloured, and immediately fell silent, apart from the occasional hiccup which set her dewlaps trembling again.

The rest was simple. We returned the way we had come. As we neared the farm, the farmer's son left us. I heard the chink of money as he clasped hands with the captain. Putting spurs to our horses, we moved as fast as we could towards Champtocé, the duenna wailing and protesting every step of the way. When we arrived, it was already night. The battlements were ablaze with torches and Jean de Craon was waiting at the drawbridge to greet us. He handed the demoiselle Catherine from her horse with elaborate courtesy, and one could see that she was already halfway reconciled to her fate. She glanced around the courtyard with a certain complacency, as if saying to herself: 'All this will be mine one day'. Even the duenna stifled her hiccups when she saw the size of the castle and the number of people who lived in it.

Jean de Craon had a young priest waiting, and we were no sooner off our horses than he shepherded us into the castle chapel. Though it was full of lighted candles I reflected to myself, a little uncomfortably, that the rule was that no marriage should be made except by daylight. I wondered why Jean had been unwilling to wait until the next morning. The priest stuttered and stumbled through the marriage service, and within a few moments Gilles and Catherine were man and wife – in the eyes of those present if not in those of the Church. We then went into the great hall, where there was wine waiting, and a joint of cold meat.

'Not much of a wedding feast,' I thought to myself, 'for the man who is heir to the richest fief in Anjou.' Catherine, however, after Jean de Craon had pledged her health and that of her bridegroom, was looking quite cheerful, thrusting her bosom out in response to each compliment the old fox paid her. Gilles, on the other hand, seemed pale and out of sorts. 'For God's sake fill this up for me,' he whispered, holding out his cup. 'I'm afraid that plump cow will smother me, once we climb into bed.'

He downed the wine I brought him in a single gulp, and I noticed he was none too steady on his feet as we moved towards the solar. Jean de Craon had surrendered it for the occasion to the bridal couple, and a huge bed had been erected, which filled up half the space. Gilles and Catherine were bedded down to the accompaniment of the usual obscene jokes, and I noted that the duenna forgot herself sufficiently to giggle at some of the saltier sallies – she, too, had refreshed herself liberally with Jean de Craon's wine. After a few minutes the old man decided that we had done enough to accord with tradition, and shepherded us firmly out of the room.

The next morning I was awoken by a loud knocking at the door of the tower room I usually shared with Gilles. 'Get up, Raoul, the master wants you in the hall!' It was still early – hardly daylight – and I pulled on my clothes and descended grumbling into the courtyard. There I found the duenna, rubbing her knuckles against her swollen eyes. 'What a head I've got this morning,' she sighed. 'I'm sure I don't know if I'm awake or asleep. What will the girl's mother say? Anyway, there was nothing I could do about it.' At this thought, she sniffed complacently. We went into the hall and found Jean de Craon waiting for us, accompanied by a band of musicians. In those days we had little music at Champtocé, and I saw that he had assembled anyone who had even minimal skill with an instrument – soldier, stable-boy, kitchen-lad, it didn't seem to matter what they were, so long as they could play a few notes. A motley lot they were, and the noise they made when told to strike up was scarcely harmonious.

They played half a tune, and Jean de Craon flung open the door that led from the dais. He then took the duenna's hand and ushered her in. The newly-weds were still in bed, lying, as I thought, somewhat rigidly apart from one another. The old man put out his long arm and twitched the covers off them in a single sweep. Instinctively, they both drew up their legs and covered themselves with their hands. The movement revealed a generous stain of red on the bottom sheet. As soon as he caught sight of it, Jean de Craon gave a grunt of satisfaction.

'There you are, madame,' he rasped to his companion. 'You may ride back to the girl's mother today, for I think there is now no necessity to detain you further. You will, of course, be able to speak of what you have seen this morning.'

Yet, after this, matters did not by any means go as smoothly as messire Jean had anticipated. Catherine's mother, who was called Beatrice de Montjean, turned out to be a tougher nut than he had thought. She refused to acknowledge the match, and she was full of shifts to delay the formal consent of the ecclesiastical authorities. The young priest who had performed the ceremony was arrested, and was given a rough time of it when he came before his superiors at Angers.

Meanwhile, the bride and bridegroom showed little sympathy for one another. Gilles usually refused to share Catherine's bed after the wedding night. 'Why should I sleep with her,' he said, 'when no one seems to know if I am really married to her or not?' Catherine kept mostly to her own quarters, and when she and Gilles sat next to one another in hall, her attitude was subtly charged with contempt. Jean de Craon affected to ignore all this, but I could tell he was worried from the number of times that he sent for me in order to interrogate me about the subject. But he gave me no sign of the surprise he had in store. About six months after his grandson's marriage, messire Jean announced that he intended to get married again himself.

When he rode back to Champtocé with his bride, I couldn't imagine what had got into him. Most people at the castle felt the same. Jean's new wife, Anne de Sillé, was a tall, bony woman of nearly his own age – so old that there was clearly no hope of his having children by her. Her clothes, as she rode into the courtyard, showed that she was not rich. Her riding-habit was old and worn, and her bridegroom had not bothered to provide her with a new one. The mare she rode was nearly as bony as herself. It was only when Catherine appeared that I got a glimpse of the old man's motives. 'Why, grandmother,' she said demurely, as she dropped a deep curtsey, sweeping her gown into the straw and litter, 'what brings you to this dreary hole? Elopements seem to run in our family.'

Anne de Sillé made no reply to this. She was a cowed, careworn creature. Jean had chosen her neither for her looks, her personality, nor her fortune, but because it gave him a firmer grip on Catherine herself. Anne's presence at Champtocé made the disputed marriage seem more respectable than it was.

From the first, Jean's new wife made little impact on his

household. Having married her, her new husband treated her quite simply as if she wasn't there. She and her grand-daughter passed a dull enough time together, sewing and spinning in a turret room which had been fitted up as a bower for the two of them. There was no question of Jean giving up the solar to their use. There was a guard posted outside the door of their room at all times, which made it clear what their position was: they were hostages as much as wives. Of course, Gilles and I could go in and out, just as we liked, but we saw little of them, for they gave us no welcome.

The main change brought about by Anne de Sillé's arrival was that, from being two, we now became three. Jean's bride brought with her (it was the one condition she had succeeded in imposing) a pair of followers. They were very unlike. One was a waiting-woman, as severe and elderly as her mistress. The other was a young man just a year or two older than ourselves. He too was called Gilles – Gilles de Sillé. His connection with the lord's new wife was left purposely undefined, but it was clear that she acknowledged him as some kind of relation. Indeed, one could see the relationship if you looked at Sillé himself, despite the differences of sex and age. He had the same kind of lantern-jaw as Anne had, and the same raw-boned figure. His forehead was marked by a deep scar. Despite his unprepossessing looks, the old woman adored him. Her face lit up whenever she caught sight of him.

I disliked Gilles de Sillé from the first. There was something about him which was simultaneously harsh and conniving. Though gruff and brutal whenever he thought he could get away with it, he proved remarkably adept at insinuating himself into the good graces of his namesake. From the moment he arrived, Gilles de Sillé was determined that Gilles de Rais should make his fortune. I noticed that Sillé took every opportunity to draw Gilles aside, to flatter him, to convince him that nothing should stand in the way of his caprices. For all his ugliness, the dark youth had a powerful sexuality, and I sometimes thought that he behaved to Gilles more like a man courting a woman than like a comrade with a comrade. Gilles had again taken to sharing a bed with me, but now there were times when he made an excuse to sleep with Sillé.

There were occasions, too, when they would absent themselves from Champtocé for quite long periods. On one occasion, at about this time, they spent a full month together in Angers. The business of Gilles's marriage to Catherine still dragged on, and Jean de Craon had sent them there to negotiate with the bishop. Gilles returned from this visit in a state of subdued excitement, and he and Sillé now had an air of complicity which I did not like. All I could get out of them was that, after two years, the union was indeed about to be given the blessing of Mother Church.

6

When it came, by the hand of one of the bishop's servants, the authorisation of Gilles's marriage was something of an anti-climax. However, Jean de Craon was determined that the occasion should be marked by a good deal of festivity. Normally, he was not a man who paraded his wealth. For him, it was enough to know that the money was there, and he saw no point in wasting it in order to try and dazzle his neighbours. But now a second marriage ceremony would be a way of announcing his victory over Beatrice de Montjean, and at the same time of making an *amende honorable* to the Church.

The preparations were arduous. Jean de Craon bought enough cloth from the travelling merchants who passed his door to make new liveries in blue and white for the men of the garrison, and even their wives were provided with enough stuff to make new gowns. For Gilles and I, and also for Gilles de Sillé, there were new doublets and parti-coloured hose. Gilles's were in scarlet (the costliest colour) with a pattern in gold. The toes of our shoes were in the most extreme court fashion – those worn by Gilles were so long that their tips had to be chained to garters just below each knee.

The bishop of Angers had been invited to perform the marriage ceremony – but here there was a hitch. Though the prelate was ready to give his dispensation, so that two persons so closely related in blood could marry, and also to forget, at least officially, what had happened in the past, he was unwilling to take forgiveness much further. One of his chaplains was delegated to do the job instead.

As soon as the man arrived, a fierce argument broke out. Was he there merely to bless and confirm the marriage which had taken place two years previously, or was he to conduct an entirely new ceremony? Jean de Craon tried to persuade him that the former would be the best course, but the chaplain's instructions were quite explicit. The first wedding had been no wedding at all, and the knot must be tied anew.

Catherine, who had been wearing her hair up and covered, after the fashion of married women, was instructed to let it down again and leave it flowing over her shoulders as it had been when she first came to Champtocé. She received these orders with a bad grace. 'Everyone knows I'm no longer a virgin,' she said, 'though I haven't had much profit, or even pleasure, out of losing my virginity.' By this time she and Gilles were scarcely on speaking terms. If they slept together once a month it was because they were browbeaten into it.

In order to assert herself, Catherine insisted on a magnificent gown of figured velvet, with trailing sleeves edged with fur and a train that stretched a foot behind her on the ground. As a consolation for Gilles's refusal to share her bed she had begun to over-eat, and the voluminous folds of material made her look blowsy. The harsh yellow of the stuff she had chosen clashed with the crimson of her cheeks.

Despite the indifference which bride and bridegroom showed towards one another both during the ceremony itself and during the festivities which followed, matters went off well enough. The marriage was followed by a feast in the great hall, and at the conclusion of this various 'subtleties' were brought in by sweating page-boys. One was a swan made of almond paste, and another was a model of the castle. They had been created by a pastry-cook specially brought from Angers for the purpose, who not only extracted a huge fee from Jean de Craon but completely upset the routine of the kitchen, so that many of the dishes came in either under-cooked or burnt to a cinder. But there was such a profusion of food, and so much wine to wash it down with, that few people noticed.

After dinner there was a joust in the lists. A special booth or tribune had been built in the middle of one long side, and hung with some of Jean de Craon's tapestries. In this Catherine, who was by now somewhat tipsy, was installed as Queen of Beauty. Gilles and I and Gilles de Sillé were to be her three champions, offering to take on all comers, and before the tournament began she gave each of us a token – to me a scarf, to Sillé a garter, and to her husband a handkerchief. As she leant down to hand it to him she deliberately blew her nose on it. Few people noticed, but I saw Gilles's face freeze at the deliberate coarseness of the gesture.

Thanks to all the wine we had drunk, the jousting was wild and rough. I knocked a couple of opponents off their horses before being toppled myself by a man twice my weight and five years older. The mêlée at the end of the joust, when the three of us pitted ourselves against the three most successful visitors, developed into a fight which was both hot-tempered and unskilful, and we were getting decidedly the worst of it when Jean de Craon used the failing light and the churned-up condition of the ground as an excuse to sound the trumpet and bring things to a halt. I had taken a blow on the head that nearly split my helmet, and a slash on the hand that bit deep into my mailed gauntlet. Gilles and Sillé were in much the same condition.

The most conspicuous absentee from the festivities was the bride's mother. Just before Jean de Craon came to terms with the Church on his grandson's behalf, we had received news of Beatrice de Montjean's remarriage. Her choice was ominous. Her second husband was a man of half her own age, a young knight who was one of the Dauphin's chamberlains. Such a man, with a foothold at court and his way to make in the world, would certainly encourage Beatrice to fight for her rights, and her failure to appear for the second wedding was a clear sign of her obduracy.

Jean was not a man to allow her to plot some new move without himself trying a counter-measure. Within a month of the marriage festivities he kidnapped Beatrice and her younger sister just as he had once taken Catherine. The only difference was that on this occasion Gilles and I were kept well out of the business. We returned late one evening from a hunting expedition to be told that messire Jean would like to see us. He looked as if he was savouring some secret joke. 'Ah, grandson,' he said, 'we have an interesting visitor this evening.'

'I look forward to seeing him in hall,' Gilles replied, rather curtly. The hunt had been long, and we had had poor sport.

'Not *him* but *her*,' the old man corrected him. 'And I am afraid the lady will be unable to join us. We must go and see our visitor instead. Come.' With this he led us towards the doorway that led to the castle prisons.

These prisons were usually well-populated. Anyone who offended the lord of Champtocé was liable to find himself locked up in them, whether there was anything legal about the arrest or not. Any merchant who dared to cheat Jean de Craon over the payment of toll, for example, was liable to be seized and kept till his friends raised a large ransom for him.

Though Jean did not believe in pampering guests of this sort, the cells were of varying degrees of discomfort. The best were above ground, and had a little light. In fact, apart from the lack of fire and furniture, they were not much worse than the rooms some of the rest of us lodged in. Beneath these ground-level cells were the true dungeons, and further underground still were the lightless stinking holes into which the privies drained on their way to final discharge in the moat.

The cell we now approached was luxurious in comparison to most of the rest. As we moved along the corridor, I heard the sound of hysterical sobbing, and then another voice, also feminine, which seemed to rebuke the woman who was crying. Jean de Craon unlocked the door with a key which he took from the pocket of his gown. Sure enough, there were two women inside. One lay weeping noisily on a rough pallet bed under the narrow window, through which the last daylight struggled. As her companion turned to face us I saw that she was dressed like a person of some quality. Her face was stony, her eyes tearless.

'Madame,' said Jean de Craon, 'allow me to present your son-in-law. I believe you have never met?'

'I've no son-in-law that I know of,' Beatrice replied. As my eyes accustomed themselves to the dimness I could see that she was a plump, handsome woman with a physical resemblance to her daughter, but marked by far greater intelligence and firmness of character.

'It is a pity you refuse to acknowledge him. If you are too obdurate, he may decide to do without you. Many people live quite comfortably without a mother-in-law. Indeed, I have heard some say they are better off without.'

Jean de Craon's voice was menacing. Behind me, Sillé snickered. I had not realised that he had followed us into the room.

'I have a husband,' Beatrice said fiercely, her chin going up.

'Much good you will be to him, sewn in a sack and thrown into the Loire.'

At the sound of this threat, the woman on the bed sat up and began to scream hysterically. Beatrice rounded on her.

'Shut up, sister,' she said. 'You're as much of a fool as my poor daughter used to be.' She turned her attention to Gilles and the clamour subsided. 'You may think you've got a good bargain in my Catherine,' she said, 'and no doubt you have, if you can hold on to her lands. But I imagine you've discovered she's stupid enough to drive any man crazy. And shrewish as well.'

For some reason this got Gilles on the raw. He stepped forward, hand on his dagger. 'I'll make you meat for the eels!' he shouted. His grandfather pulled him away.

'The lady Beatrice is not herself,' he said. 'She needs time to think about the promise I have just made to her. For the time being, at least, the eels will have to wait for their dinner.' The sister was screaming again as he closed the door after us.

For once Anne de Sillé dared to cross her husband's wishes, and it was she who persuaded Jean de Craon to listen when messengers arrived from Beatrice's new husband. Jean made quite a ceremony of their reception, enthroning himself in the great hall as he did when he dispensed seigneurial justice. There were three emissaries. The leader was a pretty young coxcomb in his early twenties – one Pierre Meschin, now Beatrice's brother-in-law. At first he tried to take a high line. His expostulations were tranquilly received.

'I don't see why the lady Beatrice should not remain here indefinitely,' Jean said. 'She is adequately lodged, and she has the company not only of her sister but of her only daughter and my wife, who is her former mother-in-law.'

'And fears every day to be drowned by your men,' Pierre Meschin answered hotly.

'I see our castle walls have ears,' Jean said, knitting his brows.

It was at this point that Anne de Sillé entered and threw herself at her husband's feet. She did it so awkwardly that it was clear that things must have been arranged, if not rehearsed, beforehand. Jean played the noble husband very graciously, raised the old woman up, and smoothly agreed to her request that Beatrice should now be released. There was a stir of surprise in the assembly.

We were doubly surprised when the two women were brought in and told they were free to go. The sister – her name was Isabelle – immediately burst into a fit of sobbing. As I had noticed before, she was not a woman who cried gracefully. Beatrice shot her a venomous look. 'You've done nothing but snivel since misfortune overtook us,' she snapped. Then, turning to Jean: 'I suppose there's some trick in this, but I'm tired of prison. When can we go?'

'Your horses are saddled and waiting.' This caused another and even louder stir, as it was now clear that Jean de Craon had planned the whole thing in advance.

'Very well. My husband's brother, master Pierre, can be our escort.' With this, Beatrice turned on her heel and made ready to go.

'Madame, I'm afraid you misinterpret me. You are free to leave. But your brother-in-law and his companions must stay with me until we reach some kind of settlement. My guards will show them to their quarters.'

I saw the coxcomb turn white as two soldiers took him by the arms. 'Since you are so good at making speeches, master Pierre,' Jean continued, in the same level tone, 'you will not mind if I lodge you in the *basse-fosse*. Our castle rats are a little crude, and need educating.'

I have heard men beg for mercy since, but the sound of Pierre Meschin's cries as they hustled him away still remains with me. He knew the reputation of Jean de Craon's justice, and he must have known, too, the unyielding stubbornness of his new sister-in-law. He realised he was about to be crushed between the upper and nether millstones of two formidable wills.

Crushed he was. By the time that Beatrice and Jean had completed their complex bargaining for possession of Catherine's inheritance, Pierre Meschin was much changed. Gilles, Gilles de Sillé and I stood on the ramparts to watch his departure, when Jean de Craon at long last decided to let him go. His two companions were pale and thin after their long sojourn in the cold and darkness, like plants that have been kept a long time from the light. But Meschin was completely broken. They carried him out of the gate and put him in a horse-litter. His wasted limbs would not support him even for the few steps that were necessary to take him over the drawbridge. He was still wearing remnants of the finery he had arrived in, but his hose and doublet were filthy, and hung in tatters from his body. His hair had grown long and matted, and trailed on his cheeks and collar like mouldy straw. His eyes stared fixedly upwards as they carried him out, and his lips were drawn back in a rictus. As he struggled to make himself comfortable in the litter, I noticed that his knees and ankles were grotesquely swollen, while thighs and calves were alike wasted to nothing. Beside me Gilles's laugh rang out.

'That poor fool won't last more than two or three days longer,' he said. 'Do you know, Raoul, I used to take a torch and go down there to see him where he stood in the darkness, up to his ankles in slime. When I first visited him, he used to curse me, but later on he begged quite prettily for his release. I always told him I'd speak to my grandfather, but of course I never did.'

Not knowing what to say, I turned my back, and heard him laugh again and make some remark to Sillé, who lounged on his other side. Later, I was incautious enough to say to the latter that I found the way in which Jean de Craon had treated Pierre Meschin disgusting, especially as Pierre had arrived equipped with a safe-conduct. I added that I was surprised at Gilles's behaviour in further tormenting the man.

Sillé gave me his insolent, lop-sided grin. 'Though you have spent more years here than I,' he said, 'you seem to have learnt little. We have a good school here at Champtocé to teach us how a true lord should behave. I advise you to profit from it, as I myself am doing.'

7

Meanwhile, the condition of the kingdom grew no better. The terrible Henry V died in 1421, and the poor mad king of France in 1422. France was now split into three realms. One, the most prosperous, was ruled by the young Duke of Burgundy. His French lands were only part of his inheritance from his murdered father. Most of the duke's wealth came from the Low Countries: from the bustling county of Flanders, from Brabant, from Artois and from Hainault. A second realm was governed by John, Duke of Bedford, brother of the dead English king, as regent for his nephew, the infant Henry VI. The English held Normandy, and they controlled Paris and much of northern France, as well as their old possessions in Guyenne. The third realm was the kingdom of Bourges, ruled by Charles VI's only surviving son. Many of us still called this prince the Dauphin, partly out of habit, partly out of doubt that he was really the king's true heir. His mother, Queen Isabeau, had long been notorious for her infidelities, and now she hinted, and sometimes more than hinted, that this enemy son of hers was none of her husband's making.

The gossip that came to us at Champtocé concerning the Dauphin's court was depressing, and not the least depressing part of it concerned Charles himself. At first he had seemed a gracious and energetic prince, struggling against the many misfortunes that had befallen him. But now he allowed himself to be governed by favourites, wicked and violent men, raised high for a few years, or even for a few months, then suddenly cast down. The Dauphin submitted himself to the rule of each in turn, but showed no sorrow when they fell.

At Champtocé, there was dissension within the walls. Gilles, who had for so long been happy to let his grandfather make the important decisions in his life, now grew restless. Sillé was largely responsible. He was always in Gilles's company, urging him to take control of his own affairs, to behave like the great lord he undoubtedly was by virtue of birth and lands. Sillé's refrain, constantly repeated, was 'You are no longer a child, Gilles. You have reached your majority. It is time to behave like a man.' Gilles's notion of behaving like a man was to quarrel with his grandfather, and sometimes with his wife. There were stormy interviews in the solar, and raised voices in the ladies' bower.

At first it seemed as if Gilles was making no progress in winning his independence. Jean de Craon was too inflexible to make any concessions to his grandson. In any case, the garrison looked to him, and he had long been used to having the mastery in his own house. The stewards referred all business to Jean as a matter of course, even where it concerned Gilles's lands and revenues.

Sillé, however, was equal to the situation. Jean de Craon continued to supply Gilles lavishly with money, and for some months Sillé saw to it that this was not spent as carelessly as before. Soon enough had been accumulated for the enterprise he had in mind. One day, he and Gilles slipped away to Angers, and, when they returned, they brought with them a retinue of lawyers. They were also accompanied by a small bodyguard, a band of ruffians which Gilles had recruited into his own service. Sillé had been given command of these, and he made a fitting captain for them.

The real point, however, was that the law was on Gilles's side, and Jean de Craon, though with a bad grace, was forced to give him the power to govern his own lands. To my surprise, we did not at once move from Champtocé to some other castle, where Gilles could set up his own household. Instead, the place was more crowded than ever, with some men responsible to Gilles and some to his grandfather. The men-at-arms in our swollen garrison often brawled with one another, and Sillé swaggered about, stirring up trouble. But then the tension was relieved by two events.

One was the latest revolution at the Dauphin's court. It brought to power a new favourite, a man rather different from his predecessors: not a handsome young adventurer on the make, but a nobleman of position and substance. His name was Georges de la Tremoïlle, and he was a man after Jean de Craon's own heart, a ruthless schemer who could be relied upon not to overreach himself as his predecessors had done, and with more than enough cash to sustain his enterprises. Better still, La Tremoïlle was Gilles's cousin. As soon as he got news

Jean dismissed his recent animosity against his grandson, and started to plan a way of using this connection to benefit the family as a whole.

The right opportunity was a little slow in coming, but it came at last, and from an unexpected quarter. One day Jean de Craon received an official letter from Queen Yolanda, his lawful suzerain and Duchess of Anjou. In ordinary circumstances a message of this kind would have been greeted with impatient contempt. Jean was quick to enforce the feudal obligations of those beneath him, but he did not like to be reminded of the service which he himself owed. Now things were different. Queen Yolanda's letter was brief and to the point. She made her 'dearly beloved cousin, Jean de Craon' her lieutenant-general in the duchy, and commanded him to raise troops and to muster her forces for a new effort against the English invader. Jean understood perfectly what she expected of him. Her feeling was that the Craon territories had not been contributing their fair share to the cost of the war. Now, as her lieutenant, Jean would be responsible for paying her troops, which were really his own.

Normally the old man would have resisted such an obvious ruse, putting an infinity of delays in the way, and raising as few men as he could, and equipping them as poorly as possible. But now he was eager to carry out his suzerain's command. It was not difficult to see why. He was too old to go to the wars himself. Yolanda would not expect that. What she wanted what he would gladly do – send his grandson in his stead. Thus the quarrels at Champtocé would be resolved, and, in Gilles's absence, control of his inheritance would revert to Jean's accustomed hands.

Far from opposing his grandfather's plans, Gilles was eager to go, and nothing Sillé could say would dissuade him. He was tired of the narrow world of Champtocé. In his mind's eye he saw himself brilliantly arrayed and playing a decisive part at court and in battles which would decide the fate of the kingdom. At the same time, I noticed that his excitement had a darker undertone. Ever since Gilles's return from his visit to Angers, he had had an air of suppressed excitement, as if he had discovered a new and secret source of energy. For the first time I felt myself deliberately excluded from something which concerned Gilles intimately. The natural assumption was that something still lay hidden between him and Sillé – some part of their plot against Jean de Craon which had not as yet ripened. Yet, though Sillé was obviously aware of what was passing through Gilles's mind, this seemed to go beyond mere commonplace mischief.

Even before the arrival of Queen Yolanda's summons, Gilles had developed a new and uncharacteristic interest in what went on at the Dauphin's court. What fascinated him most was the personality of the most-hated of Charles's favourites, Pierre de Giac, in whose downfall La Tremoïlle had played a leading part. De Giac's end had been horrible. A band of conspirators had arrived, early one morning, to snatch de Giac from his bed, and from the arms of his wife. They carried him off in his nightshirt, with one boot on and one boot off, and brought him before a tribunal of his deadliest enemies. There he was sentenced to be sewn in a sack and drowned. La Tremoïlle supervised the execution.

Gilles listened avidly to the description of the wretched man's death. The sack with the suffocating victim inside was seen writhing in the waters of a stream barely deep enough to cover it, while the executioner rode his great black warhorse in and out of the willows along the bank, waiting till the agony was over. One detail fascinated Gilles especially. It was the rumour of the prisoner's last request before they thrust him into the bag. 'He begged them to lop off his right hand before they drowned him, because he had signed a pact with the devil, and the devil would use the hand that held the pen to draw him down into hell. Raoul, do you think that's possible?'

'Do I think what is possible – that a man should use pen and paper to sign a pact with a fiend who appeared physically before him, or that the same fiend should afterwards carry him off to damnation? If one is possible, then I suppose the other is too.'

'You're not taking the subject seriously. It's blasphemous not to believe in the devil and damnation.'

'There are plenty of ways men can damn themselves. I expect de Giac went straight to hell in any case. Didn't he poison his first wife in order to be free to marry a richer woman?'

Gilles heaved an impatient sigh and turned his back – his usual way of terminating a conversation that dissatisfied him. It was clear that the subject was suddenly of great importance to him, and that I had offended by refusing to discuss it.

This slight coldness was soon forgotten, however, in the excitement of preparing for the campaign. I was put in charge of raising a new and larger company, of which I was to be the captain. Some of the men came from the castle garrison – Jean de Craon was willing to release a few of the younger ones who had a thirst for adventure. Some were younger sons of local tenant farmers, aware that there were too many mouths to feed at home, and eager to achieve some kind of independence. Since our region had as yet suffered very little from the war, these youngsters were well-fed and sturdily built. I thought it would not take very much training to turn them into useful soldiers. Finally, and somewhat against my will, I was forced to accept a number of old soldiers, men from broken companies who had come drifting down into our part of the world in search of a new employer. I did not altogether trust these, and when one of them was caught trying to rob an old woman in a nearby village, I had him hanged promptly and with some ceremony. Jean de Craon thoroughly approved of my decisiveness – he did not allow anyone to rob his own people except under direct orders from himself. To mark his approval, he made me a present of a fine horse.

Our preparations moved at such a leisurely pace that it was late in the season before we set off – we had reached the autumn of the year 1428. One last-minute hitch was caused by a little page called Poitou, whom Gilles had recently recruited into his service. It was Sillé who had called Gilles's attention to this exceptionally pretty child, as they were passing through a hamlet on the very edge of Jean de Craon's lands, in search of extra recruits for Sillé's company (he had grown jealous that my following was now substantially larger than his, and had persuaded Gilles to give him the funds to swell his numbers). Poitou was the son of a widow, just as I had been – but I gathered that she was a widow of a very different sort from my poor mother. In fact, to put it bluntly, she was the village whore, and survived by living with whatever man would give her cash, food or shelter, for as long as he would keep her. She was keenly aware of her son's attractions, and drove a hard bargain when Gilles offered to take him into his household. Poitou was worth several gold pieces to her, and security through at least two winters if she kept the money carefully.

Gilles was delighted with the child, and for a month or so before we left would attend to nothing else, putting off the day of our departure several times in succession because of some expedition he wanted to make with the new favourite, or some present he wanted to procure for him. Poitou, who had arrived dirty and in rags, was now dressed in the finest silks, and velvets, and had a handsome dappled pony to ride. He looked far more like a young nobleman than a hired servant. Gilles hated to be parted from him, and kept him in his room at night. Sillé, who was chiefly responsible for the child's arrival in our midst, now looked at him sourly, and behaved almost as if he were Poitou's rival for Gilles's affections. The page was also detested by Gilles's wife Catherine, who claimed that he had really been recruited for her own service, and that it was more suitable that a child of such tender years should serve a woman. She continually found fault with Poitou for not attending to her needs, and pinched him and boxed his ears whenever she could find a pretext.

Surprisingly enough, Gilles, who was usually so quick to take offence at any action of hers, seemed to encourage her conduct. When Poitou, who was no stoic, appeared in floods of tears after some encounter with Catherine, Gilles would take the boy in his arms and tenderly comfort him, wiping the droplets from his cheeks with his own sleeve. It was almost as if he encouraged Catherine to provide him with opportunities for ministering thus to Poitou, and deliberately sent him on errands to her, to make sure that she got the opportunity to mistreat him.

Jean de Craon was growing increasingly impatient at our long delay in setting out. The castle was more uncomfortably crowded than ever, and some of the troops were encamped in the fields around, or billeted in surrounding villages where, though they behaved quite well, they caused great unease to the peasantry. Meanwhile Jean saw his money flowing away to no purpose. The only way to keep these freshly recruited men in good heart, and on their best behaviour, was to pay them promptly and in good currency. This messire Jean did, though with increasingly bad grace. He took the opportunity to double the taxes on the merchants who passed his door, and seeing the large force he now had around him they did not dare to refuse. This was the one thing that comforted him somewhat, but he still longed to see us go, and leave him to his tyrannous tranquillity.

The situation was resolved by Poitou himself, who had been largely responsible for creating it. One day he fell violently ill, and ran a high fever. Gilles was immediately convinced that someone had tried to poison the boy: his suspicions veered between his grandfather, his wife and Sillé. An eminent physician was sent for, and meanwhile Gilles prowled round the castle precincts in a condition of pitiable anxiety. At last he turned half-angrily and said: 'Come, Sillé – even if you did this, as I think possible, you must help me undo it. Go and find the book we brought from Angers.'

Sillé at once began to protest: 'We are not skilled,' he said 'We are only at the beginning. . . .'

Gilles shot him a fierce look. 'Skilled or not,' he answered, 'we have already set our feet on the path, and there is no turning back from it. Go and get the book.'

Sillé slunk off to his quarters like a kicked cur. But by the time he came back, carrying what looked like a stout manuscript wrapped in a cloth, one of the servant-girls had arrived to tell Gilles that the true nature of Poitou's illness had declared itself. What he had was a case of smallpox. And with this Gilles's mood immediately changed. At no price now would he enter the room of the sick favourite. The clothes he wore must immediately be burned, and our troops must depart at once, for fear of the contagion. In a matter of a few hours we were riding over the drawbridge, and in an hour or two more the whole force had been assembled, and was marching upstream along the west bank of the Loire.

Just before our road began to draw away from the river-bank, we came to a little chapel, and Gilles signalled to me and to Sillé to leave the main body, and to ride with him towards it. When we got there, we found it deserted, but the priest was soon routed out of his house in a nearby village.

'What do you want, messires?' he quavered at us, intimidated by our glittering steel.

'To make our confessions to you, father, before we go to the wars, and to hear the blessed mass, and to take Christ's body and blood for the salvation of our souls,' Gilles replied to him soberly.

Each in turn we made our confessions to the priest, and then, kneeling in our armour in the shrine, listened while the mass was said. When the moment of the elevation came, I stole a glance at Gilles's face as he knelt beside me, and saw he was completely immersed in the meaning of the mystery. The old man's stumbling Latin had opened the gate to a different realm – one I could glimpse through Gilles, but could not myself inhabit.

8

Our first season's campaigning was curiously idyllic, despite the late start we had made, and the poor weather. From Champtocé we moved east and north to join forces with one of the most famous of the Dauphin's captains, Ambroise de Loré. Loré had fought in all of the Dauphin's wars, since the fall of Paris in 1418. I expected to find a scarred, soured, taciturn warrior, bearing the mark of his prince's continual misfortunes. Instead of this we were greeted by a man who still seemed young, supple and slender, with a lithe stride and an open smile.

From the first he treated us all with courtesy, and Gilles with considerable finesse. Loré was a man of good birth, and he had the tact, as well as the easy manners, of the professional courtier. He never hinted, for example, that he knew considerably more about the business of fighting battles than we did. 'You have it in your blood, messire Gilles,' he said. 'You'll take to this kind of work as a duck takes to water.' Surprisingly enough, he was right. The petulant Gilles, so ready to take offence, to whom I had become accustomed in recent years, was replaced by a cheerful extrovert. The fine surcoats produced by the embroiderers of Angers grew crumpled and mildewed in our saddle-bags, or were used to give a little extra warmth at night. Gilles now went about in the leather jerkin and leggings which were Loré's usual dress, and certainly the most practical garb for the circumstances.

We moved camp often, but the bivouacs we made were so like one another that they have become confused in my memory. We ourselves lived in low tents, patched together from scraps of canvas – very unlike the ornate pavilions you see in military scenes in prayer-book miniatures. The men lived in huts of brushwood, or else in dank holes scooped in the ground to give a little shelter from the weather. Scattered throughout the encampment were smouldering camp-fires, with men huddled round them for warmth. The smell of woodsmoke and wet leather and unwashed bodies remains with me vividly.

Our bivouacs were always full of unexplained visitors – mongrel dogs scavenging for scraps, children from the nearest village, female camp-followers, the occasional pedlar or horse-dealer. Yet Loré kept good discipline among his troops, and they were always ready to move at a moment's notice. Our own men, at first conspicuous for their neat, well-fed appearance, soon became indistinguishable from his – lean, tattered, adept at stealing chickens from the farms and tickling fish from the streams. Loré's hard-bitten Gascons had not been paid for months, but they remedied this deficiency soon after our arrival by taking most of our men's ready cash from them at dice. Jean de Craon, once he had got rid of us, sent money only irregularly from Champtocé, and we were soon in a condition of share and share alike.

At the very end of the campaigning season, as the weather worsened and the days grew shorter, Loré decided to try a stroke against an important castle held by the English on the banks of the river Loiret. 'I don't suppose we'll get into Le Lude,' he said at a council of war on the night before we moved off. 'It's a strong place and we've got no real siege machinery – just a few ladders. In addition to which the English commander, William Glasdale, is a good man, very tough, very professional. Just the kind of chap I'd like to have on my side in a fight, though of course he's not really a gentleman.' He paused, and added reflectively: 'Well, in any case it'll be fun to give old Glasdale a fright. I've had a few nasty surprises from him in my time.'

Our plan was to ride all night, and to make an immediate assault on Le Lude as soon as we reached it, shortly before daylight. We arrived on schedule, and the false dawn was just lightening the sky as we reached the river-bank just above the castle. Peering through the dimness I could make out that Le Lude was not as tall a building as I had expected. Its strength lay, not in the height of the walls, but in their thickness, and in the fact that it was surrounded by a broad moat which was fed from the river. Thanks to the recent rains, the Loiret was swollen, and the moat correspondingly deep.

Loré lost no time in giving orders to his force. 'No special order of attack,' he said. 'Just cross the moat, get your ladders against the wall, and up you go. If it doesn't work, don't try a second time. Things will get too hot if they're really ready for us.'

Gilles and I found ourselves in the leading punt. Loaded to the gunwales, it moved unsteadily across the water and scraped against the foot of the castle wall. It was at this moment that the alarm was raised. We struggled to position the heavy ladder we had brought with us. There was very little margin at the foot of the wall – half a yard at most – and this meant that the ladder had to be held at a steep angle, and braced by a couple of men so that the others could climb it. Torches blazed on the battlements, and missiles began to descend on us. At first these had an improvised character – stones, bits of wood, anything the garrison could lay their hands on. But then some of them at least managed to get their crossbows wound back, and we heard the nasty whirring of the bolts they unleashed.

I was now holding one upright of the ladder, and Gilles, who had thrust several men aside in his haste to be first, was beginning to climb it. One of the bolts caught him in the fleshy part of the left arm, and pierced the muscle through. The shock of it brought him to a halt. Then, even in the grey light of dawn, I saw his face flush, and a strange cry burst from him, an animal shriek of rage. Within a second he was at the top of the wall, and the rest of us followed him in a jostling rush. As I stumbled on to the wooden catwalk behind the battlements, I had just time to see Gilles disappearing through a low doorway.

The taking of Le Lude was quick work. Gilles's berserk assault completely unnerved the garrison. Some were so alarmed that they immediately leapt over the wall and into the moat, instead of staying to fight us. Others vanished into the depths of the building. At one corner, where there was a little turret, a knot of cooler-headed men still held out. I found myself fighting side by side with Ambroise de Loré, as we drove the enemy before us until their backs were against the turret wall. The leader of the band was a burly Englishman, wearing a helmet but no armour. Nevertheless his heavy sword was protection enough, and kept a semi-circle clear around him. He sliced the leg clean off one man who was incautious enough to come within reach of its sweep.

It was evident that he knew my companion. 'Loré! Loré! Come on!' he panted in a thick English accent. 'Careful how you tackle him,' Loré muttered to me out of the corner of his mouth. 'Glasdale is still a bit too much for you.'

What happened next happened so quickly that I scarcely saw how it was done. Loré stepped forward on the catwalk with his supple dancer's step, as if to make a stroke at his opponent. Glasdale lunged in reply. Instead of either retreating or parrying Loré moved closer still, and caught him by the shoulder. The next instant, the Englishman, off balance, was plunging over the battlements and into the water. There was a tremendous splash, and Glasdale surfaced spluttering, then began to swim away. Loré burst into a roar of laughter. 'Serve him right,' he shouted. 'The English say he never bathes from twelvemonth to twelvemonth!' He was so amused by the discomfiture of the English captain that he seemed unwilling to take any further action against him. Indeed, when one of our men started to wind back his crossbow, Loré stopped him with a gesture. 'Let him go,' he said. 'He's a good soldier, and it's bad luck for him that we caught him so much off guard. Though in one way he's fortunate that he didn't have time to put on armour. If he'd been wearing steel, he'd have sunk like a stone when he tumbled over the wall.'

Round us, the fighting had come to a halt. The few Englishmen left had thrown down their swords and surrendered. From within the castle, however, came muffled shrieks and screams and the clash of metal on metal. Anxious to know what was going on, I started to follow the noise to its source, ducking through the low doorway that I had seen Gilles enter.

Le Lude was a castle built upon a different plan to that employed at Champtocé. Though it possessed a courtyard, this was at an upper level. The whole building stood on a vast platform, and within this platform, so it turned out, was a series of large storerooms. A pair of corridors bisected one another, and met at a lofty, vaulted chamber in the very centre of the building. It was towards this that I now made my way, by the light of a pinewood torch snatched from a bracket on the wall. When I got there I was greeted by a horrific sight.

In the centre of the room stood Gilles, panting and leaning on his sword. The blade ran with blood, and the walls were splashed with great gouts of sticky red. On the cobbled floor at his feet lay a pile of hacked and gashed bodies, some almost torn apart by the force of the blows which had been rained upon them. Despite their terrible wounds, a few were still faintly twitching. The warm stench of blood filled the whole space, and I could see the steam rising from the pool of red that had accumulated upon the ground.

I raised the torch, and moved closer. Now I could see how pale Gilles's face was, and the bubbles of foam at the corners of his lips. He had torn open his leather jerkin, and the shirt beneath it, and his whole chest was bare. The white skin was marred by another great crimson splash, trickling slowly through the sparse hairs towards his belt. Yet he did not seem to be wounded, apart from the crossbow bolt which still protruded from his arm.

Seeing him sway, I came right up to him. Before I could ask if he was hurt, he tottered, and fainted in my arms.

9

The fall of Le Lude did much for Gilles's military reputation, as Loré generously gave him most of the credit for the victory. Jean de Craon was delighted by the turn of events, and the flow of money started once again. Each consignment of cash was accompanied by an increasingly urgent and peremptory letter urging Gilles to go and pay his respects to the Dauphin, so as to consolidate the good effects of the victory he had gained.

For a long time, however, Gilles was reluctant to move. His fainting spell left him listless. He seemed to recall very little of the fight which had led to the capture of the castle, and nothing at all about its closing stages. When we tried to discuss these events with him, he brushed us off. I had never seen him so introspective. He installed himself in a comfortable fortified manor not far from Le Lude, and sent to Champtocé for the now-recovered Poitou, and for some of his books – romances mostly, tales of Merlin and Arthur. But Poitou was now a little scarred, and had lost his youthful freshness, and Gilles was bored with his company within a very few days of his arrival, and soon made an excuse to send him packing again. The books, too, failed to rouse him, with one exception – a strange, ragged untitled manuscript bound in rough sheepskin. He and Sillé both seemed to take some care to prevent my looking at it, and I had a feeling that it was the volume Gilles had sent Sillé to fetch on the day Poitou's illness declared itself. Sometimes Gilles and Sillé would lock themselves up alone in a tower-room. They never offered any information as to what they had been doing there. In this fashion we celebrated Christmas Day and the Night of Kings, with little state or jollity. Outside the house, a hard winter gripped the countryside. The trees had their boughs broken down by the weight of ice, and the starving birds fell lifeless from the skies.

At last, early in January, a messenger arrived, not from Champtocé, but from Chinon, where the Dauphin now was. He did not bear a letter from the prince, but the next best thing – one from the favourite. 'Dear cousin,' wrote La Tremoïlle, 'everyone here is impatient to see you, as a new hero come to succour the kingdom in her hour of need. His Majesty commands me to send to you, and ask you to attend his court.' There could be no refusal of such a summons, and we prepared to depart.

Chinon will always be an impressive sight to those who see it for the first time. The huge castle, which is three fortresses in one, straggles along the crest of a steep hill, with the town occupying the slope below it which falls to the river Vienne, here spanned by a bridge. We approached it from the other side of the river, and could therefore see the walls rising in front of us, glittering in the winter sunlight. After crossing the bridge, we picked our way through the narrow streets of the town until at last we reached the Clock Tower which is the entrance to the Middle Castle, the most important of the three units into which the fortress of Chinon is divided.

This central enclosure is a large space, despite the presence of a chapel in the middle. All the same it seemed cluttered by comings and goings, by the great throng of people who seemed to have accumulated within the walls. We were soon to learn that wherever there is a court there is a crowd, that royalty, even when in the depths of misfortune as the Dauphin was then, attracts people to itself as surely as a honey-pot attracts the flies.

On the left-hand side of the courtyard we had entered stood a middling-sized house, with a steeply gabled roof. In many respects it was meaner than the comfortable manor we had just left to come here. Yet we gazed at it with respect, since we knew that this was the Royal Lodging, the building currently inhabited by the lawful sovereign of the kingdom of France.

It was easy enough to gain access to the king's presence-chamber – a lofty hall which occupied about one-third of the volume of the building. Hung with tapestries, magnificent enough, though a bit old-fashioned and moth-eaten, warmed by a log fire blazing in the huge fireplace that occupied most of the end wall, and filled at all hours by members of the royal guard, by courtiers and place-seekers of every variety, it held itself perpetually in readiness for the appearance of the prince. But Charles seldom cared to show himself. He lurked in the little rooms that lay hidden behind this public hall, and which were connected to it by means of a single door concealed behind the hangings to the right of the fireplace. Every time some privileged being passed in or out of this portal, the crowd stirred restlessly.

Eventually, we managed to get a message taken through it to messire de La Tremoïlle, whose full importance we were only now beginning to realise. He replied courteously, asking us to wait upon him that evening in his rooms in another part of the castle 'at an hour when I shall have a little respite from the king's business'. For the time being, we had to content ourselves with this rather distant and impersonal welcome.

La Tremoïlle had a chamber and an antechamber in one of the towers. Only later did we realise the full grandeur that accommodation of this type implied. A royal duke might, perhaps, expect a single chamber for himself and his body-servants; a mere nobleman would usually have to be content with a sleeping space in a shared room. But nobody wanted to lodge in the town, away from the source of power.

This time we waited for only a moment before a page summoned us into the favourite's presence. Gilles had decided that it gave a better impression of his own importance and dignity if Sillé and myself accompanied him. La Tremoïlle was an overwhelmingly large, even gross man, so heavy that you wondered if any horse was strong enough to carry him. As he stood up to greet us, the initial impression of grossness was replaced by another – that of physical power, and power of personality. La Tremoïlle was fat, yes, but his tremendous girth was in proportion to his height, and he was far from being flabby. His voice was a low rumble which filled the small room in which we found ourselves.

'Ah, my lord Gilles, I am delighted to see you! But I must remark you have taken long enough. What made you so shy about coming to us?'

Gilles seemed at a loss for words, and hung his head. La Tremoïlle swept on with what he had to say. It was clear that he was intent on conveying a great deal of information in a short space of time. 'Of course, certain complications have arisen since your magnificent victory at Le Lude. If you had come here at once, matters would have been different. But now the capture of one stronghold has to be put in the scales against the progress the English are making with the siege of Orléans. Before Christmas matters did not look nearly so serious as they do now.'

He paused, to let what he was saying sink in. 'There is

something else as well,' he added. 'Our lord the king does not like to meet strangers. When he dines in public, if a stranger is present and looks at him too closely, he cannot swallow, and is forced to get up and leave the table. It is a sad affliction.'

He paused once again and heaved a slightly theatrical sigh. His eyes, embedded in folds of flesh, were fixed unwaveringly on Gilles, to gauge his reaction.

'A nobleman of your birth has, of course, the absolute right to come into the king's presence, unless specifically banished for some offence, as the Constable, messire Artur de Richemont, is at the moment. But sometimes the wise man does not exercise the rights that belong to him.'

'Does that mean the Dauphin refuses to see me?' Gilles asked, his voice rising.

'We call him the king here, not the Dauphin, since the kingdom is his by right since the death of his father. And no, the king does not refuse to see you.'

'Then what is the difficulty?'

'You would serve him better, and yourself too, by allowing him to become accustomed to your presence by, shall we say, gentle stages. Leave it to me, I will manage the matter.'

'Being what I am, I should find it humiliating to be at court and yet remain unacknowledged.'

'No, no,' La Tremoïlle purred, now apparently sure of gaining his point. 'You must not take it like that. Here all newcomers go through a probationary period. The king will like you better if you do not force him. You may be present at all ceremonies. I will see to it that you are given your due precedence whenever possible. But remain a little in the background. Do not insist on kissing the king's hand till he is ready.'

'And who will be the judge of that?'

'I shall, of course. After all I know the king better than any man, and he trusts me more than any other.'

'Then I suppose I shall have to leave it to you, cousin Georges,' Gilles replied sulkily.

'Precisely what I hoped you'd say,' rejoined La Tremoïlle, immediately fastening upon the content of the answer, rather than upon its tone. 'And now we must fix you up with some lodgings. Who are these gentlemen?' he added, as if becoming aware for the first time of my presence and that of Gilles de Sillé.

'Raoul de Saumur and Gilles de Sillé, friends who always accompany me,' said Gilles, with a slight emphasis upon the second phrase. La Tremoïlle immediately caught the nuance.

This was the concession he was required to make in return for having carried his major point.

'As you know, it is not customary to offer a nobleman's retinue accommodation in the castle, that is apart from body-servants. But since you name them as friends . . .'

'Since I name them as friends I imagine you will be able to find not too uncomfortable a place for us all to sleep. Will you not, dear cousin?' With one of his lightning changes of mood, Gilles had completely recovered his composure.

'I imagine I will,' said La Tremoïlle, with a dry finality which indicated that the interview was now over.

He was, however, as good as his word, and we were provided with a semi-circular first-floor chamber in one of the curtain-wall towers of the Château de Coudray, the enclosure which lay to the west of the Middle Castle, and which communicated with it by means of a drawbridge over a ravine. The room was not large, and we were constantly disturbed at night by the soldiers coming up through it to change the guard, but in court terms it immediately conferred upon us a very considerable status. We learned later that La Tremoïlle had dislodged a bishop and his chaplain to make room for us, and had banished them at half an hour's notice to the less favoured Fort Saint-Georges beyond the Clock Tower Gate. It was less favoured simply because it was situated at a greater distance from the person of the king.

We had scarcely begun to settle into our new quarters, and to unroll our bedding and unpack our saddle-bags than we received a further summons. 'The Queen of Sicily commands the presence of the lieutenant of her lieutenant-general, and of his two attendant gentlemen.' As soon as he got the message, Gilles began to swear quietly to himself. But there was no means of avoiding the confrontation. The supercilious little page who had brought it stood waiting to conduct us to his mistress's quarters.

These turned out to consist, like La Tremoïlle's, of an antechamber and a withdrawing room. Yolanda was, after all, not only titular Queen of Sicily and ruling Duchess of Anjou, but the Dauphin's mother-in-law. She had brought Charles up, and it was generally considered that, next to the favourite, she exercised the greatest influence at court.

Her antechamber was full of women, most of them pretty, sewing, spinning and chattering. I noticed that their eyes followed Gilles's slender figure with open admiration, and that several looked at me, too, with glances that seemed to hold a promise. But I was given little time to assess either their charms or their possible intentions (though one did seem to gaze at me with especial favour) as the page hurried us to a further door, opened it, and then ushered us up a narrow but brief staircase. Reaching yet another door at the head of this, he rapped loudly, and all but thrust us bodily into the room beyond.

The chamber was not large, and it was crowded with furniture. A massive bed stood on a dais that halved the floor space, while a throne was placed beside it, under a canopy of state. There were wooden coffers with rich but sombre garments spilling out of them, and a sideboard with a fine display of silver plate.

Upon the throne sat an unusually tall middle-aged woman. We knew what was expected of us, and we all three immediately went down on one knee to her, pulling off our hoods as we did so.

'You may rise,' she said, in a slightly guttural voice. After all these years in France the Spanish accent was still noticeable.

As I got to my feet I took the opportunity to look Queen Yolanda full in the face, as I was deeply curious about this woman who was reported to have exercised so powerful an influence upon the destinies of the kingdom. It was then the convention to describe her as 'beautiful', but I did not find the adjective especially appropriate. Nor did it really seem as if she had possessed outstanding beauty, even in her extreme youth. Her countenance was handsome, but undoubtedly rather masculine. A long, strikingly determined jawbone was balanced by an equally long throat. She wore a widow's coif and her forehead was shaven, so it was impossible to see the colour of her hair. Her eyebrows were thick, and raven-black, and sloped upwards towards her temples. Beneath them was a pair of glittering black eyes.

'Gilles de Rais, you are, I believe, the duly appointed lieutenant of my lieutenant-general for the Duchy of Anjou, who happens to be your grandfather, Jean de Craon?'

'Yes, Madame.'

'Jean de Craon was always a dishonest vassal, and you promise to be a worse one. By whose command did you come to court?'

'By that of messire Georges de la Tremoïlle, who gave me to understand it was His Majesty's wish.'

'An irregular summons, since the matter has not been mentioned in the king's council. Nor, indeed, have I been consulted.'

'I know nothing of that.'

'Nor should you, since it is not your business. But tell me, having arrived here, why did you not immediately come and pay your respects to your liege lady?'

'Madame, I . . .'

'You did not think of it, because your mind was filled with the power and glory of that bad man La Tremoïlle, who is your blood relation.'

'That is not true, Madame. We have just this day arrived here. We felt we could not disturb you so late at night.'

Yolanda sniffed – it was a sceptical, Iberian sniff which said a great deal more than words. 'When do you plan to present yourselves to the king?'

Gilles began to stammer: 'We, Madame . . . I mean I, Madame . . .'

'I thought as much. The fat fox warned you off. I wonder what game he's playing?'

'He told us that the king does not like to meet strangers, that he needs time to get used to them!'

Yolanda had started to hum under her breath. 'Ah, ah,' she said. 'Perhaps *that*'s the way of it? Either Charles takes completely against you, in which case an important vassal of mine is out of favour; or else he gets used to the sight of you, and then you owe everything to La Tremoïlle's protection. We must do something about that.'

She clapped her hands loudly, and immediately the page reappeared. 'My cloak, and get a torch-bearer,' she commanded. 'And tell those idle women of mine to bestir themselves. I can't go to see His Majesty completely unattended.'

Within a few moments a regular procession had assembled outside the door of the Queen of Sicily's lodging. There were not one, but two torch-bearers, several shivering ladies-in-waiting, Yolanda herself wrapped in an immense fur-lined black velvet robe, embroidered in gold with the arms of France, Aragon, Sicily and Anjou, the attendant page to carry the train of this and keep it clear of the mud, and finally ourselves, by this time looking rather hangdog and apprehensive. We swept across the courtyard of the Château du Milieu towards the Royal Lodging.

'This way, I think,' said Yolanda, indicating a door at a lower level than the one which led into the great hall. We burst into the guardroom which occupied the space beneath it. The sleepy guard, some of whom had been playing dice, and some cleaning their armour or tending to their weapons, came scrambling to their feet at the intrusion. 'The King! I have come to see him.'

A gentleman-in-waiting, half in and half out of his doublet, met us at the foot of an internal staircase to protest that the king had retired for the night. 'Nonsense! I expect he's praying. He spends half the time on his knees nowadays. You can perfectly well interrupt him. He'd do better to spend his time raising troops for the defence of Orléans. God prefers to be thanked, rather than badgered for help.'

The rooms we now passed through were small, and the thick hangings made them seem airless and claustrophobic. The Queen of Sicily's great cloak took up most of the available area, and we stumbled along in her wake as best we could. With a gesture she halted the ladies-in-waiting in their tracks. 'You silly geese can go back to the guardroom. And take the boy with you. If the king has really gone to bed he won't want you all gawping at him as he lies there with the coverlet pulled up to his nose.'

We had come to a doorway with a couple of soldiers keeping watch outside it. They made as if to bar our way, but quailed beneath the glance that Yolanda gave them. 'Since when has His Majesty's mother-in-law been denied immediate access to his person?'

'Yes, Madame,' one of the men protested. 'But if these gentlemen are unknown to His Majesty, as I think they are, then I must ask them to surrender any weapons they may have.' The three of us took our daggers from our belts and gave them to him.

By this time our escort was already through the door, and we passed through the opening to see her just rising from a deep curtsey. The man to whom she had made it was one of the least impressive physical specimens I have ever seen, and his appearance was not improved by the fact that he was wearing only a short robe, hastily drawn round himself, and a pair of scuffed slippers. His swollen knock-knees were painfully apparent under the hem of his garment.

We knelt to him, and he started away from us as if someone had rung an alarm-bell in his ear. 'Strangers? And at this time of night?' he exclaimed. '*Belle-mère*, what does this mean?'

'Charles, Charles! Do you think that even I want to assassinate you? I've protected you often enough in the past.'

The king took a deep breath, and it was clear that he was making a great effort to control his nerves. Then he held out his hand, and we each kissed it in turn. 'If the Queen of

Sicily brings you to me, you are very welcome,' he said. 'But who are you, and what is the reason for your arrival at this late hour?'

Yolanda immediately launched into a flood of explanations. As the king listened, a smile began to appear on his face. 'Ah, Yolanda,' he murmured, 'you and messire Georges are like two dogs quarrelling over a bone. Why can't you be content that I usually obey both of you?'

'You seem to obey,' retorted the Queen of Sicily.

'At any rate, admit I do my best to content both of you.'

'Perhaps it would be better if you did more of your own volition.'

The king smiled, then sighed again. 'You know that decisiveness is not my forte.'

'Not even when the existence of the kingdom is at stake?'

'God will look after the kingdom, and the king too, if both are worthy of it.'

'You would do better to rely on good men like these, who have come here to fight for you.'

'I have had that said to me before. But those of whom it is said usually lose my battles for me and plunder the people. I expect the new friends you have just brought me will do the same.'

'You take a poor view of human nature.'

'The fact that I cannot command men does not mean that I do not know them.'

The Queen of Sicily was growing impatient with the discussion. 'Well, at any rate, now that I have presented these gentlemen to you, there is no need to get the fidgets when you next see them.'

'Oh, I expect I shall fidget, nevertheless,' said Charles, once more turning to us. 'But you will know something of the cause and you will forgive me.'

It was at this moment, I think, that we all first felt the touch of the king's strange charm. Feeble as he might appear, in spirit as well as in body, his late majesty Charles VII had the ability to touch the hearts and imaginations of men.

10

The next few weeks we spent at court in a condition of increasing discomfort, irritation and impatience. Chinon was an uneasy place to be at that time, for many reasons.

One of these was the war, and the bad news that came to us from the city of Orléans. This city was the chief possession of Charles, Duke of Orléans, the king's poet cousin, who had been taken prisoner at the battle of Agincourt, and who still languished, not too uncomfortably, in English captivity, writing verses to the daughters of his jailers. The English army had laid siege to it the preceding October, just as we were beginning our own campaign in the Sarthe which had ended with the capture of Le Lude. The enemy general was the ablest of all the English leaders, the Earl of Salisbury, who had fought with distinction in all Henry V's campaigns.

Salisbury was not a patient man. He meant to storm Orléans at once, and he began well by storming the Tourelles, the fortress on the south bank of the Loire which guarded the city bridge. But then came a set-back for the attackers. Salisbury was mortally wounded by a stray cannon-shot while he was looking out of a window of the place he had just captured. He was succeeded by William de la Pole, Earl of Suffolk, a man far less bold than himself, and the English plan seemed to change. Now they were prepared to wear down the resistance of the besieged, little by little, and they started to build a ring of forts around Orléans, gradually subjecting it to closer and closer investment. Nevertheless, messengers continued to slip in and out, bearing news from the Bastard of Orléans, the reigning duke's half-brother, who now commanded there, and it was sometimes even possible to bring fresh supplies of food into the city, since the English were short of men for the ambitious task they had undertaken, and had been forced to leave considerable gaps between their forts.

Yet because the English had been so usually successful in recent years there seemed to be a fatalistic expectation among the king's advisers that the place must fall. One problem was lack of money, It did not take us long to discover, and in the most practical way, that at Chinon the lack of cash was desperate. Gilles was still kept well supplied with money by his grandfather, and news of his affluence soon reached the rest of the court. Within a few days he, and even, to a lesser extent, both I and Gilles de Sillé, were besieged with requests for loans. The royal officials were unpaid, the ladies-in-waiting had not a decent rag to their backs, even the garrison's salary was in arrears. When the king held a state banquet in the great hall, shortly before the beginning of Lent, the occasion had its comic aspects. The splendid royal plate had to be borrowed back from those to whom Charles had pledged it – both La Tremoïlle and Yolanda, so it transpired, usually held a good deal of it in their coffers, as security for various loans – and the viands were distinctly scanty. In fact, I remember that they consisted chiefly of beans and salted mutton. But this poor fare was served with due ceremony, when all the great officers of state, or substitutes for them, standing in their places. The King's Carver, the King's Cupbearer, and the King's Taster performed their tasks with becoming gravity, and the trumpet fanfares rang out as we drank the ritual toasts in sour wine.

If it was embarrassing enough to be pestered with requests for loans by the king's servants, it was in some ways worse to get these from the king. Day in and day out one of the king's officers would be found lying in wait for Gilles at the door of our chamber. 'Would messire de Rais be so kind as to oblige His Majesty by settling an urgent bill?' On one occasion, so I recall, Gilles was asked to deal with an invoice from the king's bootmaker, unpaid for the best part of four years. 'He won't do any more work, not even repairs, unless he is paid,' the messenger reported wryly. 'You wouldn't want to see our sovereign lord going around barefoot?' Then, as Gilles put his hand into his purse, he added: 'By the way, could you be so kind as to spare me a *livre* or two extra for myself? It's not boots I lack, but hose. I don't mind being asked to expose myself in the king's service, but I must say I prefer to do it in battle.'

At first, Gilles showed a prodigal generosity in meeting these requests for money. He liked to see himself as the benefactor of all those around him. But soon enough he discovered he got little gratitude for it. Even Charles, after our first interview with him, scarcely acknowledged our presence at his court, apart from these continual requests for loans, which were always made through third parties. Gilles was not, to his chagrin, summoned to the king's council, and when the king caught sight of any one of the three of us, on the rare occasions when he showed himself in public, his little eyes slid away. La Tremoïlle, who was invariably with him, refused steadfastly to call his master's attention to us, as if to mark his displeasure that our first introduction had been performed by someone other than himself.

In those days, indeed, our best way of getting a glimpse of the supposed ruler of France was to attend the services in the biggest of the castle's three chapels – each enclosure possessed its own. At almost any hour of the day, the king was to be found in his curtained oratory, which looked into the body of the church almost as King Louis's does today at Cléry, but less secretively. If you attended the offices you could look up and see his chilblained hands and big nose protruding from between a pair of heavy curtains. But even here, if you stared too hard at him, he would become restless, pull the curtains shut, and withdraw.

Gilles attended these services far more frequently than I did. He was developing a mystical streak – mysticism was not altogether unfashionable at Chinon, and even Charles was said to be touched by it – and, in addition to this, he took great pleasure in the music of the king's choir. At least, I am willing to believe that it was this, rather than the beauty of some of the younger choristers that fascinated him. Music in those days was in the last throes of what was still incorrectly called the Ars Nova – its forced, angular dissonances, the product of a search for novelty at all costs, echoed in the vaults of the chapel roof. The sweeter harmonies of the music we use now for our liturgies were already just coming to birth at the courts of England and Burgundy; and we, though we did not know it, were musical provincials in Charles's realm beyond the Loire. Gilles, who up till now had shown scant interest in music, soon picked up the necessary terms, and could discourse learnedly about the surpassing interest of certain harmonic clashes. Sillé and I, who agreed on so little, were at least united in finding these lectures tedious.

It was to the chapel I went one morning in February, when La Tremoïlle again sent to request the presence of his cousin. Gilles returned from the interview in an irritable mood.

'What did your all-powerful cousin have to say to you?' I asked.

'He told me to stop lending people money.'

'Bravo, that's excellent advice. You'll ruin yourself, and you've already discovered they're not grateful.'

'I don't like being told what to do with my own cash. Besides, this wasn't advice, it was an order. He even ordered me to stop lending money to the king.'

'Indeed – when he lends him so much himself? Any reason given?'

'He told me I didn't understand politics,' muttered Gilles. 'And that I'd do better to keep my nose out of them.'

'You don't, and you would,' remarked Sillé, who had been listening to the conversation with alert interest.

'And I suppose you *do* understand politics, after so short a time at Chinon!' Gilles exclaimed sarcastically.

'I've taken the trouble to keep my ears and eyes open, which is more than you have done.'

'And what have you found out? As my servant you'd better tell me, if you think it's to my profit.'

Sillé ignored the implied insult. 'Oh, I think I've discovered quite a lot. Enough to make out what messire de la Tremoïlle and Madame Yolanda are up to. They both want to control the government.'

'That's obvious enough.'

'Ah, but the government each of them wants to control is quite different. Queen Yolanda believes in a coalition of the princes, united round the crown in the old style.'

'It would never work,' I interjected.

'And what kind of government does my cousin believe in?' Gilles asked, his interest at last aroused.

'One which is a business enterprise, run for his own benefit. Which is one reason why he wants the war to go on.'

'But,' I protested, 'the war is ruining the kingdom.'

'And making messire Georges richer and richer. If peace comes, the king won't need his favourite's money. By making loans to the king, Gilles, you're interfering with your cousin's chief source of power. Half the crown lands are already pledged to him.'

'Then why,' said Gilles, 'does the king prefer my cousin to his mother-in-law? It seems to me that messire Georges drives a much harder bargain.'

Sillé snickered knowingly. 'Ah, that's the really interesting part. The king would do anything and use anybody rather than fall into the power of his own relations, just because they are the blood royal. He fears men who have any claim on the throne, just because he is so unsure of his own right to it. He wants the peace with Burgundy, for example, that the Queen of Sicily is always pressing him to make. But he doesn't want it yet – only when the day comes that he feels strong enough to deal with the duke.'

'That day may never come,' I said. 'And most of the time Charles doesn't behave as if he had any strength at all, or even as if he were the true king.'

'Raoul is right,' Gilles added, now bored with the conversation. 'Our sovereign lord is a poor enough thing, as we have all seen. La Tremoïlle will govern him till his dying day. That is, unless the English take Orléans and the realm collapses altogether.'

At this time, it looked as if the second of these alternatives was only too likely. As the appeals from Orléans for a major effort to break the siege grew ever more desperate, Queen Yolanda succeeded in galvanising the king and his council into action. In the long term she was for peace, but in the short term, since the war was with us, she believed in waging it effectively. With great effort a relieving army was put together, under the leadership of the king's cousin, the Count of Clermont, and sent off to help the city. Before it even arrived there, it stumbled into an English force, far smaller than itself, which was escorting a convoy of foodstuffs to the besiegers, and was badly mauled.

This lost battle was promptly dubbed the 'Battle of the Herrings' by court wits, because salted herrings were the principal commodity carried by the English provision-carts. Lent was upon us, and troops in the field – even the *goddams* (as we called them from their favourite oath) – must bow to its austerities. The bad news came to Chinon in mid-February, a couple of days after Bures Sunday, which is the first in Lent. The week that followed was one of the gloomiest I remember. The weather, from being cold and dry, had turned wet and stormy, and the skies wept every day. Charles spent all his time in frantic consultation with his council, or else at his prayers. The dissonant strains of the Ars Nova filled the castle chapels as the Lenten offices were sung.

About ten days after the disaster, a breath of rumour reached us. The report was, at one and the same time, both ordinary and extraordinary. It was ordinary, even commonplace, because it concerned a wandering prophetess, and France had seen a good many of those since the reign of Charles's grandfather, the wise King Charles V. These women were always full of good intentions towards the monarchy, and equally full of good advice. Some were obviously touched in their wits; others were declared by the priests to be heretical. A few seemed divinely inspired, though many wondered why God should so often choose to speak to us through the mouths of the inferior sex. Even the most impressive of these prophetesses seldom came to anything. They arrived at court, unburdened themselves of some message or warning, and departed again, with a piece or two of gold for their trouble.

Now, from Gien, which was the main crossing-point on the Loire for travellers from Champagne and the north, came word that yet another of these creatures was on her way to us. What was unusual was the fact that her mission was both ambitious and specific. She was coming to the Dauphin, she announced, to relieve the siege of Orléans and to take Charles to Rheims for his coronation. We had further information about her: she was a young peasant girl from a Dauphinist district far away on the Lorraine border, and she was travelling in male dress.

What she was rumoured to have said concerning the coronation touched on a sore point. Rheims was the only place where a King of France could properly be crowned, because within it was kept the Holy Ampulla, the little flask in the form of a dove which contained the Holy Oil sent down from heaven. It was a drop or two of this unction which made a true, because God-appointed, king. But, in all the years since his father's death, Charles had never been able to get to Rheims. He held some fragments of territory in the far north – the city of Tournai, for example, still remained loyal to him – but the great county of Champagne, where Rheims was situated, was disputed territory. Though it was not officially in the grip of either the Duke of Burgundy or the English, for the most part it was subject to hostile influences. Rheims itself had admitted a small Burgundian garrison, and there was a stronger English force situated nearby at Epernay. The coronation city was considered so thoroughly hostile to Charles's followers that the current Archbishop of Rheims, who happened to be Charles's Chancellor, Regnault de Chartres, had never in fact set foot in his own episcopal see. On the other hand, the English had not as yet felt secure enough to risk taking their own king, the child Henry VI, to Rheims for a consecration which would have made many waverers accept his claims. In view of all this, it is not surprising that talk of Rheims, or indeed of coronations of any kind, was regarded as being somewhat tactless in the circle of the king's intimates.

Hot on the heels of the rumour, a letter arrived, confirming most of the things we had already heard. It was signed by the girl herself, though obviously it had been written to her dictation by somebody else, and it was brought from Sainte-Catherine-de-Fiérbois, a village with a famous pilgrim shrine about a day's travelling away from us in the direction of the Loire. The contents of this letter struck everyone as even more extraordinary than what we knew already. The sender announced herself as 'Joan the Maid', and said that she had indeed come to raise the siege of Orléans and take the Dauphin to Rheims for his anointing. She was in possession of certain secrets which she would only disclose to the Dauphin himself. If a test was required of her, she was willing to pick out Charles, whom she had never met, 'from among all others'.

The letter caused a tremendous uproar. The council went into immediate session to decide whether or not the king should receive Joan, and all over the castle people argued out the matter among themselves. I even found two serving boys squabbling about it in Charles's pantry. Every scrap of information about how the argument was going in the council itself was eagerly received, and those who went in and out of the council chamber in the Royal Lodging were badgered for information. At first it seemed as if the Maid was unlikely to be received. La Tremoïlle, for some reason, was deeply suspicious, perhaps because he had already got hold of information that she had passed unscathed through the Burgundian city of Auxerre, and had even attended mass in the cathedral there. His opposition reinforced the king's disinclination to meet anyone new.

On the other hand the king's confessor, messire Gérard Machet, was said to be in favour of at least interviewing the girl in order to see what she was like. In this he was supported by Yolanda and some of the princes, who had discovered in the matter, so they imagined, an excellent means of annoying the favourite. They counted on Charles's mysticism to overcome his phobia for new faces. 'Of course,' Yolanda was reported to have said, 'the whole thing depends on whether or not this Joan is really a virgin. The Evil One cannot abide virginity. And it will be miracle enough if she is as pure as she claims to be. We all know that these peasants begin to breed early, and in addition to that she's been travelling for a fortnight with a party of men, wearing male dress, and with no other woman near her. Luckily, I too am a female, and, if necessary, I can ascertain the truth for myself, without committing an indecency.'

At long last, a compromise was reached. The council would interview Joan in the king's absence, to see if it was proper for him to receive her. Everyone was stunned when Joan had the temerity to reject this solution out of hand. Without waiting for permission, she had ridden forward and was now lodging at an inn beneath the castle walls.

The scales were turned by three things. One was the fact that Joan had apparently come with the blessing of Robert de Baudricourt, the military commander of her native district. Someone remembered that Baudricourt was a hard-drinking, hard-swearing kind of man, unlikely to have much patience with mystagogues, or to be taken in by an obvious charlatan. Another was the arrival of a delegation from the city of Orléans, eager to see this new wonder. Despite her claim that her mission was secret, Joan had apparently talked about it quite freely at Gien – the rumour reached Orléans even quicker than it got to us, and caused great excitement. In order to quieten the townsfolk, the Bastard was forced to hold an assembly, and there it was decided to send a group of three worthy citizens to investigate the matter. The third and most powerful factor was the curiosity which by this time had grown to overwhelming proportions within Chinon itself.

At court people were certainly in the mood for a ceremony, something colourful, anything to break the monotony of Lent. The girl had proposed a test, and a test she should take. The cynical thought it would be amusing to see, at least, if she was capable of picking the king out in circumstances designed to confuse her. The devout were impressed by the many dangers she had already passed through unscathed, and were half-inclined to believe what she said. With a bad grace, La Tremoïlle gave in.

As daylight failed, as many of us as could get in crowded the great hall of the Royal Lodging. The place was packed. There were at least three hundred people present, all in their best clothes, rather than in the sombre garments prescribed by the season. Many of the women had taken the opportunity to show more bosom than was quite proper. These fine globes, and everything else in the room, were brightly illuminated by thirty torches, whose heat and smoke, added to those of the fire that burned in the great hearth, soon made the atmosphere almost unbreathable. Everyone began to sweat, and there was an acrid stink from beneath the fine silks and velvets. Pacing nervously up and down in a small space directly in front of the fire was the Count of Clermont. It was he who had been chosen to impersonate Charles, and he was wearing a fine doublet of purple velvet, sleeves slashed with gold – royal yet Lenten colours.

How many of our lives changed course that evening as the court-ushers called for silence by rapping on the floor with their staffs, as the great door creaked open, and Joan the Maid walked in! All the torch-flames wavered, and we felt a dank draught which touched our sweaty foreheads. It should have been the most solemn of solemn moments, and I find that most of those who were present now recall it as such. The truth is that an audible titter ran round the assembly.

The sight that confronted us was certainly bizarre. A pace ahead came a royal prince, the Count of Vendôme. He was short and fat, and at the best of times found it difficult to maintain his dignity. This was a pity, since he held a post that required dignity above all else, that of Grand Master of the King's Household. He was now performing his duties under protest – there had been a terrible row when he discovered what was expected of him – and he showed it with his screwed-up face, disdainfully turned away from the personage he was escorting. Nevertheless, he led her forward in the correct style, almost at arm's length, the fingertips of his right hand lightly linked to those of her left. Joan, however, was no court lady, gliding obediently in his wake. She stumped along with a slightly rolling gait which suggested that she was saddle-sore, her head cocked slightly to one side, surveying the assembly with clear eyes. Her glance made a complete circuit of the room, and I saw her expression, open and confident when she entered, seem to cloud slightly.

As Vendôme led her up the length of the hall I had just time to note that she had a compact, supple body, a face with broad cheekbones and a slightly flushed complexion, and a rather thick neck with a birth-mark on the side of it. She was wearing a man's doublet and hose, of coarse stuff, grey and travel-stained, and on her head there was a hood, rolled up in conventional fashion to make a hat, with a trailing end that fell on her shoulder.

The couple halted in front of Clermont, and Vendôme made a gesture indicating she ought to kneel to him. 'This is not my man,' she said in a soft but carrying voice, in which the rustic northern French accent was clearly audible. A confused murmuring began to fill the room. Clermont looked flushed and uncomfortable – far more so than the girl he had been meant to deceive. At this instant Sillé thrust himself forward, seized Joan by the arm, and dragged her unresisting to the point where Gilles and I were standing half-hidden in the throng. 'Here is your Dauphin,' he said roughly, pointing to Gilles. 'These people have tried to deceive you!'

The calm grey eyes surveyed Gilles, and I saw him blush to the roots of his hair and step back a pace. 'Idiot!' he hissed to Sillé, and lifted his hand as if to strike him. 'This is not my man either,' Joan pronounced, in the same decided tone. At this moment there was a stirring at the back of the assembly, just by the hidden door that led to the king's apartments.

I was told, later, by someone who was present, what those few minutes on the other side of the doorway had been like. It had been agreed that a small group would wait with the king to hear what the reaction was immediately after Joan had entered. A burst of laughter would tell them that she had undoubtedly failed her test, and the king would then appear to make her humiliation the more complete. La Tremoïlle stood blocking most of the wooden passage, idly tapping his fingers against the wall. Charles stood near him, eyes downcast, more despondent and lacking in vitality than ever. When the burst of laughter failed to make itself heard, a slight air of tension invaded the group. As the murmuring dimly penetrated the cracks of the door beside which he was standing, La Tremoïlle murmured irritably to Charles: 'Damn them! Why don't they laugh? Have your courtiers got no spirit left, your Majesty?' 'Little more than their king has,' Charles replied, in a scarcely audible voice. With this, La Tremoïlle gave the handle a violent twist and shambled his way into the hall, careless of protocol. The king followed him, like a man in a dream.

Even with a monarch as miserable in appearance as Charles of Valois, a court is immediately aware of, and transformed by, the presence of the sovereign. Immediately the king emerged, people began to make way for him, to bow and doff their hats in the accustomed fashion. With embarrassed gestures he tried to prevent them from doing this, but the habit was too deeply ingrained.

As those nearest to him fell back respectfully, Charles was left standing isolated. It was possible to take in all the details of his appearance – the knock-knees, the frail body, the big nose with eyes of no particular colour closely set on either side of it, the thick, slightly pendulous lips. Without hesitation Joan went straight up to him, went down on one knee, and with a surprisingly graceful gesture lifted her hat from her head. A look of triumph and ecstasy illuminated her blunt features.

'Please!' the king stammered, seized with his accustomed agitation in the presence of a stranger. 'You must not kneel to me. I am not the king. Look – he is over there.' With this he flapped one hand in the direction of Clermont.

'No, gentle Dauphin,' said Joan, in her sweet, inexorable voice. 'You are he and none other.'

11

Tonight, as I write this, Joan is long dead, burnt to ashes in the market-place at Rouen. There are, so they tell me, people who maintain that another woman was burnt in her place, and that Joan escaped to go to the wars again, and to marry and have children. I do not believe this is possible. There were more than ten thousand witnesses to the deed. All that remained of Joan was thrown into the Seine by Geoffroy Thérage, the public executioner of Rouen, in the early evening of May 30th, 1431.

On the other hand, I am equally certain that something of Joan lives on. Men speak of her still, and will do so as long as France is a nation. There are those who continue to think of her as many simple people did in her own lifetime: as a saint of God, sent to rescue the kingdom from its travail. And there are others, among whom I count myself, who are less confident that she now sits upon Our Lord's right hand. The Church, I suspect, will be slow to canonise her, if indeed it ever does. Churchmen are but men, and like all men they find it difficult to admit to error. The admission is made doubly difficult if it means completely reversing the collective judgement of the Church Militant, arrived at by due process of canon law. Joan was burnt, not as the enemy of the English, but as an ally of Satan. Her crime, according to the most learned doctors of the University of Paris, was the fearful one of heresy.

Even when Joan's conviction was officially quashed, some years past, by a tribunal set up on the orders of the late kings many of her judges found difficulty in denying the correctness of their original verdict. It might no longer be convenient to call Joan a heretic, but she remained a liar. One judge said that she 'feigned many things'. Another, Master Jean Beaupère, the most respected of them all, stubbornly maintained that there was 'more human intention and natural cause than supernatural cause' in the visions Joan said she had had. Beaupère made certain that the notary recorded his exact phrase. And although he was now high in the favour of the monarch he had once opposed, Charles did not disgrace him for his obstinacy. Joan's rehabilitation proceeded, not as a matter of justice, but as a matter of political expediency.

This may make it sound as if I too disliked and mistrusted Joan. On the contrary, as a witness of many of her most wonderful deeds, I admired her then and continue to do so now. Yet I never felt completely easy in her presence. There was something uncanny about this woman in man's clothing, just as there was occasionally something inconsistent about the claims she made and the stories she told. Two things, however, cannot be doubted: her physical courage, and her power to sway the minds and hearts of men.

Gilles fell completely under her spell from the moment of her appearance in the great hall at Chinon. He would talk of nothing else, and longed to be close to her, and to see her and to speak to her. For weeks he bore Sillé a grudge, for his attempt to trick Joan. 'How can I expect her to trust me?' he demanded. 'She will think I was part of the conspiracy to humiliate her.' Sillé frowned and spat. He hated Joan with a hatred at least as powerful as Gilles's infatuation.

For the first few days after her arrival, Joan was frustratingly close, yet hidden from view. The king had given orders that she was to be lodged in the donjon of the Château du Coudrai, where we ourselves had been given quarters. Everyone was impressed by the honour thus done to her. Joan's chamber, a large one on the first floor, would normally have been assigned to a Prince of the Blood. 'It would take a lot to make me sleep there,' Sillé commented sourly. 'Everyone forgets that it was once the prison of Jacques du Molay, the chief of the Templars, whom King Philip Augustus burnt. I've seen his signature scratched on the walls. Let's hope this witch from Lorraine goes the same way.'

Joan was, in fact, almost a prisoner herself. She was closely guarded, and no one saw her without permission. Two waiting-women assigned to her by Queen Yolanda kept her company at night; and a page called Louis de Coutes served her by day. This young imp suddenly found that he was a very important personage indeed. Everyone wanted to know about Joan. The merest scraps of information were eagerly gobbled up: what she ate, how many hours she slept, her reactions to the reception that had been given her. Louis reported that she seemed to take her success in recognising the king as a matter of course, and that she spent many hours kneeling in prayer, her eyes fixed on a crucifix that hung on the wall, and the tears flowing unchecked down her cheeks. But he had nothing of political importance to impart. When some great personage arrived to see Joan – La Tremoïlle, or the Queen of Sicily, or the king's confessor – he was immediately sent away, and told to stay out of earshot. Once, one of the king's guards caught him trying to eavesdrop, and gave him a resounding box on the ear. He didn't try it again.

Joan's most frequent visitor was the king himself, sometimes accompanied by his young cousin the Duke of Alençon. Ever since Joan's arrival, the king's mood had changed. He now maintained a steady cheerfulness which those who knew him best thought completely uncharacteristic. There was a persistent rumour that Joan had told him some important secret, immediately after her arrival, and that this was the reason for the transformation. 'You remember,' said one courtier, 'that a few moments after she knelt to him, they drew apart to talk in the window embrasure? What did it was a few words she said to him then.' 'You're wrong,' said another. 'It was something she told him after they had passed through the little door, and returned to the king's chamber. They talked for at least an hour in private.'

Opinions were equally divided as to what the secret was. 'She assured him he was really his father's son, despite what that bitch Queen Isabeau puts about to the contrary.' – 'But why should he take her word for it?' – 'She repeated to him, word for word, a secret prayer for the deliverance of Orléans which the king made in his oratory a few months back.' – 'He wasn't in his oratory. He was kneeling beside his bed at Loches.' – 'Why not just admit the woman has cast a spell over him?' Sillé cut in. 'If I could only get close enough, I'd sprinkle her with a few drops of holy water, as a way of putting an end to all this nonsense.'

As the days passed, there was growing agreement upon certain points. Joan had definitely told the king, and indeed anyone else who would listen, that God had entrusted her with a mission. She was not only to raise the siege of Orléans and have the king crowned, she was also to take Paris, drive the English out of France, and rescue the Duke of Orléans from captivity in England. Her instructions came to her from what she dubbed her 'voices' – St. Michael, St. Catherine and St. Margaret. She could hear these saints talking to her, and they often manifested themselves in bodily form, so that she could touch and embrace them. 'Isn't it wonderful,' Gilles said to me, 'to think that the saints can appear to us corporeally?'

'We have no proof of that,' I replied, 'since no one seems to have seen them except Joan herself.'

'It is said that the king did.'

'Well, if he has indeed seen them, no one has announced it officially.'

'The trust the king puts in her is proof enough.'

'He doesn't altogether trust her,' said I. 'That's why she's continually being questioned. Anyway, I suppose a woman who summons up the saints is a bit better than a man who summons up the devil, as Pierre de Giac used to do.'

Gilles did not answer this, but gave me a sidelong glance.

Later, Joan was allowed more liberty. She did not spend all her time shut up in her room, praying and being interviewed by great personages. Sometimes she went riding with the king, in the water-meadows by the Vienne. Despite his sickly appearance, Charles was a good horseman and had an eye for horseflesh. But Joan, as she rode by his side, proved to be more than his equal in this respect. There were plenty of experienced judges at Chinon, and all of them were impressed by the skill with which she rode. 'Do you know,' Gilles asked, as we watched her canter by, 'that she'd never even been on a horse before she set out from Vaucouleurs to come and see the king? What she says about it is: "I needed horsemanship, and so Our Saviour gave it to me." Don't you think that's impressive?'

'No, I don't,' Sillé replied. 'What *I* hear is that she spent two months as a serving-girl and ostler at an inn in Neufchâteau, when the territory round her village of Domremy was raided. She'd have learned plenty about horses there, and about men too. She's probably no better than a common tart.'

'Queen Yolanda and some of her ladies examined her, and found she was *virgo intacta*.'

'As you and I know, my friend,' said Sillé with a leer, 'there are any number of sexual pleasures one can take, without the bother of rupturing a hymen.'

This remark made Gilles so furiously angry that for several days he refused to speak to Sillé at all.

One morning, Joan asked if she could have the use of the castle lists, to practise for the coming campaign. She was lent a warhorse, provided with the lightest lances in the armoury, and the dummy was set up for her on its post. Word of what she intended got about, and the place was crowded with spectators before she appeared. Most thought she was almost bound to take a tumble. 'She's a brave girl, but she'll be nursing a few bruises tonight,' was one comment I heard.

It was Alençon who led her in, helped her to mount, and handed her her first lance. She was not of course wearing armour, as there was none to fit her, and she swung up into the saddle easily enough. The big, black stallion on which they had mounted her began to curvet, but she quietened him with a word, resting her hand briefly against his neck. There was nothing tentative about her first charge. She thundered towards the target as fast as her beast would carry her, the lance perfectly steady. Someone had fixed a ring at the end of the figure's extended arm, and it was clear that she was aiming for this. With a neat flick of the point she lifted it off the peg that held it, and sent it rattling down the shaft towards her hand as she raised her weapon in salute. She performed the same feat three or four times in succession, to show it had been no accident, before starting to ride directly at the target itself. Each time she hit it plumb in the centre, shattering her lance. 'I'm glad I don't have to joust against her,' one young squire muttered to another. 'I'd lose my horse, and my armour too.'

As Joan signalled that she had done enough, reining her stallion in, there was a burst of applause from the crowd. She looked around bewildered, as if she had not realised until that moment how many people were watching her. Then she blushed and hung her head. Tall and fair-haired, Alençon came loping out on to the churned surface of the lists to take her bridle. 'Bravo! You must have the horse. No one rides him as well as you!'

'Thank you, my handsome duke. I will ride him in Our Lord's service.'

'What's the fool doing?' Gilles grumbled beside me. 'Everyone knows he hasn't got two *gros* to rub together. That brute must be worth two hundred gold pieces.' Alençon had been taken captive at the battle of Verneuil, nearly five years previously, and had only recently been released, on payment of an enormous ransom. 'It'll be a long time before I lend His popinjay Grace any more money.'

'Why? Would you rather have given Joan a horse yourself?'

'Precisely that,' Gilles snapped, giving me a glare. Joan's relationship to Alençon had grown increasingly close in the fortnight since she had come to Chinon, and Gilles tended to behave as if the duke and he were rivals. The fact that he himself had never spoken to Joan made no difference to his attitude.

Soon, however, the rivalry was checked by Joan's departure under escort to Poitiers, where she was to be examined by an ecclesiastical tribunal. Gilles was all set to follow her there, but was prevented from doing so by orders from Queen Yolanda. She required his help in bringing together a new royal army, and the supplies to feed it. To add insult to injury, she placed him under Alençon's orders in fulfilling the task.

As we soon discovered, it was to be a task indeed. The treasury was still almost empty, and the merchants were most reluctant to provide us with provisions. A body of troops would no sooner be brought together than it would start to melt away again into the countryside, for want of pay. The news from beleaguered Orléans continued to be grim. After the Battle of the Herrings, the citizens of Orléans had sent an embassy to the Duke of Burgundy. This had left for Arras just before Joan arrived at Chinon, and throughout March, while she was at Poitiers, it continued to confer with Philip the Good. It looked all too possible that Orléans would be surrendered, if not to the English, then to the Burgundians. Early in April the Duke of Burgundy went to Paris, for a conference with the English Regent. The bulk of the delegation from Orléans was still with him, and it seemed certain that a bargain was in the offing. Burgundy would get Orléans, and the English would have the use of it. Fortunately, the two potentates quarrelled. Burgundy was too greedy, and Bedford too quick-tempered. 'I have no intention,' the Regent shouted at his ally, 'of beating the bushes so you can have the birds.' Just as Alençon and Queen Yolanda were completing their preparations, news came to us that the delegation was on its way home, and that it had left empty-handed. Escorting it was one of Philip the Good's trumpeters. Joan, her examination triumphantly completed, was on her way from Poitiers to Tours, where she would equip herself for the coming campaign. Hearing this, Gilles once again prepared to set off to join her. This time he was prevented by a summons from La Tremoïlle. He journeyed to Sully-sur-Loire to see his cousin in his own fastness.

He returned from the interview more than a little subdued.

'What happened?' I asked him as soon as we were alone together in our lodging at Blois, where the army had now begun to concentrate.

'My cousin wanted me to sign something.'

'Are you prepared to tell me what it was?'

'This,' said Gilles, pulling a little scroll of rolled-up parchment from his doublet. I unrolled it and began to read it through.

'I, Gilles de Rais, lord of . . . promise to serve my loving cousin messire Georges de la Tremoïlle . . . until death and with my life. Signed . . . Witnessed . . . Dated . . .'

After a first hasty look, I read it through again slowly, to make sure I had got the wording correct. 'Do you realise what you've done?'

'Oh, everyone makes these private alliances. It's a way of looking after one's own interests. La Tremoïlle explained it to me in detail. And he showed me some agreements other people have signed with him. You'd be surprised to know who some of them are.'

'You've handed yourself over to him tied hand and foot. Trussed like a chicken in fact.'

'The wording's vague enough. All that stuff about "until death" doesn't mean anything. It's just a formula.'

'It would provide a solid enough basis for a trial for treason.'

'Who knows what treason is nowadays, Raoul? Messire Georges is going to do something for me, and he asked me to do something for him in return. It seemed reasonable enough.'

'What is he going to do for you?'

'Stop Alençon from going to Orléans,' said Gilles.

'And who will command the army in Alençon's absence? Not you, surely? You haven't enough experience. The Council would never swallow that, however hard La Tremoïlle pushed them.'

'Yes, he explained that to me. This time there's to be no overall commander. Instead, there'll be a council of captains.'

'And you are to be one of them?'

'I am.'

'It doesn't seem an adequate return for what you've just signed.'

'I've already told you it doesn't mean anything. La Tremoïlle wanted something in writing, that was all. The real agreement can't be written down.'

'What more do you have to do, besides giving yourself to him, body and soul?'

'He wants information.'

'You mean you'll have to spy for him?'

'He simply wants to know what's going on in his absence. After all, we're blood relations. What benefits him benefits me, since we're members of the same family.'

'I doubt if messire Georges looks after anyone's interests but his own.'

Gilles gave an exasperated groan. 'Don't you see – I've got what I wanted, what really matters to me. We're going to Orléans. Alençon isn't. Joan will be there. We're going to take part in a miracle. Who the devil cares if I have to send the occasional packet of private information to my fat cousin? What he knows and doesn't know won't make the slightest difference now Joan is around. He can't stand in the way of God's purpose. And nothing I do can stand in the way of it either. It simply doesn't matter whether I spy for him or not.'

As the army gathered, it seethed with news and rumour about the new wonder-worker, the girl who called herself the Maid. Even the most sceptical began to believe that she had the power to carry out everything she promised. We heard that the king had had a suit of armour made for her by the best armourer in Tours, and that she had had a special banner painted, which showed Our Saviour as the judge of the world (and of course, by implication, as the judge of the English). We heard that Joan had taken possession of a miraculous sword – she had sent for it to the shrine of Sainte-Catherine-de-Fiérbois, and it had been discovered there buried under the floor of the church, precisely as she described. We heard that the king had now given her her own household, almost as if she were a minor prince. Tales flew about concerning the witty replies she had made to some of the churchmen in Poitiers. One asked what language her saints spoke. 'A better French than yours,' she retorted, raising a laugh at the expense of his Limousin accent. There was an especially persistent rumour that she had prophesied that she would be wounded at Orléans 'in the shoulder and above the breast', even though she was still confident that the city would be saved.

From Orléans itself we had both encouraging and discouraging news. The Duke of Burgundy's trumpeter, once he reached the city, had summoned all the Burgundian troops to leave the siege – Philip the Good's way of demonstrating his displeasure to the Regent. But the Bastard visited Blois, slipping out of the besieged city to tell us that the garrison at Orléans was at the end of its tether.

Finally, late in April, the day came when Joan arrived to join the royal army which had been brought together with so much effort.

12

The force which Queen Yolanda and the Duke of Alençon finally succeeded in raising was too large to be quartered within the walls of Blois. It bivouacked, most of it, in the fields round about, though the captains, including Gilles, were given lodgings in the town. It was towards noon, and we had ridden out towards Tours to join some soldiers of our company at the midday meal. The encampment was like most encampments, at times when no danger threatens. Some of the soldiers were playing dice; some were idly scratching themselves and dozing in the sun. A slatternly girl was mending a pair of hose for her lover of the moment, who lay with his head in her lap, somewhat impeding her efforts. A couple of other girls were tending a small fire, over which a pot was suspended. This gave out a savoury smell of stewed rabbit. From one of the untidy brushwood shelters came a noise of grunting and heaving. Another soldier, seized by the spirit of spring, had been unable to wait until nightfall, or indeed until after dinner, to enjoy the embraces of his doxy.

Suddenly we were alerted by the sound of galloping hooves, and the next moment a small party of mounted men had burst into the midst of us, scattering the gamblers and almost knocking over the cook-pot in the process. With them was Joan, riding the black war-horse which Alençon had given her at Chinon. For a moment, however, I failed to recognise her, as she was now clad in a full suit of armour, undecorated but of superb quality. Only her head was bare, though her helmet hung at her saddlebow. In her hand she grasped a standard with a long tail, fringed and divided. We scrambled to our feet as she and her party came to a halt.

'Are these some of the men who are going to Orléans?' There was a rasp in the sweet voice which I had not heard before.

'Why are they sinfully gambling, and what are these women doing here? I sent word I would have no women with the army.'

'Well, you're a woman and you're with the army,' said one of the girls insolently.

Joan's reaction was almost swifter than the eye could follow. Leaning down from her saddle, she gave the doxy a resounding blow across the face with the pole of her standard. The girl yelled, and stumbled backward, one hand to her cheek. Catching her heel on a piece of equipment, she fell against the brushwood shelter from which the sounds of sexual congress still emerged. It collapsed beneath her weight, and there were shouts of alarm from the two occupants.

With a stream of blasphemies, his hose still rolled down about his thighs to reveal a massive, half-erect penis, the soldier who had been in the hut rose to confront the cause of his discomfiture. He was a big man in every sense, and for the moment too angry to care about modesty. Legs apart, making no attempt to cover himself, he glared at Joan as she sat on her horse.

'You take God's name in vain,' she said, 'and in cursing me you curse Him, because it is He who has sent me to deliver Orléans. You defile yourself when you are called to a holy enterprise. On your knees, and ask God's pardon!'

For an instant, the soldier gaped at her, the curses strangled in his throat. Then he began to fumble with his clothes, trying to make himself decent. When he had done this as best he could, he sank slowly to his knees amid the ruins of the hut.

Gilles followed his example, and motioned to the rest of us to do likewise. 'Kneel, men,' he said. 'This is the Maid, and she does indeed come to us from God to rescue the kingdom.' I shall long cherish the look on Sillé's face, as he realised that he must either comply, or make himself uncomfortably conspicuous.

'These women must leave at once, and my confessor Brother Pasquerel will stay with you to hear your confessions,' said Joan. 'Captain, this evening I shall expect you at my lodgings in Blois, together with your colleagues. We must take counsel together about what is needed to cleanse the army, and make it fit for its task.'

Putting spurs to her horse, she galloped towards Blois at the same breakneck pace as formerly, and the rest of her party followed after her. All of them that is, except for the priest, who scrambled from the back of his hackney, and bustled forward to make a start.

The two days at Blois which immediately followed Joan's arrival were, I believe, amongst the most extraordinary of her extraordinary career. We were told to gather, morning and evening, by companies and groups of companies, in the meadows outside the walls. The gathering place was marked by a huge banner hanging from a cross-piece on a tall pole. It was just like the banners they carry in church processions, but bigger. When it was on the move, it took three priests to hold it upright and steady. On the banner was painted a terrifying image of the suffering, crucified Christ – the best painter in Blois had worked for twenty-four hours without stopping in order to produce it. Round this symbol stood all the priests whom Pasquerel had been able to gather from the churches and monasteries of Blois, from the youngest to the most decrepit. They preached in relays, moving amongst the crowd so that everyone could hear. When they had finished preaching, they asked the men to confess; and, when the confessions had been heard, mass was said and everyone received the sacrament. Joan was present to add her exhortations to theirs, and she kept a sharp eye out to see that no one approached the holy table who had not received absolution for his sins.

To my surprise, her methods were effective. The morale of the army was entirely transformed. From being idle and undisciplined, the men became full of spirit. In a twinkling they had convinced themselves that nothing could stand in the way of an enterprise which had the Maid for its inspiration and mascot.

On the third day after Joan's arrival, we were ready to march. Some of the provisions which had been brought to Blois were to go with us; the rest, notably a great herd of lowing cattle, would remain behind until we could return to fetch them. We were ten or twelve thousand men in all – a goodly host – and our progress was impeded by sixty wagons and nearly five hundred pack-animals. We moved off about an hour after the midday meal, with Joan and her priests in the lead. Her standard and their banner flapped in the mild wind, and the priests were singing, with spirit but a little raggedly, the *Veni Creator Spiritus*.

Gilles was determined to use this opportunity to improve his acquaintance with Joan, and for most of that first afternoon he deserted the rest of us in order to ride by her side. I got glimpses of him, leaning towards her and talking eagerly. Joan's replies seemed to be monosyllabic at best.

'If I didn't know it was impossible I'd say our Gilles was

suffering from calf-love,' said Sillé disgustedly. 'I've never seen him pay so much attention to a woman, certainly not to his wife.'

'Perhaps he doesn't think of Joan as a woman,' I said.

'If she is one, she does her very best to disguise it,' Sillé retorted. 'I've never seen such an unnatural creature in my life. And I've had some experience, let me tell you.' Seeming to realise that he had made one confidence too many, he then lapsed into silence until we halted for the night.

On the morning of the third day, we knew we were getting close to our objective, though Orléans was not yet in sight. Joan seemed to be irritable. As I rode up the length of the column in search of Gilles, I could hear her berating first Brother Pasquerel and then Jean d'Aulon, the steady, sensible squire in his late twenties whom the king had appointed to be master of her household.

'What's the matter with her?' I whispered to him.

'Her armour hurts – she's not used to it, and she's kept it on for two nights in succession. And her voices keep telling her we ought to be in Orléans already.'

'Have they spoken to her while we marched?'

'Quite often, she tells me.'

'What do they say?'

'That she is to trust in God, and we will raise the siege.'

'They might give us advice on how to do it.'

'The Maid would think that unnecessary. According to her – "the soldiers will fight, and God will give the victory".'

'Yes – but to whom will He condescend to give it?'

At this point our conversation was interrupted by a shout. We had started to climb a small rise, and over the brow of it came dashing a group of horsemen.

'The Bastard of Orléans!' someone cried. 'And La Hire is with him!' said another.

Joan's first encounter with the Bastard soon became famous. For it was only at this moment that Joan realised that we were on the other side of the river from the besieged city. She was disposed to blame him, first, as she thought, for arranging that she should be deceived; and secondly, for giving bad advice, which for her meant advice contrary to that of her voices. The Bastard's calm was the more admirable because he had worries of his own. His plan was to load the supplies into barges and float them downstream. But the Loire was low and the wind was contrary. So far it had been impossible to get the necessary boats to the point of rendezvous.

Then, as Joan continued to berate him, one of the more conspicuous of her 'miracles' took place. It had been fine all day, but the sky suddenly clouded over and the wind changed direction. As we descended the slope towards the bank, we could see the barges making their way upstream. The Bastard afterwards said that it was at this moment that he began to think that there might be something to be said for this termagant prophetess.

As soon as we reached the bank we started to unload the carts and pack-animals, under the Bastard's direction, and that of La Hire. The latter made a striking, if not a handsome figure, and I noticed that Joan's eyes constantly followed him. It was no wonder if she was interested in the most famous captain in the king's armies. He was a man by now almost middle-aged, with a compact, thickset body and a face reddened by drink and weather. He had one leg shorter than the other – not from a wound received in the wars, but because a stone fireplace had once collapsed and fallen on him. The injured leg was completely rigid, and he stumped about on it as if it were a baulk of wood rather than a limb of flesh and blood. It banged on the ground like the pounders people use to mend roads, when they are settling the new paving-stones. Some people said that his nickname came from this, and others that it came from the Latin *ira*, which means anger. Certainly La Hire had a bad enough temper.

Soon the Bastard was having another argument with Joan.

'No,' I heard her say, 'I cannot enter Orléans and leave all these men behind me. I have put them into a state of grace, but they are not yet steady in it. If they go back to Blois without me, they will return to their former swinishness.'

'We must all go back together,' Gilles interrupted. 'Joan will return with us to Blois.'

'God's teeth, tits and belly!' said La Hire, in his thick Gascon accent, 'I swear to you that if the Bastard and I enter the city of Orléans tonight without the wonder-working Maid, the people there will tear us to pieces, they are so impatient to see her.'

Joan's back stiffened, and I thought she was about to utter one of her stinging rebukes to those who took God's name in vain. Then she seemed to think better of it.

'Very well,' she answered. 'I will cross the river with you, since you say it is necessary. Brother Pasquerel must act in my place. He will report to me on the conduct of the men, and of the captains too.'

'Shall we cross at once?' Gilles asked. 'Or wait until the barges are all loaded?'

The Bastard gave him a long stare. 'I am afraid, messire de Rais, I shall have to ask you to stay with your company. I have room to take two hundred lances across, but in my opinion a captain should remain with his men.'

'You must not blame Gilles for his mistake,' said Joan, with what, in another woman, would have been malicious sweetness. 'You must remember that he has had less experience of the wars than you yourself – you, and messire La Hire.'

We nearly failed to return to Orléans at all. Gilles was deeply offended by the treatment he had received, and Sillé did his best to rub salt into the wound. On the road back to Blois there was mutinous talk of withdrawing our company from the enterprise, and going off elsewhere to find adventure on our own. But when we reached Blois itself, we found Ambroise de Loré waiting for us, and he soon put a stop to all such thoughts of deserting the enterprise. 'Surely, messire Gilles,' he said, 'you will want to be where things are happening? All eyes are turned towards Orléans at the moment. It's the only place where a man's reputation can be made.'

So we got together the herd of cattle that was waiting for us, loaded more carts and pack-animals, and set out for the be-sieged city once more, though this time along the north bank of the Loire. The risk might be greater, but no one fancied trying to load all those kicking, bellowing beasts into barges. Since the English controlled the north bank almost entirely, we had a bad moment when we saw a considerable force com-ing to meet us, just after we had passed the halfway mark. The next instant, however, we saw that it was the Bastard, with a force drawn from the garrison at Orléans, come to escort us into the city.

Even though we were going towards Orléans on the north bank, we did have one or two things in our favour. The chief of these was the fact that the English were rather a small army to besiege a city of this size and importance. They didn't have nearly enough men to construct, much less to garrison, regular lines. What they had done instead was to construct a number of forts around the city, some on the north bank and some on the south. But it was always possible for a body of well-armed, well-mounted men to slip in and out of Orléans, especially along the road we were now following, where there was the biggest gap in the ring of forts. This was how the Bastard had come to confer with us at Blois before we set out.

Now, as the first of the forts came in sight, the captains formed us up in regular line of march. The middle of the column was occupied by Pasquerel and his priests, with their unwieldy banner. I thought Pasquerel looked a little worried, but he swallowed bravely, sending his Adam's apple bobbing rapidly up and down, and said: 'The Maid will expect to see the priests and their banner in the midst of the host, and we shall hold it high until we carry it into Orléans.' Then he trotted off to take his place.

What followed was perfect anti-climax. We marched past the forts, encumbered by our herd of beasts, and the English soldiers stood on their ramparts to watch, but made no attempt to interfere with our progress. Just as we passed the first of their strongholds, a large group of horsemen came out of Orléans, with Joan and La Hire at their head, and rode flank-guard until we were safely into the city.

As soon as we passed through the Burgundy Gate, and saw the high-built timber and plaster houses sailing upwards and outward until they almost met above our heads, I was aware of an extraordinary atmosphere – of hope, of faith, and yet, at the same time, of anxiety and tension, as if the slightest set-back might prick the euphoria of the moment as one pricks a bubble. Joan was the focus of attention. People thronged around her in the narrow streets, eager to snatch a word, trying to kiss her hands if she dropped them lower than the pommel, prepared even to clasp her legs as she sat on her horse. I wondered at her marvellous control over the beast, as she kept it moving gently through the crowd.

We lost sight of her as we dispersed to our various lodgings. Our quarters, for once, had been efficiently seen to. A smiling woman greeted us at the door of a handsome house, and told us that we were to be her guests as long as the siege should last. 'Anyone who comes with the Maid is welcome,' she said. I was tired after the day's ride, and asked if she by any chance had a place where I could stretch myself out for an hour or so. Immediately she led me to a room which was nearly filled with an enormous feather bed. One of the servants came to help me unbuckle my armour.

My repose did not last long. It seemed to me that my head had no sooner touched the pillow than I was awakened by a persistent clamour. There was shouting in the street outside, and someone was hammering at the door of the room itself.

'Get up, Raoul!' I could hear Gilles crying. 'And get your

armour on again! The horses are being brought round to the main door of the house.'

In three minutes, with sleep still clogging my eyes, I was galloping pell-mell through the town, with the sparks flying as my horse's hooves struck the cobbles.

13

What am I to tell you about the raising of the famous siege of Orléans, through the intervention of Joan the Maid? It is a tale which, today, everybody knows and nobody knows. I could recount yet again how the English forts were taken one after another – first the little bastion of Saint-Loup, where the English garrison came out to surrender to us wearing vestments stolen from the local church, and nearly got their throats cut in consequence; and next Saint-Jean-le-Blanc and the Augustins, a couple of ripe apples falling at a touch; and last of all the Tourelles itself, where Joan was wounded just as she had once predicted, and where William Glasdale (less lucky than at Le Lude) was drowned when he fell into the Loire wearing all his armour. I could also tell the things people now like to forget – the way in which the different captains squabbled, and tried to keep their intentions from Joan, and once indeed even tried to stop her from going out of Orléans to do battle with the English. It seems to me there would be little profit in repeating here the things the chroniclers have written.

Some things, of course, stick in the memory. I remember how the people of Orléans behaved to us – as kindly and generously as if we had been their own sons. And I remember how, the night before the Tourelles fell, I went up on to the ramparts, and heard the whole town bustling below me, unable to sleep because of the excitement of the successes which had already been achieved. On one side of me, as I looked out, were lines of glimmering torches which showed where the townspeople were carrying provisions to those who held the already-captured Augustins. Directly ahead of me lay the menacing bulk of the Tourelles itself, with the occasional glitter of steel behind its battlements, where the English, too, kept watch. Far away on my other side was the glow of the main English camp. The moon was down, and there was a clear sky full of the stars in which, so they tell me, all our destinies are written. But suddenly all of these lights, both high in the heavens and beneath them, were dimmed by a huge blaze which flared downstream and upon the further bank. 'What is it?' I asked the man next to me on the rampart, whose face I could not see. 'A good omen,' he replied. 'The English must be burning one of their outlying forts, afraid that we will now come and trap them there.' It was only at that moment that I became certain we would win.

When we returned to Orléans the next evening, after the Tourelles had indeed fallen, it was to find a visitor waiting for us in our lodgings – a lean man, clad in plain and shabby black. He announced himself as a messenger sent by La Tremoïlle, and he brought with him peremptory orders from his master. Gilles was to leave Orléans at once, and make his way to the Constable of France, Arthur de Richemont, in the latter's city of Parthenay.

'Does your master know how things stand here?' demanded Gilles.

'Of course not, though he knows the Maid has already gained some surprising successes.'

'Then why is he so insistent that I leave?'

'Because he does not wish, for anything in the world, that the Constable should return to court.'

'And suppose we had been defeated today?'

'The Constable would no longer be thinking of moving, and messire Georges would have sent you another message.' The messenger smiled, and tapped his satchel. 'Indeed, I have it here. My master prepares for everything, success or failure. And he reads the Constable's mind as easily as you may suppose he reads yours.'

'Then he will know that I cannot leave until the English do, since my honour matters to me,' said Gilles curtly, annoyed by the man's insolence. The messenger smiled a secret smile, bowed and withdrew, leaving us to our own thoughts.

Early the next morning, before the sun had even risen, the watch on the walls began to shout. The English were emerging from their camp. They marched along the circuit of the fortifications, collecting men from each of their strong points on the north bank of the Loire. Those on the other side of the river were now, of course, entirely lost to them. Meanwhile, we ourselves were preparing for battle. We came out of the city by our accustomed route, through Burgundy gate, and found the enemy already drawn up in battle order about two bowshots away from us, though strangely encumbered by the sacks and bundles with which each man seemed to have laden himself. They had also brought a number of cannon out of the camp with them, and these were carefully placed on the flanks of their army. They greeted us with their accustomed cries and insults, as if they wished to provoke us into attacking them.

Though our forces were sadly diminished, through the absence of those who were still encamped around the Tourelles, we might indeed have accepted their challenge, but for the fact that Joan was also missing, and no one now wanted to begin a battle without her. Just as the men's patience was beginning to wear thin, and their ranks were starting to waver ominously towards the foe, Joan made her appearance. She was bare-headed, and wearing a light tunic of mail of the sort called a *jesseran*, not full armour. At her heels came what looked like every priest in Orléans, clad in his vestments for the mass. Being on horseback, she set a pace faster than many of them found comfortable, and they stumbled along behind her. I saw one unfortunate trip over his robes, and fall on his hands and knees in the dust. Yet, breathless as they were, the priests were trying to sing a hymn.

Beside me Sillé tittered. 'Our little innocent has a head on her shoulders,' he said.

'Why do you say that?' I asked.

'She doesn't think we ought to fight today. And she's found the best way to stop us from doing it.'

'Not fight? We beat them yesterday. It is they who should be afraid of fighting us.'

'Do you really want to charge against several thousand English longbowmen who've had all the time in the world to prepare for the assault? Remember what happened at Agincourt and Crécy. I tell you, Raoul, if we have to charge this morning, you'll find me charging the other way.'

His resolution was not to be put to the test. Joan had brought not only the priests but a portable altar with her and, brushing aside the captains who clustered round her asking for orders as soon as she appeared, she set the assembled men of God to work. 'Today is Sunday,' she said curtly to the Bastard when he persisted, 'and we have God's business to do before we tackle yours.' The voices of the priests rose unwavering into the morning air, and the French army fell silent, apparently transfixed. It was as if our opponents were no longer there, or were removed so far from us that they no longer had any power to harm.

One mass was said, while the English glared at us uneasily,

their cries of insult strangled in their throats. Joan, who had deliberately placed herself with her back to them, glanced over her shoulder and signalled for another mass to begin. The gesture seemed to break the spirit of the enemy army. There was a flurry of shouted orders, and they wheeled about and started to reform themselves into line of march, until the whole long column was moving sullenly away from Orléans. Joan remained motionless on her horse until the second mass was finished, though she must have been aware of what was happening behind her. When the last note had been sung she turned casually to one of the bystanders.

'The enemy,' she asked, 'do they have their faces towards us or their backs?'

'Their backs,' the man stammered. 'They are marching away from us.'

Only then did she tug on the rein, and pull her horse's head around. 'Let them go,' she said, her voice at last raised to carry to all the men who surrounded her. 'It is is not God's pleasure they should be fought today. You will have them another time.'

As Joan began to shepherd her priests back into Orléans, I saw La Hire beckoning to some of the other captains. He was not prepared to let our foes escape so easily. He meant to harry them along the way. Gilles was just putting his spurs to his horse to gallop over and offer his and our services in the pursuit when the messenger who had visited us the previous night materialised beside him. The man's doublet was, if possible, shabbier and dustier than ever, but I noticed that he was splendidly mounted, on a black horse any prince would have been proud to own. 'Not that way, messire Gilles,' he said. 'You are required elsewhere. Your men and your baggage already await you across the Loire. I took the liberty of ordering that everything should be made ready for your departure.'

Gilles' colour rose, and he tried to stare the man down, but the other met his gaze quite imperturbably. 'You recall the contract you signed,' he murmured. 'Should you need to refresh your memory, I have a copy in my bag. I have not of course read it, but my master tells me it is a most interesting document.'

Our ride to Parthenay was swift – swifter, perhaps, than we would normally have found comfortable. But the man in black was an admirable guide, and smoothed our path for us. The inns welcomed us at his behest. It seemed as if he was known and respected everywhere. We moved rapidly southward and westward – from Orléans to Blois, from Blois to Tours, from

Tours to Chinon. At Chinon I expected we would be summoned to an audience with La Tremoïlle, but we did not enter the town, and lodged, instead, at one of the villages outside. From here our path led to Loudun, to Moncontour and to Airvault, until at last we were within sight of Parthenay itself.

As we rode, La Tremoïlle's men entertained us with stories of the wars between his master and the Constable, who had been responsible in the first place for imposing La Tremoïlle upon the king. The tone he spoke in was detached and ironic. One would have called it disrespectful if his personality had been less impressive. 'When the Constable went to the king, and told him that he must take my master for his new guardian and favourite, the king smiled at him and said: "You may give him to me, dear cousin, but you will live to regret it. I know the man better than you".'

'Then why did he accept messire Georges in the first place?' Gilles demanded.

'Because the king must always have someone to depend on. But he hates his own dependency, and longs to throw each favourite down. That is why my master must always be on his guard.'

About the Constable himself, our guide had much to tell us. Richemont was the younger brother of the present Duke of Brittany, and had fought at Agincourt, being dragged little injured but half-suffocated from under a pile of bodies after the battle, and taken prisoner to England, where his mother Joan, the former duchess, was now the queen dowager and stepmother to the English king.

'So how was it that he came to be Constable?' I asked.

'With the full permission of the Duke of Burgundy, the king's enemy, whose eldest sister he has married,' the messenger replied. 'He is the means whereby the two parties hoped to be reconciled.'

'And why didn't that happen?'

'Because while the king half-wishes to be ruled, he found Richemont's way of giving orders too rough. His Majesty detests few men, but I believe he dislikes the Constable with all his heart.'

When we came near our destination, our guide suddenly reined in his horse. 'I must beg your permission to go,' he said. 'I cannot safely enter the Constable's town. Remember what messire Georges requires of you. Persuade Richemont it is better to stay at home.' With this, he wheeled his horse about, and in a few minutes had vanished from our sight in a cloud of dust.

'If I didn't know better, I'd say that man was the devil incarnate,' Sillé commented, meditatively gazing after him.

'Why should the devil serve as one of messire Georges' grooms?' Gilles asked laughing.

'Isn't that how the devil rules us, by pretending to be our servant?'

Gilles' face clouded, and he sat for an instant rigid in the saddle. Then he shrugged his shoulders, as if relieved of a burden. 'Come,' he said, 'it is time we paid our respects to that high personage, the Constable of France.'

Parthenay is a formidably strong town, placed where Richemont could receive most help from his friends and cause most trouble to his enemies. Chinon is not far away, and only a little further, though in a different direction, lies the southern border of the Duchy of Brittany. The town itself is built on a hill which overlooks the river Thouet, and consists of two cities rather than one: the lower, which tumbles down the slope; and the upper, called the Citadel, which fills the plateau. To reach the castle we had to pass through two sets of massive gates, before we even reached the foot of the drawbridge. Everywhere we looked we saw soldiers, well fed and well turned out. 'To keep so many men-at-arms, the Constable must still have large revenues,' Gilles said, as we looked about us.

'There is such a thing as being paid to be out of favour,' Sillé replied.

Richemont received us in the great hall of the castle, with considerable ceremony. He was not impressive-looking: a short, thickset, almost middle-aged man, with a seamed face like a peasant. 'Monseigneur,' Gilles said to him, going down on one knee. Hearing the title, and seeing the respect which the visitor was prepared to give, Richemont visibly relaxed. 'I never thought,' he said, 'that I should say welcome to any emissary from messire Georges, but since he has at least had the good taste to send me a man of breeding let me not insist. What does he want?'

The abruptness of the query took us all by surprise. Gilles remained silent.

'I will tell you what he wants,' said Richemont forcefully. 'He has sent you to warn me not to fight the king's enemies.'

'That is so,' Gilles admitted.

'Then you have delivered your message safely, and my answer is that as Constable of the kingdom I will not listen to it. Let us speak of pleasanter things. Did you have a good journey from Orléans? Is it true that the English have raised the siege?

What of this peasant girl whom the king allows to meddle in military matters?'

Before Gilles could attempt to answer any of these questions, there was a stir at the back of the dais, and a thin woman came in, with a little beaked nose and two great eyes set close on either side of it. She was splendidly dressed in harsh reds and yellows, and was followed by two cowed-looking waiting-women, who held her train. 'Ugly as an owl,' Sillé murmured in my ear. 'It can only be our host's wife, Madame de Guyenne.' We all sank to our knees again, and the princess surveyed us without pleasure. 'Why do you waste time with visitors when there is still so much to be done before your departure?' she demanded. 'If they have something to say to you, they can say it after the feast tonight. And then the sooner they are on their way again, the better.' She cast a basilisk glance in our direction, and added: 'Gentlemen, you will be hospitably treated, though your arrival here is not opportune.'

'I suppose,' said Gilles musingly, as we changed our travel-stained doublets for better ones, 'the lady thinks she has married beneath her. In her eyes, the younger brother of the Duke of Brittany cannot count for much. It is not only that she is a daughter of Burgundy, but her first husband was Dauphin of France and, had he lived, she would be queen today.'

At the feast, Richemont and his wife sat at the centre of the high table, and were served on bended knee, with fanfares of trumpets every time a new dish was presented. To our surprise, as soon as we entered the hall a major-domo led Gilles away, and placed him on the dais at his hostess's right. 'The glamour of his quarterings must have outweighed his association with La Tremoïlle,' said Sillé, as we watched from our lowlier place. Indeed, the formidable Madame de Guyenne seemed to have unbent quite remarkably, as she pledged Gilles with cup after cup, and ogled him with her owl eyes. When the meal at last came to a close, it was he who took her by the hand in courtly fashion, and led her out of the hall while the musicians played.

After this night, there was no more talk of an early departure. Indeed, it seemed as if Madame de Guyenne could not see enough of Gilles. She was constantly sending for him to come and talk to her in her chamber, and in the afternoons they walked together in the castle garden, pacing side by side between the beds of flowers and herbs. Once, as I watched from a window, I saw him stoop to pick a rose which he handed to her with a deep and graceful bow.

'What will messire Georges think of our proceedings?' I asked Gilles one night, as we prepared for bed.

'Don't worry about that,' he answered. 'I already have his approval for what I am doing here. His messenger is once again in the neighbourhood. We met the last time I went hawking. I am to stay here and keep an eye on what the Constable is up to.'

'You know well what he is up to. He leaves within three days, to join the king's army on the Loire. And all his men-at-arms go with him.'

'So do we also.'

It now seemed as if the only obstacle to this plan would be Madame de Guyenne, who was loth to part from her cavalier. But at last she too consented.

'You would have been amused by the scene we played,' Gilles asserted, scarcely able to contain his laughter. 'You never saw two such hypocrites in your life!'

'Why hypocrites?' I asked. 'I thought she had conceived a passion for you?'

'Yes, it's true I'm good with ugly women.'

'Because you don't care for women at all,' Sillé sneered.

'And that means I can be pleasant even to those women who don't attract men.'

Richemont had raised an army of more than two thousand men. It made an impressive spectacle as it took the road towards Loudun. There could be no doubt as to who commanded. The Constable's banner floated over our heads in the sunshine, and none of the petty seigneurs whom Richemont had with him would have dared to question his authority. A number, such as the Sire de Rostrenen, were in any case Bretons, not subjects of the King of France. The Constable, in his bluff way, seemed to assume that because Gilles, too, held some Breton lands, he would naturally be inclined to follow the duke's brother, and would free himself from the last vestiges of La Tremoïlle's authority. 'We Bretons must stick together,' was an oft-repeated phrase.

When we reached Loudun, Richemont received an emissary from the king. His name was the Sire de la Jaille, and he cut a sorry figure. He was ridiculous because he was deeply embarrassed by the message he had been ordered to carry. So acute were his feelings on the subject that he was too shame-faced to utter it in public, in the presence of the rest of us, but drew Richemont aside in the hall of the monastery where we had set up our headquarters and started to whisper in his ear.

'What!' roared the Constable, in a voice loud enough to turn every head in the vast room. 'You have the impudence to tell me that the king not only orders me to return to my city of Parthenay forthwith, but actually threatens to come and fight me if I don't!' De la Jaille hung his head, shuffled his feet in the rushes on the floor and finally admitted that this was the case.

Richemont drew a deep breath, and fought to swallow his temper. After a few moments the red began to fade from his cheeks and the swollen veins in his forehead subsided. Then he said, in a voice pitched to carry to everyone present: 'Tell His Majesty that what I do here is done for the good of the kingdom. That is all I have to say.' But he could not resist adding: 'And tell his councillors be damned to them all. I'll see who comes to fight me!'

His confidence was justified by the event. It was possible to cross the river Vienne by a ford, without entering any royal town, and this we did. But the mighty Loire was another matter. Here we must either be given passage, or take it by force. When we got to Amboise, and Richemont summoned the captain of the place to allow him to cross, the gates were immediately opened. The captain of Amboise, in fact, was only too happy to receive us hospitably and to give us the latest news of the campaign. What he had to say was sensational enough for anyone. Joan the Maid had been joined by the Duke of Alençon, who had been put in command of the royal army, and together they had stormed the strong town of Jargeau, upstream from Orléans, and had captured the Earl of Suffolk, the commander of the English. Now they planned to lay siege to Beaugency, on the downstream side, and were busy moving their artillery there by water.

The Constable and his men were less pleased by the news than they ought to have been. They began to fear that, before they had even arrived, the best of the campaign would be over. 'Perhaps that wench has the devil in her after all, just as the English claim,' Richemont muttered, when the captain finished his recital. And he crossed himself hastily when he thought no one was looking.

14

The night before we reached Alençon's camp before Beaugency, Gilles disappeared. He had been growing increasingly restless as we drew nearer and nearer to the Loire and the moment when we would see Joan the Maid once again. He talked of her constantly, and yet the prospect of meeting her, as it came inexorably closer and closer, seemed to make him uneasy.

'You'd almost think he had something to hide from her,' I said jokingly to Sillé.

Sillé shot me a glance from under his brows. 'What makes you say that?' he asked, with an alert sharpness in his tone.

'Nothing – merely that he's like an unfaithful husband who's afraid of confronting his wife.'

Sillé grunted, and said no more. But when the time came to set the pickets round the encampment that evening, Gilles had vanished. Richemont was extremely put out. It now seemed that he had been counting on Gilles to help him make his peace with Alençon, and through Alençon with the king.

'You must go out and find him at once,' he spluttered, his face looking redder and more seamed than ever in the light of the fire that burned in front of his tent. 'Perhaps he has ridden out, and fallen from his horse and injured himself. Perhaps he has been waylaid in an ambush. The roads hereabouts are full of masterless men. Don't wait for the morning. Take torches and go now!'

'All this is useless,' Sillé grumbled, as we began to quarter the countryside. 'There is no moon, and we shall find nothing. Either Gilles has gone off on some freak of his own, or else some misadventure has befallen him. Or perhaps both. But we certainly shan't discover the truth until we have light enough to see by.'

Indeed, as the hours went past, and no discovery was made,

it seemed to me that Sillé had spoken no more than the truth. Occasionally we saw the glimmer of torchlight in the distance, and heard the distant hallooing of those who were engaged in the same task as ourselves. And sometimes, when it was quieter, we heard the muffled cries of the predators who were still astir in the summer night, and the high-pitched shrieks of their victims. But of Gilles himself there was no sign. At last, just as the false dawn began to show, I did indeed find something. Or, rather, it was my horse that found it for me, starting and shying at something hitched in a thornbush. I lent down from my saddle, and brought the stump of my torch closer in order to see. The next moment I caught my breath painfully. The dark mass at the foot of the bush was a body, and scattered garments were caught in the branches.

'Sillé!' I exclaimed. But almost immediately I understood that this could not be Gilles. It was a child's body, not a man's. The relief was great, and yet, as my eyes grew accustomed to what they were looking at, I felt a great heave of nausea in my stomach. The corpse was that of a boy of about ten, stripped naked and marked with multiple stab-wounds. It was just beginning to stiffen, and the pools of blood that surrounded it, though already crusted, were viscous and sticky enough to attract the flies which now appeared as soon as the sun rose.

'Not pretty,' said Sillé's voice drily as he drew up beside me. 'But fortunately nothing to do with us.'

'Oughtn't we to find a priest, and see that this poor child gets Christian burial?'

'We have to get back to the camp. You forget that such things now happen in France every day.' And with this he turned the head of his horse, and made me turn mine also.

When we returned to our bivouac, a surprise was awaiting us. Gilles was there, pale and unshaven, hungrily tearing at a strip of meat he had roasted for himself on the ashes of the fire. I had never seen him behave with such lack of fastidiousness, as he gnawed at the food, spreading juice and grease on his stubbled cheeks, then wiped his fingers on his doublet.

'So you were worried about me,' he said a little defiantly. 'I rode out to meet La Tremoïlle's men, and afterwards I lingered a little. Hasn't a man the right to be alone on a fine summer evening?'

'A fine enough night for villains of all kinds,' I answered. 'We found a murdered body which might have been yours!'

Gilles paused for a moment in his chewing, and looked at me sideways. 'Well, it wasn't, was it?' he said lightly. 'Now stop trying to scold me, and go and catch up on your sleep. You look as if you needed it.'

'But Richemont gave orders that we were all to move off towards Beaugency.'

'The Constable can give all the orders he likes to his own men. Our instructions are to wait and see what happens. I hear Sir John Fastolf is bringing a fresh English army against our people at the siege. That might change everything, mightn't it?'

And with this he went back to chewing his piece of meat.

Thus it was that, despite the Constable's protestations, we refused to join him on his march towards the Loire, and so missed both his uneasy meeting with Alençon and the sudden appearance of the English army under Fastolf, which made them both realise that they must stand or fall together, whatever La Tremoïlle wished or the king ordered. On the evening of our second day of idleness a familiar figure arrived – the black-clad servitor who had guided us from Orléans to Parthenay.

'Well, messires,' he said, his head cocked a little to one side like a crow's, 'your holiday is over. It is time you packed up and went to do a little fighting.'

'Are we going to Beaugency?'

'That would make you look a trifle foolish, messire Raoul, since Beaugency is French again. My orders are to take you this very evening up the river to Meung, where the bridge we hold will soon be attacked by our enemies. The sire de La Tremoïlle would like you to have a victory of your own.'

As we marched through the night towards our new destination we became aware that the English attack had already begun, as the grumbling roar of the cannonade became louder with every step we took. But, hard as we pressed our men, we did not arrive until the sun had already risen. We strained our eyes against its level rays, trying to get our first glimpse of the fortification, and, when at last we saw it, trying to make out whose flag it was that fluttered above the battlements. Just as we came in view, the thunder of the guns had mysteriously fallen silent.

Before our hearts had sunk too far, we were able to make out that the king's standard still flew, and a subdued cheer went up. But there was no answering hail from the walls. Nor, when we finally arrived at the foot of the bridge itself, did any sentinel appear to greet or challenge us.

'Hey, men of Meung, are you all dead or asleep in there?' Sillé shouted impatiently. 'Here's help for you, to teach those rascally *goddams* a lesson!'

At last a crossbowman appeared above the gate. 'Well, you can come in if you like,' he said casually. 'But if you want to see any fun you'd better not stay with us. The *goddams* knocked at our door all night, but now the French are after them.'

We caught up with the main body of the French army at the edge of the vast forest which closed our view to the north. Some minutes before, we had seen the English column turn and disappear into it, and we feared that the French would do the same before we could get them. But suddenly the trumpets blew and the army halted. We arrived to find the leaders gathered in a circle round Alençon, who was questioning Joan. Everyone was at first too intent on her answers to notice our arrival, though the answers themselves were far from being specific. Joan seemed vague and even a little confused – I had never previously seen her hesitate, and it seemed strange and almost ominous. 'Ride boldly on,' was all she would say, 'and you will have a good guide.'

If this seemed to impress a few of her auditors, it clearly did not go down well with La Hire, who stirred impatiently in his saddle. 'We are losing time with all this mumbo-jumbo,' he grumbled. 'We shall miss the quarry.' Then, catching sight of Gilles: 'I want few men, and only the best-mounted. You, messire de Rais, and your two companions – I see you have good horses. You are welcome to join me.' And in this way he accepted us into the army again, and began to move round the circle, picking out those whom he wanted.

When he came near to Joan, she immediately put spurs to her beast and rode towards him, confident that her place was at his side. La Hire looked her up and down. 'This will not be women's work today,' he said.

'Nor was it at the Tourelles,' she retorted.

'By the Saviour's paps, that does not matter to me! Messire Aulon, I will be glad if you will keep this girl from tangling with what does not concern her.' With this, La Hire passed the Maid by, leaving her tugging desperately at her bridle, which Aulon held in a restraining hand. 'La Hire! La Hire!' we heard her cry. 'It is God's work and I must do it!'

But by this time we had already plunged into the waiting forest. It seemed to me the strangest forest I had ever been in. . . .

Dense and tangled, it was nevertheless nearly all new growth, with only the occasional tall tree, oak or elm, soaring high above the thickets. There were small clearings, where the sunlight gathered in stagnant pools, and in these we would often discover what seemed to be the crumbled remains of earthen walls. Often too, we encountered the remnants of cart-tracks, and even of paved roads, now blocked by fallen saplings and clogged by wreaths of brambles. Only gradually did it occur to me that the desolate country we were traversing had until recently been some of the best agricultural land in France. The open fields of the Beauce produced rich crops of corn in the days when the peasants found it safe to cultivate them. But gradually, as troubles increased, the area under the plough began to shrink. At first, it was still possible to till land within sight of a village watch-tower, but then the villages themselves had to be abandoned, and the cultivators moved for safety to the nearest walled town, finally sallying forth only in broadest daylight to tend the few fields which were within shouting distance of the guards. Beyond that limit, wind-sown and bird-sown trees replaced the wheat.

As we picked our way through the waste, I reflected fitfully on the course of events which had brought us here. Less than a year had gone by since we set off from Champtocé to fight in the wars, yet how tremendously all three of us had changed – Gilles, Sillé and I! Gilles was perhaps the one who had altered the most. On the one hand, he had put on the manners of a great nobleman of the court, as if these were a suit of clothes which had always been waiting for him, shut up in some chest until the moment came when it was appropriate to put it to use; and on the other hand I now sensed within him something profoundly wilder and more savage than the wildness and savagery which he had sometimes displayed during our boyhood. His infatuation with Joan the Maid had been, I now perceived, not merely the result of her sexual ambiguity but the attraction felt by one exceptional being towards another.

These reveries were constantly interrupted by new orders. La Hire made us try every path in the hope of finding some trace of the enemy. When he sent me off alone on one of these reconnaissances I became intensely aware of my surroundings. The woods and thickets might allow no glimpse of the enemy, but I was always conscious that I was being watched. La Hire, too, seemed to be uneasily conscious that the English probably knew more of our movements than we did of theirs, for eventually he ordered us to keep together and go as quietly as we could. 'By the Pope's prick,' he said, 'we don't want to play hide-and-seek much longer with these English *goddams*. If we don't find them soon they'll get clear away to Patay, and sleep in comfort while we spend a miserable night in the open. If your eyes won't serve you, keep your ears cocked, and see what you can hear.'

I listened hard as we proceeded, and for a while only the forest noises came to me, mixed with the distant drumming and jingling of our main body some way behind. And then, ahead, I caught the echo of a shout. It was so faint that I did not recognise it for what it was. It came again, and now it was unmistakeable – a hearty view-halloo. Immediately, and much closer to me, I heard a trampling in the thickets, and a great stag burst out of the trees right in front of my horse's nose. It leapt the path with one huge bound, and vanished in an uproar of snapping twigs and cracking branches. 'La Hire!' I said urgently. 'Over there, and to the right! It was Fastolf's men who put up that stag!'

La Hire gave me one swift glance from under his bushy eyebrows, and spurred his horse. In a moment we were pelting through the brambles. I felt the bile starting to rise in my throat.

The English were nearer than we had guessed. Within twenty breaths we came in sight of them. The trees thinned, and we burst out into more open country. There was a gently rising slope, and at the top of it a double hawthorn hedge. Between the two rows of hawthorn were men and horses.

'They're dismounting!' cried La Hire. 'They mean to stand and fight! Charge and take them from the sides!' Our little band of less than sixty men heard the cry, and launched itself at the whole English army. As if we had rehearsed the manoeuvre a hundred times, the squadron divided, and we wheeled left and right to take the enemy in the flanks. Gilles and I were in the middle of the line, and I saw his horse turn one way while I turned the other.

It all took place so quickly that the memory of it is even more dreamlike than memories of violence usually are. Between the tall hedges, which penned them in and prevented them from dispersing before our attack, the English rear-guard were in confusion. The mounted men were swinging down from their horses, and the pages were helping the knights to unbuckle their spurs, so that they could fight on foot. The archers had begun to plant their pikes and string their bows, and a few small cannon were being manhandled into place, slowly because of the rough ground. We rode the gunners down before they even knew what had happened. I saw one drop, his skull crushed by a blow from La Hire's battle-axe, and slashed at another with my sword. The crimson spouted from his neck in a great arc of colour. By the time we reached the centre of the position, where the men in armour stood, the enemy were already throwing down their arms; and I noticed Talbot, weaponless though once again on horseback, being led out of the mêlée by one of our own men. Then, as I drew rein, my attention was attracted by an incoherent shouting, and my eye went beyond the captive to a point where a knot of steel-clad warriors still seemed to be struggling fiercely. It took the blink of an eyelid to realise what was going on. In the midst of the group was Gilles. He was bellowing indistinguishable words, as if his tongue had swollen in his mouth and blocked his utterance. His sword flashed here and there, like a darting dragonfly, and everywhere it paused there was another splash of blood. Gilles's surcoat was sodden with it, and the blood trickled off his armour and ran down the flanks of his horse. I wondered if he any longer knew which of us was friend and which was foe. But some consciousness of the difference still remained to him, for suddenly he wheeled and forced his beast through a gap in the hedge.

Automatically I followed, and found myself in the presence of the whole English army, which was stretched out along a road which led towards the town of Patay, whose walls and church-spire were visible in the distance. It was an army in chaos. Some of the English were trying to force their way back to fight us through the wagons and heavy artillery that blocked the way. Others seemed to have taken to their heels without pausing to ask what kind of misfortune had befallen their comrades in the rear. I could see, far away, a great white banner streaming out, as the knight who bore it galloped for his life over the open fields.

The main body of the English foot huddled together quite close to me, their eyes dull and their hands hanging slack at their sides, as if they had been deprived by magic of the power to raise their weapons. It was towards these bemused soldiers that Gilles directed himself, and the dragonfly sword began to dart and flutter again, and the English stretched out their necks to receive its kiss.

Our own main army arrived on the field of Patay to find the enemy already routed. Fastolf had been forced to leave by those who surrounded him. I glimpsed him in the distance, struggling and cursing as one of his escort seized his bridle and turned the horse's head. Anyone else on the English side who had or could find a horse was busy making good his escape. The gunners cut their traces and mounted bareback, and the cart-drivers abandoned their wagons.

Seeing what the situation was, the chivalry on our side drew rein. It was hardly worth it, to blunt good steel upon such canaille, and the pursuit conducted by La Hire and a few of his men had now drawn so far ahead that it would have foundered a good horse to catch up. Our foot felt no inhibitions. With a savage cry they flung themselves upon the English soldiers who had been abandoned by their leaders.

If you ask anyone who was at Patay about the slaughter which was the main part of the day's work they will pretend not to remember. There are times when the sun shines, and God still hides his face. Since there were clearly no good ransoms to be had, our men thought it prudent to dispose of their stupefied opponents with as much finality as possible. But, even if there are willing hands and little or no resistance, it takes a long time to kill three thousand men. Our soldiers sweated as they toiled, and the butchery grew less tidy as they progressed. Joan arrived a long time after it had begun, and she wept when she saw how her prophecies had fulfilled themselves.

At the moment when she appeared on the field, her horse almost stumbled over two men, a prostrate English soldier and a Frenchman who was busy clubbing him to death. With the flat of her sword she drove the attacker off, and he retired snarling, like a dog robbed of a bone. Then Joan dismounted to try and comfort the dying man, cradling his bloody head in her arms and murmuring words he was too far gone to understand, even if he had known the tongue they were spoken in. After a while, comprehending that her efforts were of no use, she summoned the Frenchman and made him boost her on to her horse. As soon as she turned away, he came sidling back to his victim, to deliver one final kick.

Meanwhile, I had lost sight of Gilles, and I began to worry that some Englishman might at last have found the courage to strike him down as he forced his horse through the press. I rode back and forth as the massacre went on, trying to discover what had become of him. During my search, I encountered Sillé. We greeted one another with something approaching relief, and continued the task together. Gradually we moved away from the place where the main encounter had taken place, and found ourselves on the outskirts of a wood. The sun was a long way towards setting, and golden shafts of light pierced between the tree-trunks. Shading my eyes against the glare, I saw a horse which I recognised as Gilles's. It was peacefully cropping the long grass, and half-hidden in the grass itself I noticed a body with a bloody surcoat rucked up under its armpits.

We came closer, thinking Gilles must be dead, or badly wounded at the very least. But when I dismounted I found that he was breathing easily and regularly, and had a slight smile upon his lips. I shook him by the shoulder, trying to arouse him, and his eyelids flickered open, then he sighed and lapsed once more into heavy slumber.

'Go and find as many of our men as you can,' I said to Sillé. 'You remember what happened at Le Lude. This seems to be the same sickness.' He nodded at me without replying, and went to do as I asked.

Left alone with Gilles, I thought I ought to remove his surcoat, which stank of half-dried blood and crawled with flies. He was heavy and awkward in his armour, and eventually I had to cut the cloth away. I rolled the precious embroidery, sticky and ruined, into a large bundle, and tossed it some distance away from me. Having done this, I thought I ought to take off Gilles's armour as well, in case it was constricting him. After a further struggle, I managed to remove his curiass, and found that he was clad in a fine shirt of white linen, stained with sweat and stained also with rusty lines and blotches where the blood had found its way through the joints in the steel.

I put my hand to the base of his throat, to feel the pulse which was beating there, and as I did so discovered that he was wearing something hung around his neck by a leather thong. Until now it had been hidden by his shirt. I drew the thing out, and saw that it was a little bag of fine leather, tightly closed with a length of red thread, wound round and round the mouth and tied with an intricate knot. The bag was very light, and when I shook it it gave a rattle which suggested seeds, or perhaps fragments of bone. It had a strong and disagreeable scent, heavily perfumed, sweetish, indefinably corrupt. On a sudden impulse, I struggled to my feet and took a few steps into the wood. Finding a small cleft in a tree-trunk I thrust the bag into it, and left it there.

When I returned, Gilles was awake. He seemed to have come to himself quite peacefully, and looked up at me with clear eyes. 'Oh, there you are, Raoul,' he said. 'I had such a strange dream – that we fought in a great battle, and won it almost on our own. Surely that can't be true?' Then, rousing himself further and leaning on one elbow: 'Or maybe it *is* true, after all? How pleasant if it was!'

Before I could attempt a reply, Sillé reappeared with most of our men. He told me that the leaders had gone to spend the night in the town of Patay, taking with them a few important prisoners captured in the first onslaught. Most of our foot were making camp in the plain outside the town, and with unexpected tact, Richemont had volunteered to remain with them. 'Perhaps he thinks he can win the men's hearts and usurp Alençon's place,' Sillé ventured, with his usual cynicism.

It was decided that we too would do best to make camp where we were. While the camp-fires were being lit, and the bivouacs set up, I watched Gilles as he sat idly amid the bustle. Evidently he was unaware that anyone was looking at him, and his hand strayed towards his neck, as if for reassurance. It was clear that until this moment he had not realised that the amulet was missing, and a brief convulsion shook him as he discovered the fact. He mastered it so swiftly that I was sure he was already himself again. I was also certain that the little bag had been important to him.

These conclusions were reinforced when I awoke the next morning. The sun had scarcely risen, but Gilles was already stirring. I saw him a small distance away, squatting to examine something. After an instant I understood that what he was looking at was the bloody surcoat I had cut away from his body the evening before. This time he sensed my eyes upon him as he rummaged through the folds, disturbing the flies that still buzzed there. He was uneasy that I had noticed what he was doing.

'Was it you who cut this off me yesterday?' he said.

'It was,' I replied, knowing what the next question would be.

'Did you find anything entangled with it – a little leather bag, for instance?'

'No,' I said, with strict truthfulness. Then I added: 'Why – what was in it?'

'Nothing important. Something La Tremoïlle sent. Or at least his messenger gave it to me.'

'I wonder if anything good can come from that source,' I said, sitting up abruptly and staring at Gilles till he dropped his eyes.

15

Soon after the battle, La Tremoïlle summoned Gilles to come and see him privately at his castle of Sully on the Loire. Here Gilles urged him to press the matter of the coronation on the king.

'You young warriors are all the same,' La Tremoïlle grumbled. 'All you think of is your own glory.'

'I think of the king's benefit, too,' Gilles retorted.

'Surely he will be better off at home, rather than undertaking a foolhardy campaign deep into enemy country. Besides, he has no money to pay for such an adventure.'

'Haven't you seen how the people flock in to join his standard? I have even heard of gentlemen who cannot afford armour or a good horse, and who have been willing to enlist as ordinary men-at-arms. Their whole belief is now in the Maid, and they will not be content if the king refuses to go.'

'The Maid! The Maid! Why do people talk to me of nothing but the Maid?' La Tremoïlle exclaimed. 'I cannot build a policy on a prophetess. Didn't your respected grandfather tell you that miracles have no place in politics, whatever Holy Mother Church may say?'

Despite the king's hesitation, and despite La Tremoïlle's doubts, the notion grew that the king's voyage to his coronation was now inevitable. Charles and his court made their way to the town of Gien on the Loire, which would be the stepping-off point for any expedition into Champagne. The place overflowed with people. More and more of them flocked into it every day, all declaring their determination to serve under the miraculous Maid. Their murmurs of impatience grew into a swelling roar, and it seemed as if there would still be violence in the streets.

Things had reached flash-point when all three of us went to call on La Tremoïlle at his lodgings in the town. It was late morning, but he was still in bed. We had some difficulty getting past the guards who kept watch at his door. 'There you are at last,' he said angrily, heaving himself up against a mound of pillows. 'You now see what a mess you and your good advice have got us into. The king fears for his life.'

'All he has to do is take the road. The people here do not understand the delay,' Gilles replied.

'Since when must a monarch take orders from his subjects?'

'When you give them, messire!' Gilles retorted, with a flash of anger.

'And if the king refuses to budge, because he is afraid of so many strangers and such an uncertain enterprise?'

'You must find the means to make him.'

'That's more of a problem than you think,' said La Tremoïlle. 'Monarchs are like children, who have to be coaxed into everything. Why should I have to wheedle the king into doing this?'

'Because your life is in danger if you don't,' said Gilles. 'Half the people here already blame you for his refusal to set out. They think you have made a pact with the king's enemies.'

La Tremoïlle began to show signs of uneasiness, shifting his weight amid the bedclothes. 'Who has spoken to you about that?' he demanded.

'It's common gossip.'

'Of course I've been in communication with the Duke of Burgundy,' he admitted. 'That's quite normal. We've continued to exchange ideas throughout the war. After all, I was brought up at his father's court. And we both know that, sooner or later, the King of France must come to terms with his greatest vassal.'

'I thought *you* were his greatest vassal, messire,' Sillé interjected slyly.

'Only so long as the war lasts,' said La Tremoïlle, startled into candour. Then, realising what he had said, he let out a rumble of laughter.

'I'd forgotten how intelligent your comrade was, messire Gilles. He's put his dirty finger right on my problem. Can I survive the king's coronation? That's one of the things I have to decide.'

'You'll find it easier than surviving a failure to set out,' said Gilles bluntly.

'I fear you are beginning to convince me of that. So what's to be done? Between ourselves, the king is so determined not to go to Rheims that he has even told the queen to return to Bourges, instead of remaining with him here.'

At this moment, I thought it was my own turn to intervene. 'I think the solution is simpler than you think,' I said. 'You must use the Maid.'

'Use the Maid to save myself? How is that to be done?'

'If Joan sets out on the road, the army will undoubtedly follow her. I leave it to you to make the king follow the army. You can tell him he won't be king for long if he doesn't.'

'Use a greater fear to conquer a lesser one?' La Tremoïlle paused to reflect. 'Yes, that might be the way to manage it. I've done it before. Well, why are we delaying? You go and do your part and I will do mine.' And with this he started to heave himself out of bed, in an earthquake of coverlets and pillows.

Finding Joan turned out to be more difficult than I had anticipated. She had left her quarters and the first few men I questioned knew nothing of her whereabouts. At length I encountered one of Alençon's people. 'She is with my master,' he said.

'And where is that?'

'In the fields outside the town. She grows weary of petitioning the king.'

After some searching amid the bivouacs which covered the fields, I at last found a small encampment, separated from the rest, over which flew Joan's familiar banner. Joan was sitting crouched on a saddle which had been placed upon the ground. She was in earnest conversation with Alençon, who gangled miserably in front of her, like a delinquent schoolboy in the presence of his teacher. 'Let us go at once,' I heard her say. 'Our good friends in Rheims are in need of a visit from us.'

'But, Joan,' Alençon protested. 'Without the king there can be no coronation.'

'I cannot help that,' said Joan. 'My voices tell me I must wait here no longer.' Then, catching sight of me as I came up, 'Ah, one of messire de Rais's men. What have you got to say to me? Is your master ready to set out, unlike this poor duke here?'

'Ready and indeed eager,' I replied. 'All our horses are ready and our baggage packed. Indeed, I am surprised to find you still here. The word in the town was that you and the avant-garde were already on the road.'

Joan glanced at me keenly. All signs of the hesitation she had shown at Patay had vanished. 'Suppose that I had been on the road. Would you have followed?'

'Yes,' I said.

'Even with no word from the king?'

'Yes. Even with no word from him.'

'What of messire de Rais's cousin, messire de La Tremoïlle? Do you know his intentions?'

'When I last saw them, his men were busy saddling their horses.'

'Ready for a return to Bourges, no doubt.'

'No – the word was that they were to ride with their master into Champagne.'

My attention was caught by the look of utter bewilderment which was slowly invading Alençon's face. His mouth fell open, but before he could recover his composure and speak we were both of us distracted by a movement beside us. Joan had slipped forward on to her knees in the dust. Her hands were clasped in front of her, and her face was turned upward to the sunlight. I could clearly see the snail-tracks of her tears, as they went streaming down her cheeks. Eventually she stretched out her right arm, and seemed to touch something in front of her – to grasp a hand, to fondle a fold of stuff. Then she brought her palm towards her nose and breathed deeply, like someone savouring a strong perfume. It was suddenly very quiet. A summer cricket was the only sound, chirring loudly in the grass. Within my chest, my heart beat heavily.

Joan stirred, and opened her eyes, and got slowly to her feet. 'My voices say you are speaking the truth, Raoul,' she said. 'Though they do not know the reason. I am to leave and the king will follow. Everything will be as God and I desire.' Then her expression changed, and a smile which was almost mischievous spread across her face.

'Come, my fine duke. You've stood there long enough looking as though you've swallowed a fly. Have the trumpets sounded, and let us all ride forth, to accomplish the things that God commands.'

16

Our journey to Rheims was coloured by many different moods – jubilant when we set out, disappointed when Auxerre refused to open its gates to us, despondent when the city of Troyes at first made an identical refusal. At that time we seemed all too likely to starve to death as we sat in front of it, and the king's councillors spoke of turning back. But once Troyes surrendered, almost miraculously as it seemed and due to Joan's efforts, none of us had any doubt that we would reach Rheims or that Charles would have his coronation there as the Maid had promised.

It was strange, however, that the nearer we got to our destination the more fearful the king became and the more intrigue-ridden his courtiers. Charles, who before Troyes had seemed to avoid Joan's company, now constantly summoned her to his side in order to question her about what would happen next. 'Are you sure,' he said, 'that the city of Rheims wi!l admit us?' Joan gave only one reply to these anxiously reiterated enquiries: 'Have no fear, gentle Dauphin, the burgesses of Rheims will come before you.'

La Tremoïlle, on the other hand, was in his element. He had been seized by a mood of euphoria. Going to Rheims to have the king crowned was now, in his own mind at least, entirely his idea, and he considered it a masterstroke. 'Thank God I had the wit to put that girl up to it,' he confided to Gilles. 'Charles with a crown on his head and the holy unction on his brow will be twice the power he was before. After all, there's a big gap between a real king, our intermediary with God and his Mother and a mere Duke of Burgundy.'

What interested messire Georges was the way in which the spoils were to be divided. 'I'm afraid they'll be mostly symbolic,' he said, 'as the king has almost no money, and what he has is what I lend him. But we must put ourselves in a position to get the money when it comes. For you, messire Gilles, we must find something special, some reward for your heroism in the defence of the kingdom. Is it true that you killed two hundred men single-handed on the field of Patay? It's like something out of a romance!'

This conversation took place as the two men came in sight of the castle of Sepsaulx, which was to be our last halt before Rheims. It was a gloomy pile, long-neglected, which served as the country residence of the archbishops of Rheims. The hall was full of bat-dung, and the wooden shutters for the windows had long since disappeared. Many of the upper chambers in the towers were almost roofless, and smelt dank even after the many weeks of sunshine we had enjoyed. Nobody looked forward to a long wait there while the burgesses of Rheims made up their minds. 'Why can't we bivouac in the fields with our men?' said Gilles plaintively to La Tremoïlle. 'Instead of having to remain with you in this midden?'

'Because I want to keep you under the king's eye. I know how easily he changes his mind.'

We were, however, to be saved from spending the night there, for the grooms had no sooner started to unload the beasts, and the cooks to build a fire in the kitchen (where the great chimney smoked abominably since it was choked with birds' nests), when the long-expected delegation arrived.

The baggage which had just been unloaded was therefore packed up again, and we followed in the wake of Regnault de Chartres, the archbishop of Rheims, who had first to make his own ceremonial entry, since he had never before visited his city. The burgesses accompanied us, and their faces grew longer and longer as they saw, not only the full size of the king's army but the number of people who now came riding from every direction. There were too many men for the road to contain them, and they spread out over the flat countryside, trampling the vines with their horses and even managing to obliterate the boundaries of the fields.

When we at last reached the city gate, it was early evening. La Tremoïlle kept us in his entourage, and this meant that we entered the town close behind the king and the Maid, who rode upon the king's right hand. The entry was thickly thronged, and so were all the streets we passed through. The inhabitants of Rheims had brought out every kind of coloured stuff – tapestries if they possessed them, even the coverlets from their beds – and had hung them from their windows to make a show for the monarch. Women leant from their houses and threw flowers, and urchins dodged dangerously between the horses' hooves. I had never in my life heard such a clamour of shouts and bells, even upon the day we took the bridge at Orléans.

I saw the king brace himself as we went in under the arch, and the swelling roar of voices rose to meet him as he emerged again into the sunshine. But though the crowd greeted him festively, they looked with even greater curiosity at the girl in armour beside him. Joan rode with her eyes cast down, gazing at her hands, which controlled her beast with tiny movements. To those who pressed about her, who embraced her knees as she rode, who reached up to touch her steel-clad body, she made no acknowledgement, though a slight smile played about her lips. Close behind her her banner flapped, carried by the page Louis de Coutes. It seemed to overshadow the king's own standard, which was borne beside it by another standard-bearer.

We rode to the archbishop's palace, which is built beside the great cathedral, and there the tall archbishop was waiting to welcome his sovereign. 'So you came to no harm, my lord,' Charles said, slyly, looking him up and down, pleased for once to have the advantage of height as he sat on his horse. Regnault twisted his lips into the semblance of a smile. 'The Burgundians rode out at one gate as I came in at another. There are some guests one is glad to be without, even on such a day as this.'

The king and the archbishop immediately held a private council with La Tremoïlle and a few others as to how the ceremony was to be conducted. After an hour had passed La Tremoïlle emerged smiling from the Council Chamber and sent for Gilles. 'I have done better than I hoped,' he announced. 'You, cousin Gilles, are to be one of the champions who escort the Holy Ampulla from the abbey of Saint-Rémy to the cathedral. The king wishes you to be dubbed a knight on the same day as himself and will make you Marshal of France.'

'Marshal of France?' Gilles echoed. 'Why not others, who have fought longer in the wars than I?'

La Tremoïlle laughed heartily at this. 'Come, messire Gilles! I never expected any member of our family to be so modest. You are to be made marshal because I wish it, because you have kept our pact, because you have spent your own money for the king, because you are better born than most, and because none of the other captains has himself killed two hundred of the enemy in a single day and before witnesses. Aren't these reasons enough? Go and prepare yourself to keep a knight's vigil.' He paused, and turned to Sillé and myself.

'Gentlemen,' he said, 'there is much to be done and too little time in which to do it. I hope my cousin will lend you to me for tonight. In return for your work I can promise you a good place at the king's crowning.' And thus the two of us became responsible for many of the preparations for the ceremony.

It was surprising how little turned out to be lacking. From huge chests, long untouched, the archbishop's steward produced the tapestries which were customarily hung in the cathedral upon the greatest feast days. Many had not been used since the coronation of the king's father, nearly fifty years previously. As we opened the lids of the boxes some moths flew lazily out, and I feared the worst. But when we unrolled the heavy bundles there were few holes, and the gold and silver woven into the fabric was still fresh and untarnished, and the colours unfaded. The steward found a parchment which indicated where each was to be hung, and we discovered that the iron hooks to hold them still remained firm in the pillars of the church.

Having set men to hanging the tapestries under Sillé's supervision, I sent criers into the streets of the town, to say that any man who had a length of precious stuff must bring it for the king's service. To my surprise, great bolts of brocade silk were brought to me, and, better still, there were a few heavy woven stuffs from the East to cover the dais where the throne was to be put, and to lay on the stone floor in front of the high altar, at the place where the king and the archbishop must prostrate themselves.

Next, I went to interview the cathedral treasurer. He was an old man, shaky and trembling, and rheumy drops poured from the corners of his eyes as he greeted me, holding a candle in his hand. 'I don't know what's to be done,' he grumbled, 'and I don't see how you, as a mere layman, are expected to remedy the situation. The regalia is in the hands of our brothers at Saint-Denis near Paris, and that place, as you know, is governed by the English. Though we crown the king in Rheims with the crown of Charlemagne, he's supposed to bring it with him. Likewise the sword, the spurs, the ring, the sceptre and the hand of justice. All we have here are the archbishop's ornaments, the basin for offerings, and the chalice and paten of Saint-Rémy.'

I tried to insist that he should open his iron-bound chests for me, and let me see for myself, but he refused adamantly. 'It is none of your affair,' he said. Growing desperate, I sent at last for La Tremoïlle. He arrived within a few minutes, with an escort of torch-bearers, since it was by now dark. 'What's all this?' he thundered. 'D'you tell me we have nothing here to crown the king with?' In his quavering but obstinate voice the treasurer once more began to enumerate the items that were lacking. 'Open every chest,' said La Tremoïlle, with curt finality, and this time the old man obeyed.

The treasures of the cathedral, as we saw them by the fiery light of half a dozen torches, were certainly impressive, but La Tremoïlle wasted no time in admiring them for their own sake. 'The sword and the spurs present no real difficulty,' he commented. 'We have enough noblemen and warriors in the city to supply us with a good choice. As for the ring, the archbishop who left this to the church will not mind if we borrow it.' He stretched out his hand and picked out a fine sapphire ring from one of the boxes. 'Where the customary royal offerings are concerned, we must make do with the vase and the purse presented by the king's late father. The king will remember his debt in due course. The sceptre is easy – a goldsmith must cut down one of your croziers for us, and remove the crook. As for the hand of justice . . .' For a moment his voice trailed away thoughtfully, and his eyes roved over the glittering mass of metal before him. 'Ah! What's this?'

'Part of a precious canopy,' the treasurer quavered.

The object La Tremoïlle held was an ebony rod with a gilt metal hand at each end. The hands looked as if they had been designed to hold another rod, as in each case the thumb and fingers made a socket. 'Good. Just saw this in half, get the goldsmith to supply a knob of some kind to hide the cut, and the problem is solved.' The treasurer gave a little cry of anguish as La Tremoïlle tucked the rod into the sleeve of his robe.

'But what about the crown itself?' I ventured to ask him, as he turned to depart.

'Don't worry about that. I have a crown the king put in pledge to me, to raise money for the relief of Orléans. It would be ungenerous of me not to allow him the use of it on such a day. It is not the crown of Charlemagne, but it looks well enough.'

Leaving the treasury, where the treasurer had begun to babble the protests he had not dared to utter in La Tremoïlle's presence, I went again to the cathedral, to check that all was now in readiness. The tapestries were hung between the pillars, and in the choir the paving no longer re-echoed to the sound of my footsteps when I trod on precious stuffs which remained almost invisible to me in the darkness. Here and there, the priests were still lighting the candles on the altars and trimming the lamps which burned before some of the images, but I knew they would soon be gone, leaving the place empty for the king to keep his solemn vigil. Meanwhile, in some humbler church in the town, Gilles would be doing likewise; and the others who were to be knighted would watch in churches and chapels. Rheims surely had enough of these for each man to be left alone with his thoughts.

From the vast shadowy vessel of the cathedral, where the air was already tinged with the bittersweet smell of incense, I made my way to the almost equally vast kitchen of the archiepiscopal palace, where the first preparations for the banquet which would follow the king's crowning had already begun. It was surprising how many expert cooks we had been able to muster from the town, in addition to those we had brought with us, and what a variety of things there was for them to prepare. Here I saw a man who was skilfully skinning a peacock, leaving intact the sweeping tail and the head. Laying the skin flat upon a table, he began to rub ground cumin into the inner surface. In another place, a cook was beating quantities of almonds in a mortar, and my mouth watered as I thought of that delicate dish called blancmange, which is made of almonds, sugar from the East, and the white meat of a fowl. The carcasses of oxen were already being prepared and made ready to be put upon their spits, which would begin to turn as soon as the coronation service began, since it takes easily as long to roast an ox as it does to crown a king. Busiest of all were the bakers. The majority of them were making coarse bread for the trenchers which would be used at the feast, to put the meat on and keep the sauce from the linen of the tablecloth. The head baker lamented to me that, hard as he might bake them, these would not be articles of the best quality. 'You must understand, sir,' he sighed, 'that normally we keep them four days before sending them up to be used. Freshness in a trencher is no virtue, as it's the new bread that crumbles and lets the juice through.' But I knew that, for the rest of his days, he would boast of having been a baker at the king's coronation feast.

17

Because the king was already in the cathedral, keeping his vigil, the ceremony of the awakening was omitted. Once the doors were opened Charles retired to don his coronation vestments, while as many of us as could crush in took our places in the building. La Tremoïlle had been as good as his word, and found for Sillé and myself positions far better than our rank warranted. Members of his household kept them for us against all comers, until we arrived to claim them. The great church, which had seemed so huge in the darkness, now looked almost small, so packed was it with humanity – the members of the king's court, the clergy, the leading citizens of Rheims, men-at-arms who had cunningly ensconced themselves high in the triforia, and now looked down at us, their booted legs dangling and great grins cracking their stubbly faces. Shoulder to shoulder with the men of power were beggars and vagabonds who had wormed their way into the building by secret entrances. A few pockets were picked and purses slit at the king's coronation, just as one might expect.

The first procession to enter was that of the archbishop, immensely tall and stately in his mitre; and after him followed the little band of the ecclesiastical and secular peers of France – almost-equals of the monarch. Most of the former and all of the latter were substitutes. Some peers could not be present – among them the Duke of Burgundy and the Bishop of Beauvais – because they were the king's enemies. In addition, nearly all of the secular peerages had long ago fallen in to the crown. But the understudies made a brave show. Amongst the laity, Alençon took first place, and following him came the king's other cousins, Clermont and Vendôme. But La Tremoïlle too had been given semi-royal status. With his height and bulk he seemed to dwarf the rest of his colleagues, to overshadow them physically as much as he did in power.

After the peers had taken their places, two bishops were sent to fetch the king, who entered in a cloth-of-silver cloak over a white shift. After him walked La Tremoïlle's half-brother Albret, carrying upright and unsheathed the sword of the Constable. I thought how angry Richemont would be when he learned this detail. Behind Albret came two personages not provided for in any book of ritual – Joan the Maid, clad as always in full armour and carrying her banner in her hand, and beside her a thin dishevelled figure clad in the robe of a Franciscan. I gazed at him attentively, for this was the first time I had got a close look at Brother Richard, the travelling preacher who had been partly responsible for the surrender of Troyes. His neck craned and his Adam's apple bobbed as he stared around him at the great assembly. Joan, on the other hand, seemed entirely unconscious of all the many pairs of eyes which were at this moment fixed upon her. Together with the friar, she went and stood beside the dais where the king was later to be seated. Charles knelt for a moment before the throne of the archbishop. As he did so, the choir began to sing the opening verse of the *Veni Creator*, and with this the ceremony began.

The first and perhaps most necessary act was the arrival of the Holy Ampulla, which contained the oil which would make Charles of Valois forever different from the ordinary run of mankind. It was announced by a loud knocking at the closed west door. When this was thrown open the Abbot of Saint-Rémy came riding into the nave, sheltered by a golden canopy and protected by four champions, of whom Gilles was one. They too were mounted, and the hooves of their great war-horses clattered on the paving, as the congregation swayed aside to make room for them. The Abbot passed so close to me that I could have reached out and touched the Ampulla, which hung from a chain around his neck. It was a little glass flask, set into the belly of a golden dove.

When the abbot reached the archbishop, at the entrance to the choir, he dismounted and put the jewel into the latter's hands, saying as he did so: 'Monseigneur, I bring you here this precious treasure sent from Heaven to our great Saint Rémy, to be used for the sacring of King Clovis and his successors. But before I part with it I beg you, according to ancient custom, to swear an oath to return it to me again, once the coronation shall be complete.' At these words a great shudder ran through the congregation, as if it was only at this moment that we believed the event we had come to see would actually take place.

But before a king can be anointed, much less crowned, he must swear to protect the liberties of the church and do justice to the people. As Charles took the oath, making the promise no king has yet been able to keep, that he would 'prevent all men of whatever rank from committing rapine and iniquity', my glance strayed upwards, and my attention was caught, among all the dangling booted legs, by a pair clad in dusty black. Roosting there like an ill-omened crow was the man who had led us to Parthenay. Suddenly uneasy, I glanced aside, and when I looked again the man had vanished.

Now it was Alençon's duty to come forward and knight the king, putting the spurs on his feet, giving him the sword and striking him the ritual blow upon the cheek. Stripped of his silver cloak, the king knelt before the altar while Regnault blessed the crown and other royal ornaments. The archbishop then poured a drop of the holy chrism into the paten of Saint Rémy, and both he and the king prostrated themselves upon the ground. When they rose again, the time for the anointing had come. With his thumb dipped in oil Regnault touched the king upon his forehead, belly, back, shoulders and in the crooks of his arms. I saw that the white shift had been made so that it could be opened at the appropriate spots. Then, hastily, the frail body was wrapped in its royal robes and the king held out his hands to receive the last drops of chrism in the palms. The trumpets blew in the galleries, and all of us began to cheer, each man embracing his neighbour and giving him the kiss of peace as if it were Easter Day.

According to doctrine, a king is truly king once the anointing has been done. But Charles must become a monarch not merely in the eyes of God but of all the people, so now they gave him his royal ring, his sceptre and the hand of justice – all the items about which we had conferred so anxiously the evening before. They looked convincing enough. This done, the secular and ecclesiastical peers stood forth to recognise their sovereign. Regnault took the crown from the altar and placed it on Charles's head; and the peers surrounded the king, touching their hands also to the jewelled circlet. For a second time the trumpets brayed, and the great stone building seemed to rock with the cheering both within it and without, as if its pillars were trees shaken by a high wind and its vault no more than a canopy of leaves.

Guided by the archbishop, Charles mounted the steps of the dais and seated himself upon the throne.

All this time Joan had been standing on the lowest step, the tears streaming down her face. Once or twice she swayed as if she were about to faint, and her fingers loosened upon the pole of her standard. When Brother Richard tried to take it from her, however, she roughly shook him off. Now, as the king sat, she seemed to change her mind. She thrust the banner into the hands of her companion and came and knelt before the throne. The tumult of cheering died, and Joan's clear voice rang out.

'Gentle king!' she cried, 'now is fulfilled the pleasure of God, who wished that the siege of Orléans should be lifted, and that you should be brought into the city of Rheims to receive your holy consecration, thus showing that you are true king, and he to whom the kingdom of France should belong.' Regnault's brow darkened at this interruption, and beside me I could hear Sillé grinding his teeth in rage. 'The bitch!' he muttered. 'She always wants all the credit!' But these two seemed to be the only ones who were offended by Joan's act, for all around me the spectators wept as heartily as she had been doing herself.

I too would have wept with the emotion of the moment, but somewhere at the bank of my mind a voice whispered: 'Those words were too formal not to have been thought out and rehearsed'. Once more I found myself unable to reach a verdict, thanks to the mixture of simplicity and subtlety in the Maid's character. But I knew that Gilles would be weeping with the rest, despite the poor welcome Joan had always given him.

There was more to the coronation than the things I have described, but this was the nub of it. Today I am one of the few men left alive who saw the crowning of Charles VII, the Victorious, with his own eyes. Yet people will speak of it to the end of time.

Before he left the cathedral, Charles knighted those who had been chosen for the honour, striking them the same blow that Alençon had given to him. He also announced their new dignities. Gilles was henceforth a marshal of France, with a title earned in the wars to add to those he had inherited.

Without even waiting for the ceremony to be fully over I pushed my way out through a little door I had noticed. Not content with seeing the king crowned, I wanted to see him at his coronation feast. I hurried along the cloister that connected the great church with the archbishop's palace and soon found myself in the musicians' gallery overlooking the great hall. The minstrels looked at me somewhat angrily, but a gold piece to their leader and the fact that many of them already knew me, at least by sight, soon settled the matter.

The tables were still being made ready for the banquet. The

marshal of the king's household stood in the middle of the great room, and under his orders the white cloths to cover the tables were reverently unfolded. Ushers and grooms ran about. Some piled fringed napkins and towels on other, narrower tables against the walls, while others laid places for the guests with cups, trenchers and spoons. Over the whole expanse of the cloth little loaves of fine white bread were scattered, so that some would always be within reach. At the high table, at the end of the room, a single place was laid for the king.

The signal was given that Charles was approaching, and the musicians in the gallery began to play, answered by others who accompanied the royal procession. Charles was still wearing his crown, and in his two hands, folded against his breast, he carried the sceptre and the hand of justice. Behind him marched Albret, sword upright and unsheathed. The king placed what he had been carrying upon the board, and the archbishop helped him to remove his crown, which was put at the king's right as if it were another guest. Those whose privilege it was to eat with the king went to find their places.

The peculiarity of a coronation feast is that it is at least as honourable to serve as it is to eat. It was the Count of Clermont who acted as pannetier, draping a towel round his neck so that he held an end in each hand. On his left arm hung the king's napkin, balanced along his right forearm were trenchers made of gilded bread. In his left hand he carried a magnificent golden salt-cellar in the form of a ship. As soon as he appeared, Alençon and Vendôme came forward to assist him; the one to slice and shape the trenchers for the meal, the other to help the king to wash his hands. After straining the scented water from one basin into another, Vendôme put some of it into a cup and drank it down. Only then could it be pronounced fit to touch the monarch's hands.

The music played once more, and a Latin grace was sung. Only now did a second procession appear – the cooks carrying the masterpieces they had laboured through the night to produce. Here was the peacock I had seen, once more dressed in its feathers, with spread tail and gilded crest. Here too was a swan, floating white and unstained, admiring itself in a pool of green aspic. And here was an enormous pie, a model of the Tourelles we had so recently conquered. More curious even than these were the fabulous monsters the cooks had contrived by yoking one creature to another. A special madrigal sung from the gallery greeted the appearance of a pair of cockatrices made, as I soon perceived, by joining the front half of a fat capon to the haunches of a suckling pig, the whole made golden with a glaze of saffron mixed with honey.

The monarch ate and drank listlessly, not raising his eyes to look at anybody. To him this banquet was an ordeal to be endured. For the rest of those present the flesh and grease and powerful wine seemed to assuage equally powerful emotions. Even the bishops ate like men who have just enjoyed a woman, with fierce and undiscriminating appetite. Each time Charles touched his cup to his lips, and the master of ceremonies cried 'The king drinks!', the guests rose and pledged one another with a mutual love that would not last till morning.

18

As soon as the king was crowned, everyone expected him to go to the monastery of Saint-Marcoul, which lay just outside the city of Rheims. Here the monks would invest him with the last of his royal powers – the power to touch men and cure them of scrofula, the 'king's evil' which only a true king is able to cure. And after that, despite the murmurings of a few sceptics, the expectation was that Charles VII of France would take the road to Paris.

But Charles, it seemed, was in no hurry to leave Rheims now that he had reached it. He shut himself up in the archbishop's palace, talking, so it was said, with envoys who had been sent to him by the Duke of Burgundy. When he did appear in public, he seemed to shun Joan, and treated her with little courtesy.

'Now you see,' said La Tremoïlle to Gilles, 'the true nature of our sovereign lord. At first he seems to tremble before you; and then, after a while, he is gracious as only a king can be. But he quickly repents of his own kindness, and longs to cast you down. He envies his favourites for the greatness he has given them.'

'That may be true in your case, cousin,' Gilles retorted, 'but I thought it was Joan who had brought the king greatness, and not the other way round.'

'So much the worse for her,' La Tremoïlle answered sombrely.

At long last, after many delays, the day came when we set off. It was now late summer, and the weather was stifling. We all sweated miserably in our steel and leather, and stank accordingly, while swarms of flies rose to torment the horses. Joan now seemed to shun the king's company, while she was never far from Brother Richard. With them rode the princes of the blood royal – Clermont and Vendôme, and, most conspicuously of all, Alençon. Brother Richard seemed intent on working them all up into a condition of religious ecstasy. He harangued them continually, bending over the pommel of his saddle, his dark eyes flashing, his Adam's apple bobbing, his bony finger jabbing to make a point. At every little church or chapel the group would ostentatiously turn aside to make their devotions; and, every morning as we broke camp, Joan could be seen on her knees before the friar, making her confession, with the tears streaming down her face.

I had expected that Gilles would wish to ride with the princes and with Joan, but to my surprise he kept himself apart. Sometimes he even seemed to shun my company and that of Sillé. This disturbed me, and I was yet more disturbed when I returned late one night to our bivouac, after I had spent the evening with friends. A few fires were lit, since we needed light and something to cook with, but it was too hot to place oneself close to them. It was also too hot and breathless for sleep, and everywhere, throughout the army, men sat in the darkness, murmuring to one another, or occasionally whistling a snatch of melody, waiting for the night to pass and another day to come.

I had drunk too deep, and I stumbled a little as I made my way back to our own company. Then, as I tripped on a rut and almost missed my footing altogether, I nearly fell over two men who were deep in conversation with one another. I pulled myself upright and stared at them owlishly, and then at last realised who they were. One was Gilles, and the other was the black-clad man who had guided us to Parthenay, and whom I had last seen high on his perch in Rheims cathedral. As I stood there blinking, he uncoiled himself and rose to his feet, though Gilles tried to detain him with a hand on his arm. 'No, my lord,' he said, 'I must not keep you from your friend. Farewell – perhaps we shall meet one another again. On the other hand, perhaps we may not.' And with that he vanished into the surrounding darkness.

'Creepy kind of fellow,' I said as I sank to my haunches beside Gilles. The truth was that my legs would not support me any longer.

Gilles looked at me, and did not seem disposed to reply. But suddenly his attention was distracted by a fresh incident. 'Bread, good masters!' came an insistent whisper. 'Food, for the love of the Virgin!' A small claw-like hand was suddenly thrust between us. Even in my fuddled state I knew what this was. As we penetrated deeper into territory which had already been thoroughly ravaged by the war, the army attracted to it not only women willing to sell their bodies for whatever price they would fetch, but swarms of starving children, homeless and parentless, who clung to our flanks in the desperate hope of survival. As I woke in the dawn I had often seen them scavenging in our rubbish heaps for something to eat.

'Keep him away from me!' said Gilles in a low voice in which I nevertheless caught an edge of hysteria. 'Bread!' whined the child. I heard him drag himself still closer, with the seasoned beggar's instinct for the moment to strike. Hastily I dug in my purse, and found a coin. As I put it into the child's palm, he thrust his head close to mine, so close that, despite the murk, I could see every detail of his features. He was blond and little marked by starvation – as beautiful as an angel.

Gilles was lying beside me on the ground, simultaneously retching and weeping. At a loss as to what to do, I put my arm round his shoulders, leaning close to hear what he was trying to say. 'B-b-beautiful . . .' he stammered, and began to retch again. When the spasm was over, I heard him mutter under his breath: 'Yes, he said they would be beautiful.'

'What's that?'

Gilles wiped his face with his sleeve and rolled on his back, without leaving my embrace. My head was still swimming with the fumes of wine and, as I leant down towards him, it was for a moment as if we were back in our tower room at Champtocé when we were boys. It was some time since I had had a woman, and I felt my sex beginning to harden between my legs.

Gilles evidently sensed it too as I pressed against him, and he braced his palm against my chest. 'No, Raoul,' he said gently, 'the road I am now to travel is not for you. You are drunk tonight. Go to sleep.' He had a compelling, masterful sweetness I had not met in him before, though I caught the faint reek of vomit lingering on his breath.

Late the next morning I woke where I had tumbled the previous night, in bright sunshine, with the army bustling all about me, making preparations to depart. Gilles was nowhere to be seen. I soon learned what the cause of the excitement was. The Duke of Bedford, Regent in France for the King of England, had sent an insulting letter to our own King Charles. Everyone believed a decisive battle was now imminent, and the belief was strengthened when our scouts brought in news that Bedford's army had been seen up the road, where a great cloud of white dust revealed its presence.

But Bedford was a wilier fox than we gave him credit for. He made us chase him up and down in the boiling August heat, all the time drawing us further and further away from Paris, until at last we came to Montépilloy opposite Senlis, where he turned to fight.

Montépilloy is not a name that will find a place in the history books, together with those of Agincourt and Patay. The reason is that it was a battle nobody lost and nobody won. In fact, I myself was the only person to make much gain out of it, and I wasn't aware of the fact at the time. The way of it was this. Bedford had chosen a well-defended position, and we had been skirmishing with him all day, to little effect. As the afternoon wore on, everyone became more and more bad-tempered, thanks to the dust. The fields had already been harvested, and the earth was parched and dry. As the horses galloped back and forth across the barren surface, the powdery stuff rose in thick clouds to clog our throats and fill our nostrils. Soon it was impossible to see more than a few yards. The great battle-chargers loomed up out of a choking mist, and immediately disappeared into it again.

As the sun began to sink, the dust was thicker than ever, and it now took on an ominous, reddish tinge as the level rays tried in vain to pierce it. I had ridden into the thickest part of the cloud, in an endeavour to find out what was going on, when I heard a shout to my left and somewhat ahead of me. Putting spurs to my beast, I found that I had gone further forward than I knew, and was almost in the enemy position, at a point where the thorn hedges that guarded it had been completely beaten down. Close to me was a knot of savagely struggling figures. After a moment I could see that they were fighting for possession of a dismounted knight. Another moment, and I realised that the prize the two sides were disputing was none other than La Tremoïlle, weighed down by his armour and his own too abundant flesh.

Instinctively I forced my way forward, beat off an Englishman who tried to stab my horse in the belly, and reached down to grasp the fallen man's arm. It was at once clear that he was too heavy for me to hope to drag him on to my horse's back. 'Grip the stirrup, my lord!' I shouted, and at once he obeyed. His mind, at any rate, was never less than rapid. 'And you there!' I called. 'Take him under the other arm!' In this way we half-dragged, half-carried him the few necessary yards to safety. Soon a page came up with one of the massive cart-horses La Tremoïlle favoured, and a dozen obsequious pairs of hands were ready to help hoist his vast bulk back into the saddle.

He settled himself into place, and, restored to a height a

little above mine, took the opportunity to identify me. 'Ah, Raoul de Saumur!' he panted, briefly raising the visor of his helmet. 'You seem to have a talent for making yourself useful.' His page handed him a lance, and he dipped it to me in formal salute before he lumbered away.

19

Having resisted successfully all day at Montépilloy, the English nonetheless decided to pack up and go next morning, leaving us, to our surprise, the masters of the field. Senlis opened its gates to the king's troops, and the bulk of the army was quartered there, while Charles went to Compiègne to continue his interminable negotiations with the Burgundians. Joan mercilessly badgered the king to continue the campaign and attack Paris, but he resisted her importunities. Meanwhile the troops grew more and more restless and more and more ill-disciplined.

One day Joan completely lost patience, and browbeat Alençon into calling the army together and setting out for Paris without the king's orders. A few days later the bulk of our forces were at Saint-Denis, and the advance-guard was at the little village of La Chapelle, which is practically within bow-shot of the walls of Paris. Gilles insisted on his full rights as a newly made Marshal of France, and, as a result, he and I and Sillé found ourselves bedding down in a flea-ridden one-room hovel at La Chapelle when we might have been sleeping snug at Saint-Denis. Charles had not yet arrived to join his captains, but was reported to be reluctantly on the road.

Anyone who sees Paris for the first time must surely experience a feeling of awe. The city is much larger than any other in France – which means that it is much larger than any in Christendom. It seems to belong to an altogether different order of things from the other cities of men. When I first went out from La Chapelle to look at it, it was almost sunset. As far as I could see, both to my left hand and my right, there stretched a seemingly never-ending wall, pierced here and there at long intervals by massively defended gates. In front of this wall there was a ditch, in which I could see the gleam of water; and behind were roofs, the green tops of trees, and almost innumerable church towers. These towers impressed me almost as much as the length of the wall itself, since they seemed to symbolise the huge numbers of people who lived in the city, and who needed all these temples in which to worship. Paris was not silent as I gazed at it. I heard the ringing of the church bells – the irregular tolling which is the signal of alarm. The gates were firmly shut, and behind the parapet of the wall I caught glimpses of figures moving. Then there was a whirring sound, and a spent cross-bow bolt dropped at my feet.

Joan got rid of her nervous energy as best she could, chiefly by provoking a series of skirmishes at a windmill that lay midway between La Chapelle and the city walls. Our men had easily the best of these, but petty victories did not satisfy her. She began to go round the captains, talking to them one by one in private. She said the same thing to each of them. 'We have come all this way. Are we to turn back without at least trying to do what we came for? God will not be pleased with us if we give up the enterprise.'

'And the king and messire La Tremoïlle will not be pleased with us if we don't,' Sillé retorted when he heard what she had been saying. But it was clear that Joan would soon goad us into taking action, whether Charles gave his permission or not. Preparations for an assault were nearly complete: the siege ladders had been made, great faggots of wood had been prepared for use in filling the moat, and wagons had been brought up. It was with a sigh of relief that we heard that the king had made his way to Saint-Denis. Relief was followed by euphoria. The fortifications which had seemed so formidable when we first looked at them now struck us as things of small account. All the captains who were at La Chapelle decided to ride back in a body in order to pay their respects.

The distance from La Chapelle to Saint-Denis is so short you would not have imagined that Joan could find an opportunity to get into mischief while going from one to the other. But so it turned out. We were halfway to our destination when she spotted one of the camp doxies in the furtive embraces of a soldier. They were so absorbed in what they were doing that they did not notice our approach. Joan threw her reins on her horse's neck and slipped from the saddle. When she was only a few yards from the couple, she pulled her great broadsword from its sheath and began to shout. Startled, the culprits drew apart from one another. Ignoring the man, Joan caught the woman a great thwack across the backside with the flat of her blade.

'Enemy of God!' she bellowed. The girl gave a cry of pain, and began to stumble away from her assailant. The fact that she was heavily pregnant made up for the disadvantage Joan was under because of her armour. In a few strides she had caught up with the enemy again. 'Satan's bitch!' she cried, and gave her another blow. The guffaws going up from the spectators were instantly silenced when it was seen that Joan's sword had snapped cleanly in half. She stood staring stupidly at the stump she held in her hand.

'An evil omen!' muttered a voice behind me, but when I twisted round in my saddle I was unable to identify whose it was. It was in a very subdued mood that we continued on our way to Saint-Denis.

And it was in a very subdued mood that we were received there. Somehow the news of what had just happened had already reached the king and his courtiers. Joan knelt before Charles, and I could see that his knees were knocking together so fast that he could hardly stand upright. The monarch, now everywhere successful, had never looked more miserable, even in the dark days at Chinon. For once he did not bother to mask his displeasure. 'The sword is gone,' he kept repeating. 'The sword you told me you had from God! Why didn't you take a good stick to beat that woman with!' Standing in the background, La Tremoïlle and Regnault de Chartres murmured together, and were scarcely able to conceal their smiles of satisfaction.

That night, when we returned from court, Gilles asked me to go with him to the chapel that gave the hamlet its name, in order to pray for victory on the morrow. The building had been long neglected, and much of the painted glass that had once adorned the windows was broken. Even though it was a warm, still night the draught stirred the candles that burnt within, before the altar. Gilles knelt, and I with him, and, for a moment, thanks to the shifting patterns of light and shadow, I was unaware that anyone else was there. Then I saw Joan, too, was present, kneeling beside us, her eyes fixed on the wooden image of the crucified Christ. For long minutes I tried to pray. The words formed in my mind, but would not loosen themselves from my earthbound spirit and rise towards God, as I commanded them to do. After a while I gave up the attempt, and began to glance to left and right of me at my two companions, wondering how it was with them.

The candle-flames gilded the two profiles, which were so very different from one another. Gilles's winged brow and fine nose proclaimed him what he was, a nobleman and a warrior, a man whose ancestors' names were remembered since the days of Charlemagne. And Joan's, by contrast, had no subtlety of contour, though the set of the mouth revealed her imperious will. I had expected to see that she was weeping, as she often wept in church when she gazed at the holy images. Indeed, there were the drying snail-tracks of tears on her cheeks. But now the expression on her face was that of a woman beyond tears, slowly coming to terms with grief.

Glancing to my other side I looked at Gilles, whose expressions were so much more familiar to me, and was surprised to find that he too wore a look of stoic sorrow. After a while he stirred, and started to rise to his feet. As if the movement had roused her from her reverie, Joan followed his example. 'So that's that, then,' I thought I heard him mutter under his breath. When the three of us emerged from the chapel he stooped and swiftly took and kissed her hand, like a man saying farewell to a loved friend whom he will never see again. She made no comment on his action, and did not try to snatch her hand away.

The next day, despite all these discouraging omens, our first move against Paris was a success. We attacked one of the gates and, though we failed to breach it, we took and burned the outwork that protected it. But our second assault, made against the wall itself, wavered to a halt before we had even reached the edge of the moat.

It was at this moment that Joan appeared, apparently tranquil and untroubled. She got from her horse and shouldered her way through the ranks. Gilles was standing near me, and she marched straight up to him. 'Well, Marshal,' she said, with a touch of her old contempt for him in the way she stressed the title, 'are you willing to come forward with me, and see how much or how little we have to do?' And without waiting for his reply she continued on her way, a lance in her hand to replace the sword whose empty scabbard flapped against her thigh. Her standard-bearer followed, with her banner in his grip, and after him went Gilles, then Sillé and I, as if mesmerised by the few words she had spoken. A hail of projectiles descended on us, and I remember wondering why none of them reached their mark.

When we reached the moat, we found it consisted of not one but two ditches. The ditch nearer to us was dry, and Joan immediately scrambled down into it, then climbed again to stand on the ridge which divided it from the second, which was full to the brink with murky-looking stagnant water. Seeing her standing there, unscathed and apparently unconcerned, the men behind us took heart. We heard shouts of abuse being hurled at the defenders, and the hasty trampling of feet. Soon the reverse slope of the dividing ridge, which offered a little shelter from the missiles pouring down on us from the wall, was packed with soldiers, many of whom had brought with them the ladders and corded bundles of wood we should need for the next stages of the attack. With a mighty shout the first faggot was raised and toppled into the water. It sank for a moment, then bobbed to the surface and started to float away. A derisive yell went up from the ramparts above us. More and more faggots were thrown in, with precisely the same results.

Joan meanwhile was unconcernedly probing the moat with her lance, to see if it was less deep in some places than in others. As the storm of insult and counter-insult died away for a moment she looked up and called in that clear, sweet, carrying voice: 'Men of Paris, think again! Wouldn't it be better to surrender now, before nightfall, than to wait and have your throats cut in the dark?'

A burly cross-bowman was leaning perilously outwards, straining to get a good shot at her. 'Cut mine if you can, you bloody whore!' he yelled, and loosed his bolt. It sped true, and I saw Joan's legs crumple beneath her as she fell backwards into the dry ditch. At the same moment her standard-bearer got a bolt in the foot; and then, as he lifted his visor to look at the damage, another full in the face. He, too, dropped beside Joan.

Scrambling along behind the shelter of the ridge, the three of us made our way to Joan to try and discover how badly she was injured. The standard-bearer was dead (the second bolt had caught him neatly between the eyes), but Joan's wound, though disabling, was not as bad as it might have been. The missile had pierced the flesh in the meaty part of the left thigh. She was a little shocked, but coherent. 'Don't let them give up the attack!' she pleaded. 'We'll win here as we won at the Tourelles when I was wounded!' Gilles made no direct answer to this. 'We can't move her yet,' he said to me. 'They'd get us at once. Will you stay here with the Maid, while I do what I can to rally the men?' Together the three of us dragged her to a position just below the crest of the ridge, where there was most shelter, and Gilles and Sillé set off on a zig-zag scrambling run to the rear.

The next three hours have a nightmare quality in my recollection. Several times our men came past us to make another attack, but never with any success. Each time they came there were fewer of them, and the dwindling numbers could not be accounted for solely by those who were killed or injured, and scattered the slope near us or rolled helplessly down to the bottom of it. Each time a new assault started, Joan would raise her head and try to encourage the men with her usual exhortations and promises of victory, but they paid less and less attention to her, sometimes trampling over the two of us as if we were mere corpses. Meanwhile Joan was tormented by the flies that began to buzz about her wound, and I could see her eyes were bright with fever and her lips parched by lack of water. I had to hold her up with all my strength to stop her falling to the bottom of the steep slope on which we rested.

The last assault was made by a pitiful handful, just as dusk was falling. A moment after the men stumbled past us up the slope, almost too weary to walk, they were coming down it again, defeated. One man, clutching an injured arm from which the blood trickled in thick streams, almost tripped over us as we retreated. He swayed, recovered himself, then bent down with the elaborate care of a man far gone in drink to see what the obstacle was. Sure enough, I caught the heavy smell of wine upon his breath. Rage slowly flooded his coarse features as he recognised Joan. 'So you're the one who promised us we'd take Paris and live like kings forever after,' he said. 'I'll show you what I think of your promises!' And he spat in her face. Joan did not attempt to reply, but stared at him fixedly, with the gob of spittle sliding slowly down her cheek. For the first time I could not deny her the wholehearted loyalty and admiration I had never been able to give her before, but at the same time I could find no words to express it.

It was shortly after this that Gilles came to find us. In the half light he looked haggard and weary. 'I did my best,' he said, but at first Joan turned her head away and would not acknowledge his presence. With Gilles were a number of the other captains – chief among them Alençon and Ambroise de Loré. It was as if none of them wanted to face Joan alone with the news they brought. Alençon cleared his throat, and the others looked at him. 'We have orders to carry you back to La Chapelle,' he said. 'By the king's command the attack on Paris must now cease.' He signed to some of the others to pick her up.

For a moment Joan tried to resist. 'By my staff, one more

assault and we would have taken it!' she murmured, in a voice so parched and hollow that it certified the contrary. Once out of range of those who were still shooting at us from the top of the wall, Joan was laid on the ground to wait until a horse could be brought. She closed her eyes, as if to shut out the fact of defeat and those who surrounded her. For a moment her face remained clenched with the physical and mental pain she was enduring, then it relaxed and softened, and I saw her reach out her hand, as once before at Gien, to touch some person or thing which remained invisible to the rest of us. Instinctively Gilles leaned down, and took that seeking hand in his. Slowly she opened her eyes again, and looked at him. 'Thank you, messire,' she said gently. Then, looking round at the rest: 'Very well, you may mount me now. I have been given permission to go.'

part two

20

Who or what was it that gave Gilles and I permission to go, and to leave behind us the king's court and its intrigues? In my own case the answer was very simple, if also unexpected. Our departure from Paris in mid-August was followed by an immediate retreat to the Loire. Though no enemy pursued us, this retreat resembled a rout. The king kept the army on the move both by day and by night in his impatience to be home. The territories we crossed were already devastated, and the men's morale was low. They plundered whatever had not been laid waste, and gradually our proud army became a rabble of bandits and robbers. In the midst of the throng I sometimes caught a glimpse of Joan, riding as if in a trance, her eyes fixed straight ahead, seldom bothering even to answer those who addressed her.

At Gien, from which we had originally set out, the retreat was finally halted, and the men began to disperse to their own districts, while Charles made ready to go to Bourges. I was asleep one night when La Tremoïlle sent for me. He received me surrounded by papers, and it was clear that he was heartily glad to be back in his own element of receipts and quittances, letters and reports. Our conversation was brief and to the point.

'I believe I owe you a debt,' he said.

'I was not aware of it, my lord.'

'You saved me from capture at Montépilloy. What do you think that is worth?'

'If I had thought it was worth something, I would have asked you for it.'

'The point is that *I* think it is worth something, even though you are too honest a man to be of much use to me. I estimate my ransom at thirty thousand *écus*.'

I bit my tongue, knowing that the English would gladly

have asked messire Georges a great deal more than that, had they had the good luck to capture him. But I still couldn't see what La Tremoïlle was driving at.

'One might argue, of course,' he added, 'that you only saved half of me. There was, after all, that soldier who took my other arm. Unfortunately I have been unable to trace him. And in any case I expect to pay less to my friends than my enemies. Otherwise there would be no reason to make the distinction.'

'As your lordship pleases,' I said, not knowing what else to reply.

'No, Raoul. On this occasion it is as you please. Are you willing to become my vassal?'

The question took me so much aback I could only goggle at him.

'I have here the papers which will put you in possession of a small fief. It is worth fifteen thousand *écus*. It is in Anjou, a long way from my other possessions and a long way from the war. Do you accept?'

There was only one answer a landless man could make, and I knelt before him and put my hands between his, ready to take my oath. And this was how I came to take my leave of the court and of Gilles, and to marry the lady-in-waiting of Queen Yolanda's who had once looked at me with favour. The Queen was not sorry to see one of her own women wed to one of La Tremoïlle's men, especially when the husband held land within her own duchy. As a way of keeping the balance equal she gave my wife a handsome dowry. I retired to my new estate and had no reason to think that great events would ever touch me again.

The one person whose reaction I had worried about was Gilles, but he took my desertion quietly. 'Sillé will look after me,' he said. 'Perhaps he knows me better than you.' Sillé's mask did not alter, but I could imagine how happy he was to see the back of me. Our boyhood rivalry was at last resolved in his favour.

Of course, my retirement did not prevent news from the outside world from reaching me. Some of it concerned Gilles, and some concerned Joan the Maid. First I heard that Gilles, too, had retired from court and gone to his own lands. Then, at Christmas 1429, I heard that his wife, Catherine de Thouars, had borne him a daughter. The timing puzzled me, as, quite apart from his dislike of her, he could hardly have been there at the time of the child's conception. But there was no talk of it being repudiated. At about the same time news came that Joan, in a bitterly cold winter campaign, had failed to take the town of La Charité on the upper Loire. Next I heard that Gilles was supposedly short of money, and had been selling one or two outlying properties. I imagined that in the end his military adventures must have cost him more than he or his grandfather expected.

The tidings that came in the New Year touched us more nearly. La Tremoïlle and Queen Yolanda had quarrelled, and despite the war that the king still waged against the English, were engaged in a private war of their own. For a month or so I lived in dread of being asked to furnish men to one or the other, but gradually it became clear that I was so neatly balanced between the parties that neither would turn to me for the little help I could give.

Early in June news arrived which shocked me more though it concerned me less. Joan the Maid had been captured at Compiègne in an attempt to drive off the Burgundians who were laying siege to the town. I had prayers said for her in our village, and was told later that similar prayers had been said for her throughout all that part of France now in obedience to the king. It was only Charles himself, and Archbishop Regnault, and messire Georges who seemed quite unmoved by her capture. Our invocations did not prevent the bargain whereby Joan's captors sold her to the English. In December of that year, a passing traveller told me that Gilles, who had fought for La Tremoïlle against Yolanda, had composed his quarrel with his suzerain and was now at Louviers in Normandy, the nearest French-held town to Rouen where Joan was imprisoned. For a few weeks, we lived in the expectation of hearing that the Maid had been freed by the captains who fought with her at Orléans and Patay. But hope slowly died, and when the fatal month of June came round again we heard for certain that she had, on the previous thirtieth of May, been publicly burned as a heretic.

I was surprised to find how moved and shaken I was by the news of Joan's death, and how sharply the event brought back to me everything that had taken place in the months between our arrival at Chinon and the retreat from Paris. It was only now that I fully realised that I had taken part in something which had a legendary dimension, and that I was therefore a different man from that which my destiny had first intended. At the same time, I found that every thought of Joan raised an uneasy echo in my mind. It was as if, though dead, she had not yet done with me, and meant to reach beyond the fire to disturb my life once more.

By the autumn of 1431 this vague sense of unease was displaced by a very different and more personal preoccupation. My wife and I had as yet no children, though we were perfectly happy in every other way. Now my darling came to tell me that she was pregnant with our first baby. Throughout the late winter and early spring I watched her belly swelling to ripeness. The child was due in June, and by April she was visibly very heavy. But pregnancy suited her. Never had she seemed more blooming, more lively, more vivacious. She joked about the fashions she had worn as a court lady, which made even a virgin look as if she was gravid. 'Perhaps that's why your Joan insisted on wearing men's clothing,' she said with a smile. Often she would touch her stomach contentedly and murmur: 'At last I feel complete, with this new life that we and God have made stirring within me.'

When her labour began it was punctual, and I feared nothing. A woman who had carried her child so easily up till now would surely have no difficulty at the last. In a few hours my son (for we were both sure it must be son) would be bawling loudly in my arms. Even when the contractions prolonged themselves for hour after hour I was not at first worried. Nor was the midwife. Then she began to grow alarmed, and insisted that I send for a famous physician, then resident in our nearest town. The weather was good and the roads fast, but it was several hours before he arrived. My wife was by this time grey with exhaustion and pain, almost without the strength to cry out as each new convulsion racked her. Meanwhile the contractions themselves were growing weaker, though there was as yet no sign of the appearance of the baby. The doctor came straight in to see the patient, who lay in our great bed in the solar behind the hall. After a moment he asked all of us except the midwife to leave. 'You, too,' he ordered, looking at me from under the level line of his black eyebrows.

It seemed a long time before he came out to me again. 'Send for the priest,' he said. 'I cannot save her, though there is still a chance that I can save the child.' But even this was not to be.

The next few months passed in a heaviness of grief for me which has blotted out almost every memory save that of grief itself. However, I vaguely remember hearing, at the very end of the summer, that Gilles had been responsible for a brilliant victory at Lagny, on the Marne near Paris, and that the general whom he had vanquished was none other than Bedford himself. The news seemed to refer to a man I had known, not merely in a different existence, but in a different universe.

In October 1432, I was startled to receive a letter direct from Champtocé. It was written in an almost illegible hand, and it came, not from Gilles, but from Jean de Craon. After a long struggle with the handwriting, I managed to puzzle out what it said:

My dear Raoul,

No doubt you will be surprised to hear from me, and yet more surprised to learn that I write to implore you to come to me here, at my castle of Champtocé. As you know, I am accustomed not to beg but to command. But I beg you nonetheless, despite your recent sorrow, to ride here at once. You will perhaps understand what I mean when I say that Gilles has learned all the lessons I once tried to teach him. He has learned others too, from what tutors I know not. More I do not wish to write. Come now, as soon as you receive this. I am a dying man.

The signature was even more illegible than the rest, but it was still unmistakeably Jean's – a wild, exploding parody of the bold flourish with which he had signed the letters and documents which kept half a province in subjection. It did not take me twenty-four hours to decide to go.

21

Champtocé, when I reached it, seemed scarcely to have changed from the days when I left it to go to the war. It was still a house divided. Gilles's men-at-arms and those of Jean de Craon still glared at one another in the courtyard; Catherine de Thouars lived isolated in her tower. Some shifts in the balance of power soon became apparent, however. Gilles's men were now notably more numerous, and it was they who were the masters, pushing Jean's servants out of the way, running the place to suit themselves. And there were some new personalities to be taken into account. One of these was Gilles's brother René. He had been a plump child when I left, now he was a sturdy young man. The family resemblance between him and Gilles was very much apparent, yet René did not carry with him that atmosphere of the extraordinary which surrounded Gilles from the first moment I met him. This was simply a very commonplace young nobleman – good-looking enough, well-mannered enough, who spent his days at the hunt and his evenings drinking rather more than was good for him. The only strange thing about him was the way in which he and his elder brother managed to live in the same castle without, apparently, ever acknowledging one another's existence. If they met, it was by chance. And had they collided physically – for example, had one of them been coming in over the drawbridge and the other leaving by it – one would have expected them to pass right through one another, like two beings from different dimensions.

But in speaking of this, I am getting ahead of my story. Upon my arrival, my first duty was to present myself to Jean de Craon, who had sent for me so urgently. When he heard what my mission was, the captain of the watch became almost truculent, but he admitted me nonetheless, and I made my way through the familiar hall, and thus to the door at the back of the dais which led to the old man's quarters. To my surprise it was guarded by two men who crossed their halberds in front of me and refused me admittance. I suspected that neither of them could read, and in any case I was reluctant to show Jean's strange letter to anyone, and certainly not happy to display it to menials. A noisy argument developed, watched with some amusement by passers-by who had been drawn into the hall by the sound of raised voices. At last the sound penetrated the thick planks of the door itself, and I heard the sound of bolts being drawn on the other side of it. The door opened a crack, and an indignant elderly head appeared and started to curse me roundly. But, though the man was much changed and worn, I recognised him. 'François!' I exclaimed, in a momentary pause in the flow of words. 'Has it taken you so short a time to forget Raoul de Saumur, whom you helped to bring up?' The old man fell silent and stared at me, then slowly nodded his head. Then, still without saying anything, he shut the door in my face. The two guards sneered at me derisively. Their expressions changed a moment later when the door once more opened a crack and a skinny arm beckoned to me. I eased my way through the narrow opening, and the planks slammed behind me, as if the devil might be on my heels.

The room was so dim that it took some time for my eyes to become accustomed to the lack of light. The first thing that struck me was therefore the smell. A great fire was burning in the fireplace, though the weather was warm for autumn, and the atmosphere was not only intolerably hot, but close and fetid. Someone had been burning incense, and the scent of this lay heavily on the air. Beneath this smell, there was another – the acrid, sick-room taint of herbs and drugs. And beneath that, barely discernible, yet another smell – the sickly odour of corruption.

Now that I could see, I noted that the furnishings of the room had altered. In place of the large table where Jean had sat to conduct his business, there was now an even vaster bed, perhaps the one where Gilles and Catherine had spent their wedding-night, piled with furs and coverlets. Here lay Jean de Craon, propped, however, against a vast mound of cushions and pillows, so that he was in fact sitting almost upright. For a moment, I could scarcely believe that this was the fierce old man whom I had known and feared throughout my youth. The complexion was yellow, the eyes dull, the mouth hanging open to show gums which were almost toothless, and the neck was now so thin and scrawny that it scarcely seemed able to support the weight of the head. The upper part of his torso was skeletally thin; his belly, by contrast, was hideously swollen.

'Who is it?' he whispered, seeming not to recognise me, though I knew that François must have told him who I was.

'Raoul, messire,' I replied. 'You summoned me to come here.'

'So I did. So I did.' It seemed for a moment as if he had no further comment to offer, and I stood there staring at him.

'Did you have something to say to me?' I prompted.

'Yes.' But once more he did not continue. His breath rattled in his throat. I could see the sand pouring through the neck of an hourglass which stood on a table beside his bed.

Then his lips moved as if to form words, and I leant forward to hear what he had to say. 'You know Gilles,' he muttered. 'That is the reason. You know Gilles.'

By this time I was almost convinced that he was delirious. All at once he seemed to pull himself together. His eyes became as penetrating and fierce as I remembered them. 'You know Gilles,' he repeated, in a voice which was almost resonant. 'The question is – do you know him well enough?' And, in a lower tone, as if to himself: 'I need time, and God will not give it to me.' Then, once again, his manner altered. 'François! François! Turn the glass!' The old servant bustled forward to do as his master commanded, and Jean painfully turned his head on the pillows to look broodingly at the trickle of sand.

'Well, at least there is the child,' he said. 'I made him accept the child. Someone for the lands to go down to. I wish they could go to young René.'

'Is that what you wished to tell me?' I persisted. A faint shadow of the old cunning passed across his face.

'No, maybe you are not the solution. I acted too hastily. You are not one of us, Raoul. An upstart, that's what you are! We should keep it in the family. Work the thing out for yourself – you'll find out what I mean, if you stay long enough. Can you really be as stupid as you look?' He went off in a long derisive cackle of laughter which ended on a cry of pain.

'Quick, François – my drink! Who is that man? I don't know him. Get rid of him at once!' But I had already turned and was making my way to the door.

No doubt I would have mounted my horse and returned straight home, but as soon as I emerged from the great hall into the welcome sunshine of the courtyard I was waylaid by a personage whom I did not recognise.

'Here!' he said. 'He wants to see you!'

The speaker was a somewhat shifty-looking adolescent,

richly, even elaborately dressed, but without the aura of a gentleman. It took me a moment or so to recognise Gilles's page Poitou.

'Messire de Rais?' I asked.

'I don't know what the fuss is about, but he says you're to come at once.'

There could be no question of evading the summons, however discourteously delivered. I followed in Poitou's footsteps towards the entrance to the keep. Once we entered it, he preceded me up the narrow staircase to an upper floor. Without bothering to knock, he flung open a door, and we entered.

Several people were in the room, which was much smaller than Jean de Craon's chamber. Indeed, that and the hall were the only two really large rooms at Champtocé. Gilles himself was reclining on a pile of silken cushions which had been thrown on the floor, which itself was covered with a luxurious Eastern cloth. Seated upright behind him was Sillé, and standing before them in the centre of the chamber was a blond child, who looked very much as Poitou himself had done when we left Champtocé to go to the king's wars. The child had been singing, while Gilles accompanied him on a viol, but now he stopped abruptly, disconcerted by the interruption. It was clear that Poitou was delighted to have produced this effect.

'The person you asked for, messire,' he announced, putting a world of insolence into this simple statement.

Gilles rose languidly from his position on the floor. 'Raoul!' he said, and embraced me. As he put his arms about me my nostrils were filled with the scent of the heavy perfume he was wearing. 'Let me look at you!' And he disengaged himself and held me at arms' length.

I don't know what changes he saw in me, but I certainly saw some in him. It was now more than three years since we had last been in one another's company. He was even thinner than he had been formerly, and he had reverted to the rich clothes he had worn before he became a warrior. A fine sapphire, almost like a bishop's ring, gleamed upon his finger, and over his mulberry-coloured velvet doublet he wore a gold chain and a richly enamelled belt. But these were not the chief changes. There had been an almost indefinable alteration in his personality. He seemed more self-contained, yes, and more certain of himself. He also seemed to have acquired a steady control of the magnetism which before he had possessed only in gleams and lightning-flashes; it now fixed your attention on his every gesture and action. For a strange, uncomfortable moment he reminded me of Joan the Maid. He had acquired a touch of her ambiguity, of her unconscious assumption that she belonged to another sphere.

'So you have come to be the light to my shadow!' said Gilles.

It was not merely the extravagance of the phrase which took me aback, for I supposed that Gilles must already be aware that I had been summoned to Champtocé to see his grandfather. Indeed, his next words made it quite plain that he knew all about my visit.

'It was good of you to pay your respects to messire Jean,' he said. 'I fear you found him much changed.'

'So I did,' I admitted.

'Well, having seen that he no longer has his wits about him, there is no need for you to trouble yourself further. Come, sit down and let's talk. Or will you allow Henriet here to finish his song?' He picked up the viol, and I realised that the subject was closed.

I doubt if I would have stayed at Champtocé, had I not had another interview with Gilles the next morning. He roused me at dawn, rapping at the door of the bedchamber that was assigned to me, which happened to be the one that he and I had occupied together in the years when we were growing up.

'Raoul!'

'What is it?'

'Come hawking. It's a beautiful day.'

'My horse is tired from the journey yesterday.'

'I have another saddled and waiting for you. Will you get up, or do I have to come and tip you out of bed?'

Seeing that resistance was useless, I rose grumbling.

Three or four grooms accompanied us, and there was no sign of either Poitou or Henriet. For a while Gilles rode companionably by my side, occasionally whistling through his teeth, and scarcely bothering to let loose the little hawk he had on his wrist, even when the occasion presented itself. But though he seemed contented enough with our outing, it was also clear that he had something on his mind. At last, about nine o'clock, after we had stopped and broken our fast, he said: 'I have something to say to you. Let's send the others back.'

'Is it safe for the two of us to ride alone?'

'Safe enough. Things have quietened down remarkably since the days of Joan the Maid.'

'Very well,' I said, not liking to ask which days he meant, those of her victories or those which had followed her burning.

For a while Gilles watched the little group of grooms going

off into the distance. When they had entirely vanished, he gave a little shrug of his shoulders and murmured close to my ear: 'I saw her burnt, you know.'

'Who?'

'Joan the Maid.'

'I knew you were at Louviers, but how did you get to Rouen?'

'Ssh!' said Gilles, in a soft but agitated tone. 'There are those who may be listening to you!'

A pause ensued, as if my untimely question had made him decide not to continue the story. Then he said, in a more normal kind of voice:

'It was surprisingly easy.'

'What was surprisingly easy?' I asked, bewildered, but sensing that the conversation was of great importance to him.

'Getting into Rouen the day she was burnt. The English were anxious that as many people as possible should see it happen. They sent messengers into the countryside, to tell the peasants to come. I went, and several other men from the garrison at Louviers. We slipped into the city in peasants' clothing. Of course by that time we knew the king would do nothing.'

'Why go then?'

'It seemed necessary to be there. Something was being concluded.'

'And the others?'

'Oh, I imagine they hoped we might rescue her. I knew from the start that that was impossible.' He paused again for a moment, awaiting my reaction. When none came, he said, almost petulantly: 'Don't you want to hear about it?'

'Only if you wish to tell me,' I said.

'It will explain certain changes you may have noticed.'

'In you, Gilles?'

'Yes, and at Champtocé.'

'What has that to do with Joan the Maid?'

'You'll understand, if only you'll listen.'

'Very well,' I said listlessly, as a sudden wave of my own private grief rose to overwhelm me.

'We were standing in the market-place. We came into Rouen with all the others, as soon as they opened the gates in the morning, and we had to wait for quite a while before she appeared. I heard afterwards she took a long time making her confession. There were four platforms altogether – one for the judges, one for the bailiff of Rouen and all his people, one for the preacher, and one built up very high on a plaster base. That was for the stake. There was a big guard of English soldiers round it, but they'd built it up so the crowd could see everything. When Joan came, they brought her in a cart, which also had two priests in it. She wore a black shift, and had a kerchief round her head. There were more soldiers round the cart, but I was close enough to see that she was weeping.'

'You saw her weep often enough before.'

Gilles ignored this interruption.

'The fool of a preacher took an hour over his sermon, and the English soldiers started to get restless. They wanted to get it over with and go home to their dinner. And then the chief of her judges, Bishop Cauchon of Beauvais, insisted on having his say. And then Joan was crowned with a canvas mitre, with some writing on it to say why she had been condemned. She knelt down, still weeping, and started to beg for pardon. But they couldn't get a word out of her against the king, even though it was Charles who had deserted her.'

'I hear it was your cousin and my overlord who saw to it that he did.'

'La Tremoïlle?' said Gilles. 'Oh yes, he was glad enough to get rid of her. But no more eager than our noble sovereign. It's not a pretty thought, to think that a heretic put the crown on your head.'

'You believe she was heretical?'

'Raoul, let me finish my story. It's the only way of telling you what I thought and still think. At last the English soldiers got so unruly they dragged Joan to her feet and took her over to the bailiff, who was supposed to read out the sentence. But her guards shouted at him so he just waved his hand and let them take her to the stake. As soon as that happened all the judges climbed down from their platform and fled as if the devil was after them. Priests aren't allowed to watch that kind of thing, you know. Not unless they are actually comforting the prisoner. Then they can stay and watch as much as they please. Only the two who'd actually been in the cart remained. As she felt the chains go round her, Joan straightened her back and said, as if she couldn't believe what was happening to her: "Ah, Rouen, shall I die here?" And she looked up into the sky as if she expected an angel to swoop down and rescue her. One of the priests had climbed up on top of the pyre and was talking to her, and he wouldn't get down till the soldiers threatened to light the fire under him. So he scurried away and got a processional cross on top of a long pole. He held it up so that she could kiss it, and then the executioner fastened her hands and put his torch to the wood.'

'Did she die bravely?'

'She cried out a lot and begged for holy water. It seemed to take a long time. The place smelt terribly of roast pork when it was over.'

'Gilles, why are you telling me this?'

For the first time since the conversation began Gilles looked at me directly, and gave me one of his most seductive smiles.

'Don't you see, Raoul? I believe that there is a God and that Joan the Maid came from him in order to rescue the kingdom. But that day at Rouen taught me there's a devil too – a devil far more powerful than God would like us to know. Sometimes it's difficult to choose between them.'

'I hope I am on God's side,' I said, 'and I hope that you are too.'

'There are those here at Champtocé who do not have that wish for me. That is why I want you to stay with me now whatever may happen. Will you do that?'

'There are duties – '

'None that you cannot leave now your wife is dead,' said Gilles with cool finality. 'Don't you think it's more important to rescue a soul here on earth than to spend your time brooding over one which is already in Paradise?' And suddenly he drew back his arm and released the hawk from his wrist. 'Holla! Quarry! Bring her down, Isabel, bring her down!' And the bird went soaring after a pigeon fluttering in the blue.

22

We spent the next three weeks waiting for Jean de Craon to die. He never sent for me again, and, though it troubled my conscience, I made no further attempt to see him. The only people who went in to Jean were his old servant François, from time to time a physician and, at the end, an attorney and a priest. Every day, while Jean lay in the next room and made hard work of leaving the body which now brought him nothing but torment, we dined ceremoniously in the great hall. Gilles sat at the centre of the high table, with his own wife Catherine on his left hand and his grandfather's wife Anne in the place of honour on his right. His brother René de La Suze also had a seat there, next to madame Anne; and I, now that I was a lord of lands, was honoured too, and had madame Catherine for my partner. No one looking up at us from the tables in the main body of the hall would have suspected anything strange about the relationships between those present, though Anne de Sillé was greyer and more ghost-like than ever. She seemed to have sunk into a kind of dotage, and moved her lips continually and shook her head. Gilles, speaking in a low voice, amused himself by constructing a courtly dialogue between himself and her. He took the old woman's nods and becks as cues for his replies, which grew more outrageously high-flown and amorous as the meal wore on. René, meanwhile, either glared in embarrassment at his trencher, or held out his cup to be refilled.

That left Catherine and I to talk to one another, since Gilles, though without making the fact obvious, never addressed a word to her if he could help it. She was poor company, for more than one reason. In the first place she mistrusted me, as a friend and ally of her husband. In the second, she made it plain that she thought of me as an upstart, whose true position was below the salt. She ate more grossly than ever, never wiping her mouth and covering the front of her dress with spots of grease. Young as she still was, she now had a fine collection of dewlaps and double chins, and her cheeks, always high in colour, were beginning to be mottled with broken veins. Like her brother-in-law, she was continually calling the servitors to fill her cup with wine.

It was the liquor that loosened her tongue. By the beginning of the second week, looking at me sideways out of eyes imprisoned in rolls of fat, she had begun to flirt with me. I responded as best I could, thinking it unwise to antagonise her. Then, with a sure instinct for taking revenge upon my lack of interest, she began to harp upon the subject of my dead wife and child. From thence, by inexorable, perhaps unconscious stages, she moved to the subject of her own infant daughter, whom I had never seen, though the sound of the baby's crying sometimes carried down from some upper region of the castle into the courtyard.

What was she trying to tell me? At first I was not sure. Buried deep in the maternal gush there was an element of sly boasting about the child's illegitimacy – never openly referred to, but plainly hinted at in the emphasis she put upon its lack of resemblance to Gilles. But beneath that there was something else. She seemed to long to tell me more about her daughter's parentage, yet caution kept her back. It seemed impossible to know what she was hinting at, and every time she came near to speaking more plainly Gilles would abandon his game with Anne and interrupt to turn the conversation. It was clear that he kept one ear cocked to listen to what Catherine was saying. These interventions, though always courteous, had a strange effect on his wife. At one moment she was almost drunk, loud and indiscreet. At the next, sober and reflective. Yet Gilles did not, even in the most oblique way, seem to threaten her. Rather it was as if he grimly reminded her of a bargain which neither party was in a position to break.

I reflected long and hard about the problem, and came to a conclusion for which I had no proof. Catherine's daughter was the child of René de La Suze, and it was Jean de Craon who had bedded them in Gilles's absence, to make certain of an heir. My conviction was strengthened by René's attitude towards Catherine, and hers to him. They did not spend much time together. He never, for example, went to visit her in her chamber, even in the presence of her waiting-women (news of that would soon have gone round Champtocé). Their meetings were public and largely accidental, and when they encountered one another each had a hangdog air. They seemed to be careful never to touch one another – René, for example, always left it to me to take Catherine by the hand and lead her to her place at table, although the right and precedence were his. Yet at the moments when the two of them so ostentatiously turned away from one another you could feel the erotic current flow.

The true mystery was why Gilles tolerated a situation so humiliating to himself. I knew of his contempt for procreation, but could not think what had induced so proud a man to acknowledge a child whom most people knew not to be his. All his fortune must eventually go to this cuckoo, unless he bred a male heir to replace her. That seemed scarcely likely if Catherine remained his wife. True, he would not get rid of her easily. The Church would obviously be reluctant to dissolve a union achieved with such difficulty and amid so much scandalous publicity. And much of what Gilles held, was nominally Catherine's, and would go with her if a divorce was pronounced. Even if he rid himself of the burden by other and more drastic means (and I believed him capable of this), Catherine's possessions would descend to her daughter, unless the latter's legitimacy was challenged. Yet all these reasons, powerful as they were, did not seem enough to account for his inertia. At last it occurred to me that Gilles might not be altogether unhappy to find his wife and his brother linked to himself in a conspiracy of ill. One day René so far forgot himself as to query some decision Gilles had made. 'Ah, dear brother,' the latter purred, 'you needn't think you can salve your conscience, even in small things, at the expense of mine.' René started back as if Gilles had stung him, and an angry blush suffused his face.

The three weeks passed, and Jean de Craon found his release. His will was a surprise. Messire Jean, for all his wealth and power, had little room for manoeuvre in the disposition of his main assets. Their destination had been settled long ago – they went to Gilles. But two symbolic gestures Jean was free to make. His sword and curiass he left, not to the marshal whose prowess as a warrior was famous throughout France, but to the untried René. And he asked to be buried humbly, and with as little pomp as possible.

Gilles greeted this second condition with a sardonic grin. 'Far be it from me,' he said, 'to stand in the way of my grandfather's last wishes.' So Jean was wrapped naked in his shroud and put in a cheap coffin. On a wet November day, with the help of one priest, we hurried him into the ground. The hole the grave-diggers had made was already half-filled with water, thanks to the driving rain; and the clods of earth which Gilles and René and I picked up to throw on the coffin-lid dissolved and turned to mud in our hands.

His grandfather was no sooner buried than Gilles was anxious to be gone. 'I have lived here too long,' he said. 'And the whole place stinks of that pestilential old man. I wouldn't be surprised if he climbed out of his grave and came to haunt me. I am a man of many castles. Where shall we go?'

To everyone's surprise, his choice fell on one of the remotest of his possessions, and the one apparently least suitable to the season of the year. 'Let us pay a compliment to my other liege-lord,' he said. 'Let us go to Machecoul in his duchy of Brittany.'

It fell to Sillé to organise the journey, and a considerable task it was, since Gilles was determined to augment his household, and also to take with him everything which might make life at Machecoul luxurious. In particular, Sillé received orders to find Gilles experienced clerks to train the choir of children which the latter meant to build up there. 'Not Henriet alone, but a whole company of little Henriets!' Gilles exclaimed enthusiastically. 'What a pity it is that they last so short a time, and one must always be looking afresh!' The remark struck a strange echo in my mind, but I thought no more of it. It was true that Henriet's voice was already showing signs of breaking, though this did not seem to deprive him of Gilles's favour. Indeed, the lad was well on the way to becoming as unbearably insolent as his comrade Poitou.

Finding the necessary clerks did not cause Sillé as much trouble as another item which Gilles had ordered. He was determined to have a portable organ in the latest fashion, with a set of pipes and two pairs of handles to carry it. But every time we sent to Angers to enquire from the craftsman how the new toy was progressing, the messenger returned with yet another set of excuses – either the lether for the bellows was of the wrong quality, or properly seasoned wood for the framework was lacking, or one of the metal pipes had a flaw in it and must be remade. 'The truth is,' said Sillé wearily, 'that the man was tempted by the great price Gilles offered him – he knows that a thing as intricate as this cannot safely be made so rapidly. But Gilles is determined to keep his Christmas in Brittany.'

Sillé, like others at Champtocé, was much changed, and had I ever liked him I should have felt sorry for him. If Sillé had seen me go with a light heart, in the certainty that he would now exercise an unchallenged dominion over Gilles, the years that followed had clearly disappointed his expectations. Once he had been treated (as indeed I also was) as a landless gentleman attendant upon a great lord, not equal in fortune, certainly, but almost equal in birth. Now he was something not far removed from a steward – a mere drudge, a man to fetch and carry. Today he seldom offered an opinion on any subject – he, who had been so free with his opinions before – but compressed his lips and did as he was told. Even his appearance was conspicuously altered. He was the only shabby man whom Gilles allowed in his vicinity, and his worn garments made a striking contrast with the opulence of the two pages, who treated Sillé with open contempt.

Nevertheless, it was chiefly thanks to his efforts that we were ready to start by mid-December. Gilles had made it plain to his brother and his wife that he did not expect them to accompany him. 'My dear René,' he said, once more with the hint of a purr in his voice, 'I give you the captaincy of Champtocé, which is a great charge for a man as young and untried as you, and in addition I leave my dear wife in your keeping. I am confident you will know how to look after all her necessities.' Neither René nor Catherine tried to pretend that this decision was anything other than a relief, though I noticed that they still looked at one another askance. When they came out on the walls to see us go, they stood ostentatiously apart from one another.

It was a long procession that set out for Ingrandes and the bridge over the Loire. I was struck by the contrast between the state which Gilles now kept and the comparatively small entourage that had seemed to content him before. We travelled not only with a strong company of men-at-arms, but with grooms and pages and clerks and singing-boys, and men to look after the hounds and others who were in charge of the hawks, and a head cook and three assistant cooks and a gaggle of cooks' apprentices and even a pair of turnspits. There were few women, for Gilles had given orders that as many as possible should be left behind. 'All members of that sex are much the same,' he said. 'There will be plenty more of them, alas, when we reach Machecoul.'

Our journey was smooth enough. We travelled downstream for a while, along the south bank of the Loire, then we made our way through unremarkable country to Clisson, which stood at the confluence of two smaller rivers called the Sèvre and the Moine. The strong castle there belonged to the Duke of Brittany, and his captain there greeted us courteously and entertained us well, though I could see he was astonished by the splendour with which Gilles surrounded himself. 'One would say messire de Rais was a sovereign prince!' he exclaimed naively. 'Well, at least he is richer than some who are sovereign,' I retorted. The duke's perpetual lack of money was notorious.

Past Clisson the landscape changed. It gradually became wetter and more spongy until, after only a few leagues of travel, we found ourselves in a place where it was hard to tell if land prevailed or water. We now picked our way along the tops of great dykes. From these, as far as the eye could reach through the wintry haze, we saw a huge expanse of marsh, sometimes choked with reeds, sometimes showing a regular pattern of salt-pans and oyster-beds, sometimes opening out into brackish estuaries. The sharp saline smell that came to our nostrils was quite different from that of inland streams. It was plain that the territory was densely populated. Wherever a small islet or even the conjunction of two dykes permitted it, there were low cottages, thickly thatched.

As we paused at one of these villages, Sillé came to find me. 'What do you make of all this?' he asked abruptly. The enquiry was so general I did not know what to reply.

'I think we'll all have to turn into fish – salt-water fish at that – if we're to live here happily. The men will hate it. It's going to be hell on steel and leather.' I could already see the rust spots forming on my own breastplate.

'The men will have to put up with it. Don't you realise this is where most of the money comes from? No man can live without salt, and what would Fridays be without oysters?'

'Is that why Gilles is dragging us all this way? To take a closer look at his own particular pot of gold? It doesn't seem like him.'

'No, it doesn't, does it, Raoul?' Sillé countered, looking as if he hadn't received quite the response he expected. Then he added: 'Did you know he's sent a message to the local bishop, asking permission to change the dedication of the castle chapel?'

'What is it to be?' I said incuriously.

'The Holy Innocents,' Sillé replied, and began to force his way through the throng towards the head of the column.

23

When we arrived at Machecoul, it was easy to see how a castle had come to be built at that spot. The place where the buildings stood was scarcely higher than the rest of the surface of the marsh, but it was firm ground, an islet which once, perhaps, had been surrounded not by bog, but by the clean waves of the sea. The castle occupied all the surface available to it, defended not by high walls (though a wall of sorts did defend the periphery of the island), but by tidal streams which filled and emptied with the movement of the invisible ocean. Next to the castle, on another patch of dry ground, was a populous village, whose inhabitants came crowding out to witness the arrival of a lord so long unknown to them.

They were a handsome race, the men of the Marsh of Machecoul – tall and slim and fair, with a dextrous grace which showed itself at its best when they manoeuvred their flat-bottomed wherries along the open canals or drove them in among the reeds. Every household in the district seemed to own at least one of these boats, and even quite small children knew how to use the long poles with which they were driven along. A man, or for that matter a half-grown boy, could easily manage an ordinary wherry on his own, but there were other, larger ones, which were used for the transportation of heavy loads, and these needed up to four people to propel them. Our men-at-arms were at first inclined to mock this way of getting around, but they soon learned that the management of the pole on a muddy bottom called for a special knack. Quite a few of them, trying to discover how the thing was done, were left clinging to it, while the wherry shot from beneath them.

The Christmas we kept that year was the most lavish I ever remembered, and traders came flocking to his remote domain to supply Gilles with the luxuries he required. But he was not content with fine things for his own use alone – silks, furs, spices, perfumes, tapestries, jewels – though these, it seemed, were now brought to him from every quarter of the known world. His men-at-arms, too, must be dazzlingly equipped, with surcoats emblazoned with the Rais arms and weapons and armour in the latest Italian fashion. And, above all, those connected with the castle chapel must have nothing denied to them. From every silk-merchant Gilles bought materials to make vestments. I often found him in the great hall with the bales of precious stuffs undone and spread before him, a spectrum of all the colours of the liturgical year. The silks were no sooner chosen than they were put into the hands of the embroiderers, of whom we now had a whole colony in the village outside the gates. Relics aroused Gilles's enthusiasm almost as much as vestments did. He wanted to collect enough of them to make the Holy Innocents of Machecoul a place of pilgrimage for pious people throughout France. He bought a piece of the True Cross, a splinter of Holy Thorn, the arm of one saint, the great toe of another. 'Since the devil is so powerful, we must strengthen God in every way we can,' Gilles commented.

The men who peddled such goods were strangely furtive – priests without parishes who arrived just as the gates were about to close for the night and vanished with heavier purses at dawn the next morning. Every relic purchased meant a new commission for the goldsmiths, to provide a reliquary befitting its importance.

But it was not only silks and relics that Gilles needed for his chapel. He collected people too. There was talk, once the act of foundation had been properly promulgated, of appointments for a dean, an archdeacon, a treasurer, a little flock of canons. Gilles was already receiving solicitations from all of Britanny and half of France, seeking to engage his interest on behalf of deserving persons. These enquiries did not interest him. 'There is time enough for that,' he would say, casting aside yet another letter with a noble or episcopal seal on it. His passion was for singing-boys. His whole household was instructed to scour the countryside for likely candidates. It was even hinted to me that I might like to make myself useful in this fashion, a hint I ignored, as it seemed to me there would be no lack of supply.

Indeed, the little singers were not slow to offer themselves, or to be offered by their parents. The prospect of a place in the household of a noble as rich and generous as the Marshal of Rais was an alluring one. Gilles insisted on seeing and hearing all the candidates himself, and the chantry priests would often be seen leading some new candidate into the solar. I noticed that it was the more angelic-looking as well as the more angelic-sounding of them who were retained for Gilles's service.

One day, when an especially large number of candidates arrived, Gilles decided to audition them, not in the chapel, where he usually tested their prowess, but in the great hall. Some had their parents with them, or some female relative (the men would most of them be at work in the salt world of the marsh); others seemed to have come alone, carrying their possessions tied up in little bundles in case they should be chosen and allowed to stay in the glamorous world of Machecoul. One by one the boys mounted the dais, and the choirmaster struck his tuning-fork to see how well they could match the note. Afterwards the group of musicians sitting to one side played a simple air so the candidate could try a verse of it.

Gilles listened attentively for a little while, but then grew restless, and began to wander up and down in the body of the hall. Some of the boys looked at him boldly, others shrank back towards the wall, or clung to their mother's skirts. It was these shy ones who seemed to attract him most. He came close to them, and pinched their cheeks and fingered their plump arms. His matter-of-fact yet greedy inspection of the tender wares which were offered for sale reminded me of some housewife shopping for apples in a market.

With such a plethora of children arriving at Machecoul at all hours, with or without those who should have been responsible for them, it was perhaps natural that one or two should have become mislaid. Most turned up again, having seized the opportunity to play truant, but I heard rumours in the village that several had disappeared completely. The best-substantiated of these concerned a boy of about twelve, who vanished shortly after our arrival. He was not, as it happened, one of the children being considered for service in the chapel, but an apprentice to a furrier who had settled in Machecoul to be close to such a fruitful source of patronage. The story went that Sillé, visiting the shop on business, had asked if the boy could run a message for him to the castle, and that, somewhere on the brief journey, the child had melted into thin air. The men on guard denied having seen the child arrive, but then, why should they have paid attention to such a visitor? Sillé (I was later told, for I never questioned him on the subject) alleged that the errand was a much longer one, to Tiffauges where Gilles had another castle, and said that, since his message had never got there, the child must clearly have been kidnapped by marauders on the way. It would have been a common enough thing, even here in Brittany.

It so happened, however, that the furrier's wife was childless, and had had a greater fondness for the boy than women usually do for their husband's scapegrace apprentices. She raised such a fuss that Sillé made the mistake of trying to stop her mouth with a few pieces of gold. This made her more truculent than ever, and it was from this moment that the rumours began to grow and people to look askance at us in the village. But at the time I was not troubled, for the castle walls kept out what was being said.

What did trouble me was a change in Gilles. Whereas at Champtocé he had left it to his wife and his brother to keep the cup-bearers busy at every meal, now I noticed that he was downing great draughts of heavy wine unmixed with water. The wine had a strange effect on him. It inflamed, not his temper, but his passion for religion and for music. He had the children brought in to the great hall to sing elaborate graces to us, and woe betide the soldier who belched or whispered during the performance. And, half-drunk, he would go to chapel to hear the offices sung, and when some anthem particularly pleased him would insist loudly that it be repeated. At other times, however, he would show what seemed an exaggerated spirit of penitence for his sins, would wear a hair shirt and urge his confessor to heap penances upon him.

I once asked what drove him to these agonies of repentance. 'Surely,' I said, 'there is a kind of presumption in claiming to be so much worse than other men?'

Gilles looked at me sombrely. 'I am nothing if I am not the first,' he said. 'Who would dare claim to be the first in virtue?'

The remark seemed to me so strange I could make no sense of it, and it soon slipped from my mind. Gilles's excessive drinking I attributed not so much to an uneasy conscience, as to the rawness of the winter climate at Machecoul, for the months after Christmas were plagued by a cruel wind that swept across the marsh and chilled us to the bone. At night, I began the habit of having a cup of mulled wine brought to me in my chamber, to warm me before I slept. On occasion it worked even better than I anticipated, as I woke only late in the morning, feeling heavy and drugged. When I jokingly complained to Gilles about this, he began to tease me, saying: 'Ah, Raoul! You always were a heavy sleeper. On campaign we always used to say you could sleep through a battle or a murder. Don't you remember?' I didn't remember any such thing, but let the matter pass. Even when the cold relaxed its grip, I still had these occasional heavy nights, and went so far as to consult Gilles's physician, but he assured me I had no reason to worry.

Little by little, the grief I had felt at the loss of my wife and child had begun to soften. It was replaced by a curious feeling of mental rather than physical lassitude. Never, in all the years I had known him, had I felt closer to Gilles, even though we no longer shared the same room or the same bed. Whereas his attitude towards Sillé had become both peremptory and contemptuous, he treated me quite differently, with a caressing charm which was almost a kind of courtship. He seemed to seek my approval at all times, and yet was at pains to exhibit small faults to see if I would condemn them, or, rather, to see if I would continue to love him in spite of them. I cannot say that I was insensible to being courted in this fashion. I felt a delight in the fact of Gilles's presence, a fascination with his bodily grace, which reinforced the flattery he lavished upon me. At the same time I felt a powerful reawakening of physical urges, which I satisfied with some of the women living in the village. Not with peasants, for I had no taste for those, but with the merchants' wives, some of whom were young and handsome. At that time I was a good-looking man, not endowed with Gilles's elegance of bearing, but healthy, muscular and well set-up. As a seigneur, I did not expect any resistance to my advances, nor did I meet with any. Yet I sometimes wondered at the reticence these women showed – a reticence which could resemble fear when I first approached them, and which never entirely dissolved, however vigorously I pleasured them. It was for this reason that I went from one to another, never settling for one sole mistress. Once I was startled to discover, after I had been with a woman, that Gilles had sent her a substantial gift of money, almost as if it were he himself who had bedded her the previous night.

We remained at Machecoul the whole of that year, and the best part of another. During our second summer, news came to us of the fall from power of messire Georges. Like his predecessors, he was tumbled from his place at the moment when he was least expecting it, surprised at night, by a band of conspirators in his rooms at Chinon, wounded in the belly, held prisoner for a while and made to pay a ransom, then forced to promise he would absent himself from court. The king, it was reported, saw these events with the same apparent indifference as he had the fall of all his previous favourites. Queen Yolanda now ruled in La Tremoïlle's place, and by slow stages was managing the Constable's return.

More weeks passed, and now a messenger arrived, to announce La Tremoïlle's intention of coming to see us. Gilles received the news with a bad grace. 'Why must he come here?' he said. 'His disgrace will come with him, to trouble our tranquillity.' As for the pact he had once signed with La Tremoïlle, this seemed to interest him not at all. 'My cousin is less great,' he remarked, 'so he cannot expect me to do such great things for him.'

Indeed, La Tremoïlle when he arrived was by no means changed in bulk, but nevertheless strangely diminished in personality. He had aged and carried his hands folded over his vast belly as if to protect the spot where the wound had been. Sudden noises startled him. When one of the servitors dropped a metal dish behind his seat while he was dining with us in hall, he flinched visibly. He treated Gilles with a kind of deference which surprised me, since he remained, after all, as great and almost as wealthy a noble as the Marshal of Rais. Charles VII had stripped him of power, but had let him retain his riches.

The purpose of his mission soon emerged. He wanted to use Gilles as a means of currying favour with the king, and thus, perhaps, of regaining some part of his former influence. There was a town called Grancey, in Burgundy, which did not belong to Duke Philip the Good, who had therefore, quite logically, sent some of his forces to besiege it. 'And you,' he urged his host, 'must take these splendid men of yours and lift the siege, which will give great pleasure to our royal master.'

'When did he ever take pleasure in anything?' Gilles retorted. 'These fine fellows of mine are much too good for journeyman warfare of that kind. Do you realise what it costs to equip four hundred men in best Milanese plate?'

La Tremoïlle persisted, and at last managed to wring a small concession from his reluctant host. 'Very well, let my brother René take a few of the men of Champtocé to the siege. They are old, and know too much about warfare, and he knows too little. Between them, they should make a fine mess of it.' After this he refused to discuss the subject again.

The big man lingered for some days more at Machecoul, though Gilles did little to make him feel welcome. It was fine late summer weather, calm and hazy, and one day, evidently at a loss for something to fill his time with, he came to me and said: 'Raoul, let us ride out for the day. There is something here that makes my skin prickle even more than it did in the darkest times at the king's court.'

I consented, since there was no reason not to go. I supposed that La Tremoïlle would want to go hawking, since the marsh often provided fine sport with herons and other wild fowl. He accepted the presence of the falconers without comment, and we flew our birds companionably until the time came for the noonday halt. After the meal, he asked: 'Do you mind sending all these people home? I have a fancy to do something I have never done.'

Intrigued, I consented, but suggested nonetheless that we keep two grooms. I had already discovered that it was not wise to ride alone into the maze of pools and dykes, without taking someone with me who knew the paths. 'Just as you like. It would not make much difference now if I sank into a quicksand. There are people who might even thank you for it.'

'Where do you want to go?' I said, to turn the conversation. 'Towards the ocean. I have never seen it.'

I was ashamed to admit that I had never seen it either, in spite of having sensed its presence and felt its influence during all the months I had lived at Machecoul.

The two grooms received my instructions without expression, and one of them turned to lead us swiftly through the labyrinth. At first the marsh seemed to grow denser and more intricate. There were fewer dykes and fewer signs of man's handiwork. Naked expanses of mud alternated with stagnant pools and tall thickets of reeds. Occasionally there were what seemed like green stretches of meadow, but the groom waved us peremptorily away from these. He always seemed to know where it was safe for a horse to set his foot, even a horse as heavy as the one La Tremoïlle was riding. After about an hour the ground seemed to grow drier, though we were now riding beside a stream which flowed in the same direction as the one we ourselves were taking. On my right hand a sandy bank seemed gradually to raise itself out of the level surface of the marsh. Our guide halted, and waited for me to catch up with him. He pointed, and at the same time lightly touched my horse's rein. 'Up there, messire,' he said. 'Yves and I will wait till you come back.'

Obediently I took the direction he indicated, and La Tremoïlle followed me. We climbed the ridge, and then a second and taller one. I heard a hushing and swishing sound which could only be the voice of what we had come to look at. Putting my mount's head towards it, I climbed a third barrier, one still taller than the rest, and made this time of loose sand which crumbled under the horse's hooves. Behind me I could hear my companion swearing at his mount as it stumbled and threatened to unseat him.

Coming to the crest of the dune, we were able to gaze at what, until now, had been a name to both of us. The haze clung to its surface, and at first it was difficult to make out what it was like. When at length my eyes grew accustomed to its appearance, I was disappointed. This faintly stirring, form-less greyness did not seem worth having come out of one's way to see.

Beside me, La Tremoïlle sat immobile, staring towards the horizon. 'So that is how it looks,' he said. 'You must be sure to describe it to my cousin Gilles.'

'Why?' I asked, startled by his reaction.

'He still thinks of the world as clay that he can form, one shape becoming another if the first should happen not to suit him.'

'I believed vou thought the same,' I said.

'So I did.'

'And now?'

'Now I think it is as easily changed and moulded as that ocean.'

24

After La Tremoïlle's departure, Gilles's attention was con-
centrated, not on the declining fortunes of his brother at
the siege of Grancey, but on his own negotiations with the
chapter of Saint-Hilaire at Poitiers. These began in the autumn,
and continued throughout the following winter and into the
spring. They involved the dispatch of many lavish gifts, and the
traders who had settled at Machecoul did better than ever.

Gilles's object was to be made a canon of Saint-Hilaire. The
barrier to this was not the fact that he was a layman. Saint-
Hilaire is one of those ancient foundations which has the right
to confer a semi-sacred status upon certain lay-protectors. But
these protectors are by custom men of royal blood, which itself,
according to the old belief, gives a sacred and inviolate character to the man whose veins it fills. Gilles might be noble, but
he was not royal. A genealogist was hired from Nantes, and
put to work in the muniment-room at Machecoul, tracing
Gilles's descent from the old Dukes of Aquitaine and even from
the Merovingian kings. His discoveries, combined with the
magnificence of the gifts which were continually sent to them,
were enough to beat down the resistance of the men of Saint-
Hilaire, and Gilles was at last invited to come to Poitiers for
his installation.

I could not understand why the honour meant so much to
him, and was tactless enough to tell him so. Gilles looked at me
astonished. 'Don't you see, Raoul,' he said, 'that as the founder
and patron of the chapel of the Holy Innocents, my life already
has a priestly character? Unworthy though I am, am I not the
protector of these little ones?' And he waved a slightly tipsy
hand at a couple of his choristers who, according to established
custom, were making music with him in the solar. The notion
was too much for my equanimity, and I burst into a loud guffaw.

For the first time since I had returned to live with him,

Gilles was seriously offended. He refused to speak to me for some days, and even when he consented to make up our quarrel, he decided that I was not to travel with him to the installation ceremony. 'You can be captain of this place in my absence,' he decreed. 'I would rather leave Machecoul in your hands than any others.'

Thus it was that I formed no part of the procession which, late in July, marched out of the castle gate on its way to Poitiers. It made an impressive spectacle. Gilles himself, superbly mounted on a bay horse, was dressed in sober grey, and it would have taken a sharp eye to detect from a distance the quality of his horse-trappings and of the enamel on his belt. But only a blind man could have missed the brilliance that surrounded him. His guard, all tall and handsome men, wore their Milanese armour and emblazoned surcoats. At the head of the procession went Gilles's herald in his tabard. Following him were the musicians, and then the chantry priests and children. All the people belonging to the chapel were on horseback, and they were dressed in a uniform which Gilles had had made for the occasion – long robes of scarlet cloth, and hats of grey and white fur. The effect was splendid, though the children and their mentors looked ready to melt in the heat. Behind them was carried the portable organ which Gilles had had constructed in Angers. In the damp climate of Machecoul it had long since ceased to work, but its gilding and its painted decoration were still in good condition, and it made an eye-catching item in the show.

Not long after Gilles's departure, I received a message from Sillé. It was brief and to the point. It said: 'We owe four hundred *écus* for food and lodging. Please remit them by the hand of this messenger.' Puzzled that Gilles should be short of what was, for him, so trivial a sum, I went to see the old clerk of accounts who was one of the few members of Jean de Craon's household Gilles had brought with him from Champtocé. He peered at the letter and sighed. 'Well,' he said, 'whom shall I borrow it from this time – Guillaume the goldsmith, or Pierre the silk-merchant, or even Isaac the Jew? We pay less interest to Christians, but they are more reluctant to lend.'

'Has this happened before?' I demanded.

'Of course,' he said, his eyebrows flying up till they almost reached the top of his bald cranium. 'Messire Gilles recently discovered that one of the advantages of wealth is that you can borrow money. I don't think he has yet discovered that you have to pay it back.'

'What about the expenses of the castle?' I asked, as another thought struck me. 'Did he leave enough in the coffers for that?'

'Not in ready money. But see for yourself.' And he offered me his bunch of keys and gestured me towards the strong-room.

It was true that the money chests were empty, though there was still an immense mass of valuable things in store. In the end we decided to pawn enough old-fashioned plate to carry the establishment through until the next lot of salt revenues began to come in. I sent Sillé's messenger off with the sum requested, but prudently said nothing about the much larger reserve I had managed to obtain.

I had reason to congratulate myself on my own foresight, for within six days I received a message from Gilles himself, asking me to go to Orléans, to arrange accommodation for himself and for his entire household, as he would be joining me there shortly.

In fact he had left me with very little time to make the trip and do what was necessary. Part of the journey, however, I was able to make in a boat up the Loire, and this made things less fatiguing. Orléans, when we came in sight of it, was simultaneously familiar and unfamiliar. All signs of the English fortifications had disappeared, and the ruined churches they had once surrounded had for the most part been rebuilt. The Tourelles, too, had been completely repaired, and the ducal banner flew proudly over it, though Duke Charles remained a prisoner in England – his captivity had lasted ever since Agincourt. There was a great bustle of traders over the bridge, and within the town the streets were thronged with people of all kinds. The shops overflowed with goods. Paris had not yet been recovered by the king, and Orléans was making the most of its position as the principal trading city on the Loire, which remained the chief highway of the kingdom.

Since I knew that Gilles would be bringing a considerable body of men-at-arms with him, I thought it best to take myself to the town-hall, to acquaint the chief men with his intentions. Their reaction was more favourable than I expected. 'The Marshal of Rais has shown himself a good friend of this city,' one of them said, 'and we see no reason why he should not bring in whom he likes – provided, of course, that he is prepared to feed and lodge them at his own charge.' And with this he gave me a leer which was almost a wink. I saw that news of Gilles's prodigality had travelled more swiftly than he did.

Even so, since the place was crowded with people, I had considerable difficulty in finding enough accommodation. For

Gilles himself, I hired a fine mansion, 'The Golden Cross', which belonged to the widow of a rich burgess. She was all prepared, partly from good-will but also from curiosity, to remain there herself and act as housekeeper, and I had great trouble in persuading her to move out, as I knew that this arrangement would by no means satisfy Gilles. In the end, she contented herself with charging me an extra sum for her absence, 'in view of the damage you will certainly do, if I am not there to oversee things'. For the singing-boys and their mentors I hired most of the rooms in one inn and half of another. Even so, the list of people to be disposed of remained formidable – the captain of the guard, the herald, the armourer, servants, grooms, men-at-arms, a professional book-illuminator whom Gilles seemed to have acquired in Poitiers. It was even a problem to find sufficient stabling for the horses.

At last everything was done, and word came that Gilles was approaching the city. I watched from the roof of the Tourelles as the long procession made its way towards the south bank of the river, along the road from Poitiers. It certainly made a splendid sight, with the many-coloured surcoats of the warriors and the moving ribbon of scarlet which was, I knew, the Chapel of the Holy Innocents in its travelling dress. Having looked as long as I dared, I slipped down the turret stairway and made my way back to the house where Gilles was to lodge. There had been some disagreement amongst the members of the council as to whether or not he was to be offered a ceremonial flagon of wine, and in the end it had been decided not to do so, since he was coming as a private person, however richly attended. But some of the rich burgesses had come on their own account, to pay him their respects.

As Gilles's household made its way through the narrow streets, people crowded to their windows and doorways to see him pass. It was nothing like the welcome Orléans had once given to Joan, yet there was stir enough, and I could see Gilles was pleased with the effect his return to the city was making upon those he saw around him. He thrust his hand into his purse, and scattered a fistful of coins for the children to scramble for, crying at the same time: 'Alms in the name of Joan the Maid!' The scramble turned into a near riot when it was seen that among the silver coins were some gold ones.

Once installed in the house I had rented, Gilles seemed to have two preoccupations. One of these I might have anticipated. He embraced me as soon as he had descended from his horse, and as he did so he murmured in my ear: 'Well, Raoul, have you found me a good Jew?' I saw that we would soon have a long conversation on the subject of money. However, before he settled down to his tête-à-tête with me, Gilles turned his attention to the city fathers who had been waiting to meet him. His manners were at their most seductive, and they fell over themselves to tell him everything he wished to know. Yes, it was true that on the eighth of May each year, the anniversary of its deliverance from the English, the city marked the day with a solemn procession and other celebrations. Yes, it was also true that, during the celebrations, the custom had grown up of performing a mystery which represented the principal events of the siege.

'Surely,' Gilles enquired, 'you cannot do that without giving some credit to the Maid? But the Maid is still condemned as a heretic.'

'Here in Orléans we think of her as a saint!' exclaimed one of the burgesses fiercely.

'And we noticed, messire, that you gave alms in her name,' chimed in another.

'Quite so,' said Gilles. And then, as if changing the subject: 'I hear that I too am represented in this mystery of yours?'

The burgesses cleared their throats and shuffled their feet, and at last admitted this to be true. Gilles smiled a small and secret smile.

Even when everybody had settled in to the lodgings allotted to them, his household continued to make an impact on the life of Orléans. It was soon a familiar sight in the streets when the children of the Chapel of the Holy Innocents took part in some religious procession. Gilles was always willing to pack them off to help one of the parish-churches celebrate a saint's day. The men-at-arms, generously paid, became favoured customers in the best taverns. Whenever Gilles himself moved through the streets, it was with a glittering escort, and he was always surrounded by a throng of people hoping for a fresh distribution of alms. They were seldom disappointed.

It was only Sillé and I who knew how some of this magnificence was paid for. Out of their travelling chests came some of the embroidered vestments Gilles had had made for his chapel, still fresh and for the most part unworn. At night we would take them off to old Aaron in his secluded house, and Aaron would count out his gold pieces in exchange. I sometimes wondered that he was so willing to buy the merchandise we brought him. 'Oh, we are good friends, the men of the church and I,' Aaron would murmur deprecatingly. 'They know a good thing when they see one just as well as I do. These embroideries are exquisite, exquisite!' And he touched them gently, with his fine ivory-coloured hands.

Gilles had added yet more people to his household while he was at Poitiers. One of these was a boy called Jean Rossignol – aptly named, for he sang as exquisitely as any nightingale. Gilles was besotted with his voice, and for a while Poitou and Henriet had their noses quite out of joint. 'Imagine,' I overheard one of them murmur to the other, 'our little song-bird has been given a prebend at Saint-Hilaire. I wonder what he had to do for our master the canon in order to get it.' 'I wish I had done as little to get as much,' the other answered. 'But sometimes messire de Rais takes payment in instalments.' Whereupon they both began to snigger and to dig each other in the ribs. For my own part I had a soft spot for master Rossignol, and my weakness was shared by nearly everyone else at the Golden Cross. His manners were so innocently free it was impossible to take what he said or did amiss.

The case was different with Eustache Blanchet. Blanchet was a priest, a man of the same stamp as those who used to come and sell us relics at Machecoul. Aged about forty, he was not attractive physically – tall, bony and clumsily built, with disproportionately large hands and feet, he had a greyish complexion which always seemed to be on the point of pouring with sweat. He emitted a faint, sour, subtly offensive odour. All the other members of the household detested him. Gilles, on the contrary, seemed to be fascinated with him, and often saw him in private. At the same time he did not treat Blanchet with respect, and seemed to take an uncharacteristic pleasure in keeping him short of money. Occasionally the priest would come to me begging for a loan. I gave it to him, and repaid myself from the household coffers, since I soon learned that for Blanchet 'loan' and 'gift' were synonymous. I once asked Gilles why he did not pay the man a regular stipend. 'You could appoint him to some post in your chapel,' I said, 'and that would solve the problem quite neatly.' Gilles looked at me sidelong, as if wondering what to reply. 'No, I don't think the chapel is master Eustache's *métier*,' he answered finally. 'In any case, I prefer to pay him by results.'

One strange thing I noticed about Blanchet was his power of melting into thin air just when one would most expect to see him. The house itself had a small chapel, but I never saw him there, even though he was so much in evidence at other times.

Nor did he show himself when the Holy Innocents paraded in their scarlet robes.

I might have paid more attention to this and other facts had not the arrival of La Tremoïlle, accompanied by Gilles's brother René, driven most other things from my mind. The longer La Tremoïlle was kept from the centre of power, the more he seemed to fade and wither. Now he had actually lost weight, and the skin hung from his neck in wrinkled folds. From being a man of masculine power, he was suddenly transformed into an old woman. And, like an old woman, he nagged and wheedled Gilles to return to the military life. 'The moment is almost gone,' he whined. 'We must act now, if we are ever to return to influence. By the autumn of next year Charles will have reached a settlement with the Duke of Burgundy. He is already negotiating with the duke's ambassadors.'

'Was there ever a moment when he *wasn't* negotiating with them?' Gilles retorted.

René de La Suze was in Orléans to add his own solicitations to those of La Tremoïlle – or this, at any rate, was the story he gave out. I was soon to discover that his real purpose was rather different. He sent one of his servants to ask me to come and see him at the inn where he lodged, the Little Salmon.

René kept a very different kind of state from his magnificent brother, and he himself was considerably changed from the last time I had seen him at Champtocé. The attempt to raise the siege of Grancey might have been unsuccessful, but the experience had clearly toughened and matured him. It was a coldish evening for early autumn, and René sat before the fire in the inn's best room, a flagon of wine in one fist and a half-gnawed chicken leg in the other. His legs were comfortably propped on the table in front of him. His face was still ruddy, but now it was the healthy ruddiness which comes from sun and wind, not the alcoholic flush that had marked it formerly. He was coarse, solid, earthbound and not entirely unformidable.

'Let me be frank, Raoul,' he said, waving the chicken leg at me for greater emphasis, 'I don't see why any decent man should stick to my brother. But you seem decent and nevertheless you've stuck to him.'

There was no useful response I could make to this, and therefore I made none.

'No comment, eh? Well, I don't blame you. Maybe you know some things and maybe you don't.'

'I try to mind my own business,' I said levelly.

'And it's business I want to talk to you about. Mine rather than yours. You know Gilles is in debt?'

'Yes.'

'I heard you'd been to see the Jews for him. Got rid of a few expensive bits of frippery did you, and took a big loss in the process?'

'You could put it that way.'

'I am putting it that way. And I'm telling you it won't pay the bills for long. The next moment he'll be selling land. He's got rid of one castle already.'

'To pay for his part in the campaign that relieved this city and got the king crowned.'

'I'd expect the king to pay *me* for my help, not the other way round.' René took a bite of chicken, and I saw his strong white teeth tearing at the juicy meat, to free it from the bone. He continued only when he had thoroughly masticated and swallowed the mouthful. 'Selling fripperies is one thing. Selling land is quite another.'

'It all belongs to Gilles.'

'That's where you're wrong, my dear Raoul. It belongs to Gilles, but in a broader sense it belongs to his whole family – to everyone who might have a claim on it if Gilles were to die tomorrow.'

'He shows no sign of doing so.'

'Who knows? This is an extremely fickle and changeable world. Or that's what the good priests are always telling me. I don't want to wake up one day, to find that Gilles is a corpse and I'm a pauper.'

'What do you expect me to do about it?'

'Try to restrain my brother. Persuade him to renounce some of his more expensive amusements. Also some of his more dangerous ones.'

'I'll do my best. But I doubt if I have much influence over him.'

'I don't know anyone who has more – anyone whom I could speak to as I'm speaking now to you. Sillé is completely under Gilles's thumb. And I'm damned if I'll address myself to two creatures like Henriet and Poitou. My flesh creeps when I see them.'

'And if I cannot change Gilles's ways?'

'Then leave him and go back to your fief. No one will blame you for it. You're standing under a tree the lightning is bound to strike. If not today, then certainly tomorrow.'

With this René tossed the chicken bone he was still holding into the heart of the fire. It sizzled, and gave off an acrid stench. For a moment I thought it smelt like burning human flesh.

25

By dint of much nagging, La Tremoïlle eventually persuaded Gilles to go on an expedition with him to the north of France, where the war still raged. René de La Suze retired to Champtocé. From the moment the enterprise was agreed, I was doubtful as to its prospects. It was already winter, and the weather was cold and wet. Gilles continually changed his mind as to when he would set out. Christmas came before he had fully decided what to do, and it was in the midst of the Christmas feasting that he sent for Sillé and myself, to tell us his plans. The first surprise was to find a notary also waiting for us. To start with, however, Gilles did not explain why the man had been summoned.

It was to me that he turned first. 'Raoul, I have decided to keep our lodgings here in Orléans, as it will be easier than looking for fresh ones when I return, and we are now all used to them. The people of the chapel, and the domestics can stay here. You can look after them while I am gone, and live as magnificently as you like for your trouble.'

'Yes,' I said, 'if you will be kind enough to leave me the money with which to pay them.' We had already got so used to the topic of Gilles's debts that it had become a subject for jesting.

'Don't worry, I have made arrangements for that. Sillé here will not be coming with me either. I have another job for him. See what you both think of my new plan. Notary, will you be so kind as to read the document?'

The man duly began to read. As clause followed clause, all in proper legal phraseology, I began to doubt the evidence of my own ears. The parchment contained a proxy made out to Sillé. It gave him the right to sell, or failing that, to pledge, any of the lands which belonged to Gilles in Brittany. This was sweeping enough, but there was also a sting in the tail. Sillé was specifically authorised to negotiate a marriage for Gilles's daughter Marie, to whomever he thought suitable.

Gilles was as pleased as a child with what he had devised. 'Of course Sillé won't sell all my lands,' he explained. 'But this sets him free to sell whatever property he can get a good price for. It's the best way of getting money quickly, don't you agree? After all, I can't always go on borrowing.'

'What about the marriage of your daughter?' I ventured to ask.

'Daughter!' exclaimed Gilles, heedless of the notary's presence. 'You know as well as I do that brat is not my daughter! Never mind, people think my wife's bastard is heir to all I have, and who am I to disillusion them if I can get a good price for her marriage? Time enough to disinherit her later. In fact, Sillé, I think you'd better begin with little Marie. Four is a ripe age at which to plight your troth, for a girl as rich as she's supposed to be!'

As I put my hand to the deed as witness, I thought of the explosive effect this would certainly have on René de La Suze, and indeed on all of Gilles's kinsmen, and wondered if the lightning René had mentioned was already about to strike. Nevertheless, when Gilles fixed me with his blazing, excited eyes, I felt I had no choice except to sign.

Gilles scattered sand on the document and shook it off, then handed it to my companion. 'There, Sillé, get it properly sealed, and go at once to Machecoul. I shall expect great results by the time I am back. I have much to do that cannot be done with an empty purse.'

The expedition, however, had scarcely taken the road before Gilles was with us once again and Sillé was recalled from Machecoul with his commission cancelled. The reasons for this precipitate return were soon made clear to me. 'How could I be bothered with all that wearisome marching back and forth?' said Gilles to me rhetorically. 'There are more urgent things to be thought of here in Orléans. Others can play at soldiers just as well as I, but only I can see to it that the Maid is properly honoured at her festival.' From the moment he came back it was the celebration planned for the eighth of May that seemed to occupy all of Gilles's thoughts.

One morning early in March I came into the solar to find him turning the leaves of a bulky manuscript I did not remember having seen before. 'Well,' he said cheerfully, 'I managed to get it out of them. They were so reluctant you would have thought the whole thing was a state secret.'

'What is it?' I asked.

'The text of *The High and Powerful Mystery of the Siege*, written by the town poet. Of course, it's wretched stuff, but I think it has possibilities. Here, listen to this:

> Glasdale and you other lords
> Of might and great renown,
> You waste your strength and blunt your swords
> In trying to take this town.
> So leave these errors and go back
> To England whence you came,
> Or else I'll give you such a thwack
> You'll never be the same.'

'Wretched stuff!' I agreed, laughing. 'Is that supposed to be Joan, shouting across to the garrison in the Tourelles? I doubt if she'd recognise herself.'

'There's no time to get it rewritten. And I doubt if the city fathers would thank me if I found them a better poet. They like their mystery just as it is.'

'So where are the possibilities?'

'The point of the whole thing is the spectacle, not the words. People look more than they listen. They like action and colour. That's the way to commemorate the Maid and make people remember what she did.'

'Gilles, what have you done?' I said, my heart sinking.

'I've offered to help the corporation of Orléans make this the most magnificent mystery in the whole of France.'

Thus it was that I found myself once more trying to raise money. Gilles was determined to lay his hands on a considerable sum, and the disposal of surplus vestments would not provide what he required. 'We must sell some of the relics,' he said finally. 'Messires the saints will not mind their bones being put on the market for such a good purpose.' This led to a long debate between us as to which relic in particular it was best to get rid of. Finally the choice settled on the head of Saint Honoré – a fine silver bust, parcel gilt, wearing a coronet studded with pale sapphires. The coronet hid the fact that the object was made in the form of a box, where the relic lay wrapped in fine silk from Byzantium.

'Must it be that?' I protested. I did not believe in all the things Gilles had brought from his middlemen, but this I revered, and I could not touch it without feeling the vibration of its holy power.

'It looks impressive and it has a pedigree,' said Gilles coolly. 'In fact we can be more certain that this is really the skull of the blessed Saint Honoré than we are that our sovereign lord the king is really the son of his father.'

My first thought was to take the object to Aaron the Jew, with whom I had done business before. When he saw what I had brought him, he shook his head regretfully. 'No, my friend, this is going too far. Pious people would never believe that such a relic could come from me, intact and unmeddled with. They'd accuse me of substituting pig's bones for the authentic ones, and burn me in the nearest market-place most likely.'

'What shall I do?' I asked, disappointed.

'I will introduce you to an Italian banker who, if he purchases the goods you have to sell, will allow me a small commission.'

'Why an Italian?'

'You will see for yourself why such a person is the most suitable.'

I knew that Italian merchants and bankers lived in most of the great cities of France, just as Italian soldiers of fortune served as captains in both the king's and the Duke of Burgundy's armies. But until now I had never had much to do with them. Messire Lodovico's house, from the outside, was like that of any other rich trader. Inside, it surprised me by its lightness and spaciousness, its air of ordered luxury. Messire Lodovico himself, short and middle-aged, was more like an aristocrat than a merchant. He took his hands from his sleeves, picked up the reliquary and examined it in silence. Then he glanced at the papers and parchments I handed to him. Only as an afterthought did he glance at the contents of the box. He wrinkled his nose a little and dropped the lid again swiftly.

'In principle, I do not like this kind of transaction, but I am willing to help.'

'You come straight to the point.'

'It is the modern way of doing business.'

'That suits me well enough.'

'There is one thing I ought to tell you. I am buying a handsome piece of goldsmith's work and a miscellaneous collection of documents. The rest is of no interest to me.'

'You will return the bones to my master?'

'If he insists. They are of no value by themselves.'

'Don't you believe in the miracles of the saints?' I exclaimed angrily.

'What I do or don't believe is of no consequence. It's what other people believe that matters. Without this fine container and these writings the relics of Saint Honoré would not be relics at all. It is a simple matter to find substitutes.'

'Is this the new philosophy they teach men in Italy?'

'It is an old philosophy which we Italians think has been too long forgotten.'

'I will remember that next time I meet one of your countrymen!' But it was to be some time before I had cause to think of the incident and what had been said.

Meanwhile, Gilles was busy pushing forward his plans for the mystery. He held a series of meetings with the representatives of the city guilds – for it turned out that it was these guilds who were responsible for the annual celebrations. The tradesmen and craftsmen were flattered that they had attracted the attention of so great a man. At the same time, they were not sure that they relished his interference. The whole enterprise began to lead us into a maze of conflicting jurisdictions and petty rivalries. I realised that the Orléans I was now seeing was one I had never encountered before. Was it a matter for the hatmakers to provide all the hats that would be required? Would the carpenters abate payment for erecting the scaffolds because this was a municipal show? Who would be responsible for providing beer for the trumpeters? It was clear that all these matters had been argued about on previous occasions. but they were quite happy to argue about them again.

The guildsmen were not pleased, however, when Gilles wanted changes in the text. 'If the poem was good enough for us last year, and the year before that, I don't see that we need to alter it now,' one of them asserted sulkily.

'But surely,' said Gilles, 'we want to give the best account we can of the miraculous deliverance of this city?'

It soon became apparent what kind of alterations he wanted. The scenes that concerned himself were the ones which drew his fascinated attention. At first he began by insisting that this or that detail be corrected, and then he started enlarging his own role. The text must be altered to make it plain to all who came to see the mystery that it was the Sire de Rais who had led the king's army when it accompanied Joan to the rescue of Orléans. And into his mouth must be put all the most pious and elevated sentiments, until he seemed like an incarnation of St Michael himself.

The guildsmen acquiesced in these changes, not so much because they agreed, but because they had no language in which to discuss such matters with a man as great as Gilles. They muttered mutinously after every meeting they had with him.

If the text of the mystery caused difficulties, much greater ones arose from the allocation of parts. Since the entertainment had now been given for four years in succession, various people in the town had established their claims upon the principal roles. A lame tailor played La Hire, because the man whom he represented had a similar affliction. A bullying innkeeper had usurped the part of the Bastard of Orléans and scrivener had been awarded that of Ambroise de Loré. To those of us who remembered the originals, the contrast between them and these vulgar impersonators was almost too ludicrous to be borne. Yet many people in Orléans, who had lived in the city throughout the siege and had seen these warriors passing every day through the streets, and who had even fought side by side with them at the Augustins and the Tourelles, swore that the resemblance was perfect. Gilles soon discovered that it was impossible to dislodge those who had taken possession of the chief parts if the mystery was to be presented at all.

He did, however, declare that he must be allowed the choice of the man who was to undertake his own role in the drama, and everybody agreed that this was reasonable. The only person to be dissatisfied with the decision was the burly horse-meat butcher who had previously shouted the speeches of the heroic Marshal of Rais, and had waved sword and banner (either alternately or together) to his own great satisfaction. 'There's a lot of book-learning in it,' he grumbled, 'and they'll never find anyone else who can manage the book-learning and do all the horseback-riding and fighting as well.'

It soon began to look very much as if he was right. A succession of would-be actors was paraded in front of the exigent Gilles, who found them too fat or too thin, too tall or too short, too bandy in the legs or too squeaky in the voice, or in some other way disqualified from the task.

After a number of failures, he turned to me and said, as if it were the most natural thing in the world: 'Of course the solution to our problem is for me to act myself.' It took a day of argument to convince him that a man in his position could in no circumstances consent to mount a scaffold and entertain the vulgar. 'Unless the day comes when they decide to execute me!' he exclaimed ruefully, when at last we brought him to see the force of our arguments. 'Noblemen are not exempt from entertaining the vulgar then.'

The lot fell at last on a young sergeant among Gilles's own men-at-arms – an unusually handsome as well as an unusually intelligent specimen of his kind. At first he was very reluctant to agree to do it, for fear that his comrades would laugh at him, but the problem was solved with a substantial increase in pay. 'Everyone respects money,' Sillé remarked, with a return of his old mordancy, as he went to Gilles's treasurer to confirm the arrangement. Since the sergeant could neither read nor write, a man had to be hired to teach him his verses, parrot-fashion.

There was almost as much discussion about who was to be given the role of Joan. 'It has to be played by a boy, just like the part of the Blessed Virgin and those of the female saints,' Gilles remarked, condescending to my ignorance. 'We couldn't allow a woman to flaunt herself in public.'

'I see enough women already flaunting themselves in the streets,' I retorted. In prosperous Orléans, it was sometimes difficult to tell a rich burgess's wife from a prostitute.

'Oh, Joan always wanted to be a male. Why shouldn't she have her wish?' said Gilles equably.

The hobbledehoy who had played the part previously was now, by universal consent, too old for it, and in any case his voice had broken and the first whiskers were sprouting amongst the pimples on his chin. So the role must go to somebody new. It was at this moment that Gilles proposed that the part of the Maid should be given to Rossignol. I suspected that this was what he had had in mind all along. The child was sent for, so that the guildsmen could take a look at him. He came into the large hall of Gilles's house, and stood quietly on the dais, waiting for whatever instructions his master would give him. A ray of light fell from the tall window behind him, and touched his hair, which was of that silvery fairness which is usually seen only in certain Flemings, and in people from the extreme north, the regions of ice and snow. His blue eyes outshone the blue of his doublet, and his expression, usually merry, was for the moment solemn.

'Sing something for us, Rossignol,' Gilles commanded.

'Can you give me a note, messire?'

A servant came and put a small harp into Gilles's hands. He touched the middle string. Immediately the boy's voice soared like a crystal jet towards the high roof of the room. He sang first a slow melancholy song, a plaint to the Virgin; then immediately changed to a popular, jigging air, something I had heard sung in the streets, a girl abusing her lover.

When he finished, there were murmurs of applause. The leader of the guildsmen cleared his throat and looked round at his fellows. Seeing the same verdict on all their faces he said:

'If you will lend us your page for this, messire, I think we all feel it will be for the good of the mystery.'

'But who is to teach him his part?' another of them chimed in, and again they all looked at one another. I spoke instinctively, before anyone else could provide an answer.

'If you will give me a copy of what he has to learn, I will be happy to undertake the task, as my contribution to the enterprise.'

26

The *Mystery of Orléans* opened such a wound in Gilles's finances that I thought it might prove mortal. For the sake of the new enterprise everything must be sold if necessary. We ran up and down, getting what prices we could for jewels, plate, precious manuscripts. Latin historians, French poets, the Fathers of the Church, books of hours and books of profane verses – they followed one another pell-mell to the pawnbroker. Soon nothing was left but what was necessary to make a show, to keep up the illusion of wealth. Meanwhile Sillé rode back and forth, finding buyers for a manor here, a parcel of good agricultural land elsewhere, and borrowing on the security of what he could not sell. Some instinct had made Gilles change his mind, however, about selling what he had in Brittany. It was chiefly possessions in the kingdom of France which he chose to put on the market.

As soon as it came in the money was immediately spent upon the play. The armourer Gilles had brought with him worked full time at providing real suits of armour, of the best make, for the scullions and pastry-cook's apprentices who were to represent the chivalry of France. The tailors of the town worked equally hard to fit them in clothes as fine as those Gilles wore himself.

The guildsmen were not slow to take advantage of his generosity. They soon discovered that their new patron would provide them with anything they told him was necessary to the enterprise. One day a whole delegation of them came to see him with long faces.

'Why do you look so gloomy, gentlemen?' Gilles demanded.

'Messire, it's about the cakes.'

'The cakes?' Gilles echoed mildly. 'As far as I remember we did more fighting than eating when I first came to Orléans.'

'The free cakes, to be given out when the mystery is played.'

'The free wine, too,' added a man whom I knew to be a prosperous vintner, in tones so sepulchral they might have come from his own cellar.

'It is, of course, customary,' added a third.

'They do it very magnificently at Laon,' said the original spokesman.

'Then we must do it better. Certainly what is given out must be worthy of the spectacle we plan to present. Perhaps you will be so kind as to go and see my treasurer, with an estimate of what is needed.'

No estimate thus presented was ever refused.

At last the month of May arrived, and with it the fine weather. I had taught Rossignol his lines, and had felt a strange pang when our sessions were ended, and he went off to join the other actors in rehearsing the piece. However, the child seemed to like my company, and now often sought me out. I looked for him every day and was disappointed when he did not spend a moment or two chattering to me. Now he came to me and said: 'Come, messire Raoul, we must go and look at the scaffolds. The carpenters are putting them up this morning.' Confident that I would go with him immediately, he put his hand into mine.

Long before we reached the place where the performance was to be given we heard the noise of vigorous hammering and sawing. The scaffolds were being built in the dry ditch of the Tourelles earthwork, on the other side of the river. The space was a long oval, like the pictures of Roman circuses I had seen in one of Gilles's books, and in the middle of this an earthen platform had been made, with wickerwork hurdles to hold the earth in place. Around this was a broad pathway, and then, to make the outermost boundary and close the arena in, there was a set of tall scaffolds, with plank floors at different levels.

'Look,' Rossignol explained, 'sometimes we stand up there on the platforms to say our verses, and sometimes they give us a ladder and we come down into the centre. There is a man called "the leader of the mystery", and he stands in the very middle with his book and staff, and reminds us if we forget our words and at the same time tells the public what we are going to do.'

The mystery was so long that it was to be given over several days. When the first of these arrived I made my way through the city streets with Gilles, and crossed the bridge which was already thronged with people. The crowds grew thicker still as we made our way into the arena. Gilles was immediately led to one of the scaffolds, now richly covered with tapestries and silken stuffs I thought I recognised. Some scaffolds were already occupied, others awaited the presence of the actors. These latter were designed so that they could, from time to time, be closed off with curtains.

'I think you should see well from here, messire.'

'What are those?' asked Gilles. He pointed to a boy who carried a large tray. As he moved through the throng he offered its contents to the spectators.

Our guide seemed a little embarrassed. 'Those are the free cakes your worship was kind enough to pay for.'

'May I have one, please?'

The youth was summoned, and a specimen cake was handed up to us. It was an appetising golden colour, and had been baked in a mould stamped with the arms of Rais.

'How nice!' said Gilles, as he bit into it. 'It's almost like eating money.'

Before I could decide what the correct answer to this was, or if, indeed, it needed an answer, the performers marched into the arena, with the leader of the mystery at their head. God the Father and various saints scrambled up into their places, followed by a bevy of angels, amongst whom I recognised many members of the Chapel of the Holy Innocents. Below them, the English, in suitably villainous tones, began to make plans to lay siege to the city.

The first day's performance was nearly over before Rossignol made his entrance. His first scene was as Joan the peasant girl, whose mission is announced to her by the Archangel Michael. Michael was superbly dressed in fluted armour, with a great pair of wings on his shoulders constructed from wire and swan's feathers. Joan was wearing her long red peasant's dress. As she knelt in the centre of the arena there was a sudden hush among the spectators, who had until now been moving round as they pleased and chattering loudly to one another. From beneath one of the scaffolds came the notes of a hidden organ. In the silence which followed, Michael began his speech:

> Fear not, oh gentle Maid!
> For I come from Our Lord.
> Whatever now is said
> Take as His Holy Word . . .

I found myself gazing at Rossignol's slight figure with unexpected intensity. I had to admit that he did not look in the least like the Joan I so vividly remembered. Where her hair had been black and cropped brutally short, his was fair and fell in curling ringlets. Where her complexion had been tanned, his skin was transparently pink and white. Where her body had been strong and sinewy, his gave the impression of being soft and graceful. There was something troubling about his appearance. Far more than Joan, he gave the impression of being androgynous, of possessing the essential qualities of either sex. 'Not a young faun, but a young hermaphrodite!' Gilles muttered in my ear, as the people all around us began to applaud. I cursed him silently for his devilish perspicacity.

The splendour of the spectacle he had contrived, and the enthusiasm with which the spectators received it, put Gilles into a high good humour that evening. But it was the succeeding days which had the most powerful effect on him, for it was on these that the story of his own part in the siege was unfolded. He could scarcely tear his eyes away from the handsome young sergeant who (it must be admitted with a certain stiff self-consciousness) re-enacted his own feats at the Tourelles and later at Patay. The assault on the Tourelles was particularly well done, for here the whole cast left the arena and swarmed over the building itself, performing acrobatic feats which none of us would have dared to attempt when we were in actual peril of our lives. The scene ended with a most convincing bonfire under the Tourelles drawbridge, so that for a moment I feared that it would catch alight in good earnest. Glasdale and those who were with him plunged into the smoke, and in a moment we heard a great cry, and the splash of something heavy falling into the river. But it was only sacks full of stones which had gone to meet their death by drowning, and at the end of the proceedings Glasdale and his comrades reappeared with broad grins and soot on their faces to take a special bow.

The battle of Patay, on the other hand, was nothing like the bloody massacre I still had imprinted on my memory. Nor did Gilles's part in it have the slightest resemblance to what had actually happened. In this version the two armies, the English and the French, made a fine spectacle as they advanced towards one another in ordered ranks, with the trumpeters blowing flourishes from the upper level of the surrounding scaffolds to urge them on to combat. The French side was splendidly arrayed, with the Rais arms so prominent upon their surcoats that anyone would have concluded that these were all the Marshal's men. In truth, most of them were. The men-at-arms Gilles had brought with him to Orléans had most of them been commandeered to add numbers to the spectacle. They, at any rate, looked as if they felt at home with their military accoutrements, whereas many of the other actors were ill at ease, and carried their swords and banners in the oddest fashion. I knew what a handful of good troops would do to such a rabble, were the battle to be fought in earnest, and so too, from the looks on their faces, did the real soldiers interspersed among them. I saw some ill-suppressed mirth in the ranks, and some surreptitious jostling. More than one famous captain was to be seen clutching nervously at the pommel of his saddle, or gripping his horse's mane, as the two armies drew together.

Gilles did not seem to notice any of these details. Patay was what pleased him most in the whole five days that it took to present the mystery. 'What marvellous times we lived through!' he said to me exultantly, 'and how lucky we are to have them recreated thus before our very eyes!'

When the mystery at long last came to an end, it was with a triumphal procession over the bridge, and a service of commemoration in the cathedral. The citizens turned out in crowds to see the actors and the rest of us go by. Naturally Gilles attracted the best of their attention. It was the mummer-Marshal who passed them first, with the genuine article bringing up the rear, surrounded by the glittering escort of his guard. As he turned each corner and came into sight of yet another group of spectators, we could hear the exclamations. 'How handsome he is! How nobly he carries himself! Anyone could tell true from false!' Gilles preened in the sunshine of their admiration.

That night, as he sat alone with me in the solar of our rented mansion, I said: 'There, Gilles! The thing is done, and the Marshal is even more of a hero than he was before to the people of Orléans. Was it worth all the gold it cost?'

Gilles gave me a sly look. 'Who said it was over?' he asked.

'Surely the mystery will not be played again till the next Feast of the Deliverance?'

'It will be played again next week. And again the week after that.'

'For God's sake, why?'

'Because I am paying for it. And because I wish it.'

Gilles's will prevailed, even though he had a tussle with the guildsmen to achieve his end. Their objections were twofold. First that to repeat the mystery out of season was something unheard of. Second that those who took part had their normal lives and occupations to return to. The first objection Gilles simply swept aside, and the second he countered by offering to pay the actors good wages so long as they continued to appear in the play. Where the players were apprentices, as many of them were, then their masters would be handsomely compensated for the temporary loss of their services.

The summer wore on. May became June and June July. Still, week in and week out, the *Mystery of Orléans* continued to be acted in the arena beside the Tourelles. The silks and tapestries that draped the scaffoldings became progressively more faded and tattered, and the way in which the actors delivered their lines more and more careless and lackadaisical. Yet Gilles did not seem to notice this, and almost every day he went to see his own life replayed.

Soon, however, he was the only person of quality to go. The place became a resort for a handful of idlers, who would repeat the verses in chorus with the players, and amuse themselves in other ways by trying to disrupt the course of the play. It was the place to find every rogue and thief in Orléans, especially at the moments when the free cakes continued to be distributed.

The town council was becoming increasingly concerned by the bad reputation the arena was getting, and were trying to get up their courage to tell Gilles that the whole business must be brought to an end, when the mystery was halted in a more dramatic fashion.

It was early morning on a hot July day, and the household at the Golden Cross was just astir. I was leaning out of an upper window, enjoying the sunshine, when I saw and heard a commotion in the street below. A small crowd was following on the heels of two men. One was an official-looking personage in royal livery; the other a trumpeter in a surcoat ornamented with the royal arms. The trumpeter halted directly in front of the doorway of the mansion, and blew a long, deliberate blast. Then his companion pulled a parchment from his sleeve and began to read from it in a loud, bullying voice. He seemed to be directing what he said, not to his increasing throng of auditors, but to the building in front of him. Gradually, as the words drifted up to me, I began to piece together their meaning.

'We, Charles, King of France, by the grace of God . . . forbid . . . Gilles of Laval, Marshal of Rais . . . to sell, pledge or otherwise dispose of . . . territories, movable goods . . . no contract . . . valid . . . with the said Gilles . . . given under our great seal . . . Amboise . . . and hereby witnessed . . .'

As the words rolled unctuously out I understood that our time in Orléans was now over, and that a new phase in all our existences was about to begin. René de La Suze had at last found a most effective way of putting an end to his brother's proceedings.

27

Before we could leave the city, however, there were other dramas to be played out. The most urgent necessity was to find the money for our journey. Gilles's coffers were almost empty, and we had all of us been living from day to day on whatever Sillé could provide. An anxious conference was held in Gilles's room.

'We'll go to Brittany,' he said. 'I can do what I please there. It's outside my grateful sovereign's jurisdiction.'

'Fair enough, messire,' said Sillé. 'But how do I pay for it all? There are debts to be paid here before we go, and more than five hundred men to move to Machecoul.'

A long silence ensued. It was I who broke it by saying: 'Gilles, have you received the act of incorporation for your Chapel of the Holy Innocents?'

'Some time ago. But what does that have to do with our present problem?'

'Get someone to bring the act,' I said.

Sure enough, as I suspected, it turned the chapel into a separate legal entity, capable of holding property.

'I still don't see what you're after,' said Sillé.

'Gilles here cannot even sell an old doublet to get us out of this fix. But there's nothing to prevent the chapel from pawning anything it owns.'

'Such as?'

'What would you say to a pair of golden candelabra?'

The chapel's proudest ornaments, and almost the most beautiful things Gilles owned, were a pair of massive candelabra made of pure gold. They went with him in boxes wherever he travelled, and hung from the ceiling wherever his chapel was set up. Their spreading branches were aflutter with tiny angels, the sculptured likenesses of the children who sang beneath them.

Because the idea had been mine, it was I who was deputed to take them to the banker Lodovico. I waited until it was dark, and the streets were empty, as I knew there would be much curiosity about the movements of Gilles's household on this particular day. The tradesmen had already begun to come in to present their bills, and the plan was that we would begin to pack up before dawn, so as to be out of the city at first light the following morning. With four men behind me to carry the heavy cases, and a guard of four soldiers, I made my way to the house I had visited before. Lodovico opened to us the moment I knocked, as I had already sent a messenger to tell him of my coming.

'Welcome, messire Raoul,' he said, 'but I hope you will forgive me if I say I may now find it difficult to help you. As a stranger here, I have to be even more careful in my dealings than the king's own subjects.'

'First see what I have brought,' I replied. The candelabra were made so that they could be taken to pieces, and I opened one of the boxes and began to put the elaborate structure together. Messire Lodovico stopped me with a gesture.

'I have seen these already, hanging in the Marshal's chapel. They are very fine, but I cannot buy them from you or even take them as a pledge. As his property they are worth nothing after the king's decree.'

'Then let me show you something else,' I said, and pulled out the parchment which contained the act of foundation. 'I seem to remember you have an affection for documents. What you have is the original, but I have also brought with me a certified and notarised copy.'

Messire Lodovico read what I had given him, and read it again. Then he gave me a tight-lipped smile. 'You are a quick student, Raoul.'

'Why do you say that?'

'Last time we met, you objected to my views. But now you are acting according to my own principles. So long as these beautiful things *appear* to have another owner, I am free to lend you money. Shall we put them on the scales, and then I will tell you how much extra I can give for the workmanship? It is not Italian taste, but it has a certain quality.' And he touched one of the little angels with a possessive finger-tip.

As soon as I saw that, I knew I would make a good bargain; and we returned to the Golden Cross even more heavily burdened with gold than we had left it.

Would that I had sought my bed as soon as my task was

accomplished! It was a burning night, too hot to sleep, and in addition I was possessed by a restlessness I would not admit I recognised. I decided to take a last stroll through the narrow streets of Orléans, since I had a premonition that I would not soon see them again. Gradually, however, my footsteps took me closer and closer to a place I had visited far more often than I had the house of the banker Lodovico.

Orléans, like every large town, has a multitude of bath-houses. They are one of the luxuries which mark the difference between city and country living. If you go to a bath-house, you do more than wash yourself. There are tubs of hot and cold water, and also a place where they put large stones, which are first heated red-hot on the fire, and then dowsed with water. This makes a steam which fills the whole of the room and draws the dirt out of the skin better than scrubbing. Respectable bath-houses have separate times of admission for men and for women. As most men know, however, there are other houses with the same apparent purpose which in fact cater for different necessities. They, too, are called 'stews' in the language of the streets, but with a special emphasis. It was towards one of these that I was now making my way.

I have said that at Machecoul I had already felt an upsurge of animal appetites, and had lain with some of the merchants' wives. No doubt I could have continued to find my satisfaction in the same way when I got to Orléans. Yet now the prick of desire was sharper. I did not want to go through even the few ceremonies which had been required of me before. I wanted only to find a willing body and slake my lust upon it. One easy way to deal with my necessity was to go to the bath-house I was now approaching. Its peculiarities were threefold, and shared with all establishments of its sort. First, it catered only to men. Second, the fee for admittance was substantially higher than that charged by more common-place counterparts. And third, each bather was provided with a female attendant.

The shutters were closed when I arrived, but I could see chinks of light and knew from experience that the place would be open for business. I knocked on the door and, after I had been scrutinised for a moment through a peep-hole, was admitted. The room I entered was a kind of ante-room, with curtained cubicles in which to leave one's clothes. Here the illusion of modesty was jealously preserved. In each compartment a small oil-lamp burned. As I undressed, my body threw grotesque shadows on the ceiling – their motions were a mocking rehearsal for what was to happen next. Then I wrapped a large sheet round myself and mounted a few steps to go into the bath-house itself.

There were oil-lamps here, too, casting a glow through the steam, but it was almost too dim for me to see anything, at least at first. As soon as I came in a soft hand touched my arm, and I was aware of a naked female body beside me. Gently her hands divested me of the cloth, though I still had a small napkin tied around my loins, and she led me forward to where the tubs of hot water were placed. In a business-like way she began to wash me; then gradually, but still in a manner which was perfectly matter-of-fact, began to excite me. The long fingers strayed under the napkin and massaged my member, which obediently stood to attention. I touched her breasts and she deftly undid my last covering. They were full, but not pendulous, the breasts of a woman who has not yet had children. Responding to my gestures she turned to present her back to me, and the next instant I was taking her dog-fashion.

As our flesh slapped together I was intensely aware that we were not the only couple enjoying this pleasure. The room was full of dimly perceived bodies coupling in various permutations. A grossly fat man loomed up in front of my partner, and she bent over still further to take his penis in her mouth.

As I walked home through streets and alleys which were now almost entirely deserted, finding my way thanks to the full moon which had risen above the rooftops, I wondered why I found this kind of experience so exciting – to the point where I was lured back again and again to the same establishment, though each time I went I vowed that this must be the last occasion. Now that the last occasion had finally come, its finality was not of my choosing. Had we remained in Orléans, I would have continued to go to the place. Tonight, as I moved away from it, I felt a kind of numb shame which overlaid but did not disguise the satisfaction of physical appetite. But was the appetite itself as purely physical as I pretended? Did I not find, amid the steam of the bath-house, a cruder version of what I had so often found during my life with Gilles: the pleasure of seeing events taken to some uncontrolled extreme – so uncontrolled, indeed, that I could continue to feel detached from them?

When I arrived at the Golden Cross the house was dark and apparently silent. I knocked, and at last a surly porter appeared who seemed reluctant to let me in. 'We thought you had gone out for the night, messire,' he said accusingly, holding the door open but still barring the way with his arm. I could see beyond his shoulder, in the moonlight that flooded the inner courtyard, boxes and bundles already stacked up for the morrow's departure. And now I could hear the stirring and stamping of horses in the stables, as if they already knew we would soon be making a journey. Impatiently, I pushed the man aside and went in.

Like many large town mansions, this one was built round a pair of courtyards. At the back of the first courtyard stood the high range of buildings which contained the great hall and the lord's living quarters. Though no lights showed, I had the feeling that people were astir within it. Somewhere just on the threshold of hearing I seemed to catch the sound of muffled droning or chanting. On impulse, I crossed the courtyard, towards the door of the hall. The porter followed me. I was aware now not merely that he wanted to conceal something, but that he was afraid. In fact, I could smell the stink of fear coming from his flesh. 'What d'you want to go in there for?' he whined. 'Anyway, it's locked.' I tried the handle, and sure enough it was. I shrugged my shoulders and began to make my way to my own quarters, which were in a lower building at right angles to this one. As I turned on my heel, I thought I caught a sigh of relief from the spot where the porter still stood.

It was this sigh of relief that perhaps decided me. The Golden Cross was a house built at many epochs, and the rooms communicated with one another in strange and unexpected ways, often by means of staircases within the thickness of the walls. When I decided to rent the place for Gilles, the landlady had insisted on showing me all these different routes. 'Why, it's fit for a king!' she exclaimed. 'He could keep his mistress here, and no one would ever know!' It would be easy enough to make my way into the hall-range and find out what had made the porter so anxious.

I found a rush-light in my chamber, and lit it. Shielding the flame with my hand I began to travel the circuitous route I had already mapped out in my head. The landlady had thoughtfully provided me with an extra bunch of keys – 'Just so you can keep an eye on things for me,' she told me, with a roguish wink – and it was these that I used to unlock the numerous doors I encountered. Many of these were hidden behind the tapestries, and I suspect their existence had remained unknown to the rest of the household. The locks, at any rate, were so stiff that I surmised they had not been turned since my initial tour of the house.

Gradually, with many changes of level, I approached the solar that lay behind the hall, coming towards it from the other side. I knew that the last staircase I took would lead me down in a tight corkscrew spiral to a cramped storehouse, once perhaps an oratory, which was never used, and thence through a low door beside the fireplace and into the solar itself.

When I reached the store-room, I paused. The sound of chanting was now definitely audible, though I could not distinguish the words. But odour as well as sound came seeping into the space. The mingling of scents was so complex that I was hard put to it to identify them all – there was the bitter tang of myrrh, for instance, and the sweet, slightly oily smell of sandalwood, together with a vinegary scent which was either vinegar itself or the lees of wine, and finally there was the unmistakable odour of burning sulphur.

At this moment I should have turned back. It was the last instant at which I could have said: 'The knowledge which will come of this is not for me'. But I have never been able to refuse knowledge. I was drawn towards the door that led to the solar as irresistibly as I had been drawn towards the bath-house earlier that evening. Silently I moved towards it and pressed my ear to the crack. What was being chanted was now clear, though I still did not recognise the voice:

'By the dreadful Day of Judgement, by the Sea of Glass which is before the face of the Divine Majesty, by the four Beasts before the Throne, having eyes before and behind, by the Fire which is about the Throne, by the Holy Angels of heaven and the Mighty Wisdom of God.

'By the Seal of Basdathea, by the name Primematum which Moses uttered and the earth opened and swallowed up Corah, Dathan and Abiram, answer all my demands and perform all that I desire. Come peaceably, visibly and without delay!'

At this point the dust in the room and the sulphur seeping through the door-crack combined in my nostrils to produce a mighty and irresistible sneeze. The chanting voice stumbled to a halt, and another voice asked urgently: 'Is he come? Is he here? What do you see?' This speaker I had no difficulty in identifying. It was Gilles. I turned the key in the lock and entered the solar.

Immediately I found myself enveloped by a swirling cloud of fumes and smoke, thicker, even, than the steam in the bath-house. My eyes watered and I began to choke. As I coughed, the light in my hand guttered and went out in the foul atmosphere. I moved to one of the windows, flung it open, and leaned out of it, gulping down great draughts of the night air outside.

When the smoke in the room had cleared a little, I turned back to look at what was going on. In the four corners were four braziers, still pouring out their fumes. In the middle, an elaborate circular design had been drawn on the floorboards in red paint. Here stood a fifth, smaller brazier, also smoking, and the area within the circle was scattered with bunches of wilting herbs. A black cock squawked and fluttered, blundering sightlessly from one wall to another – sightlessly because its eyes had been put out. In the midst of the circle stood two men. One, the taller of the pair, was Eustache Blanchet, dressed in priest's robes and with a wooden wand held in his right hand. He gaped at me in a dazed kind of way, like a man just roused from sleep. The other was Gilles, whose expression was a mixture of amusement, disappointment, irritation, and – yes – a tinge of malice.

'Ah, Raoul,' he said urbanely, 'you are always welcome, but you have spoilt our incantation. Or are you by any chance the demon whom we have been trying to conjure up?'

28

Why did I stay with Gilles after I discovered that he was a practitioner of the Black Art? I knew that every day I remained with him put my soul more dangerously in peril. Looking back, I find I have excuses, but not reasons, for my actions. Inertia and habit, for example, kept me at Gilles's side – I had spent the major part of my life with him, and now my wife was dead there seemed no other place to go. Then, too, there was a heavy indifference in my spirit which seemed to put it already beyond the reach of good or evil. This indifference was ruffled by few emotions. One, as I have hinted, was a strange curiosity, always eager for the next event, yet willing to find it trivial and meaningless as soon as it arrived. The other emotion, in this case, was relief. There was something about Gilles's personality which had increasingly oppressed me. Here was a plausible explanation for this sensation. It was the more acceptable because, though I knew the Black Art to be evil, Gilles's involvement with it seemed not only unsuccessful but ridiculous. Because I so often found it risible, it did not appear to threaten me.

When we returned to Machecoul from Orléans, it was not to take up the old way of life. News had already reached the little colony of merchants that the once magnificent and spendthrift Marshal was now in need of funds. Since there was no more profit to be had, they packed their baggage and departed. The Machecoul peasants would no doubt have liked to follow the example set them by their betters, but had no opportunity to do so. Gilles, who up till then had been a comparatively just and merciful lord, now began to follow the tactics which had once been pursued by his grandfather at Champtocé, and to squeeze his tenants for every sou that could be extracted from them. The men of the garrison ceased to be idle ornaments, but rode out almost daily to see what pickings could be found, Their fine accoutrements settled into comfortable shabbiness.

Though their discipline continued to be lax, laxer certainly than Jean de Craon would have permitted in his day, the men seemed more contented with their lot. They preferred bullying peasants to making an exhibition of themselves in the *Mystery of Orléans*.

Sillé, too, changed under the stress of the new dispensation. Our shabbiness was now a match for his, and it was he who usually took charge of the garrison's forays into the countryside, and showed a finely tuned judgement as to how much pressure could be applied to any particular tenant, without either crippling him physically or encouraging him to run away. As his spirits revived he grew more arrogant, and it was against me, in particular, that this arrogance was directed.

'My poor friend,' he said to me one day, 'do you mean to tell me that you managed to remain ignorant all this while of Gilles's traffickings with the devil? Don't you remember when he and I used to go off and stay for a month at a time in Angers? It wasn't merely for the opportunity to do interesting things to each other in bed.'

'No, you could do those at Champtocé,' I retorted.

'There was a knight imprisoned at that time in Angers castle on suspicion of sorcery. We used to go and see him in his cell. It was he who showed Gilles a book he had had smuggled in to him. It was full of incantations.'

'So that was when it all started.'

'In a manner of speaking.'

'But so far the incantations have been without success, if all messire Blanchet could manage to conjure up was me.'

'Complacency has always been your fault, Raoul,' said Sillé curtly, and turned his back. I congratulated myself on having been able to score off him so easily.

It was true that Gilles seemed dissatisfied with the results of his magical experiments. He now searched for new necromancers as obsessively as he had once looked for new splendours with which to adorn his chapel, or new ways of elaborating the *Mystery of Orléans*. Perhaps influenced by the fiasco in which I had played an unwitting part, he decided that the priest Blanchet did not have the gifts necessary to make a successful magician. Nevertheless he kept him in his service, and now employed him to hunt for other practitioners of the same art. New candidates were continually presenting themselves at the gates of the castle, but each in turn was tried and found wanting. I was often invited to be present at their conjurations, and found them the more doleful and ludicrous every time I attended one of their ceremonies. The only one who impressed me at all was a kind of hedge-priest in a tattered habit whose claim to magical skills seemed so improbable that Gilles only allowed him to try his luck because he was bored and restless on the day the man arrived.

The hedge-priest proved no more successful than the others in achieving the wished-for results, and Gilles dismissed him with thinly veiled contempt but nevertheless with a handsome present. To his surprise the man, who seemed near to starvation, returned the purse he had been negligently given after taking from it a single coin.

'This is for my journey, messire,' he said, 'and it is enough for those who travel through the world as I do. The rest I do not deserve, since I have not been able to accomplish what you desired.'

The man intrigued me, so I made a point of waylaying him as he made his way out. 'Let me ride a little way with you,' I said. 'The soldiers of this place are not always as courteous as they should be to their master's guests.'

'Thank you for your kindness,' said the priest, as he climbed on to the back of an old mule as bony and dilapidated as he was himself. 'But I fear your beast will find it hard work to go as slowly as mine. If he gets impatient, leave me. We must be kind to animals too.'

We went a little way without talking, riding along the tops of the dykes. After we had gone about a quarter of a league, my companion said in a neutral tone: 'You wished to ask me something, of course.'

'Yes,' I admitted.

'Why? You have just seen me fail in the art I claim to practise. And I think you do not much believe in it in any case.'

'In general, that is true. But I think you are nearer to having a talent than any magician I have yet met.'

My companion hesitated, then bent his head over the neck of his shambling beast, muttering something I could not catch.

'What was that?'

'I said the gift comes and goes as it pleases. We can never be sure of it.'

'And it deserted you at Machecoul.'

'I am not a true summoner of demons, but usually I can get people to see what I want them to see.'

'But not the Marshal of Rais?'

'He seeks for demons when they already dwell within him. I had no power over him, but feared he would have power over me.'

I would have thought longer about this somewhat disturbing conversation had I not found Gilles in a state of great excitement when I got back to the castle.

'Excellent news!' he cried. 'That wretched fraud must have brought a little luck with him after all! My brother has been turned out of Champtocé, and my men there have succeeded in catching Michel de Fontenay.'

'Michel de Fontenay?' I echoed.

'Surely you remember? He was the priest who beat me so unmercifully when I was a child. You saw him when he brought me to my grandfather. Don't you recall how the captain of the guard gave his mule a great thwack on the rump and sent it bolting off over the drawbridge? And how much we laughed to see him nearly fall out of the saddle?'

'He must be an old man now.'

'Oh, he still has enough life in him to suffer a little,' said Gilles, his tone hardening. 'Even if I'd forgiven what he did to me years ago I have another score to settle with him.'

'Indeed?' I said, my heart sinking, as I knew that to meddle with a venerable and respected cleric would bring us all nothing but trouble. Times had changed since the days of Jean de Craon. Soon after we had left Orléans, for example, the king had signed the long-awaited peace with the Duke of Burgundy at Arras, and the royal authority was once again being felt almost throughout France. But Gilles seemed unconcerned about all this.

'It was Fontenay who presided at Champtocé when they read the letters forbidding me to sell my lands. He and René and the rest – they want to turn me into a child again.'

If Gilles was heedless at first of the kind of scrape he had now got himself into, he was soon to be made aware of what he had done. The road to Machecoul was suddenly thronged, not with practitioners of the Black Art, but with delegates from the University of Angers, with emissaries from the bishop, and finally with men bearing summonses from the king. The tone in which these were written was by no means conciliatory.

Soon Gilles was forced to relinquish his prey, and Michel de Fontenay was released, a little shaken perhaps, but not really the worse for his experience. Gilles himself became increasingly irritable after this check. He took to accompanying Sillé when the latter rode out to remind the local peasants of the duty they owed to their lord, and some of the stories the men-at-arms brought back with them were rather ugly. Even my by-now hardened conscience was pricked.

It was fortunate that a diversion arrived, in the person of yet another magician. Jean de La Rivière was one of Blanchet's discoveries, and the two of them made a strange contrast. Where Blanchet was tall, La Rivière was short, with a consider-able corpulence and tiny hands and feet. He was not a priest, but a doctor, and claimed to have studied medicine at the best Italian universities, at Padua and at Salerno. He had a honeyed tongue and Gilles was instantly delighted with him.

At once he started making plans for a new series of evocations. Meanwhile La Rivière bustled round the castle, a notebook in his hand and an ink-horn in his belt, making his notes and calculations for the work to come. The garrison was at least partly aware of his activity, and some of them made a practice of greeting his appearance with derisive whistles. La Rivière would ruffle his feathers and stick his nose in the air, without deigning to reply to these rude greetings. 'If that stuck-up little doctor is a friend of Satan,' the captain of the guard remarked to me, 'then I have no fear of hell-fire.'

Perhaps because of the persecutions the men-at-arms subjected him to, La Rivière eventually announced to Gilles that the atmosphere of Machecoul was not suitable for his purpose, and that this was why previous magicians had so consistently failed to produce results. 'Of course, if they had known their craft,' he said disdainfully, 'they would have known from the start that the place is too full of watery humours. The beings with whom we wish to converse are creatures of fire, and the opposite element is inimical to them. Air and fire are what we need, not earth and water.'

'The sweet air of Champtocé,' commented Sillé when he heard of this, twisting his face into the cynical grimace which was now habitual to him, 'and the warm hearth-fires of Angers. I think our learned doctor is starting to be a little home-sick for civilisation.'

If La Rivière had hoped to engineer a return to the softer regions on the other side of the Loire, he was to be cruelly disappointed. Gilles accepted his proposal that the ceremonies should be held elsewhere with enthusiasm. 'We will go to Pouzauges,' he declared, 'the remotest of all my castles. It is time the people there had a visit from their liege lord.'

The ceremony was to be held at the autumn equinox and September had already begun. So once again there was that hasty packing of baggage which had become so familiar a part of our life with Gilles, and we set off for our chosen destination. Our route lay along the course of the Sèvre – first to Clisson, and then to Gilles's massive castle of Tiffauges. It was the first time I had seen this fortress, and the sight of it struck me with an uneasiness I could not explain. Its massive walls crowned a bluff above the river, and encircled a court-yard which was almost as big as the area covered by the two main encientes at Chinon. Tiffauges was a truly royal possession, but its atmosphere was mournful and sinister. I was glad that we were only to stay there for one night.

My feelings of disquiet were partly confirmed by an incident which took place during our stay. Though he had taken fewer people with us than usual, since accommodation at Pouzauges was said to be limited, Gilles had insisted that we bring with us some of the children of his chapel. 'I must have some of my innocents with me, to divert me with their music when I am sad,' he said, in a tone which permitted no further argument. Rossignol was one of the children chosen to come with us, and another was a fragile, pretty boy called Jeannot, who had only recently entered Gilles's service. In the morning Jeannot was missing.

I had slept heavily that night, as heavily as I sometimes did at Machenoul in the days when we first came there, and when I made my appearance in the morning the others were already almost ready to depart. It was then that I noticed the boy was no longer with us. I suggested that someone be sent to search the children's sleeping quarters, to make sure the boy had not overslept as I had done myself. One of the servants shrugged, and went off with dragging feet to undertake the task. A moment later, too soon for him to have looked with any thoroughness, he returned to say there was no sign of the child.

'Why not send a messenger into the village,' I suggested, 'and ask if anyone has seen him there?'

An awkward silence ensued, which was finally broken by Gilles himself.

'Oh come!' he said harshly. 'We can't hang about all day waiting for a stupid child. Either he's run off, in which case good riddance, or the men here will send him on to us if he turns up.' With this, he gave the signal for the cavalcade to move off. In the back of my mind stirred the memory of the apprentice whom Sillé had once sent to take a message to Tiffauges, and who had never been seen again.

After Tiffauges, the character of the landscape changed, and became increasingly wild and hilly. The hills were criss-crossed by hedges which divided even the steepest slopes into fields, and groves of trees crowned the summit of each hill. Though we had not yet reached the middle of autumn, a keen wind had begun to blow, and we felt it more as we climbed higher.

Pouzauges, when we reached it, was a small stone-built town, the biggest we had yet encountered in the region, but still hardly bigger than a large village. Its houses clung to the side of an exceptionally steep hill, and the castle stood, not at the top, but at a point before the summit. The crest of the hill was crowned by one of those groves we had already seen elsewhere, but one with memorably tall and beautiful trees.

'See,' said Rossignol to me as we dismounted, 'they couldn't build the castle any higher up, because the old ones didn't want it.'

'Why do you say that?' I asked.

'I can feel them watching us.'

Tease him as I might, he refused to be laughed out of his fantasy.

The people of the town turned out into the streets to see us pass, and from their expressions of curiosity, it was evident that it was a long time since they had received a visit from a great lord. Gilles was at once put into a good mood by the amount of attention we received, and this mood was not shaken by the sight of the castle itself. This had been built simply for defence, with no thought of commodity. It consisted of an enclosure fenced in by strong walls, with a few bastions at the weaker spots. On the side towards the town there was a small, square keep of archaic aspect, with a large chamber on each of three floors. There was a staircase in one corner turret, and a set of garde-robes in another.

Our first night, heaped up together in a single room, wrapped in our cloaks and with saddles and saddle-bags for pillows, was so uncomfortable that we all of us, I think, felt thankful that our stay was not to be of long duration. The ceremony was planned for the next evening. Meanwhile Gilles, to conceal the true purpose of our visit, busied himself with the castle accounts, with inspecting the equipment of the garrison, and with doing justice to the people of the town – in fact, with all the traditional duties he could so seldom be bothered with at home.

It was late afternoon before La Rivière decided he had need of a curiass and then, because of his stoutness, none could be found to fit him. The fashionable wasp-waisted Milanese armour of our own men-at-arms was something he could not get into at all. Eventually, after much searching, an old-fashioned breastplate and backplate were found in the castle stores. With the aid of new straps these could just be fitted round him, though a great gap was left at each side where the soft flesh could be seen bulging through.

'If he was an oyster I'd throw him away,' commented the castle armourer, after all the adjustments had been completed. 'The ones that gape open before you even take a knife to them are the ones that make you sick.'

'And where are you going to talk to the devil, messire doctor?' enquired the irrepressible Rossignol. 'Here in the castle, where we all of us can see him?' La Rivière flushed, and made an instinctive gesture as if to box the boy's ears. The pinching of his curiass, however, seemed to restore him to prudence. The sweat broke out on his forehead and in a subdued voice he asked us to leave him alone for an hour or so, in order to prepare himself for the ceremony. Soon afterwards, I saw him pacing the ramparts and looking increasingly often towards the grove which crowned the top of the hill. Behind it, the sun was just beginning to set.

29

The sun had long dipped behind the high curve of the summit when we set out from the castle. We were a strange-looking party – the elegant Gilles, myself, the two magicians La Rivière and Blanchet, the ever-obnoxious Henriet and Poitou, and last of all Rossignol, who had finally obtained permission to come by threatening to climb over the walls and follow us. Four impassive men-at-arms were paraded to act as our body-guards.

La Rivière had insisted that we were to walk to the spot where the invocation was to take place, perhaps because he did not fancy trying to manage a horse in the dark once he was strapped into his ill-fitting curiass. It was one of the soldiers who went in front, holding a sputtering torch, and after him stepped the doctor, panting a little with the effort of the climb and holding a drawn sword in his right hand and a little shield in his left. The rest of us followed in no sort of order, with the other three soldiers bringing up the rear. As we climbed, the sky seemed to lighten, and as we approached the skirts of the wood we saw that the sunset, after all, was not entirely over. The hill on which Pouzauges was built was the last of a range, and from its crest the land dropped downward to a vast plain. On the farthest rim of this the last sliver of the sun's disc could still be seen, but almost as soon as we arrived it vanished, leaving only an afterglow of green rays, rising up like the ribs of a huge scallop shell.

With a gesture, La Rivière brought us to a halt. 'We must wait here,' he said, 'until the day has gone entirely. The creatures of the night will not consent to make their appearance while the sun still lingers.' We did not have to wait long. The conflagration in the west burnt itself out with astonishing suddenness.

'You still cannot go forward,' announced the fat little doctor.

'The risk is mine. Stay for me here at the edge of the wood. Do not come further than this, whatever you hear.' I was standing next to him, and it seemed to me, in the hazy light of a three-quarter moon, that I could see the pearls of sweat once more beginning to roll down his face. He turned on his heel, and with his naked sword pointed in front of him, vanished into the darkness of the grove.

I don't know how long we waited huddled together in a group on the outskirts of the wood. Though it seemed like much longer, perhaps it was half the time that an hourglass takes to run. Then came the sound of an unearthly cry. Every nerve in me shudderingly responded. My right hand felt a smaller hand creep within the palm, as if for shelter, and nestle there. Rossignol. At the identical moment my gaze fastened on Gilles's dimly visible profile, and saw how the upper lip lifted to show the teeth, in a wolfish spasm. The tension broke. 'Oh, it's only an owl!' the boy murmured beside me, at the same time withdrawing his fingers from my clasp, as if ashamed of the impulse that brought them there.

As if the owl's screech had been a signal, uproar immediately broke out in the heart of the wood – incoherent cries, and the noise of metal clashing on metal. La Rivière came stumbling out to us as if pursued, with a great dint in his shield and his hand flung up in front of his face. 'The leopard! The leopard!' he babbled, and collapsed in an untidy heap at our feet.

On the way back to the castle, with the doctor trailing behind us, half-supported by the soldiers and ministered to by the hangdog Blanchet, Gilles fell into step beside me. 'At least he had the grace to try and give me a good performance,' he said in a low, carefully neutral tone which seemed to mask a great weariness.

'Give up the search, Gilles,' I said urgently.

'So you've felt it too,' he countered, almost in a murmur.

'Nothing happened. Isn't that the point?'

'But you were convinced something was about to happen, till that rogue started caterwauling and banging his sword on his shield? You felt it growing, like something inside you?'

'Yes, I did,' I admitted sullenly. I still felt hanging in the air the sense of some momentary change in the natural order of things, like the tingling of the skin I sometimes experienced after a thunderstorm.

Perhaps without the disturbing sense of a brush with the supernatural the thing which happened later that night would not have taken place. The keep at Pouzauges, when we returned to it, seemed a more uncomfortable place to sleep in than ever. The wind was now blowing at gale force and it rattled the ill-fitting shutters. Icy fingers of could air seemed to seek us out wherever we lay. Rossignol had placed himself beside me, instead of sleeping in a puppyish heap in a corner with the other boys, which was what he had done on the previous evening, and I offered him a share of the warm cloak I had had the forethought to bring with me. He pulled a corner of it over himself, and seemed to go to sleep contentedly enough. I, on the other hand, remained wakeful, and lay on my back for a while listening to his light, regular inhalations and to the snores of the others lying around me.

After this, I too must have slept for a while, for the next thing I knew was that I had woken, to find myself no longer in the same position, but resting on my side, with Rossignol pressed closely against me, his back touching my chest, and the rest of him fitting closely into the curve made by my body. I was at once keenly aware of his mixture of strength and delicacy, of the fine architecture of his childish bones and the fine texture of his young flesh, even through the thicknesses of clothing that separated us. He stirred and sighed, pushing his backside more firmly against me, and I felt a fire beginning to burn in my groin. My sex stiffened and pressed urgently against the fabric that constrained it.

Rossignol stirred again, and this time I knew what he was doing was deliberate. With stealthy movements he undid the points of his hose. When the last lace was loosened, he paused, as if to see how I would respond. When I did not stir, his hand crept to my thighs and began to loosen my garment as well as his own. With fierce eagerness my rod came bursting out of its confinement. The boy turned fully towards me and his fingers closed briefly round its root and afterwards caressed its tip, as if to make sure of its condition of readiness. Then, with langourous slowness he once more presented his back.

I could not have refused to penetrate him if all God's saints had appeared in the room and forbidden me to do so. I am largely built, and I felt his brief spasm as I first possessed him, but then he twisted a little and made a reciprocal movement which was an unmistakable command to continue. It was part of the erotic quality of the moment that there were other people all around us, and that each thrust, which longed to be violent, must still be as slow and unobtrusive as possible. Any doubts I might once have entertained about Rossignol's past or present role in Gilles's household were dissipated. Yet even before the act was over, I felt my heart beginning to fill with a doomed, melancholy passion for him.

It was perhaps foolish to imagine that the night's proceedings would remain unknown, however stealthily we took our satisfaction. The others may not have noticed, but Gilles certainly knew. He did not allude to the matter, but from the time we rose the next morning there was a subtle change in his attitude towards me. He henceforth took a rather cruel pleasure in parading his amours in front of me, caressing Poitou and Henriet in my presence, and discussing with them the sexual skills of his other 'innocents'. Underlying these remarks, though never directly expressed in them, there was always the threat that he would deprive me of Rossignol and return him to his former duties. I, who had so long enjoyed a kind of quasi-independence from Gilles and his caprices, was now no longer free.

For the time being, however, these manoeuvrings were pushed aside by the grave news that reached us as we were on our way back to Machecoul. Sillé, who had been left in charge of the castle in Gilles's absence, reported that he had received a surprise visit from the Duke of Britanny, almost as soon as we had left the place, and that the duke had insisted on receiving an oath of fidelity from Sillé himself, as acting captain. 'I hear,' Sillé added in his letter, 'that the duke has now gone to most of the other places that belong to you within his dominions, and has exacted the same oath. My belief is that he has got wind of some new proceedings on the part of your brother, and means to forestall him by seeing to it that, if the apples fall from the tree when it is shaken, they fall to his own dukedom and not to some other power.'

30

We had to wait some time for the blow to fall. In the floods of February, René de La Suze returned to Champtocé and seized possession of it. Gilles greeted the event with a theatrical display of rage which, knowing him as I did, I was convinced was hollow. The loss of Champtocé was followed, not by preparations to win it back, though Gilles still kept a considerable number of men-at-arms in his service, but by agitated and apparently purposeless activity within Machecoul itself. There was a great scrubbing of rooms and changing round of apartments throughout the spring and summer, almost as if the place was being made ready for new occupants. The only person who was not encouraged to take an interest in all this work was myself. I noticed that Gilles was continually inventing excuses to get me out of the way, and very often he would tell Rossignol to accompany me, using the child as a kind of lure to get me to do what he wanted.

I took the bait he offered willingly, and looked forward to the nights I spent with the boy at one or other of Gilles's lesser castles – at Saint-Etienne-de-Mermorte, a few leagues away, at Le Lorroux-Bottereau, or at Pornic on the sea-coast, where the fortress dominated a fishing village where nothing but the Breton tongue was spoken. Seeing these mighty buildings it was hard to believe that the splendid Marshal of Rais was now a man on the very brink of financial ruin, unable to pay his garrisons regularly, offering cheer in the hall which varied from feast to fast not according to the progression of the religious year, but according to the amount of money Sillé had been able to scrape together from the few money-lenders still willing to do business with a man who was known to be in desperate straits.

Luckily, the money from my own small fief continued to come in, though in reduced quantity since I had neglected my lands for so long. This gave me a limited freedom, and made me shut my eyes to the signs of ruin which existed all around me. Besides, I had little inclination to think of anything else but Rossignol. The relationship gave me a mixture of pain and joy. The pain came from the knowledge that the boy would soon be grown, and that when he grew our special kind of tenderness must inevitably come to an end. Even more acutely, it came from the knowledge of what Rossignol had been before he came into my hands. This child, who seemed so spontaneous and innocent, who delighted me by the freshness of his reactions to everything and everyone, must nevertheless contain, however well-hidden, a small seed of corruption.

Our attitudes towards those we love with the love of the body are often expressed most truthfully without the use of words. My love-making with Rossignol was not gentle. It was as if, each time I took him, I had to compensate for the constraints of our first night together. He accepted this physical harshness without complaint, indeed, there were even signs that he tried to provoke me into it. When, sometimes, I uncovered him in the morning light, and saw the bruises I had made, I began to fear my own nature. He, at these moments, was never more sweetly tender and affectionate.

One day we returned to Machecoul from Pornic to find the castle had received two unexpected visitors. Not the least unexpected thing about them was that they were middle-aged women. The Dame de Jarville and Madame d'Arraguin were connections of Sillé, distant cousins upon his father's side. They laid claim to the hospitality of Machecoul apparently without the least suspicion that it might be refused to them, and imposed themselves so confidently that no one dared to point out that they were far from welcome. At dinner, they sat at the high table with Gilles and matched him cup for cup, and during the rest of the time they wandered around the castle sticking their sharp noses into everything. You would find them in the kitchen, bothering the cooks; and in the stables, interviewing the stableboys about the health of the animals. They cawed and chattered together like a pair of rooks, and the resemblance was increased by the fact that, being widows, they both of them wore the coif and dressed in black. Widowhood, indeed, they regarded as being the highest estate of woman. The ideal, according to them, was to have achieved marriage, but to be free of its responsibilities.

Their attitude to their relative Sillé was that of a pair of meddling aunts. They would never leave him alone, and dogged his footsteps as he went about his duties. To my suppressed amusement he was reduced to the condition of a sulky schoolboy, unable to resist their demands, yet loth to comply with them.

One day the Dame de Jarville said to him: 'We see you've been clearing out the lower room of the tower beside the great hall.' The tone implied that he had been trying to conceal something. 'A curious job for a man who isn't a servant,' Madame d'Arraguin commented. 'Why doesn't your friend Gilles get himself a housekeeper? Perhaps one of us could do with the job.' They both cackled with malicious amusement, and Sillé seemed to think for a moment that they had done with the subject. But this was by no means the case.

'I think we'll come along and see if you're throwing out anything useful,' announced the Dame de Jarville.

'We're only dealing with some builder's rubbish. It's due to be burnt – that's all it's good for,' said Sillé, a note of desperation in his voice.

'Nonsense! I already saw a perfectly good chest coming out of there. You men are so wasteful. You never know what's useful and what isn't.'

'We insist on coming along. We're bound to find some pickings,' added Madame d'Arraguin.

'Otherwise we'll find out where you've dumped the stuff and go through it all afterwards. Much better to look now. We might upset the men, if we happened to ask about it.' This apparently innocuous comment inspired both the ladies to a further bout of sniggering. Sillé's mouth set in a tight line. 'I'm afraid there's no room for you in the tower,' he said, as if to settle the argument. But this apparently was the response his tormentors had been waiting for. 'Oh, we *know* that!' they cawed in delighted unison. Then the Dame de Jarville moved in swiftly for the kill.

'But we did find this little window, didn't we, Jeanette?'

'We did indeed.'

'It's a bit high up. But it gives quite a good view.'

'We took it in turns. One of us had to hold the other.'

'Which was a trifle tiring.'

'So we thought . . .'

'You might be kind enough to lend us a ladder,' the Dame de Jarville concluded triumphantly. 'Then we could be sure of spotting anything we wanted.'

Sillé's expression was one of mingled fear and rage, which seemed to me an over-reaction to the trick they had played on him. Nevertheless, later in the day I saw one of the men-at-arms carring a stout ladder in the direction of the tower.

The rubbish which was burnt after this particular bout of house-cleaning seemed to contain a high proportion of animal bones, and the stink of them hung over Machecoul for several days. The evil smell did, however, bring one advantage in its wake. It performed an act of exorcism which had until then seemed impossible. No sooner did they sniff it in the wind than the two widows decided to take their departure. When they made their farewells, I thought they were, for them, a little subdued.

The castle received no more visitors until late in November, and when they arrived they too came unexpectedly. René de La Suze and his allies had now been inactive for so long that Gilles was lulled into false security. He passed the time in his usual pattern of activities. He and Sillé squeezed the local peasantry for as much as they could provide. He dallied with Henriet and Poitou, and listened to the children sing. And he sent out occasional emissaries in search of really well-accredited magicians, though these, for some reason, were reluctant to come forward. Gilles seemed to have tried all the existing stock, and to have found them wanting.

One blustery night I was roused from sleep by a grating sound above my head. The chamber into which I had been moved as a result of recent changes at Machecoul was in the top of one of the towers, and in the ceiling there was a trap-door which led by means of a ladder to the roof and the parapet walk. This trap-door was now being levered up. Almost as soon as I realised what was happening, the catch broke and it sprang open, and a man dropped heavily into the room. An arm was extended to him from above, and from it he took an already kindled torch. As he held this up I recognised that it was René de La Suze. At the same instant René recognised me.

'I'm sorry to disturb your slumbers, messire Raoul,' he said, 'though equally sorry to see that you have acquired some of my brother's habits,' and his glance indicated Rossignol, who was struggling into wakefulness beside me.

'Why are you here?' I asked, gaping at him.

'To take possession of the heritage my brother squanders so stupidly,' said René. Then looking upward, he called: 'It's all right, men. No resistance. You can come down.' At once the room was filled with a rush of soldiers. The next moment, however, it was empty again as they found the door and clattered their way down the stairs.

'What was that?' asked Rossignol timorously.

'The castle has been attacked by messire Gilles's brother.'

'Will we be killed?'

'No. All they want is to see the back of us. Pull on your clothes and come with me to the rear postern.'

As we crossed the courtyard I saw desultory fighting, but it was evident that the garrison did not have their hearts in it, and were putting up some kind of resistance only for honour's sake. Most of the inhabitants of the castle had evidently had the same idea as ourselves and were crowding towards the postern-gate. Among them was Gilles, wrapped in a great cloak, beneath which he appeared to be naked.

'Can't we fight them, Raoul?' he asked.

'Not a chance. Anyway they don't want to kill us. Why tempt them into it?'

'I could speak to my brother.'

'Do you want to conduct a family quarrel in front of a rabble of men-at-arms?'

Gilles did not reply to this, but bowed his head in acquiescence.

'Where to now?' asked someone. 'It's impossible to get at the horses.' Indeed, we could see the invaders already beginning to lead them out of the stables.

'We could go by boat to Saint-Etienne-de-Mermorte,' I suggested.

'There are no boats here.' This time I recognised the voice of the captain of the guard, whose duty it had been to protect us.

'There are plenty in the village,' I said impatiently. So a motley group of us – children, priests, men-at-arms, scullions – began to make our way along the muddy canal-bank in the direction I had indicated. A heavy rain beat in our faces, and soaked us to the skin.

When we reached the point where the village wherries were moored, and started to untie them, there was a great clamour from the local curs, who had detected the presence of intruders. Soon the villagers who lived nearest the mooring came running from their huts to investigate what was happening. There was just enough light for them to see what was going on, though it took a moment or two for them to recognise who we were. When they did, and when they saw the state we were in, this, instead of quietening them, seemed to arouse a passionate hostility.

'It's the monster of Machecoul!' shouted an anonymous voice in the darkness.

'All right! Here's a chance to show what you think of him!' cried another. A fistful of mud came sailing towards us, and caught Gilles full in the face. This early success seemed to encourage our assailants, and soon all of us were thoroughly splattered. The mud began to be followed by stones.

'Let's deal with one or two of them,' said a man-at-arms who stood close to me, facing about and raising his sword-point menacingly.

'No!' I put my hand on his arm. I suspected that in a moment or two all the inhabitants of the village would be roused. It was likely their mood would be the same as that of the men who were now attacking us. We were not in a condition to put up much resistance, even to these peasants.

As the flotilla of boats at last drifted free, and out of range of the missiles, I thought that Gilles's fortunes must now at last have reached their lowest point.

31

Christmas found us at least nominally in better circumstances. Gilles had been asked to keep the feast with the Duke of Britanny at Vannes. The Duke, ever alert to profit, thought there might be some pickings to be had from Gilles's misfortunes. Meanwhile negotiations were being pursued for the restoration of his properties. René de La Suze, it seemed, was not unwilling to listen to reason. All he wanted, so he declared to the duke's emissaries, was a compact fief which was entirely and indisputably his own. Then, as he put it in his bluff way: 'My brother can go to the devil in any fashion he chooses.'

I had long been curious about Duke Jean V, who now seemed likely to exercise such a powerful influence over our lives. Yet I had to admit, having seen him, that I found him disappointing. The duke was not a man whose personality impinged on you once you were out of his presence. Now, at this distance of years, while many of the other personages in my story still inhabit an old man's memory with perfect clarity, Duke Jean slips out of focus. He was the Constable's elder brother, and one thing I do recall is the family resemblance, so much so that it is Richemont's face that superimposes itself when I try to think of the duke. The latter was like a blurred copy of his sibling, even though he was in fact the elder of the two. Where Richemont's countenance, seamed and ugly as it was, mirrored a fierce and rigid will, Jean's reflected nothing but a wavering though still persistent cunning. He flattered Gilles because it was his nature to flatter, but also because he meant to ruin this spendthrift to his own advantage, rather than to allow the ruin to be accomplished, and the profit taken, by other hands.

Some of his flatteries were already dauntingly expensive – to Gilles certainly, not to himself. As soon as we arrived in Vannes, the duke began to harp on the glories of Gilles's chapel, about which, he said, he had heard so much. The children who had sung for us at Machecoul were, of course, scattered to the four winds. Only Rossignol and a few others remained. Yet Gilles was at once determined that the duke should have proof of how glorious the choir of the Holy Innocents was. Soon he was busy recruiting new singers from among the duke's subjects, and ordering splendid robes for them, improved versions of those which the original Holy Innocents had worn on their journey to Poitiers and Orléans. Luckily, the tradesmen of Vannes were still in a state of comparative innocence concerning Gilles's financial situation, and allowed him lavish credit. The choir was clothed and trained in time for the Christmas festivities, and sang before the duke in the ducal chapel. Jean showed his appreciation of their musical skill by nodding gently off to sleep in the middle of the most florid of their motets, but he was quite clever at finding the right remarks to make about their performance afterwards.

He rose still higher in Gilles's estimation when, thanks to his ambassadors' solicitations, René suddenly decided to surrender Machecoul. After Christmas we returned to a house which had been thoroughly plundered, and which was now as scoured and empty as a seashell. Gilles, strangely, showed no inclination to restore it. He preferred to spend more and more of his time at the ducal court, at Nantes, at Vannes, or at Rennes. At Machecoul itself, Sillé and I were often left to enjoy one another's company. Perhaps because we were now thrown together so much, Sillé became more communicative than he had been in recent years.

'I think we shall soon undertake an enterprise against Champtocé,' he said to me one late spring evening, as we paced around the courtyard.

'Won't that mean harder fighting than Gilles's men have stomach for?'

Sillé laughed briefly, like a fox barking. 'No, not at all. We shall be playing in a comedy arranged for us by the Duke of Britanny. Gilles is to take Champtocé by permission of his brother René. René is to get the independent fief he always wanted. Gilles will then get a hundred thousand *écus* as a loan from the duke. And after a decent interval the duke himself will get the castle Gilles has so dramatically retaken.'

'Why not buy it from René outright?'

'Because the King of France would object. Champtocé is the key which opens the door between Britanny and Anjou. Here, look at this.' He picked up a fragment of pointed stick and started to draw a map for me on a patch of bare earth. 'Amusing, isn't it?' he said, with a hint of bitterness in his tone. 'Gilles could have been a great man if he'd wanted, as great as La Tremoïlle once was. But I expect he'll find his own way of being remembered.'

Sure enough, Sillé proved to be a true prophet, at least for the short term. In the month of May orders came for him to join the captain of Pornic and twenty men in an assault upon Gilles's lost castle. In my own case, it was not orders I received, but an appeal.

'My dear Raoul,' wrote Gilles, 'this is to beg you to go with the men who are going to get back for me my castle of Champtocé. I would not ask you to trouble yourself with what is really a piece of family business, but for one thing. My liege lord the duke insists that my men be accompanied by his chancellor, the Bishop of Nantes. I have told him that this is not priest's business, but I fear he does not trust me to keep my side of the bargain. Sillé may have told you what this is. The duke is now unwilling to wait until I put the place into his hands, as I have sworn to do, and wants the bishop to take formal possession of it at once. Your part must be to act as the chancellor's escort, and to see to it that he neither comes to, nor does, any harm.'

Sillé swore out loud when I showed him this message. 'The duke is almost as big a fool as our friend Gilles,' he said. 'He makes all these elaborate arrangements to cover his own tracks, and proceeds to bring them to nothing because he is too mistrustful and too impatient. And this priest will be a burden to all of us. Do you really want to undertake such a tiresome errand? I suppose your famous curiosity won't permit you to stay at home?'

In fact it was less the prick of curiosity than loyalty to Gilles which made me resign myself to doing as he wished. And as soon as I encountered the bishop, and knelt to kiss the ring he held out to me, I began to regret my decision. Jean de Malestroit was one of those clerics who cast a perpetual gloom around them. His thin face radiated a settled joylessness, and I wondered why he had consented to come on this expedition at all, since he so clearly disapproved of it. On this subject at least Sillé was able to enlighten me: 'The duke owes him money, just as Gilles owes money to the duke. No doubt he has been promised first call upon the salt revenues, and he is going to protect his own interests. There will be such an outcry in France over this piece of double-dealing that maybe only the presence of the Chancellor of Britanny himself will serve to enforce the duke's right.'

Perhaps it was his fondness for money, but Malestroit kept little state when he was travelling. Two servants and a chaplain were all the household that accompanied him. 'Your men should be enough to protect me,' he said to Sillé with a wintry smile. 'Though I should be quite happy to rely on my office. The man who attacks a priest, much less a bishop, is an enemy of God.' At this the chaplain, who was as plump as his master was lean, uttered a little cluck of approval. 'I did not ask your opinion, sirrah!' said Malestroit, shooting fire from under his brows.

The now familiar journey between the two castles passed uneventfully. At Ingrandes, however, there was a surprise. We were joined by Henriet and Poitou. They had now become handsome blond young men, muscular and well-made. What spoilt their looks was not any physical defect but the expressions they wore, or, rather, their singular lack of expression. No emotion ever ruffled their features. Yet I always remained conscious of the malice that dwelt in both of them, waiting for an opportunity to show itself.

Malestroit disliked them for a different reason. 'Ah, messire Gilles's lackeys, whom he is pleased to call his chamberlains,' he said as he surveyed them sourly. 'Why does he not choose lads from some noble house as his attendants, instead of these? There are plenty of boys of good birth in Britanny, who would benefit from the kind of education a man like the marshal could give them.'

Henriet and Poitou were not interested in the bishop's opinion of them. They had come to hold an urgent conference with Sillé, and they drew him aside from the rest of us as soon as they could. Sillé listened to what they had to say with a deepening frown. 'All right,' he said at last, 'have the beasts ready for our return to Machecoul. I think the three of us can do the job.'

The assault on Champtocé was pure farce – except, that is, as far as Malestroit's chaplain was concerned. He came with his master shivering and shaking, and protesting under his breath that men of the cloth had no place in such warlike enterprises. The attack was to be made at dawn, when the watch would have a rope ready to let down to us. It also had been arranged that they would leave a couple of boats on the far side of the moat. The boats were there, sure enough, when we arrived, though it would need a couple of trips before all the men were across. As Sillé and the last group were about to embark, a soldier turned and said sneeringly: 'Well, priests, are you coming with us?' The chaplain uttered a squeak of alarm, and started trembling worse than ever, while Malestroit remained disdainfully silent.

'Surely you don't mean to ask my lord bishop here to shin up a rope?' I asked. 'That would hardly be suitable.'

'No,' said Sillé impatiently, 'the rest of you can remain here until we get the drawbridge down. But don't try to cross it until René's men have gone their way. It wouldn't do for you to meet in the middle.'

Soon I and my unsympathetic companion, accompanied only by his own attendants, were standing deserted on the shores of the moat. The plash of oars diminished into the distance, and through the morning mist we saw the last of the men at-arms disembarking at the foot of the castle wall. There was a sharp whistle, and the promised rope descended jerkily to meet them. They began to swarm up it, and soon the last of them had vanished from view.

'They understand, of course, that there must be no bloodshed?' remarked Malestroit suddenly. 'If there was to be bloodshed my position would not allow me to take part in such an affair.'

'I think you can count on that,' I said, watching René de La Suze's banner beginning to flutter down from the pole at the top of the gate tower. After a moment, Gilles's flag replaced it. Everything still remained silent – only the movement of the flags suggested the castle was inhabited. Then the main gate was opened, and the drawbridge came down with a great clatter. René's garrison had obviously passed the night merrily enough waiting for us to arrive, and most of them were now so drunk they could hardly sit on their horses. They reeled over the bridge with shouts and cat-calls, which redoubled when they saw the Chancellor of Britanny standing there rigid in his black robe.

No doubt this incident did something to increase his habitual ill-humour. After we had entered the main courtyard, he prepared to read the proclamation he had brought with him, taking possession of Champtocé in the Duke of Britanny's name, while at the same time Gilles's banner, so briefly triumphant, was hauled down once again and replaced by that of the duke. But Malestroit did not care to perform without an audience, and he insisted that everyone be present to hear him. The men-at-arms were rounded up easily enough. They had been searching desultorily and without much hope for a little loot, but the previous occupants had left them nothing in the way of pickings. It was Sillé, Henriet and Poitou who were nowhere to be found.

'Send people to look for them,' the bishop commanded. 'You go, messire Raoul. It is you, after all, who know the place best. Tell them they are showing disrespect for me, and also of course for my master.' I agreed to see what I could do to flush the culprits out, and set off without the smallest enthusiasm for my task. Champtocé was a vast structure, and a search of its more secret places might easily take several hours.

As it was, I discovered the truants rapidly enough, guided by a slight sound of scraping which seemed to come from the lowest storey of the keep. I made my way down to a room which, when Gilles and I were boys, had been used as a store-room for old and unwanted things – too worn to use, yet not dilapidated enough to throw away. It was also the room in which, long ago, Gilles had been beaten by Pierre Cardinal. As I reached the door, which was a little ajar, I heard the murmur of voices and knew that my guess had been right, though I couldn't imagine why the three had made straight for this unlikely spot as soon as the castle fell into our hands. I called out, and reached out my hand to thrust open the door. There was a violent exclamation, and a moment later I heard the bolt being pushed home. I paused, bewildered, and wondered what to do. Whatever was going on was clearly none of my business, and still less was it the business of the Bishop of Nantes. I battered on the wood and shouted, to be greeted only by silence.

As I crept back to the bishop with my tail between my legs, certain phrases in Gilles's letter returned forcefully to my mind. Clearly there was a mystery here, and one that Gilles was anxious Malestroit should not penetrate. The situation was immediately made more difficult by the latter's refusal to believe my excuses. 'How can they have made their way to the village,' he snapped, 'when all of us here, standing in the courtyard, would have seen them go?' Like a child caught out in an obvious lie, I maintained my story the more stubbornly, the more Malestroit strove to demolish it. At last he seemed to realise that he was not the only one who was being made to look foolish, and he consented to unroll his proclamation and begin.

Once he had formally taken the place into the duke's hands he was luckily only too anxious to get rid of anyone associated with Gilles. He consented, though even then reluctantly, to keep the captain of Pornic and his men, to serve as a castle-guard until ducal troops could be sent to relieve them, but as far as Sillé and myself were concerned he made it very clear that our absence would be more welcome than our presence. I was equally glad to be rid of his company, even at the price (as seemed likely) of riding back to Machecoul with Henriet and Poitou for companions.

This supposition was immediately confirmed when I saw the cavalcade the next morning. For some reason of his own, Sillé had insisted that we leave very early. 'If my lord bishop is so anxious to get rid of us,' he said, 'let's do him a favour and be away as soon as we can.' He even arranged with the captain of Pornic that the horses should be loaded and the drawbridge lowered before day had fully broken. We assembled in the dim light of the false dawn. In addition to the four of us there were two pack-horses, each loaded with two small wooden chests – confirmation, if any were needed, that Sillé had not only sought for, but found something during his twenty-four-hour visit to Champtocé.

Since such a mystery had been made about it, it was natural that I should wonder what the chests contained. Clearly it couldn't be gold or silver. Though the chests were small, treasure even in that quantity would have relieved the most immediate of Gilles's financial necessities, and thus there would have been no reason for him to hand over the castle itself, had he been certain of laying his hands on such a large sum of money. Then, too, the two pack-horses did not move as if they were burdened with a heavy weight of metal. The clinching argument, however, against the chests containing money, or anything worth a great deal of ready cash, was the fact that we were to travel without a guard. Whatever else I thought about Sillé, I did not think he was rash.

He was in too much haste to get started for me to be able to ask any questions until we were well on our way. At last, after we had crossed the ford at Ingrandes, I sidled my horse next to his and said, in as level a voice as I could muster: 'Those chests we've got with us look like the kind of thing that would have interested the Dame de Jarville and her friend.'

The reaction to this was immediate. Sillé jerked so hard on his horse's bit that the poor beast reared up on to its hind legs. At the same time, as if instinctively, he pulled his sword halfway from its sheath. 'What the devil made you say that?'

I was so surprised I could only goggle at him. 'Why nothing.

It's just that I remember the way they went on about "useful chests" when they were at Machecoul.'

Sillé let out a deep breath, and steadied his horse. 'I suppose you think they're full of gold and silver?'

'That's the one thing I *don't* think they're full of.'

'So why pry into what doesn't concern you, if there's no money involved?'

'You know I'm not interested in money.'

'Only very untrustworthy people say that,' said Sillé, touching his sword again. Then he seemed to think better of whatever he had been about to do, and forced an unconvincing smile on to his face. 'As a matter of fact, the chests are full of old parchments. Gilles was willing to give up the castle, but he didn't see why the duke should have all the records of Rais family history.'

Long as the antipathy between the two of us had been, it was the first time Sillé had bothered to tell an outright lie to me. Indeed, he had often seemed to take pleasure in rubbing my nose in the truth, whenever he thought this might upset me. In the circumstances, I knew I would be wise not to contradict him. But I did recall one fact, which was that the records at Champtocé had been lovingly kept in a special fire- and damp-proof muniment room of their own, and had never been left lying jumbled in a store-room at the base of a tower, where the mildew would be certain to get at them.

As we rode the long miles back to Machecoul, those chests and whatever was in them began to oppress my spirit to a quite extraordinary extent. I didn't know why, but I wanted at all costs to be out of their company. So when we were three-quarters of the way home, I made my excuses, and, for want of anything better to do, turned my horse's head towards Nantes, where I knew Gilles to be staying.

32

Gilles received me cordially enough, in the town house that had come to him as a small part of the great possessions he had inherited. It was called the Hotel de La Suze, and I wondered how Gilles felt about living in a mansion which bore the name of a brother he was now on bad terms with. Yet the thought of changing its appellation did not seem to have occurred to him. In plan it was rather like the house we had inhabited in Orléans, but everywhere there were signs of neglect. The tapestries were moth-eaten, the sparse furniture was dull from lack of polish, old-fashioned and often broken. Gilles, who had once been so fastidious about his surroundings, did not seem to care about any of this, either. Instead, he resembled a man in a drugged dream, tranquil, careless, and euphoric.

He also had a considerable surprise in store for me, but it did not explode for some days. As usual, there were new faces in the household. People came and went. Mostly they came because of the rumour of Gilles's carelessness with money, and went when they discovered that this extended to not paying their own wages. There was still a swarm of children in the place, and some of these were still designated as the singers of Gilles's chapel, but they now sung little enough.

One morning, soon after my arrival, Gilles said to me: 'You will be interested to meet my new herald. He is away carrying a message, or you would have encountered him before.'

'Why should I be interested in that?'

'Only because he is an old acquaintance,' said Gilles, and lapsed into one of the dreamy silences which were now habitual with him.

When the man arrived, I did indeed recognise him instantly. He was the individual whom I had always thought of as 'the

man in black', who had fetched us to Parthenay on La Tremoïlle's behalf, and whom I had encountered on several occasions since. He looked not a day older than the last time I had
seen him, in half-darkness on the road to Paris, though that was
nearly ten years ago. And it seemed as if he still wore the dusty
black clothes I had always associated with him, though these
were now partly hidden by the gaudy tabard of a herald. With
him, as he rode into the courtyard of the Hotel de La Suze, was
an exceptionally pretty child, mounted on a pony, and wearing
clothes which were obviously new.

'So you managed to get our little angel back from his parents,'
said Gilles coming to meet them. His voice betrayed eagerness,
but underlying it was a surprising trace of deference. He did
not sound like a great lord speaking to one of his men. But then
the man in black had managed to impose a kind of equality –
or maybe it was a version of his own superiority – right from
the start.

'Indeed I did,' said the other. 'It was just that that Scottish
captain of yours over-reached himself, by speaking so soon of
taking little Hubert here to a distant country. But the pony
and the fine clothes had a good effect. Just keep him around in
Nantes for a few days more, where they can actually see him
going in and out, and they will be entirely reassured.'

Gilles, for some reason, seemed little inclined to protest at
this. 'But you know why we agreed to speak of the journey . . .'
he began. The herald silenced him with a gesture. 'Have no
fear, messire,' he said. 'You know you may trust me to deal
with that when the time comes.' Then he turned from Gilles to
me, like a monarch dismissing one courtier in order to greet
another. 'Raoul de Saumur!' he exclaimed. 'It is an honour as
well as a pleasure to meet you again!' At that moment, instead
of resenting his familiarity, I felt a strange and powerful attraction. He seemed to draw me to him with his eyes. As if he had
thought better of whatever he had been trying to do, he dropped
his glance, and lightly dismounted from his horse. It was
ridiculous to feel simultaneously disappointed and relieved by
such a small incident.

A few days later, the herald made an opportunity to have a
brief private conversation with me. It was not in Gilles's
mansion, but in a little tavern a few paces down the street.
'These people know me as an old friend,' he said, looking around
him a little complacently. He got in reply an assenting chorus
which seemed to my ear just a trifle too unanimous and eager.
I remembered the place had a slightly bad reputation, and

wondered what hold he had been able to establish both over those who owned it and those who came there. But my train of thought was interrupted as he went on. 'I hope we shall get on as well together as we always did before.' I didn't know what to reply to this, the tone of condescension was now so marked. Yet it was obvious that a reply was expected, even demanded. 'Do you know, I don't know what your name is,' I managed to get out. 'I have always thought of you as being simply "the man in black".'

For some reason this made my companion roar with laughter. 'I like that very much,' he said, 'and maybe I shall find occasion to use the designation on my travels. Here they know me as Princé.'

'That has a royal sound to it.'

'Yes, it does, doesn't it? But I leave it to others to make up their own minds.'

I immediately had the feeling that I was being warned about something, and that Princé, as he called himself, had invited me to drink with him simply in order to bring the conversation to the point it had now reached. But I was unwilling to leave matters there.'

'What did you call yourself when you were in the service of messire de La Tremoïlle?' I asked.

'D'you know, I've quite forgotten,' he answered with an apparent carelessness which I knew to be feigned. 'Why do you ask me that?'

'I was wondering why you decided to leave messire George's service?'

'The life he lived was no longer truly interesting. I go where my services can be of most use.'

'Let me guess,' I said, 'where you worked before you entered La Tremoïlle's employment. It was for that favourite of our sovereign lord the King of France whom messire Georges sewed in a sack and cast into the river. I believe people said he made a pact with the devil?'

'Indeed you have a long memory!' exclaimed Princé, staring at me with eyes which were no longer seductive but simply hostile and opaque.

During the period after Princé's return, Gilles's household was dominated by the presence of the little Hubert. Not since Rossignol first caught Gilles's attention had any one infant exercised such a spell over him. The boy ran in and out of all the rooms in the mansion, and at first his mother and father came most days to see him. They were unusually anxious, protective parents, and Gilles chafed at their rivalry for the child's attention. Every time they came, he tried to make the boy forget their visit by immediately giving him some new treat or favour. We all of us knew, at the Hotel de La Suze, that Hubert had shared Giles's bed since two or three nights after his return in Prince's company, but this was one fact of which the child kept his parents in ignorance. Little by little these became easier in their minds, and eventually they stopped coming so regularly. After they had both been absent for a complete week, Hubert disappeared.

Noticing that he was missing, I waited a day, then asked Gilles what had become of him. 'I expect he's run off, as so many of them do,' he answered. 'You recall that ungrateful young Jeannot at Tiffauges? But this one will come to no harm since his parents live so close. I expect he's returned to them.' I was astonished that the matter was being taken so lightly, since the boy had been, up to the very moment of his disappearance, the very centre of Gilles's affections.

After another couple of days had passed, however, Gilles seemed ready to bestir himself about the absence of his new favourite. 'Go and see the parents and tell them to send the boy back,' he commanded Prince in my presence. 'After all, they agreed to the excellent arrangements we made for the child's future.' Prince received the order with a low and silent bow which aroused my suspicion that this was a comedy being acted for my benefit. A little while later he returned.

'Well, have you got young Hubert?' Gilles asked sharply.

'No, messire. The father seemed thunderstruck when I asked for him. The parents thought their son was still with you.'

'So what will they do now?'

'I am afraid they were not as reasonable as I had hoped. In fact the father said to me that it was I who had taken his child, and that it was now up to me to find him and bring him back.'

'I don't think they'll get very far with that, do you?' said Gilles.

Hubert's parents, so it turned out, were unwilling to take no for an answer. Once they heard that their precious boy was missing, one or other of them used to appear at the Hotel de La Suze every day, where the scenes they made grew increasingly desperate and violent. It moved me greatly to see their grief, but I hesitated to intervene, because I found myself very confused in my own mind about young Hubert's fate. There was, after all, no proof that any harm had come to him.

'Why won't you see the boy's mother and father?' I asked Gilles one day, after they had once again failed to get in to see him.

'The whole business upsets me too much. And there's no point. The boy's gone forever. I'll tell Princé to deal with them next time they come.'

Whether by chance or design, it was indeed Princé who appeared to confront the couple, who on the next occasion appeared together on their obsessive mission. As soon as she caught sight of him the mother began to shout: 'There he is! There he is! The devil who took our darling boy away from us! Get out of the way! I want to see your master. I've got a question or two to ask him.'

'No question I can't answer,' said Princé calmly, barring her way.

'Well, tell us this, then,' said the father, a big, burly rough man who looked like a shoemaker or a carpenter. 'What's happened to our son?'

'You know as well as I do.'

'Know as well as you do?'

'Didn't I come and ask you what had become of him?'

'Yes, you did. But I don't believe it was an honest man's question. I think you knew all the time.'

'Well, we have been able to make certain investigations,' said Princé blandly, for a moment taking the aggrieved couple aback.

'So now the devil admits he's been lying to us all along!' screamed the mother.

'We had to satisfy ourselves first.'

'*Satisfy* yourselves? It's to us you'll have to give the satisfaction!' The distraught woman made a move as if to claw the eyes out of Princé's face, then just as suddenly stopped in her tracks, her sobs stifled in her throat. The herald had scarcely deigned to glance at her.

'You'll never see your son again,' he said evenly, not a trace of emotion in his voice. 'You remember that Scottish captain who first came to see you?'

'And wanted to take our little Hubert away with him to his own cold country?' said the father in a numb voice.

'I'm afraid that's just what he's done. He's run off from messire Gilles and taken the boy with him. Since he seems so fond of him, I expect he'll care for your darling well enough.'

33

This encounter was not quite the end of the story of the missing Hubert, though of course we never saw him again. Having failed to gain any satisfaction at the Hotel de La Suze, his parents went to seek for justice at the court of the Duke of Britanny. And the duke, after having let them beat upon his gates for a suitable length of time, affected to take pity on them, and let them come in to speak to him. He listened as they told their story, and said finally: 'It is a grave matter for common people to bring an accusation against a nobleman as great as the Marshal of Rais. But since it is your son who is in question, I will think about it. Return to see me in a month's time.' With this they had to be satisfied.

The duke did not need nearly a month to make up his mind. Having extracted the thing he wanted most from Gilles, namely Champtocé, he was quite glad to see the back of him for a while. The time would certainly come again, and sooner rather than later, when Gilles needed money. At that moment, the duke would be no doubt glad to tell the spendthrift what the price for further help would be. But until then, let him go. It was intimated to Gilles – delicately but not so delicately that the meaning would be misunderstood – that he and his followers were beginning to disturb the peace of the dukedom, and that it would be as well if he lived elsewhere, at least until he was invited back.

Gilles took the news quietly enough. 'Very well,' he said, 'let us rid his highness of the burden of our company. I shall be glad to live as I please and do as I please, without having to dance attendance on other people or pay attention to their ideas of what I ought or ought not to do.'

'Where will you go?' I asked, a dull sinking feeling in the pit of my stomach.

'To Tiffauges, of course. That is out of the dukedom.'

'But within the kingdom of France, where I think you are also not very welcome.'

'Pooh! The king's power gets weaker the further away from himself that he has to exercise it. Tiffauges is on the very frontier of the kingdom. Charles will not trouble us there. And if he does, the castle is strong enough to withstand anything he may send against us.'

I was deeply troubled about whether or not I ought to accompany Gilles on the next stage of his life's journey. I had a fair idea (so I thought) of how he would find means to live at Tiffauges. And there was something else, some horror in the back of my mind, something which was so dreadful that I did not dare to form it into words – even words which reverberated in the strict privacy of my own head. Hubert's disappearance had something to do with it, and so had the four chests we brought from Champtocé, and the smell of burning at Machecoul which so rapidly persuaded the Dame de Jarville and her companion to make their farewells to us. And other incidents too, suddenly arising from the fog of the past, which can seem to cover everything yet will suddenly part to reveal some insignificant detail clearly.

Gilles seemed to sense my internal struggle. 'You will come with us, Raoul?' he asked on more than one occasion. And the last time he added: 'Well, if you won't come for my sake, come because your precious Rossignol will be there.' It was true that Gilles was gathering together all his remaining followers – Sillé had been sent for from Machecoul, Blanchet had reappeared, Henriet and Poitou had rejoined the household and were in higher favour with their master than ever. I knew Rossignol was in no position to refuse his master's orders, even if he had wanted to. And I even suspected that he would not be wholly reluctant. Like me, he felt the fascination of the man who had once been his lover.

But perhaps it was not the lure of Rossignol that decided me. There was, too, the feeling that some great drama was still proceeding, and a desire to know what the next development would be. It was a sick and sickened curiosity which would not allow me to refuse.

Tiffauges, when we got there, was as gloomy as ever, and Gilles set about making a living as I had suspected he would. No longer was there any pretence, as there had been even in our latter days at Machecoul, of collecting dues and tolls to which some semblance of legality could be given. Gilles and his men extorted whatever they could, and robbed anyone who was not strong enough to withstand them. When he got drunk, which was often, Gilles used to rail at me for refusing to join these expeditions, calling me 'lily-livered'. Once, when my small income was being delivered from my own fief, he even robbed the courier, and beat him as well, in an effort to make me see the error of my ways. Nevertheless, I stood firm and refused to participate. If I rode out, it was only to go hawking or hunting, for my health's sake, and even this I did less and less often, for I too often came across scenes that sickened me – burnt farms and half-dismembered corpses. In addition to this, the mere fact that I came from the castle put my life in danger with the peasants unless I rode with a strong escort, and this made even the simplest expedition cumbersome in the extreme.

Once I ventured to remonstrate with Gilles – not about the inhumanity of his proceedings, for I knew that would have no effect – but about the way he was laying the countryside waste around us. 'If you go on,' I said, 'we'll get precious little to eat next winter.'

'Next winter won't matter,' Gilles retorted, 'for within the next few weeks Blanchet will have returned with what I sent him to fetch.'

'Not another sorcerer!' I exclaimed. 'You know how little success you have had with them before!'

'Not a sorcerer – an Italian alchemist,' Gilles replied, not a bit put out. 'A man who knows how to transform base metal into gold. Think of it, Raoul – I shall be rich again, rich enough to tell these kings and dukes who now plague me exactly what they can do with themselves. Rich enough perhaps to pay the devil his due, and make him serve me as I wish to be served!'

Blanchet, it was true, had again been missing from the household for a long time, and Gilles had been looking anxiously for his return. But at last word came from the other side of the Loire that the priest was safely back from Italy, and that he had brought with him the very thing that Gilles so much desired: 'A most learned alchemist, my lord, who will I am sure accomplish everything you wish. In addition, he is very skilled with incantations, and can conjure powerful beings out of the earth to do him service.'

After receiving this letter, Gilles was almost beside himself with impatience. Nothing would satisfy him but that Henriet and Poitou should set off immediately, in order to escort the newcomer safely to Tiffauges.

When the stranger arrived, he was not at all what I expected. Francesco Prelati was a handsome man, and still young –

perhaps twenty-five years of age. He had raven hair, cut short in the warrior fashion, laughing black eyes, fine teeth and a smooth olive complexion. He was of middle height, and his body was muscular and beautifully knit. With his quick gestures and his slightly harsh Italian-French he reminded me of a spruce young crow, comfortably nourished on food stolen from other people. Almost from the moment he arrived his self-possession and his self-confidence were absolute. There was only one instant, and that was at the very beginning, when I saw it slip. This was when he encountered the herald Princé. As he first clapped eyes on the latter who was standing in the court-yard to welcome him, the colour drained from his face.

'Haven't I seen you somewhere before?' he stammered, without preamble.

'You may have done,' said Princé tranquilly, not a bit put out. 'I have seen service almost everywhere.' And he made the newcomer an ironic bow. 'You may of course know that fact,' he added, and Prelati for a second time turned pale.

The Italian had an extraordinary effect on Gilles, and soon established a powerful hold over him. The truth was, indeed, that Gilles fell head over ears in love with him, and it was not long before Prelati openly moved into his master's bedchamber, and shared his bed. This was astonishing, because in recent years Gilles had confined himself mostly to young boys, most of them below the age of puberty, though I suspected he also had the occasional fling with Henriet and Poitou, for old times' sake. Wherever he chose to bestow his affections, he was both physically and mentally the dominant partner. This was clearly not the case with Prelati, who had a slightly swaggering masculinity which made Gilles look feminine; and who, in addition, soon showed that he knew exactly how to wind his supposed master round his little finger.

In fact, he displayed a cool cynicism which amazed me. I had met many wicked men in my life. Indeed, I had a suspicion that I had now, by degrees, allowed myself to become one of them. But Prelati was not bad in that sense, because to be bad you have to believe in something, you have to choose evil, consciously or unconsciously, because it is the opposite of good. For Prelati, neither of these poles existed. He lived in a moral universe which was governed entirely by immediate practical convenience – his own convenience, naturally. The best course of action, whether upon his own or anyone else's part, was the one most likely to benefit Francesco Prelati. When I tackled him about this, he gave me one of his dazzling smiles.

'But of course, my dear,' he said. 'I am one of a new race of men. All that nonsense about God and the Devil is over. There are many others who think like me in Italy, and soon there will be more in France. We are a dominant strain. We breed fast, and soon the world will be full of us. I am glad I am one of the first.'

When Gilles insisted that Prelati conduct some invocations, in his impatience because the alchemical apparatus was not yet finished, the latter treated the business with levity. The first of these occasions was very much like the ceremony I had interrupted at Orléans, only now, as an initiate, I was allowed to assist with the preparations, and to see how the magic circle was first drawn with the point of a drawn sword, and what mixtures of spices and herbs were used in the braziers. Prelati had no intention of asphyxiating himself, however, and he ordered that the four windows of the room below the great hall at Tiffauges, where the ceremony was held, be opened to their fullest extent, to let out the more noxious of the vapours. This meant that we others, who stayed outside while he and Gilles remained within, could hear snatches and more than snatches of what was going on.

'What nonsense it all is!' said Prelati afterwards, without troubling to lower his voice. 'My poor friend goes to all this trouble to sign away his soul, and stands there like a fool with the contract in his hand, and nobody comes to take him up on it.'

'Don't you feel responsible for the fact that nothing appeared?' I asked.

Prelati shrugged gracefully. 'Not at all. What devil would be mad enough to sign a contract in order to get what he can already have for nothing?'

Two further ceremonies were undertaken, and they ended rather differently, though still in a fashion which was unsatisfactory for Gilles. One invocation was out of doors. It was held not far from the castle, and near one of the farms which Gilles and his men had burned and looted. This time Prelati insisted that he would take Poitou as his assistant, and that Gilles must remain at some distance. The night was fine and clear when we rode out, and I was surprised to see Princé at the last moment attach himself to the rear of the party, though he had not been given specific permission to come. Prelati did not notice his presence until we had actually reached our destination, and, when he did so, he was a little put out, or pretended to be so. However, after some persuasion, he consented to go on with the ritual. This time the circle was dug in the ground with the aid of a knife, though the same herbs and spices were burned. There was also a certain amount of hocus-pocus with a lodestone. Poitou was plainly terrified by all this – it was almost the first time I had ever known him to exhibit emotion – and his teeth were chattering when Prelati signed to us to withdraw, and the ceremony itself began. It seemed that the name of the demon he wished to evoke was 'Barron', as this word, uttered with tremendous emphasis, carried to us very clearly in the midst of the chanting.

At about the fourth or fifth repetition, something very strange happened. The sky which had, up till then, been clear and tranquil, suddenly clouded completely over, and within moments a tremendous storm had begun. The wind tore at us, the lightning flashed, the thunder roared, and we were pelted with hailstones as we tried to make our way back to Tiffauges. We arrived very disconsolate, and soaked to the skin. The only one of us not to suffer these inconveniences was Princé, who said he had become bored, and had slipped away shortly after the chanting had begun, and had thus escaped a drenching. Prelati told Gilles, though without putting any stress on the matter, that the wretched Poitou had begun to cross himself as the invocation increased in vehemence; and Gilles seized on this as a reason to blame his young chamberlain for the failure. Poitou was out of favour for quite a few days. I could see that Prelati did not believe in this explanation himself, and that indeed he was troubled to find one. His eye slid to Princé, but he shook his head and obviously tried to put the matter out of his mind.

The third magical ceremony of which I will speak had, on the face of it, similarities to what had happened at Pouzauges, when he went there with the good doctor La Rivière. Prelati, this time, had chosen once again to conduct his business in the big room below the great hall, but this time insisted that he must enter the magic circle alone. The rest of us, including Gilles, were banished to an ante-chamber. Blanchet, who for some reason was offended with Prelati, chose this moment to go on an errand into the village, and departed as soon as the latter locked himself in and began his preparations, leaving the windows open as before. Soon we heard the expected rhythmic chanting, growing louder and louder and more and more urgent as Prelati urged the fiend Barron to appear to him. The tension built up as the chant continued, seeming to shake the very planks of the door behind which we listened.

Beside me Gilles started to tremble with eagerness. 'Can't you feel the power beginning to flow?' he whispered. 'Something is going to happen in a minute. It must! It must!'

All at once there came a frightful cry, and what sounded like the sound of blows and of furniture being smashed. There were more shouts, as if Prelati were now begging for help, and then for mercy. The smashing continued, and then the whole uproar died down as suddenly as it had begun. There came a silence, followed by a series of incoherent groans. A little wind seemed to blow very gently through the room in which we stood.

I must admit that I was frightened enough myself. I felt the hair prickling on the back of my neck. And when I looked at Gilles I saw that he was terrified, rigid in every muscle and with his eyes starting out of his head. When the power of speech returned to him, he said: 'Someone must send at once for Blanchet.'

'Why? One or other of us can easily get a ladder and enter through one of the windows.'

'No, not that!' Gilles exclaimed sharply.

'I can't see any reason . . .' I began.

'Don't you understand? Some traces of the emanation may remain.'

So Blanchet was duly sent for, while the two of us remained behind the locked door and listened to Prelati groaning. When the priest arrived, and heard what had taken place, he was notably reluctant to undertake the task assigned to him. 'Oh come, my poor Eustache,' said Gilles briskly (for he had by now recovered from his discomfiture), 'I know you may not be much of a magician, but surely you're capable of saying a few protective spells? Even a sorcerer's apprentice ought to be able to manage that.'

Blanchet saw there was no further room for argument, and girded himself to mount the ladder that had been brought. In a few moments we heard the sound of the bolts being drawn, and Blanchet's long whey face appeared as the door opened. 'We will need a doctor,' he said. 'I think poor master Prelati is in a bad way.' As I entered, to see what could be done to help the victim, my eyes encountered an extraordinary spectacle. Every piece of furniture in the chamber had been smashed and this included a massive wooden table which had stood against one wall. The braziers had been overturned, and live coals were scattered everywhere, though, since the floor was of stone, there was little danger of fire. The magic circle was smeared, and the figures within it were half-effaced. The blade of the naked sword Prelati had been using instead of a wand was snapped in half, and the two pieces lay on either side of his prostrate body.

The condition of the victim was in fact a little less serious than it looked at first, though he was only half-conscious and had clearly been badly beaten up. He had a cut on his forehead which had bled profusely, a black eye and a split lip. His torso was badly bruised, so much so that I wondered if he might not have broken a rib. But there was in fact nothing wrong with him that time and rest would not cure.

He stayed in bed for a week, until he looked presentable again; and it was Gilles who insisted on nursing him, as if to make amends for his earlier failure to come to the rescue. Gilles was now utterly convinced of Prelati's powers as a magician. 'What went wrong,' he declared, 'was that Francesco did not succeed in controlling the power he had conjured up. But it is clear that he has great gifts.'

For my own part, I had doubts, and these doubts were reinforced by my memory of what had taken place in the wood at Pouzauges. Could Prelati have been desperate enough to injure himself so severely in order to convince his patron? Somehow I doubted this – yet I knew he was capable of much if he thought the end he had in view would justify it. Oddly enough, he seemed, when we had a conversation in private, almost over-anxious to convince me that the whole business had been of his own doing. 'Don't you think I'm a good conjurer?' he said complacently. 'It's quite a trick to break a heavy oak table into splinters, with nothing to help you but your bare hands. You must let me teach it to you one day.' But I did notice one small change in his behaviour. If he had mistrusted Princé before, he now seemed to go out of his way to avoid him. Princé, on the other hand, seemed to take an especial pleasure in tormenting Prelati with unexpected confrontations, as they both went about their business.

34

Prelati had now established himself in a position where whatever he wanted would be given to him. What he wanted, it seemed, was to start what he called 'the great work', the effort to transform base metal into gold. Since I judged Francesco to be a trickster (and indeed he had given me every encouragement to make the judgement), I was surprised by how seriously he seemed to take this enterprise. When I challenged him on this, he said: 'This is nothing to do with magic, though of course I have to make our friend Gilles believe that it is. It is a question of the nature of materials, and the logical order of the universe. The transformation of one metal into another is something which wise men have been trying to accomplish for centuries, and I believe we are now very close to being able to do it. There is no real secrecy about the processes we use.' And to prove his point he proceeded to treat me to a long lecture on the subject. What he said was so complex that I have forgotten all of it, but it was clear that, for once, he believed everything he said.

What Prelati required was soon being installed at Tiffauges. Great furnaces were built, stocks of wood were laid in, glass and metal vessels were procured. A building in the second court, as far from the main gate as possible, was adapted for his use. Rossignol took a great interest in all this, and, to my surprise, but also somewhat to my relief, Prelati asked if the boy could serve as his assistant. Rossignol was no longer the charming infant I had first known. His voice had broken, and he was on his way to manhood. But he still possessed, indeed perhaps he now had it to an even greater degree, the ambiguous physical charm which he had always had. We still remained lovers, and he continually surprised me with his amorous ingenuity when we were in bed together. The physical pleasure he brought me had never been sharper. Yet my delight in him was mingled, as it had been from the very beginning, with secret and inexplicable anxiety. I feared for Rossignol, but what I feared was something I had still not discovered. I did know that Gilles, after a long period of disinterest in the boy, was now beginning to notice him again, and this made me doubly uneasy because the interest was covert, and Gilles was at some pains to conceal it. But I knew him too well not to notice what was going on.

Just as the preparations were complete, and alchemical operations were about to begin, a message arrived at Tiffauges. It was from the king of France, summoning Gilles to attend a States-General at Bourges 'so that we may benefit from your counsel and good advice'. At the same time it ordered the Marshal of Rais to raise three hundred men-at-arms 'for an enterprise we have in mind to make against Le Mans'.

'All that's easy enough to interpret,' said Sillé, when Gilles showed him the letter. 'The king's son Louis is nearly grown up, and there've been rumours for a long time that he's a restless, ambitious young man, and that he's been conspiring with some of the great nobles, such as our old friends Alençon and Clermont, and even with messire Georges, to put his father in tutelage. Charles wants all the help he can get, and he's even willing to look to you for it.'

'Do I have to go?' asked Gilles lugubriously.

'You must, unless you're ready to offend the king.'

Much against his will, therefore, Gilles was forced to depart for Bourges. Meanwhile Prelati pushed forward with his alchemical experiments, and the air at Tiffauges was black with the smoke of his furnaces. Gilles was naturally anxious to have news of what was going on, and Prelati sent him letters in code by frequent couriers. I formed the impression that these contained, not only tantalising hints of imminent success, but demands for money. 'Gold cannot be made without gold,' as Prelati once said to me, smoothing his black hair with a gesture that always reminded me of a bird preening its feathers.

Perhaps the Italian pitched his demands too high, or perhaps his absence had helped to clear Gilles's head a little, but when the latter at last returned he was in no very good mood, either with Prelati or with the rest of us. One special cause of grievance was an amulet which Prelati had sent to him. Apparently this consisted of a silver tube filled with some sticky aromatic substance, within a silver case. Gilles had been given instructions to wear this round his neck. 'But I felt no special good from it, and so after two or three days I threw it away,' he now said curtly. 'You say your devil Barron brought it to you in person – I can't see why he didn't appear when I was present, instead of waiting till I was away from home.'

All Prelati could do was to claim that he had, as the result of further practice, gained greater control over the infernal powers. But it was clear that a special effort was required. It was at this juncture that he decided to take Rossignol into his confidence. Rossignol afterwards relayed the conversation to me, half-flattered at having been made the repository of an important secret, half-frightened of what the consequences might be if anything went wrong.

'Prelati says,' Rossignol murmured, as we lay side by side in our great bed, 'that he is confident of achieving success with his alchemical process, if Gilles will give him time. But since time is what he cannot have, he means to do something which will impress Gilles enough to get him to allow the experiments to continue. "You have been an actor," he keeps cawing in that funny accent of his, "and in Italy I have been a maker of theatrical machines. We are more advanced in that than you are in France, just as we are more advanced in most other things. Together we will devise something." '

When it came, the show Prelati put on was spectacular enough to satisfy almost anyone, and I was forced to admire the cool nerve with which he carried out his deceptions. A ceremony was arranged which was to take place in the laboratory itself, or, rather, in an ante-chamber which led to a room where the furnaces were. In order to give the matter as much verisimilitude as possible, several of us were positioned in lesser circles outside the main one, which was occupied by Gilles and Prelati himself. Gilles insisted that, in order to protect themselves, the spectators should be provided with relics, selected from among those which remained in his collection. I was given a fragment of the True Cross, wrapped in a little piece of linen and sealed with sealing-wax. Its unimpressive appearance had caused several Breton merchants to doubt its authenticity when Gilles tried to raise money on it after the fall of Machecoul, but he still preserved a stubborn faith in its miraculous virtues. Sillé was more awkwardly burdened. He was made to clutch in his arms a wooden statuette of the Virgin, which was said to have, enclosed within it, a small piece of her veil.

The business began about midnight, with the ritual chanting I now accepted as something almost commonplace. The braziers burned sulkily, and every now and then Prelati would sprinkle them with a pinch of one or another substance. Some of the things he put on the coals were herbs or gums, each identifiable by its own characteristic aroma – myrrh, aloes and the rest – but once he added a pinch of what must have been metallic powder, which sent off a cloud of bright, multicoloured sparks. The heavy beat of the chant grew louder and louder, and in spite of myself I began to be affected by it – the percussive syllables seemed to attune themselves to the rhythm of my body, to my breathing and the pumping of my heart.

Just as it seemed as if my nerves could stand the swelling crescendo of noise no longer, the door which led to the furnace-room and which had previously been locked and bolted, flew open with a crash. Through it, a slim, winged figure could momentarily be seen illuminated in a sudden flare of light. Prelati gave a triumphant cry: 'Barron! Barron! Obey my command! Bring us the gold!' The figure vanished and a darkness which seemed all the blacker because of the previous burst of brightness filled the archway of the door. But within a moment this was replaced by a spreading glow, within the centre of which there seemed to be a small pile of golden ingots.

The sight of the wished-for gold was too much for Gilles's composure, and he broke from the protective circle with a shout. But Prelati was ready for him, and grabbed him by the arm: 'Be careful, messire. Be careful! Do you not see the guardian serpent!' And he reached out and swung the door shut, but not before Gilles and the rest of us had caught a glimpse of a green and fiery creature, coiling in circles upon the furnace-room floor.

By this time Gilles was completely beside himself. I had never seen such an amalgam of rage, cupidity and terror. He wrenched his arm from Prelati's grip and began to curse him roundly, then cried: 'A relic! A holy relic! That will protect me from whatever is in there! The gold! I must see it – handle it!' He darted towards Sillé, as if to snatch the statuette of the Madonna from his clutch, then seemed to change his mind and threw himself towards me, fumbling for the linen packet which I held.

'The spirits do not like the presence of holy things!' exclaimed Prelati, warningly, though he must have known Gilles was beyond heeding him. Once more the door flew open, and Gilles precipitated himself into the space beyond, which was again completely dark. He tripped over something, and fell full-length with a tremendous crash.

It took some time before torches could be brought, and the place illuminated. Of the glowing ingots of gold there was no sign, nor of the devil Barron, nor of the fiery serpent. What remained were a few traces of what seemed like burnt paper, and a strong smell of chemicals. But there was also something more. Smeared on the palms of Gilles's hands, where he had put them out to save himself as he fell forward, there were substantial traces of what could only be gold-leaf.

Dawn had almost come by the time the excitement had died down. By the time I got to my chamber I expected to find Rossignol already safe in bed. But in fact he arrived some moments later, just as I was beginning to worry about his safety. His face and hands were smudged with soot, and his clothes were dirty.

'Where have you been?' I demanded.

'Hiding in one of the furnaces. We didn't think you'd look there. It was a tight squeeze, I can tell you!' Then, as I asked no further questions, he said, in a slightly disappointed tone: 'Didn't you like our firework display?'

'It was certainly impressive,' I answered, as drily as I could. 'That rascal Prelati clearly learnt a thing or two from his Italian masters. And I thought you made a very pretty devil. But the best touch was the gold-leaf.'

'The gold-leaf?' Rossignol echoed blankly.

'Yes, the gold-leaf Gilles found on his hands when he grabbed for the gold. Just as if it had left something of itself behind in vanishing.'

'I don't know anything about that,' said Rossignol, in a slightly troubled voice. 'And I'm sure that if Prelati had thought of it he would have told me. He's so conceited about his own cleverness.'

However they got there, the small fragments Gilles found clinging to his palms after his failure to seize the gold played a large part in bringing him back to a belief in Prelati's powers. And Prelati was not slow to rub the lesson in. 'If you hadn't been so quick to start brandishing that piece of the True Cross,' he said scoldingly, 'everything would have gone right. You didn't give the gold time to stabilise itself. Now we must go the long way round because, after such rough treatment, Barron will be reluctant to come again, however urgently we summon him.' By way of punishment, Prelati imposed a strange ritual on his master – I took it that it was chiefly a means of demonstrating his own power. Anyway, a little time after the abortive ceremony, he announced that Barron had appeared to him in a dream, and had said that, in order to show his repentance, Gilles must promise to give a banquet henceforth to three poor men, three times a year, on three of the great feast-days of the Church – Easter, Ascension and All Saints. He indicated that the first of these banquets must take place more or less immediately, on the All Saints Day which was nearly upon us, and devoted a great deal of energy to devising humiliating rituals for Gilles to perform. In the event, the ceremony was nearly cancelled for want of guests. Poor peasants and beggars were none too anxious to enter the portals of Tiffauges, and three wayfarers had to be more or less kidnapped for the purpose. They sat at the high table, while Gilles waited upon them, shivering and trembling, obviously convinced that their last hour had come. Indeed, they only believed they were to be allowed to go free and unharmed when the guard booted them out of the gates after everything was over. I suspect that kicks never felt sweeter than did the ones bestowed upon the Marshal's All Saints Day guests. Yet Gilles himself had tended them with a humility and devotion which seemed quite unfeigned, and, as so often before, I wondered at the power of good that lived on within him, despite his effort to repress it.

Some visitors still came willingly to Tiffauges, as we were soon to learn. One day towards the end of November, when All Saints was nearly a month forgotten, a spruce herald in royal livery rode up to the gates. The personage who had sent him to announce that he would soon be with us was Louis, Dauphin of Viennois. Gilles, at first, was not inclined to take the Dauphin's visit seriously. 'What can that brat have to say to me?' he cried. 'A prince who is no sooner out of swaddling bands than he tries to go to war with his own father?'

Within a few days, however, he had begun to change his tune, as news started to come in of Louis's proceedings in Poitou. King Charles had just at that moment published the kind of ordinance which, in the days before he made his peace with the Duke of Burgundy at Arras, would have made him the laughing-stock of that part of the kingdom he still ruled. In sonorous language, it commanded that an end be made to the great excesses and pillagings which still desolated France. But now it seemed as if the king had found the means to put teeth into these pious wishes. His chosen instrument was the son who had so recently rebelled against him, and who might so easily rebel again. Whatever his own secret thoughts in the matter, Louis clearly found a relish in his work; the gibbets were heavy with bodies wherever he had been. As he drew closer and closer to Tiffauges, Gilles's nervousness increased. Three days before the prince was due to reach us, he ordered the destruction of the furnaces and other alchemical apparatus.

Prelati watched impassively as the work of destruction went forward, and, when I asked him later what his feelings were, he shrugged and said: 'I think it is a lesson to me, in case I needed one, not to act like an honest man. We seekers for the secret must always rely upon others, since the business is so laborious and so expensive, and they always betray us before our researches are carried to a conclusion.'

The rooms where Prelati and Rossignol had worked were scarcely restored to their former state before the Dauphin appeared at Tiffauges. Louis came with a considerable retinue and he made it plain that he expected us to treat him with the greatest reverence. 'I have not come,' he rasped, 'to exchange meaningless civilities. I have arrived to do justice for the king and for the kingdom.'

These words were pronounced as he sat stiffly upright in an armchair under an improvised canopy of state. Round him clustered his guard, and the retinue of clerks whom he had brought with him. His people mingled with ours, as if to make certain not one of us could make a false move as he surveyed us from the dais. From the first moment of his arrival, it had been evident that Louis was no more trustful than his mistrustful father.

If I hesitate to describe the impression which the prince made upon me, it is because he now reigns in France, and everyone knows him to be a most redoubtable monarch. If I thought there was any risk of this manuscript falling into his hands, I would not write about him at all, as I have no wish to end my days hoisted in an iron cage in the midst of one of his dark dungeons at Loches. Yet my story would not be complete without a picture of the young Louis and his proceedings.

My first impression of him was that he was ugly. My next was that he was intelligent. My third was that he, despite his youth, was both infinitely subtle and infinitely dangerous. In Louis, all his father's physical defects reappeared, and in exaggerated form. He had his father's close-set eyes, pendulous nose and thick lips, but he was both shorter and swarthier. The father was knock-kneed, but in the son this characteristic was so much exaggerated as to amount to a deformity. Louis seemed even shorter and more stooping than he actually was, thanks to his sidewise, shuffling gait. When he moved, it was always suddenly, almost at a run, so that he reminded you of a spider scrambling along a wall, going from one place of concealment to another.

When he stopped, he had a formidable stillness. He never fidgeted or plucked at his clothes. Only the eyes moved, and these were often concealed by the shadow of the hat he wore pulled down over his forehead.

He made it clear to Gilles, when the latter tried a compliment or two, that he had not come to Tiffauges to listen, but simply to speak. 'Evil things are said of you, Marshal,' he declared. 'Worse perhaps than of any man in France. They are no concern of mine, except in so far as they affect the peace of the kingdom. I am told you live here like a robber, that you rob men upon the roads and hold the villages to ransom. There is no place for that any more. Great lord you may be, but if you disobey henceforth, it will be my pleasure as well as my duty to hang you.' He paused, and I saw the flash of his eyes, as they moved beneath the brim of his hat. Then, lowering his voice, he spoke to the captain of his guard who was standing beside him. 'Arrest that man,' he said, pointing to Sillé. 'It may be too early to hang a Marshal of France, even one as dissolute as this, but I can see no objection to hanging one of his men as an example.'

35

The Dauphin's visit to Tiffauges set the wheels of fate in motion, not only for Gilles, but for all of us who surrounded him. Thenceforth things had their own inevitability, like a great clock preparing itself to strike. The immediate consequence was Gilles's decision to leave the kingdom of France, and return once more to Machecoul. Tiffauges, after all, had not been far enough from the sources of royal power, and he preferred the sly and covert ill-will of the Duke of Britanny to another confrontation with Louis. But not all of us were to go with Gilles. Two of our number, not one, had departed in the Dauphin's train. Sillé went as a prisoner, his arms bound behind him and his feet roped under his horse's belly; and from day to day we waited for news that his neck had been stretched for him. And the herald Princé had decided to change his employment, and to wear the royal livery. As was his custom, he scarcely bothered to make any farewells – indeed, had I not happened to run into him just as he was saddling up, I should not have known of his departure until long after he was gone.

'So you are changing masters?' I said sarcastically. 'Or is it that you are changing servants?'

Princé looked up from tightening the girth on his horse, and a faint grimace of amusement twitched his thin lips.

'You do me too much honour,' he said. 'Let us just say that my presence here has become superfluous. As far as messire Gilles is concerned, things can now look after themselves.'

'Shall I see you again?' I asked, not knowing why I put the question.

'Not unless you take the trouble to summon me,' said Princé, as he swung his lean body into the saddle. 'And both you and I know you are not likely to do that.'

Another missing member of the household was Eustache

Blanchet, and it took us some time to discover what had become
of him. The truth was that messire Eustache had run away –
but not completely. Perhaps because he had nowhere of his
own to run to, he had simply removed himself to another of
Gilles's castles, and refused to leave despite his master's
blandishments. The extent to which this desertion affected
Gilles surprised me. Blanchet's absence seemed to fill him with
a secret anxiety, which occasionally burst forth in ugly outbreaks
of rage. I could not understand why Gilles missed the company
of the renegade, still less so why he seemed to fear some harm
this miserable creature might do him.

The mood in which we all reached Machecoul was therefore
a gloomy one. Yet in my case it was alleviated by my relief
and pleasure that we were no longer to live at Tiffauges,
whose atmosphere had perpetually weighed upon my spirits.
Another man not wholly depressed when we left Poitou
behind us and returned again to Britanny was Prelati. He
seemed to have recovered completely from the check to his
plans which had been brought about by the destruction of his
furnaces, and his bond with Gilles was clearly closer than ever.
He was delighted with the strangeness of the landscape that
surrounded Machecoul, and fascinated by such things as the
method used for making salt. Another thing which seemed to
give him pleasure was the absence of Princé. He several times
made me repeat to him all the details of the last conversation
I had had with the departing herald. 'So he said he would not
come unless he was summoned,' he mused. 'There's something
to be careful about.'

Meanwhile. Gilles was becoming restless. In part this was
because he still fretted over Blanchet's absence; but also he
seemed to long for new faces of any kind. Henriet and Poitou
were sent off to interview the renegade priest, and were told
to use any effort which might be needed to persuade him to
come back. For Prelati and myself Gilles had a different task.
'This place is melancholy without the presence of young people,'
he proclaimed. 'I cannot get through the winter without some
fresh and charming company. It is up to you to go and find
me some guests.' As he asked me this, smiling into my eyes as
if the request he was making was the most natural thing in the
world, I felt a kind of deadness fall upon my heart.

More than two years had passed since the fall of Machecoul
had driven Gilles into the arms of the Duke of Britanny, and
it was the morning of Christmas Eve when I came out of my
quarters into the courtyard, to find my horse already saddled

and Prelati waiting for me, wrapped against the weather in a great cloak. Though snow is rare in the region, it was bitterly cold, and a fine white powder was sprinkling down from the dull grey of the sky. A thin layer of ice had formed over the puddles scattered on the ground, and where the horses had broken it with their restless trampling it was already starting to reappear.

'Which way shall we turn?' I said to my companion.

'Towards the village.'

'I fear the Marshal's men do not have the best of reputations among the villagers.'

'We shall do well enough,' said Prelati with a laugh.

As we rode through the settlement clustered on the banks of the mere a little way from the castle, I thought how altered it was from the days when I had first come to Machecoul. The merchant's houses were closely shuttered now, and many showed signs of crumbling into ruin. Nobody cared to come to this remote part to do business with Gilles any more, whether it was to buy or to sell. Smoke still rose from some of the humbler huts, making its way out through a hole in the centre of the roof, and here and there I could sense, rather than see, an eye peering at us from a door kept slightly ajar. Behind a fence a dog howled and rattled its chain. Nowadays the people of the place kept out of sight as much as they could when the Marshal's men passed.

'Where now?' I asked.

'To Saint-Etienne-de-Mermorte.'

On either side of the dyke the frozen reeds stuck up stiffly from water which was just starting to congeal. The snow fell more thickly, driven by a keen sea wind, and I was forced to bring my cloak up to cover the lower part of my face, peering out of the narrow gap between my forearm and my hat. Even so, the crystals began to cake upon my eyelashes.

'It's no weather to be wandering the roads,' I grumbled. 'Gilles will have to wait for guests until another day.'

'Not so!' Prelati exclaimed, and pointed with the little whip he was carrying. 'They are coming to meet us already.' At first I could not make out what he meant, and then I saw, as I peered through the snowflakes, what looked like a strange two-headed beast, struggling and swaying along the ridge-top towards us. As the beast grew closer, I could make out that it in fact consisted of two children who had wrapped themselves in a single length of rough cloth. One of them carried a basket.

Prelati reined his beast to a halt, and waited until they drew level. Now that they were close, I could see that their faces were blue with cold, and that the smaller and weaker of the two seemed near to fainting. 'B-b-bread!' stammered his companion, half-raising the basket in a movement filled with pathetic hopelessness.

'We'll take you to where bread is,' Prelati offered. They were pretty children, and did not seem badly nourished, and I wondered what had brought them to such a pass. But before I could pursue these speculations, the child was replying to Prelati's invitation. 'Not to a big castle!' he exclaimed. 'I've heard of a big castle where bad things happen.'

'Bad things like a bed and a fire and something to eat?' said Prelati smiling. 'Is that your brother? He looks as if he's about to fall.' And indeed at that moment the younger child uttered a faint cry and slumped unconscious to the ground. Instantly Prelati was off his horse and gathering the boy into his arms.

As we rode back towards Machecoul, with the two children mounted before us on the pommels of our saddles, and rapidly reviving thanks to the warmth which we, our beasts and our cloaks provided, the Italian began to tease me a little. 'Don't worry, messire Raoul,' he said, out of the side of his mouth, 'you haven't seen another specimen of my supernatural powers.'

'I doubt if I've seen one yet,' I answered.

'So how did I know where to find our guests?'

'I haven't the slightest idea,' I said.

'You should take more interest in what goes on in the district. After all, I've only just got here. When a man marries a jealous woman there's bound to be trouble.'

'I don't see how that applies here.'

'Sometimes she's jealous, not of other women, but of the children he's had by a previous marriage. These are the sons of one of Gilles's tenant farmers by his first wife, who died some two or three years ago. Since then, he's married again and had another child.'

'What are you trying to tell me?' I asked, though I was beginning to have an idea.

'Simply that we met these two children here by arrangement. Obviously the second wife didn't want to deliver them straight to the doors of the castle. That would have been too crude.' He seemed to wait for some kind of response on my part. 'You do understand, don't you?'

'I understand she sent them out to get bread in the middle of snowstorm, and told them not to return without it.'

'Small chance of that,' said the Italian, almost under his breath. Then, after a further pause, he began to whistle jauntily, beating time in the snow-laden air with his whip. It took me some time to recognise the tripping tune for what it was – '*Dies irae, dies illa* . . .' As the Latin words insinuated themselves into my head, with their pitiless promise of a day of wrath, my blood seemed to run colder than the water which filled the ponds and canals that everywhere surrounded us.

36

I come at last to that part of my story which I would rather not tell, even though it makes the keystone for the rest, and the reason for telling it. When we returned to Machecoul, Gilles received his two young guests with extravagant pleasure. 'We will keep the twelve days of Christmas together,' he declared, 'and it will be a merrier one than you have yet had in your lives. Until the Night of Kings you shall be the two monarchs of the feast, and sit at the high table with me for every day's dinner.' And that first day he was as good as his word. The time was long gone when the master of Machecoul could keep in his service cooks skilled in producing those master-pieces of pastry and spun sugar which had once adorned his table. But we ate well enough, for all that, and there came a long succession of dishes appropriate to the season – oysters served half a dozen different ways, in broth, in pastry, or on skewers; and every different kind of wild fowl the marsh could provide, from snipe to heron; and there were beef and venison, too; and salted mutton; and winter salads for roughage. At the end of the meal came a surprise: candied plums from the Levant, which the men of the garrison had robbed from some unhappy merchant.

The two boys did full justice to everything that was offered to them; and their host saw to it, too, that they drank their share of wine. Long before the meal was over, their faces were flushed and their eyes were heavy. After the plums had been served they could keep sleep at bay no longer, and their heads gradually sank until they were touching the littered board. Gilles smiled, and put his cup once more to his lips, and sig-nalled to two of the servants. 'Put them in a truckle bed in my own chamber,' he said in a low voice. 'I will see to them later.'

Just at this moment there came a distraction. A stir down at the end of the room announced some new arrivals, even though the meal was by this time almost over. The newcomers pushed their way towards the dais, between the tables which held the men of the garrison and the members of the household – greasy menials, most of these, as most of the functionaries had long ago found reason to desert an employer who not only did not pay their wages, but openly despised all their high mysteries of book-keeping, clerking and accountancy. The only men of letters Gilles now had time for were those who could read a magician's *grimoire*.

A howl of derision went up as one of the three who had come in was recognised. Blanchet had never been popular with the men-at-arms, who thought he combined the worst qualities of the sneak and the sorcerer. A hail of leavings began to fly about his head, bespattering his face and his gown. Behind him, Poitou and Henriet hung back so as to avoid the missiles. Gilles stood up in his place at the centre of the high table, and raised his hands for silence.

'So the prodigal has returned to us,' he said. Blanchet hung his head and did not reply. From the slight quiver of his garments I could see that he was trembling.

'What shall I do to this man for defying me?' he asked, raising his voice a little. A dozen suggestions were shouted back – some ribald, some (and these were horrible enough) seriously intended. Gilles seemed to consider them for a moment and Blanchet's trembling visibly increased. 'No,' he said at last, 'even drowning in horse-piss is too good for you. You may return to us, messire Blanchet, and will take part in all you used to take part in.'

Since the men had had a lot to drink, there was a further outcry from the body of the hall at this apparently feeble and ambiguous verdict. Tormenting the wretched priest would have provided a good winter afternoon's sport for the type of man Gilles now recruited for his garrison. But Gilles simply sat down and sat toying with his wine-cup until it had died away. It was clear that he had said all he meant to say upon the subject. I noticed that Blanchet, who should have been relieved at getting off so lightly, acted almost as if a sentence of death had been passed upon him. His legs seemed too feeble to carry him, and he sat down heavily on the nearest bench without asking leave, the sweat-drops blossoming on his brow. Gilles, too, observed his distress, and a sly smile passed across his face, which he masked by taking a gulp of wine.

After the meal I felt so heavy with all I had consumed, and also (though I would not admit it even to myself) with the burden of guilt and anxiety I felt weighing upon me, that I went to my chamber to rest. Perhaps my emotions should have kept me awake, but instead they had the opposite effect, and combined with the food and wine to make me fall asleep as soon as I lay on the bed.

I was awakened by someone shaking me. 'Rossignol?' I muttered, trying to get the sleep from my eyes, and thinking he had come to find me.

'No, not your precious Rossignol,' said an instantly recognisable sardonic voice beside my pillow.

'Sillé. Why I thought –'

'You thought I had been hanged, and small grief it caused you,' said the man himself, releasing his grip on my shoulder. 'I gather it's a day for returning prodigals, and that Blanchet is back with us already.'

'He had to be brought; but you, I gather, came of your own free will,' I said, recovering my wits a little and struggling into a sitting position.

'If it's free will to choose to escape rather than be strung up,' Sillé answered drily. As I looked at him now I could see that he looked aged and worn, and that his clothes still had dungeon filth on them. 'But I won't be staying here long,' he added.

'Why not?' I exclaimed, as this sudden declaration astonished me more, perhaps, than Sillé's sudden reappearance. I had always thought of him as Gilles's alter ego, absent only on his master's business.

'I had time to do a little thinking in the Dauphin's prisons. And I came to the conclusion that, if I'm to save my own hide, Sillé must vanish utterly, just as if he'd never existed.'

'But you're in Britanny,' I protested, my head starting to spin again, 'outside the Dauphin's jurisdiction.'

'Now you're talking as I used to do. The clever, clean-cut solution to the problem. Much good it did me.'

'Then why come back here at all?'

'For two reasons, my dear old friend,' said Sillé in a tone which was the closest to caressing that I had ever heard from him. 'First, I need money. Vanishing is an expensive business, unless one is a better magician than messire Prelati.'

'I cannot give you much. What I have I will give you willingly.'

'Bravo, Raoul! Always the altruist. I have no need to turn to you for cash. Through the years I have put away a little here, a little there, cheating where I could and saving where I could. Much of it is hidden here at Machecoul. Why did you think I was always so badly dressed?'

'I never thought about it!' I cried defensively.

'Oh yes, you did,' said Sillé, his voice hardening. 'You were perpetually creeping, and prying, and wondering, and trying to make out other people's reasons for doing things. But the one important thing, the thing which would really upset you, was the one you were careful never to find out. And that's the second reason why I've come back. To make sure you touch pitch before I go. Why should you persuade yourself that you've always been Gilles's good angel, trying to rescue him when men like me made him wallow in filth to serve their own purposes?'

'I don't understand.'

'Not understanding has been your weapon. So long as you pretended not to see certain matters, Gilles felt free to plunge deeper and deeper into them, taking you for the image of the world's deliberate blindness. Come with me!' And he pulled a dagger from his belt and pointed it at my throat.

Even if I could have resisted, I would not have done so. I moved like a man still asleep, feeling the dagger now and then pricking at my ribs to warn me to change direction. We crossed the courtyard, which was deserted in the early darkness, though we heard occasional sounds as the garrison continued to carouse in their own quarters. We passed through a door which led into the space under the great hall, and here Sillé found and lit a lantern. We then started to mount a stair within the thickness of the wall, which I knew would lead us eventually to Gilles's chamber. Before we reached that level, however, the stairway branched, and Sillé murmured to me to take the other limb of the fork.

'But this leads only to the privy,' I whispered.

'Trust you to know that.'

When we reached the privy, Sillé stood on the stone seat, and reached to push aside the boards which made a rough ceiling. To my surprise, they moved quite easily. He thrust his hand still further upwards and then sideways, and a knotted rope tumbled downward.

'Up you go,' he said. 'It's quite safe even in the dark. Stop when you reach a ledge.' I did as he instructed, finding the climb easier than I thought it would be. When I reached the ledge he spoke of, the stone I touched felt warm, as if there was a fire burning somewhere on the other side of it.

Sillé joined me, the lantern glowing where it dangled from his belt. He unhooked it and held it up. 'Step across the gap,' he ordered. By the uncertain lantern-light I could see another ledge facing the one on which we crouched. It was possible – just – to scramble across from one to the other. I hesitated, and once more the point of the dagger pricked me through my doublet.

The ledge on the other side was not just the lip of a hollow scooped out in the thickness of the wall. A short curving passageway led away from it, and finished in a minute domed chamber. 'Ingenious, isn't it?' said Sillé pleasantly. 'I discovered it when I was looking for a good place to hide my money. My little nest-egg was quite safe when René de La Suze and his men came here. The vent we've just climbed goes up between the two chimneys, the one in the hall, and the one that leads from Gilles's own chamber. Now look here.' And he touched a small wooden shutter I had not noticed, sliding it back to reveal a small opening, at the height where a kneeling man might put his head. A dim ray of light stole through it. 'Down and look your fill, Raoul. I think I may have chosen a good night for my return.'

I hesitated, and a faint cry floated through the orifice, the cry of a child in fear or pain. The dagger probed the nape of my neck.

What I had, when I knelt down, was a bird's-eye view of Gilles's room, which was dimly lit by the roaring flames of the fire which burned in a fireplace almost directly beneath me. One or two thick wax candles further dispersed the gloom, but I knew that my spy-hole was so high up that it would be totally invisible in the shadows that clustered under the beams of the ceiling. My point of view was nevertheless not ideal, as I could only see about a quarter of the floorspace. Much of it was blocked from view by the angle at which the spy-hole was set and by Gilles's great bed.

There was a small creaking noise, like the sound of a rope going over a pulley. What looked like a bundle of clothing swung into view at the end of a cord. In another instant I perceived that it was the elder of the two boys Prelati and I had found on the road that morning, choking horribly in a noose. 'All right, Henriet,' said Gilles's voice. 'Let him down.'

As the wretched victim dropped limply to the floor, it seemed as if he must be dead. Gilles now came into view, loosening the cord round the child's neck, massaging the mark it had made. 'Good! He still breathes.' The boy stirred feebly and began to sob with terror. Immediately Gilles caught him in an embrace and began to cover his face with kisses. 'There,' he murmured. 'Don't weep. It was only a game.' At the same time, however, he disengaged one of his arms and put it behind his back, gesturing with his fingers as if he wanted to receive something. Someone whose face I could not see leaned forward and put a long knife into his hand. The blade glittered in the fire-light. With a sweeping motion Gilles brought it forward and opened the boy's torso from crotch to chest. There was an agonised scream. But the business was not finished yet. The knife fell with a clatter to the floor and Gilles, kneeling astride the prone body of his victim, was loosening his own garments with bloody hands, and freeing an erect member. As the dying flesh twitched beneath him, he swiftly brought himself to the point of ejaculation, mingling his semen with the child's blood and excrement.

'Now let us see how they compare. Bring me the head of the other one to put beside this.' The helper who had given him the knife moved fully into view, carrying the severed head of the younger of the two brothers by its hair. Even at that moment I was praying selfishly for some small mercy to myself. But the acolyte who stepped forward so calmly and gracefully was not Henriet, nor Poitou, nor even Blanchet. It was my own Rossignol.

37

By what means Sillé got me down from that secret room I shall never know. When I began to recover myself a little we were in my own chamber. At first, my reaction was to throw myself upon him in berserk rage, but he coolly held me off. Then, when I was quiet again, he sat beside me on the bed and enquired, still with a touch of mockery in his voice: 'Are there any questions you want to ask me?'

'How many and how long?'

'None of us will ever know how many. Some hundreds at least. He has been doing it since just before his grandfather died. I think the old man found out, and that was what helped to kill him. Those chests we took from Champtocé were full of children's bones. And it was children's bones I burnt for him here at Machecoul. The two old women discovered a bit more than they bargained for.'

'So that was why they left so hastily.'

'With a story they couldn't pass around. At least, not in so many words. Very frustrating for two professional gossips.'

'And Rossignol?' I whispered, self-pitying tears coming to my eyes.

'As guilty as the rest of us. Gilles would have killed him in Orléans, but spared him for his voice and for his looks. Rossignol knew the danger he'd been in, and chose the only way of avoiding it permanently. After all, he'd nowhere else to go. He's been slipping from your bed for years to lend a hand.'

'With Poitou and Henriet.'

'And me, and Blanchet and Prelati. Princé, too, sometimes, I have no doubt.'

'How could you do it?'

At this enquiry, Sillé actually burst out laughing. 'Don't be silly, Raoul! After you've done a thing a couple of times, you get used to it. There've been plenty of horrors in France these past years, and none of us wanted to become masterless men. I suspect even Prelati's made Italy too hot to hold him. We didn't even have to bother to keep the thing quiet.'

'I didn't know about it,' I said sulkily.

'That was because Gilles thought that one ignorant man in his immediate neighbourhood gave a kind of cover to his activities. We all had strict instructions not to tell you anything. But the peasants know. That's why they curse us – not only because we rob them, but because we take their children. And the Duke of Britanny knows, though he isn't admitting that he does. And I imagine the Dauphin Louis has as much information as he needs – which is why he didn't even bother to question me about it when he had me in prison.'

'Then why doesn't somebody act?'

'Because Gilles is a great lord, and because the tree isn't ripe for shaking. Though it will be soon, I think.'

'Is that why you're taking your leave?'

'Of course,' said Sillé calmly. 'I don't want to get hit on the head when the apple falls. And nor do you.'

The upshot of this conversation was that Sillé did not leave Machecoul alone, when he rode out of it for the last time in the grey dawn of a Christmas morning. It was I who went with him, though I now hated him as much as I have ever hated any man in my life. It did not help that he knew about this hatred and revelled in it. The garrison saw us depart with bleary indifference. They may even have imagined (and the thought made me shudder) that we were going off to see if we could lay our hands on fresh victims to satisfy their master's appetite. The groom who saddled our horses, grumbling at being put to work so early on what should have been a day of rest, even ventured to remark: 'No peace for the wicked, eh, messire Sillé? I'd have thought you deserved a holiday after the time you spent with my lord Dauphin. But I suppose the Marshal hankers for a Christmas treat.'

'Have I changed so much?' I said to Sillé, once we were out of earshot. 'A day ago, that man would never have dared to speak thus in front of me.'

He cocked his head to one side, and looked at me closely before answering. 'I suppose knowledge carries its own atmosphere with it,' he replied. 'I assure you Gilles would have you playing the butcher with the best of them, if you decided to stay here. A good reason, perhaps, for making you remain behind.' At which, hating him still, I began to plead with him not to desert me, as if it was only in his company that I could feel certain of getting away from Machecoul at all.

It was only after we had crossed the Loire that we at last parted from one another.

'I suppose I shall never see or hear from you again,' I said.

'Never, I hope.'

'That is my wish also.'

And with this we turned our backs upon one another, and rode off in opposite directions, without another word. For a while I rode without purpose and without direction, anxious only to put as many leagues as I could between myself and the man who had been my friend for the best part of my life. But then I came to my senses again, and pointed my horse's head in the direction of the fief I had not seen since the dying Jean de Craon summoned me, more than nine years before. Going slowly, stopping at small inns where landlord and customers alike were too befuddled by the Christmas celebrations to notice who I was or what I did, I arrived at last at my own manor, to the great consternation of the bailiff I had put in charge of it. Not only had he moved out of his own house and into my more commodious one – 'just so as my wife could be here to look after your things', he said to me resentfully, as his flock of children tumbled amid the ruined furniture – but he had been milking my rents for his own benefit. And there was something else as well. The rumours concerning the Marshal had travelled thus far, too, though it was a long time since he had been even as close as Champtocé. His name was used by mothers as a bogey to frighten children with. I, because I was known to have lived with Gilles for many years, smelt of brimstone to the people of the district.

Once I was home, I settled down to wait. What I was waiting for I did not know. At first I thought it was a message from Gilles, or even some attempt on his part to pursue me, as he had pursued his wretched Blanchet and forced him to return. In my dreams (and I had many nightmares) it was always Rossignol who rode up to my door to deliver the letter of summons. But nothing happened. People talked, not of Gilles, but of the second rebellion that the Dauphin had made against the king. La Tremoïlle was in the thick of it, and so were Joan's two paladins, Alençon and the Bastard of Orléans, and the Duke of Britanny was giving them covert help. It was only by chance that news reached me, at the end of May, that Gilles, far from learning his lesson from the business of Michel de Fontenay, had taken a priest prisoner in the church itself at Saint-Etienne-de-Mermonte. The Duke of Britanny might, if it suited him, try to overlook such a piece of sacrilege; but I doubted if the same could be said of bishop Jean de Malestroit. Yet for the time being nothing further happened.

At the end of August came word that the Constable had seized Tiffauges. Almost as if he had been present bodily before me, I heard Sillé's voice murmur: 'It won't be long now. They are already starting to divide the spoils.' Gilles was arrested at Machecoul on the fifteenth of September 1440.

Even here, where I lived, a long way across the Breton border the shock caused by the news was tremendous. It unleashed all the rumours which people had perhaps murmured under their breaths before, but now dared to discuss openly. There were civil accusations against Gilles, but the main charge was heresy. He was to stand trial for his life before Malestroit, as Bishop of Nantes, and before a certain Jean Blouyn, vicar of the Chief Inquisitor of France.

As soon as I heard what had happened, I knew that Gilles was lost. It passed through my mind to wonder if I might not be lost also, in view of my long association with him. Poitou and Henriet, Blanchet and Prelati had all of them been arrested along with Gilles. Of Rossignol's fate there was no word. He had vanished as completely as Sillé had done before him. The days passed, and no one was sent to trouble my repose. Only the great flood of rumour continued. It seemed as if every mother and father in Britanny who had lost a child in the past nine years was now converging upon the court at Nantes to cry for vengeance. As all this reached me, I grew more and more restless. My old itch of curiosity returned to torment me. By early October I knew I had to go to Nantes and see and hear for myself what was going on, though I might be putting my own neck in a noose if I did so.

38

I reached Nantes on the thirteenth of October, and put up at an inn, giving a false name. As I expected, Gilles's trial was the only topic of conversation in the hostelry. 'Ah!' said the landlord, shaking a massive head as he brought me my supper. 'If you're going to get in to see it, it'll cost you gold not silver. The men they've got on the door are making a fortune out of people who want to take a look at the monster of Machecoul. And I can't say I'm doing too badly either. It's an ill wind –' And here his voice tailed off in meaningful fashion.

When I asked him to sit beside me, and offered him some of his own best wine, he became more loquacious. 'I don't know if you haven't already missed the best of it,' he said. 'This morning there was a real uproar in the court. As I hear it, the way of it was this. They brought him in, and read him all this rigmarole – I think they call them articles – pretty strong stuff let me tell you, to do with all kinds of witchcraft and sorcery, and murdering the poor little children too, of course. And the Marshal gets up on his hind legs, all high and mighty, and tells the bishop and the inquisitor that they're no judges of his, and that they're a pair of rogues and money-taking thieves to boot. In fact, he even said: "I'd rather be hanged by the neck, than submit to be judged by a pair of miserable priests like you".'

'Messire de Malestroit can't have liked that,' I commented.

'He didn't,' said the landlord, smacking his lips. 'He rose up, white as a sheet, and told the Marshal to recognise the court or take the consequences. And the Marshal refused. And then they argued a bit more, and the bishop excommunicated him. Excommunicated him right there in the court! He's cut off from the comforts of the church, as he sits there in that big room they've given him in the Tour Neuve, and tomorrow the excommunication will be proclaimed in every church in the diocese.'

With this piece of information to sleep on, I passed a restless night; and next morning I wandered out early to sniff the air and see what arrangements I could make to get myself into the court for its next sitting. Gilles was being tried in the great hall of the ducal castle, next door to the Tour Neuve or New Tower where he was confined. When I got to the castle, one of the guards tried to stop me going into the courtyard. 'No show today!' he said roughly. 'And if you try tomorrow you won't get in. We're all of us bothered enough as it is.'

'I'm sure you prefer people who bother you with money,' I said, and showed him a silver piece. 'That's yours, if you find the captain of the guard for me.' As a result he went off, though in a somewhat surly manner, to do as I asked.

The captain, when he came, was a pleasanter individual – a bluff old soldier, somewhat out of his depth amidst all the excitement. 'Yes, what is it?' he said, looking me up and down and straightening himself slightly as he recognised that I was some sort of a gentleman.

'I want a place at tomorrow's session.'

'That's going to be difficult enough – ' he began, but came to a stop when I produced a small purse from my sleeve.

'How much have you saved towards your retirement?' I asked.

'Well, to be truthful, not very much,' he said, his eyes fastening on what I held in my hand.

'Here's one *écu* for you now,' I said, handing him a gold coin which he palmed as soon as it was offered to him. 'There'll be six more of them when I go through the courtroom door tomorrow.'

It was at this point that our conversation was interrupted by a call from behind me. 'Raoul de Saumur!'

I turned, and to my horror saw that the person who had addressed me was none other than the Dame de Jarville. With her was her inseparable companion, Madame d'Arraguin. 'Raoul de Saumur, what a surprise to find you here!'

'Or perhaps it isn't,' said Madame d'Arraguin drily. 'After all, he's got at least as much interest in this business as we have.'

It was at this point that I felt the beginnings of uncontrollable panic. My knees started to tremble as they had never trembled when I went into battle. The back of my throat became dry, and already I had begun to envision myself, not as a spectator at Gilles's trial, but flung into a ducal dungeon and left to await my own turn. I still don't know what I would have done if the two women had not had their attention distracted. It was the captain of the guard whom they had come to see, and it was evident that he was all too familiar with them. He seized his chance to slip away, giving me an apologetic look and a shrug as he did so.

'Here, Captain! Captain!' said Jeanne de Jarville, making an unsuccessful grab at his sleeve. 'Come on, Thomine – tell him he's got to come back!'

As the captain fled into the safety of the castle, I took to my heels in another direction. I could hear the two women calling after me, and they even made an unsuccessful attempt at pursuit till their long skirts tripped them up. In a moment I had lost myself in the narrow, bustling lanes of Nantes, hurrying along as best I could, dodging the market-porters with their heavy burdens, tripping over a child playing in the gutter, cannoning into a fat bourgeoise sailing along in rich brocade with her maid tripping behind her. It was the sour look the mistress gave me which made me slow my pace. People would wonder what it was that made me run as if the devil was after me. And the last thing I wanted was to attract attention.

I wandered the streets for a couple of hours, trying to decide what I should do. Gilles's description of Joan the Maid's terrible end returned vividly to me, and I thought that, if I were once arrested and accused of complicity in Gilles's crimes, I stood a good chance of sharing a similar fate. At length, lacking even the resolution to leave the city at once, I crept back to my inn and shut myself in my room, pretending to be ill. Indeed, the deception soon became almost fact. I spent each day trying to nerve myself to pack my bags and order my horse to be saddled, and my nights dreaming evil dreams. In these I saw, not only the dying child at Machecoul, with Gilles crouching over him; but earlier, half-forgotten sights as well. There was Gilles on the battlefield of Patay; and Gilles at Le Lude, in the blood-splashed room; and I saw again the sack of puppies, faintly stirring and squeaking on the edge of the moat at Champtocé.

One afternoon, I heard an agitation downstairs, and raised voices, one of them terribly recognisable. 'I don't care what you say, my man! I know he's here. If not under his own name, then under some other. And I mean to search every room until I find him.' Resigning myself to my fate, I opened my door and went out on to the landing. The Dame de Jarville was already halfway up the staircase.

'Ha!' she said, looking up at me. 'A fine dance you've led us. Did you think we were going to have you arrested?' Then, seeing my expression: 'Of course you did! What terrible cowards men are! It was just that we thought it was time that we had an exchange of information. Well, aren't you going to ask us in?' Numbly I held the door for her, and she swept into it, Madame d'Arraguin hot on her heels. 'Now send for some wine, and let's have a proper talk.'

At last, when I had at least partly satisfied their appetite to know all about Gilles's proceedings – at Pouzauges and Tiffauges, at Machecoul and Champtocé – they began to take pity on me. 'Well, he's not an entirely satisfactory informant, is he, Thomine, but I suppose he's done his best?'

'I suppose you could say that,' Thomine assented.

'So perhaps we can tell him a thing or two in exchange.'

I began to protest that I was not in search of information, and indeed couldn't understand their perpetual thirst for it.

'Nonsense! Everyone wants to know as far as possible what's going on. It's only human. Besides, you wouldn't be here if you weren't interested in Gilles's trial, even if you've been too frightened to go to it.'

'For my own peace of mind, I need to know the end of the story,' I said.

'Well, we can't tell you quite the end,' Thomine interjected, with a touch of grotesque coyness, 'but we can tell you what has been going on since Gilles was brought to Nantes.'

'There was a fine scene yesterday,' said the Dame de Jarville, smacking her lips reminiscently.

'You must realise that, up till then, he had always refused to recognise the court.'

'Simoniac rogues, that's what he called them. He said he had rather be hanged by the neck until he was dead than answer their questions.'

'So they excommunicated him on the spot.'

'But now, when bishop Malestroit asked if he was still of the same mind, he fell to his knees and cried for mercy, asking pardon for all his insults and saying that he would admit to whatever crimes he had committed.'

'It's all over, then?' I asked, with a strange mingling of sadness and relief.

'Oh, no!' exclaimed the two ladies together, just as if I had uttered an indecency. And Jeanne de Jarville added: 'You'll see – there's a whole rigmarole to be gone through yet.'

It was clear that they meant to allow me no escape – I was to accompany them to the next session of the trial.

Though it was a full three hours before the court went into session, there was already a crowd building up outside the door of the great hall of the castle when the three of us arrived in the chill light of the next day's dawn. The crowd rapidly grew, pushing and murmuring, and shoving those of us who were early arrivals against the wood. I noticed that there were numerous women in the crowd, in addition to my companions, many of them rich bourgeoises, careless of the way their gowns were being crushed and their headdresses knocked askew. When the door was at last unlocked, there was a Gadarene rush towards it. But here stood the captain of the guard whom I had already encountered, with a couple of stout fellows to help him. The sheep were not too gently separated from the goats, and only those whom the captain gave the nod to were allowed in. I heard the frequent chink of coins as the favoured were allowed to pass. When my own turn came, I held out the six coins I had originally promised him, but his arm still barred my way. 'Are these ladies with you, sir?' he said. Reluctantly I doled out another helping of largesse, thinking that I knew one reason at least why my two companions had had such a desire that I should go with them.

Within the hall itself, two chairs had been placed upon the dais, and a great crucifix had been hung on the back wall between them. On either side of the chairs had been put some stools. These, I knew, were for those whose duty it was to act as advisers to the court. In the body of the hall, and somewhat at an angle to the dais, was a table, with another stool behind it. This, I supposed, would be for Gilles. Then, filling part of the room, a set of benches, one with another table set in front of it for the notaries. And finally a rope behind which the public might dispose of itself as it pleased.

The session began with the entry of the assessors, followed by the vice inquisitor, and by Malestroit, who looked sourer than ever. I thought how much he must be enjoying the occasion in his heart. There was a sudden stir. The door at the back of the dais was flung open, and Gilles entered, ducking his head because the lintel was so low. He was preceded by a tipstaff, and followed by two guards.

Gazing at him across the room, I wondered at the way in which an absence of nine months had changed how he appeared to me. Until I left Machecoul for the last time, I had always thought of Gilles, and indeed had continued to see him, as the handsome, slender young man whom I had accompanied to the king's wars. But though he was still slender, and had the remnants of good looks, Gilles no longer carried with him the air of youth. He looked, in fact, older than the thirty-six years the calendar now gave him. The dark hair was flecked and plumed with white, the forehead was deeply lined, the cheeks were hollow and the eyes sunken in their sockets. He wore a close-fitting doublet of black velvet, and black hose, which accentuated the greyish pallor of his complexion. He seemed very nervous, and his hands were constantly in movement, twisting and knotting a handkerchief he carried. When he had been brought to his appointed place, Malestroit rose and glared at him. 'Are you ready to take your oath?' he asked.

Gilles silently nodded his head, and a clerk brought the gospels to him. Lifting his hand, he swore to reply truly, in a voice so feeble that it scarcely carried to the back of the room. Then another clerk began to read aloud the many articles of accusation.

Listening to this apparently endless rigmarole, this roster of things done and not done, big sins and little ones, I wondered at the industry of Jean de Malestroit's emissaries in gathering all this material together in so short a space of time. Or perhaps it had been collected over many years, until at last the opportunity came when those who hated Gilles could make use of it. I realised at last how many men he had offended by his wealth and arrogance and carelessness, rather than by his crimes.

When at last the reading came to an end, Jean de Malestroit cleared his throat, and said, in a clear, level voice: 'Well, Marshal, how do you reply?' It was the tone of an executioner rather than a judge.

Gilles seemed to hesitate for a moment, and moistened his lips with his tongue. 'As regards some of these matters . . .' he began.

'The court requires you to answer 'yes' or 'no' to each of these accusations. Do you wish them to be read to you again?'

'No, my lord bishop, that will not be necessary.'

'Do you affirm the truth of all that has been said?'

'My lord . . .'

'Remember we have heard witnesses whom you did not contradict.'

'Am I a man to have to answer them?' It was suddenly the Gilles I knew, with more than a touch of his old fire.

Malestroit ignored him, and turned to confer for a moment with his fellow-judge, who slowly nodded his head. Then he spoke directly to the prisoner. 'We judge you to be contumacious. Our decision is that you be put to the question, that the pain of your body may serve for the salvation of your soul.'

The blow was so sudden that Gilles evidently did not realise the full meaning of what had been said. He gaped at Malestroit silently, in a kind of rictus of astonishment, while a low murmuring filled the room. Even here, with Gilles a prisoner before them, people found it difficult to realise that the brilliant Marshal of Rais could now be racked like any common felon. The first to recover themselves were the two guards, who moved forward to take Gilles by the elbows. They missed their grip, for in that instant he was grovelling on the floor.

'Mercy! A little mercy! Give me time to recollect myself!'

'We will show more mercy than you did to others,' said Malestroit with unctuous relish, as if all along he had been preparing for this moment. 'You may withdraw, and we will send you those who will advise you, to bring you to a better frame of mind.' As the guards led Gilles away, he beckoned to two of the assessors, who first conferred with him in low voices, then followed the prisoner through the dais door. Malestroit made no attempt to end the session of the court, but sat back in his seat and folded his hands into his sleeves. The gesture told us that we had not long to wait.

But we were due for a surprise, for when the door opened, it was not to admit Gilles. Instead, Francesco Prelati stood there on the threshold. He was blinking a little, as if they had just brought him from some dark place, and his black hair was ruffled. Yet his quickness of reaction had not deserted him. Seeing where he was, he immediately straightened himself, and his hand went to his hair in a familiar gesture. His lips twitched into a faint smile as a murmur of 'the Italian astrologer' went round the room. The door opened for a second time, and Gilles reappeared, followed by his guards and by the two clerks who had been sent to counsel him. His eyes moved to where Prelati stood, and it was as if all the rest of us vanished – Malestroit, the vice inquisitor, the assessors, the notaries, the guards and the whole throng of spectators. With a single swift step he crossed the dais, and folded Prelati into his arms. Almost casually, the latter pushed him away, as if Gilles was a too-enthusiastic acquaintance whom he had met in the street.

'Farewell . . .' Gilles began, and stumbled to a halt, as if Prelati's reaction had taken him entirely by surprise. Then he spoke again, but now as if the words were something he had carefully learned by rote: 'Farewell, François my friend. Never again shall we meet in this life. But I now pray God to give you good patience and knowledge. And be certain, providing you have these and hope in God, that we shall meet again in the great joy of Paradise. Pray for me, and I will pray for you.'

Prelati's smile broadened, but he said nothing in reply, but instead looked at the floor like a girl who has been paid a compliment. It was Malestroit who spoke. 'Well, you have seen him now,' he said, 'just as you have so frequently requested. So let him leave us, and make his way to my lord Duke, who today has business with him.' Still without uttering a word, and without showing the least astonishment at the turn events had taken, Prelati bowed formally to the bishop, then started to push his way through the crowd towards the main door of the hall. The court officials and the guards made no attempt to stop him.

Gilles gazed after him for a moment, and then, with a face drained of all emotion, turned back towards Malestroit, who was looking at him expectantly. 'Well, my lord bishop,' he said, 'upon advice given by those you sent to counsel me, I am willing to make a full confession before all these who are present to hear me. Are you willing to listen to it?'

'It is what I am here to do,' Malestroit replied.

Without preliminaries, and in a soft, rapid, scarcely varying tone, Gilles began a catalogue of crimes – killings, mutilations, burnings of bodies, conjurations, evocations of demons. It was more and worse than even I had known. Whenever he reached some especially horrible episode, he seemed intent on elaborating it, as if to make it seem even more dreadful than it was. The spectators were mute, not whispering, scarcely stirring, as if frozen by the horror of what they were being made to hear. At first Malestroit, too, sat rigid in his chair, but then, as the recitation continued, I saw a muscle working in his jaw and the light moving in the sapphire of his ring as his hand tightened upon the arm of his chair.

Then, explosively, he was on his feet and shrugging off his fur-lined robe. 'No, no!' he exclaimed. 'It is not fit that such things should be said in the presence of the image of God!' And he turned to veil the crucifix with the piece of cloth he had torn off. Gilles waited quietly till he had done so, and then said, as if making an observation about a matter that had little to do with him: 'Nevertheless, my lord, in these cases I believe it is a judge's duty to hear the prisoner out, and a priest's to hear the confession of one who wishes to make it. You will not mind if I now continue with what I was saying?'

At first I was not certain if I would remain in Nantes to see the last day of my friend's life, though I knew that I myself was in no danger. Of all those who had been close to Gilles, only Poitou and Henriet were to die with him. Prelati was rumoured to be already busy building alchemical furnaces for the Duke of Britanny. The Dame de Jarville and Madame d'Arraguin were predictably insistent that I ought to stay. 'You'll never forgive yourself if you go now,' said Jeanne. 'It will be the most edifying spectacle of this century. The nuns we lodge with are aflutter at the thought. Do you know that he has asked for a general procession to be made, to bring him to the place of execution, and to pray that he and his servants be maintained firmly in their hope of salvation?'

'More than that,' said Thomine, 'he has condescended to ask to be hanged first, so that Henriet and Poitou may be certain he will not escape from judgement.'

'The judges are now so impressed with his contrition,' Jeanne went on, 'that Gilles is to be hanged only and not burned. Or at least the body is to be cut down before the flames have consumed it, and is to be buried in holy ground. There's been a lot of competition for the burial, let me tell you!'

'But you still haven't told him the best of it!'

'Ah, yes!' Jeanne de Jarville exclaimed, looking as coy as her normally forthright expression would allow. 'Thomine and I are to have our own little part in the proceedings. Once Gilles is dead, and the fire has singed him a little, his body is to be given to four highborn women to be placed in its shroud and taken away to its sepulchre.'

'And you are among the number?' I asked.

'We are indeed! And don't look at us so strangely, my dear Raoul. Our blood is at least as good as that of the other ladies who are to be found in Nantes. And haven't we deserved this honour? Think of the interest we have taken in the whole business from the very first.'

When the day of execution dawned I was up early, and crossed one of the bridges to the immense meadow which lies across the Loire upon the south side of the city. Here the gibbet had already been set up, with three ropes dangling from it for the three victims, and an immense pile of wood for the burning afterwards. A few soldiers loitered round to see that no one interfered with the arrangements, and some spectators had already gathered to make sure of a good place. But most people had preferred to remain behind, in order to take part in the procession.

Now the bells of Nantes began to toll through the October mist, and I heard the sound of solemn chanting as the dark pageant began to cross the bridge. First came a detachment of men-at-arms, helms and breastplates glittering in the morning sunlight. Then, behind them, a double file of churchmen, lay and monastic, singing an anthem and carrying a banner with the Crucifixion in their midst. The variety of different habits showed that every religious order in Nantes had turned out to do Gilles honour. Then more men-at-arms, surrounding the executioner's cart, in which were Gilles, Henriet and Poitou, together with a Carmelite friar to comfort them. Gilles seemed to be talking earnestly to the other two, who hung their heads as if in disbelief at what was happening to them. It was possible to see that their hands were bound behind them, while his were not. Behind the cart came a sumptuous bier, as yet unoccupied, carried by two horses, one before and one behind, with liveried grooms to guide them. Next, mounted on dark-coloured hackneys, were four ladies, too deeply veiled in black for me to be able to distinguish one from another. After them, two pretty pages carried an immense drapery of white silk which I knew to be Gilles's shroud. And last an immense crowd of townspeople, many in mourning dress, telling their beads or praying *sotto voce* as they walked.

When the cart reached the place where the gibbet stood, Gilles rose to his feet, and motioned to the Carmelite to descend. The procession broke its ranks and formed an immense circle round him and round the gibbet, with the men-at-arms facing outward to prevent the crowd from coming too close. But instead of speaking directly to the people, he began to address Henriet and Poitou who were beside him.

'My poor servants,' he said, 'you must be strong and virtuous in the face of the temptations the Devil will still hold out to you, in the few moments you have to live. Not only must you feel that great regret and great contrition for your crimes which both of you have already shown, but you must, as well, have confidence in God and believe that there is never so great a crime that a man can commit, but God in his goodness will be able to forgive it to him, provided always that he truly and persistently cries for mercy in his soul. You should thank God who lets you die now, in full possession of all your faculties, and with full awareness of what your sins have been, instead of cutting you off one day, suddenly and unexpectedly, with the burden of your crimes still upon you. We, who have done evil together, shall, as soon as our souls have been separated from our bodies, meet one another again in the presence of God, and in the glory of Paradise.'

At this the two wretches began to blubber copiously, the tears and snot streaking the faces they were unable to wipe. With the grace of an actor, Gilles sank to his knees, joined his hands and began to pray, looking for all the world like the kind of statue that might soon adorn his own tomb. Then he rose again, and favouring the bystanders with a dazzling smile, called out: 'Brothers – for being a Christian I am your brother – pray for me now, and beg God to pardon me, and to show me His mercy as you would wish it shown to you.'

By now nearly all those around me were in tears, and I thought Gilles must be well contented with the impression he was making at his exit. He stripped off his doublet (the same doublet of black velvet I had seen him wearing at his trial), and gave it to the executioner, saying: 'Your perquisite – a pity to have it singed, perhaps?' and the man adjusted the knot around his neck. Then, in a lower tone: 'When I give the signal!'

'Yes, messire,' the executioner answered, then returned to his place in the driver's seat, leaving Gilles poised on the cart's tail. 'Now!' cried Gilles, and the whip cracked.

The thing was done so quickly and expeditiously that one had to admire the smoothness of it. Gilles was no sooner jerking at the rope's end than the executioner had flung the reins to his deputy and jumped down to pull the victim's legs. There was a distinct crack as his neck broke. The next instant men were piling the faggots and kindling beneath the body as it dangled, and the flames went up with a roar. But the wood was no sooner properly ablaze than the executioner and his assistants were scattering the bonfire and stamping out the embers. Gilles was cut down, with a few scorch marks here and there, and the noble ladies came forward to perform their office, wrapping him in the shroud, which in turn was placed upon the waiting bier. The procession re-formed with the body in its midst, and turned once again towards Nantes.

All this time, Henriet and Poitou had been sitting waiting in the cart, slumped and motionless, scarcely lifting their heads to watch as their master exercised his right of precedence. As the bulk of the crowd streamed away, the executioner remembered their existence, and began to manoeuvre his vehicle back into position under the gallows. 'Up, my lads!' he said, prodding them with the toe of his boot. 'Can't have you keeping his lordship waiting – can we? – wherever it is he's gone to.'

Then he dropped the two remaining nooses over their heads and drove away in the customary fashion.

No one bothered to pull Poitou's and Henriet's legs for them. They danced a long time, until at length the front of their hose was stained with that last ejaculation which hanged men have. The small group of spectators jeered to see it. Then, while the corpses were still twitching, the faggots were again heaped up and duly set ablaze. But now they were allowed to burn until the ropes charred through and Henriet and Poitou plunged down into the heart of the fire. More wood was piled on top of them, and the fire spat and seethed as the fat began to run out. I knew it would be kept going until almost nightfall, when nothing recognisable would be left. The ashes from the heart of the fire, and the few scraps of charred bone mixed up with them would be raked into a sack by the executioner and his people, and the contents of the sack would then be thrown into the Loire. This was all the burial Henriet and Poitou would ever know.

As I walked away alone from the place where their bodies were still burning, with the stench of their passing in my nostrils, and the noise of it in my ears, I thought of these two, whom I had despised and sometimes feared. I thought that my friend Gilles had killed them both just as surely as he had killed the children he had used for his pleasure. And if the soul can die before the body, then the souls of Poitou and Henriet had long since ceased to inhabit the fine temples that God made for them. Gilles would be lucky to meet his servants in that Paradise whither he was bound, nor (it occurred to me) did he truly expect to do so. An audience of angels would hardly have places for Poitou and Henriet.

As I write these words it is cold and dark. I can hear the rain lashing the stone tiles of the roof. Soon my monks will be moving through the door of our great shadowy church, each man sheltering his candle with a cupped hand. It will be time for us to sing another office, to send our prayers and praises up to a perhaps merciful God who perhaps listens. As the light strengthens and creeps through the windows, the candles – all but these that burn on the altar – will be snuffed between thumb and forefinger. It will be I who give the signal, when I think the moment has come. Economy in all things.

And now, as the bell strikes, I must scatter sand on this final page, and go down. I have travelled through many years since the day I saw Gilles die in Nantes, and Poitou and Henriet after him. Now I am a servant of servants, bound even more tightly than those I nominally rule to the way of life we have all vowed to follow. The lord abbot must not keep his men waiting, even for a moment. I have purged myself of everything that was evil, received absolution and done the penance imposed on me. Yet, when I came here at first, it was in the hope of escaping responsibility, and yet a different kind of responsibility has inexorably sought me out. In this community, everything moves thanks to my decision, thanks to my will.

Why, then, have I chosen to write down a story which could cause so much harm if it fell into the wrong hands? It is not as if I am unaware of the risks I have run. When I first entered the life of religion it did not take me long to discover the great vice of monks. It is curiosity. Living here, apparently so openly, so closely with one another, we perpetually suspect secrets. Leave your missal on a window-ledge, and you may be sure that at least one set of fingers will have riffled through its pages before it is returned to you. Looking for what? Even the man who leafs it through could not tell you. Maybe the corner of a page turned down, the mark of a thumb-nail against a particular prayer.

Once, not long ago, I remember, I came in here, to the room where I sleep and write, and found the novice who that week was assigned to clean it. His back was turned, and he was just trying the cupboard door, giving it a little tug, to see if by any chance it was unfastened. We walk silently in our sandals on these stone floors, and he did not hear me enter. Rather than announce my presence, I turned on my heel and left him to it. After all, the door was securely locked, the key safe at my belt, and no harm had been done. But what a disaster had I been careless! For he would then have been free to peruse some few at least of this great stack of parchment sheets. And there is matter here to disturb the most settled and prudent.

If I fear the possible consequences of writing this, why have I been so insistent on completing the task? I have used good wax, which might have made candles to burn before the holy images, and goose-quills we might have sold for the profit of the monastery, and I have spoilt much expensive parchment. The store-keeper has been grumbling for months about the quantity of such things I demand, and use to no visible result. When the manuscript is at last finished, I shall parcel it up, and send it away, to save my brothers in religion from the dangers I know it contains. It will not go to be copied by a professional scribe. The Lombard banker who deals with the monastery finances (the son of a man I once knew in the city of Orléans) will send it over the Alps for me, to our father the Pope. Not that the Pope will read it. Nor any of his cardinals. His librarian will glance at a page or two, then consign the parcel to his remotest shelf. But I still have the feeling that the poison this writing contains is of the kind that changes its nature slowly over the passage of years. In the Pope's library my tale can mature, as a vintage does in a cellar, until at last it is ready, healthful rather than harmful. People may profit from knowing the truth about the splendid and infamous Marshal of Rais, my friend Gilles who sinned greatly. Like that of Joan the Maid, his story may tell them what mankind can be and is. For my part I still mourn for Gilles despite his crimes, and continue to pray for his soul. I fear he has not yet been released into the Paradise which he believed to be his by right.

PRINCIPAL CHARACTERS

The narrator
Raoul de Saumur – a nobleman from a good but impoverished family, who first enters the household of Gilles de Rais as his whipping-boy, and who remains with him almost throughout his life.

The family of Gilles de Rais
Gilles de Rais – the richest nobleman in France, companion-in-arms of Joan of Arc, created Marshal by Charles VII.
Jean de Craon – Gilles's grandfather, responsible for bringing him up.
René de La Suze – Gilles's younger brother.
Catherine de Thouars – Gilles's wife.
Anne de Sillé – Jean de Craon's second wife, and (by a previous marriage) grandmother of Catherine.
Gilles de Sillé – a distant relation of Anne de Sillé and contemporary of Gilles, who joins Gilles's household and becomes his close companion.
Beatrice de Montjean – mother of Catherine de Thouars.
Pierre Meschin – brother-in-law of Beatrice de Montjean by her second marriage.
Georges de La Tremoïlle – a cousin of Gilles de Rais, and for a while, all-powerful favourite of Charles VII.

The royal houses of France and Britanny
Charles VII – King of France.
Yolanda of Aragon – Duchess of Anjou and titular Queen of Sicily. Also mother-in-law of Charles VII.
The Duke of Alençon and the Counts of Clermont and Vendôme – princes of the blood.
The Bastard of Orléans – illegitimate son of the king's uncle, the murdered Louis of Orléans. Representative of his brother, the captive Duke Charles, who fell into English hands at Agincourt.

Artur de Richemont – Constable of France and younger brother of the Duke of Britanny.

Madame de Guyenne – wife of the Constable, sister of the Duke of Burgundy, and widow of Louis de Guyenne, Charles VII's older brother, once Dauphin and heir to the kingdom.

Jean V – Duke of Britanny.

Louis, Dauphin of Viennois – the only son and heir of Charles VII. The future King Louis XI.

Joan of Arc and her household
Joan of Arc – the Maid of Orléans.

Jean Pasquerel – her confessor.

Jean d'Aulon – the master of her household.

Brother Richard – an itinerant Franciscan friar and powerful preacher, who attaches himself to Joan after the surrender of Troyes.

The household of Gilles de Rais
In addition to Raoul de Saumur and Gilles de Sillé, this includes the following at various times:

Henriet and Poitou – two pages, later chamberlains.

Rossignol – a singing-boy.

Princé – a herald.

Hubert – another page.

Eustache Blanchet – a priest turned practitioner of the Black Art.

Jean de La Rivière – a fraudulent magician.

Francesco Prelati – an Italian alchemist.

High ecclesiastical personages
Regnault de Chartres – Archbishop of Rheims and chancellor of France.

Jean de Malestroit – Bishop of Nantes and chancellor of Britanny.

Professional soldiers
Among them:

La Hire and Ambroise de Loré – professional captains for Charles VII.

William Glasdale – an English captain, commanding at Le Lude and then in charge of the fortress of the Tourelles at Orléans.

Pierre Cardinal – Jean de Craon's Captain of the guard at Champtocé.

Sundry clerks
Among them:
Michel de Fontenay – tutor to Gilles de Rais when the latter was a child.

Ladies of title
Among them:
Jeanne, Dame de Jarville and her friend Thomine d'Arraguin – two noble widows.

other recent fiction from GMP:

Agustin Gomez-Arcos
THE CARNIVOROUS LAMB
translated by William Rodarmor

Into a shuttered house in Franco's Spain, where the ghosts of past rebellion and present defeat still taint the air, Ignacio is born, the carnivorous lamb of the title. His father stays locked in his study, amid memories of political failure. His mother, vague but implacable ruler of her shadowy domain, refuses to acknowledge her son's existence. Only his brother Antonio is real – father-surrogate, teacher, protector and eventual lover. Their relationship is the centre of this story of one family's suffocation under an intolerable regime, which is also an incisive, savagely funny, but not entirely despairing look at post-Civil War Spain.

Born in 1939, Agustin Gomez-Arcos has been living in France since 1968. Before his exile from Spain, he received the Lope de Vega Prize for two of his plays and was widely acclaimed for his translations from French. Despite this, his works were banned and he left the country. *The Carnivorous Lamb*, written in French, appeared in 1975 and received the Prix Hermès for the best first novel of that year.

"A carnal poem, frank, provocative, triumphant . . . and a dirge for Spain" – *Le Monde*.

"Extraordinary, beautifully constructed. Agustin Gomez-Arcos extends and deepens his sexual themes until we realise that the entire bizarre tale is a metaphor for the future of Spain" – *San Francisco Chronicle*.

ISBN 0 85449 019 1 (paperback)
       0 85449 018 3 (cloth)

Kay Dick
THE SHELF

"The shelf" is a repository in the coroner's office where Cassandra's letters to Anne had first been lodged – as well as that other, unposted letter found in Anne's handbag. It was all so long ago – back in the 1960s – but Cass has not been able to forget the passion Anne engendered in her; their brief affair; and the mystery that surrounded it.

"Recalls writers like Elizabeth Bowen, Rosamund Lehmann and Elizabeth Taylor. What these writers have in common with Miss Dick is a willingness to regard the intricacies of love, the shifting patterns of light and shade in the relationship of one person to the other, as being of prime importance. The stylish economy of Kay Dick's writing places her firmly in that tradition. It is a book you are not likely to forget" – Allan Massie, *The Scotsman*.

"Theme, manner and writing evoke Colette" – *Daily Telegraph*.

"A tour de force, powerful in its evocation of relationships and the gradations of passion. This work places Kay Dick in the same category of sensibility as Jean Rhys, Katherine Mansfield and Ford Maddox Ford" – Gillian Freeman.

ISBN 0 85449 002 7 (paperback only)

Tom Wakefield
THE DISCUS THROWERS

Considered by many critics to be one of Britain's most
original contemporary writers, Tom Wakefield's *Mates* and
Drifters have been widely praised for the way they depict the
humour and pathos of human relationships. His latest novel
continues in the same vein, following the progress of five
everyday figures who react against the social conventions that
shackle their lives.

"Wakefield is an accomplished narrator; detached, witty and
knowing" – *The Times*.

"There can be no doubt that we are in the hands of a finely
perceptive and sensitive writer" – *Guardian*.

"Delicate marquetry of the domestic and everyday in his
characters and plot, richness of detail, and sheer, irrepressible humour of character and viewpoint. This is a lyrical,
magical novel, and a warming shot of sentiment in a climate
of cool" – *City Limits*.

ISBN 0 907040 79 9 (paperback)
    0 907040 80 2 (cloth)